KK

I know your secrets. And you know mine.

Jean-Paul's gaze rose to meet Britta's. "What does the writer mean by that? He knows your secrets?"

She remained so still that he didn't think she was going to answer. But fear momentarily settled in her eyes. "I assume he's referring to the magazine," she said in a low voice. "My column is called 'Secret Confessions.'"

Liar. "It sounds more personal." He closed the distance between them. "I think you know more than you're telling. You may even know the killer. At least, he knows *you*."

She lifted her chin a notch. "A lot of people who write to the magazine think they know me."

"You're hiding something, Miss Berger." He leaned across the desk, so close his face was only a breath away. So close he inhaled the hypnotic scent of her perfume.

So close he felt the tension vibrate in her lean muscles.

"But secrets have a way of coming out. And before this investigation is over, I will find out exactly what you're keeping from me."

D0030431

Other titles by Rita Herron

RITA HERRON

SAY YOU *Love Me*

HQN™

ISBN-13: 978-0-373-77193-6
ISBN-10:   0-373-77193-2

SAY YOU LOVE ME

This edition published by arrangement with Harlequin Books S.A.

® and TM are trademarks of the publisher. Trademarks indicated with
® are registered in the United States Patent and Trademark Office, the
Canadian Trade Marks Office and in other countries.

www.HQNBooks.com

Printed in U.S.A.

Dear Reader,

I have always loved New Orleans, and like so many people across the States was greatly saddened by the destruction, devastation and loss of lives and homes that Hurricane Katrina caused. The culture of the city is unique and fascinating, and should live on.

At the time the storms hit, I was working on this book, and was so moved and concerned that I put the story on hold. Like so many others, I wondered what would happen afterward—if the city would be rebuilt, if Mardi Gras would return and what changes might be made. But after a long talk with my editors I decided to finish the book in honor of the city, people and culture of New Orleans that has offered inspiration to so many writers over the years. I hope the story will not only entertain, showcase the wonderful culture and sights of the city, but also capture the positive spirit and fortitude of those who suffered, survived and are rebuilding their homes and lives.

The colorful characters, setting, atmosphere and Mardi Gras celebrations of New Orleans and the bayou made a perfect backdrop for this romantic-suspense thriller *Say You Love Me*, and triggered my imagination into overdrive. As a fiction writer I took some privileges in adding my own folklore to the legend surrounding the swamp, but I think the swamp devil I created and the eerie serial killer stalking the heroine make for an exciting and interesting read. Mixed into the blend is a religious cult that should also raise the hair on the back of your neck.

Of course, the romance writer in me decided that I needed not only a strong hero, but a hero with two hot Cajun brothers. All three men are tough, brooding, strong and in law enforcement. And all three are suckers for a woman in trouble.

In *Say You Love Me*, you'll meet Detective Jean-Paul Dubois, a sexy tortured hero who lost his wife to the terrible storms, a man who has given up on love, but who will give his life to save the citizens of his beloved hometown—and of course to protect the heroine, feisty, troubled Britta Berger, a woman with disturbing secrets in her past.

And for fans who like trilogies, look for the two brothers' gritty, dark romantic-suspense stories to follow!

Happy reading,

Rita Herron

To all those who lost and suffered during the hurricanes. New Orleans is a beautiful place. I hope you find love and happiness in your future!

SAY YOU
Love Me

PROLOGUE

Black Bayou

THE BAYOU KILLED.

But it also gave life. And it was home.

As was the covens.

They thrived in the swampland, creating their black magic just as they would tonight as he began his own private kingdom.

The magic circle had been formed. The mandrake root had been pulled, a task that had put him at risk for death. But he had withstood the maddening shriek as he'd confiscated the plant, knowing the importance of it for his ritual.

At sixteen, he was finally a man.

He studied the thirteen-year-old girls as they were brought before him, the flames from the open fire illuminating their pale, frightened faces. They stood shivering in thin white virginal dresses, their heads bowed in fear, yet sublimation. Symbolic, yes. But the translucent cotton also offered a reprieve from the vicious heat of the bayou and teased him with a peek at the supple bodies that lay beneath. Two blond girls studied him as if he had not earned the right to be a man.

But he had.

Just as the full moon glowed—hypnotic, beckoning the animals to prowl, the wild to hunt, the men to mate. Just as the drums of Mardi Gras pounded out the ancient voodoo-priestess spells.

It was time for the passage.

And he could choose among the girls offered.

Automatically one stood out. He'd watched her for ages. Known he wanted her. Her eyes haunted him.

Adrianna Small.

Her hair flamed as red as the sunset on the deep murky Mississippi River. Her temper matched it.

She was a bad girl. Defiant. Adversarial. A fighter.

One who needed to be broken.

He met her gaze and held it, uncertainty gnawing at him like the mosquitoes clawing at his bare legs. He could never please his father. Wasn't tough enough. Big enough. Enough of a fighter. The other boys laughed at his artwork. Called him a sissy and other vile names.

Would he be man enough for Adrianna?

Yes. He had spread the mandrake root oil on his body, inhaled the intoxicating aroma, grateful the aphrodisiac would entice Adrianna to succumb to his wishes. She just had to get near him….

A frog croaked from the depths of the backwoods. An alligator lay stone-still, searching for his own prey. Waiting, watching, ready to pounce. The mysteries of the wild surrounded him, the scent of jasmine, marshy land, danger. Spanish moss draped the cypress trees along the swampland with gnarled witchlike fingers, hiding its secrets, ready to snatch another lost soul to the tangled wild vines and brush of the backwoods. Yet honeysuckle and verbena sweetened the air.

"Now, son." His father, tall and commanding, placed

his hand on his shoulder. "You have chosen the first, the one to begin your kingdom?"

"Adrianna," he said, his palms sweating.

Drums pounded as the masked musicians and the clan danced around the fire. The witchdoctor screeched his secret chant. Sobek had to be pacified tonight.

"Ahh, the feisty one. The one with the witch's eyes." An odd expression replaced his smile. "She would be the perfect sacrifice to the Crocodilian gods."

He trembled at the thought. "No, father. I want to keep her for myself."

"No, son. She has the evil in her just like her mother."

His father gestured toward Mrs. Small, a frail woman who'd been drugged since her arrival. His father had found her on Bourbon Street and brought her and her daughter to safety with the clan. The tenth woman his father had added to his own kingdom.

Now he knew his father's true reason.

Adrianna's mother brushed her daughter's hair from her cheek in a loving gesture, then suddenly pushed her forward. Did she know the extent of her offering?

His father jerked her up beside him and the voodoo priestess doused her with oil and whispered a spell of love and fertility.

Adrianna's icy look chilled his blood as if she had silently cast a death spell upon him. Maybe she was a secret member of one of the covens, a witch who had enticed him for her own sick motives. Or maybe she was born of the swamp devil himself. After all, no one knew her father's identity.

The clan surrounded them, chanting and clapping to the beat of the drums, urging them to start the celebration into adulthood. Snakes hissed and spewed venom from the depths of the fiery pit. The crude carvings of the crocodile surrounded them. The battle between good and evil.

He reached for Adrianna, the special necklace he'd crafted for her dangling in his other hand. His gift—the serpent swallowing its tail—symbolized the great work of alchemy: the transformation into a higher form already inherent within it. That was his present for Adrianna. If evil possessed her, he would cure her of it. Then he could save her.

But she screamed in protest, then threw the necklace into the dirt and spit at him. His father slapped her and she wrenched free, grabbed a rifle near the fire, raised it and a gunshot blasted the air. The bullet slammed into his father's chest and sent his body flying back. Shouts and cries erupted. He went numb at the sight of the blood spilling from his father's crumpled body. Like a scarlet river, it ran down his father's white shirt and splattered onto the ground.

"I could never love you," Adrianna screamed at him. "You can't make me."

Then she turned and ran into the bowels of the bayou. Like predators ready to swallow her, the weeping willows and gnarled branches of the oaks and cypress trees captured her in the black abyss.

Chaos erupted. The witchdoctor knelt to tend to his father. His father's wives surrounded him, as did the rest of the clan.

"He's dying," someone whispered frantically.

The still waters of the bayou that had lain eerily quiet mere seconds ago, churned to life. The gators' yellow eyes pierced the blackness, searching for prey. One crocodile shot forward, his teeth gnashing.

Adrianna had crossed into the unknown part of the swampland—where danger awaited.

The bayou took lives. The animals, the plants, the heat—it was relentless. She didn't even have water. And the snakes and alligators lay waiting for their next meal. Then there was the fabled swamp devil who met at Devil's Corner. He would eat her alive.

There was no way she would survive the night.

He knotted his hands into fists. After what she'd done, she didn't deserve to live. She deserved to be punished. To suffer the bayou.

One of the men shouted that they had to find the girl murderer. He ran for a *pirogue* to take on the river to search for her.

Although if the swamp devil or the gators got her first, there would be nothing left to bury, nothing but mutilated flesh, bones and tissue....

No, he'd find her first. Then he'd make her pay for killing his father.

CHAPTER ONE

New Orleans—thirteen years later
One week before Mardi Gras

"I KNOW YOUR secrets. And you know mine."

The hairs on the nape of Britta Berger's neck stood on end as the note slipped from her hand to the wrought-iron table. She'd already sifted through a half dozen letters for her Secret Confessions column at the magazine she worked for, *Naked Desires*. All erotic. Some titillating, others romantic as they described various private confessions and sexual fantasies. Some bordered on S and M. And others were plain vulgar and revealed the debauchery of the South's sin city.

But this note felt personal.

An odd odor wafted from the envelope, a scent she vaguely recalled. One that made her skin crawl.

Powdery sugar from her morning beignet settled like snowflakes on the charcoal-gray paper as she glanced around the crowded outdoor café to see if someone was watching her. A drop of sweat trickled into her bra, a side effect of the record high temperatures for January.

Or maybe it was nerves.

The French Quarter always seemed steeped in noise, but today excitement buzzed through the air like mosquitoes on a frenzy. The twelve days of partying and parades leading up to Mardi Gras had already brought hordes of masked creatures, artisans, musicians, voodoo priestesses, witchdoctors, tourists—and crime. Bourbon Street fed the nightlife and drew the tourists with its infamous souvenir shops, voodoo paraphernalia, palm readers, street musicians, strip clubs, jazz and blues clubs and seedy all-night bars. And then the hookers…

The massive crowd closed around her as the sidewalk seemed to move with them. Any one of them could be the enemy. Any one of them could have sent her the note.

Battling panic, she reread the words. *I know your secrets. And you know mine.*

Yes, she'd done things she wasn't proud of. Things no one else must ever know. They would say she was a bad girl. But she had done what she had to do in order to survive.

The very reason she was the perfect editor for the Secret Confessions column. She wanted her privacy. Understood that the written word could be evocative. But the fantasies deserved to be kept anonymous.

Just as she tried to do with her identity. Always changing her name. *Running.*

And what better place for her to hide than in the heart of New Orleans, so near to where it had all happened? Working for this magazine was the perfect cover, the perfect way for her to blend with the masses.

But how could the person who'd written the note know about her past? The horror. The shame. The lies.

They couldn't. It was impossible. She'd never told a soul.

Furious, she stuffed the note inside the envelope. It

was probably just a prank from some sex-starved fan who wanted to win her attention——like the pervert with the fetish for penis rings who'd exposed himself to her in Jackson Square last week.

Just because she printed sexually explicit material, some people thought that she understood their individual desires. Condoned their behavior. And that she wanted them personally.

Shivering at the thought, she tried to shake off her anxiety. No one knew the real Britta Berger.

And no one ever would.

She took a deep drink of water to swallow the remnants of the beignet which had lodged in her throat. In the background, the singer drifted into a slow tune, crooning out his heartache blues. A tall man, around forty with a goatee and wire-rimmed glasses, strode by and stared at her. She froze. Was he going to stop? Tell her he had sent the note? That he'd been following her? Waiting to watch her reaction?

Oddly, though, he winked at her and strode down the crowded sidewalk toward the Business District. She breathed out a sigh but forced herself to take a mental snapshot of the man in case she saw him again.

Time to let old ghosts die. Move on.

Shaking off her paranoia, she started to close the envelope but a photo fell into her lap. A picture of a dead woman or some kind of sick joke?

Her heart pounding, she examined the picture more closely to see if it was real.

A naked woman had been tied to a four-poster bed. The bedding appeared rumpled and stained with blood. The woman's eyes were wide-open in terror, outlined in crudely painted-on black makeup, her slender young face contorted in agony. Ruby-red lipstick covered her mouth, and was smeared as if she'd hastily applied it. The remainder of her makeup was grotesque, overdone to the point of making her look like a whore. And the bloodred color of the lipstick matched the crimson red teddy that had been ripped and lay at her bare feet.

Where had the photo been taken? She scanned the room for details. An alligator's head hung on the scarred wall in the dilapidated shanty. A snake was coiled by the bed.

A lancet pierced her heart.

Inhaling sharply, Britta zeroed in on the necklace dangling around her bruised throat. The black stone was shaped like a serpent swallowing its tail.

Britta had seen that same necklace before. Years ago....

The man had tried to make her wear one, but she'd thrown it into the dirt and run.

The scene moved in slow motion in her mind. The scents of rotten vegetation, blood, mutilated animals. The marsh rose from the depths of her darkest hours to haunt her. Like quicksand the muddy soil tried to suck her underground. Alligators and snakes nibbled at her heels, begging for dinner. Bones crunched where one had found his feast.

She closed her eyes. Banished the images and sounds. Visualized herself escaping. Slowly, her breathing steadied and the panic eased in her chest. She was overreacting.

The picture was probably fake.

But the yellowish-blue tint to the woman's skin and the blood looked real. And Britta's gut instincts told her that the woman had been murdered.

DUSK DARKENED THE SKY around the backwoods, blurring the lines between day and night as the murky Mississippi churned and slapped against the dilapidated shanty.

Detective Jean-Paul Dubois stared at the crime scene in disgust. The woman had been viciously murdered. Blood covered her bare chest and had dried onto the stained sheets of the bed. A scarlet teddy lay at her feet, which were bound to the footboard with thick ropes, and her hands were tied to the headboard. Whoever had killed her had defiled her body—left her naked, bound, posed, her heart literally ripped apart with some kind of ancient spear.

His gaze fell to the serpent necklace and he recognized the symbolic meaning. Good fighting evil.

Apparently the evil had won this time.

The CSI team arrived but he held up his hand for them to wait, then bowed his head for a moment, silently offering a prayer of reverence before he allowed them to move forward. With two sisters of his own and the never-ending guilt of his wife's death on his conscience, seeing any female hurt and stripped of her dignity grated on his soul. At least Lucinda had not suffered rape or this humiliation. But still her death had cut him to the bone.

He had to put her out of his mind. Had to work, keep busy, pay penance for his mistakes by saving others.

The Dubois men were cut from Cajun cloth. Had shady characters in their own ancestry. But today's Dubois men spelled law. All three of them. Himself, Damon and Antwaun. He'd do his job and find out who had made this woman suffer.

He mentally cataloged the crime scene while his

partner Detective Carson Graves searched the exterior. The room reeked of raunchy sex. Her face was painted with makeup in a grotesque style. Especially her eyes.

Then her heart had been brutally slashed. The killer had intentionally left her vulnerable and exposed as if to shame her. Worse, he'd left her deep in the bayou where the vermin might eat her before her body could be discovered.

It appeared ritualistic. Had he murdered before?

Or had this sicko just come to New Orleans?

Bourbon Street, Mardi Gras…as much as Jean-Paul loved his home in the bayou, something untamed in the land and climate drew the crazies like flies to sweet maple syrup. And with the pre-Mardi Gras celebrations, crime would only escalate.

Still, he did things by the book. No man was above the law. He had to make sure the investigators did everything right.

Flies and mosquitoes swarmed inside. The sounds of the woods croaked and buzzed around him while the muddy river carried vines, broken tree limbs and God knows what else upstream. Shadows hugged every corner, offering a hiding place for predators.

The stench of death from the victim assaulted him, along with another strange odor that he didn't quite recognize. The female CSI officer paused, stepped outside for air, then returned a few seconds later, looking pale but determined.

Judging from rigor and her body's decay, she had been here at least a couple of days. In fact they might never have found her had a local fisherman not noticed a faint light from an old bulb shining in the darkness and decided to check it out.

"At least he left her inside the cabin," Skeeter Jones, the head CSI officer, murmured.

Yeah, or the gators would have fed on her already. Then no one would ever have found her.

The medical examiner, Dr. Leland Charles, leaned over to examine the body. "The chest wound looks bad. A wide blade, lots of bruising. Looks as if he twisted it. He wanted her to suffer. Her coloring is pale with a yellowish tint."

"We'll check and track down where he got the lancet." Jean-Paul stooped to study the spear. "They sell them in the gift shops in town."

"Hell, a man could have his pick of murder weapons from the street vendors," Charles muttered.

"So, what was the cause of death?" Jean-Paul asked.

"There are no ligature marks on her neck so I'd rule out asphyxiation. She might have bled out from the chest wound, but I want to check the tox screens." Charles noted more bruises on her body—her ribs, abdomen, thighs. "She did fight back," he murmured, "as much as she could in her position."

Jean-Paul wondered if she had agreed to the bondage, then changed her mind later. Or she could have been unconscious when the perp tied her up. "I want the cause of death as soon as you finish with her. And make sure to send me the result of the full tox screen and rape kit. We need to determine if the sex was consensual."

Charles nodded, then dabbed a Q-tip across the woman's abdomen and bagged it. "It looks like he rubbed some kind of oil on her body. Maybe one of those love potions or sensual oils they sell in the market."

Jean-Paul scanned the room for a bottle. "So our guy uses massage oil as if he wants the woman to enjoy sex, then kills her? I don't get it. Maybe he was conflicted?"

Charles muttered a curse. "Figure out what makes this one tick and you'll catch him."

"Maybe the night started out with romance, then things got rough."

"And something she said or did triggered the man to snap and he killed her," Charles added.

Jean-Paul shook his head, not buying it. The scene seemed too posed. Too planned. "No. The serpent necklace and lancet indicate he came prepared." And what the hell did the mask of that crocodile head mean?

A tech motioned toward the medical examiner and Jean-Paul narrowed his eyes. "Did you find something?"

She shrugged. "Boombox is still warm. Found a CD in it called 'Heartache Blues.'"

"Symbolic or what?" Dr. Charles commented.

"She ripped out his heart, so he did the same to her." Jean-Paul made a sound with his mouth. "Could be his motivation."

"Check out the artist," the tech said. "Some newbie named Randy Swain. I saw a write-up about him in the paper. He's here for the music festival."

Along with a thousand others. All strangers, which made their investigation more difficult. "Of course." Jean-Paul made a note to question the singer Randy Swain. And to question a couple of guys who made masks and sold them in the market.

The woman bagged the CD, dusted the boombox, then tagged both items for evidence.

"Anyone find the girl's identification?" he asked.

One of the CSI techs shook his head. "Not so far."

"Where are her clothes?"

"We didn't find them, either," the CSI tech replied. "No clothes. No condom. Nothing personal. Not a toothbrush, comb or even a pair of underwear."

"This guy knows what he's doing," Jean-Paul said. "He's meticulous. He cleaned up. Didn't leave any trace evidence."

"There's usually something—a hair fiber, an errant button, thread off a jacket," the female crime scene investigator said. "If there is, we'll find it."

Jean-Paul nodded and studied the victim's face again. Woman? Hell, she looked so damn young. Like someone's daughter or little sister. Except for the grotesque makeup.

Had she been a hooker or had the killer only painted her to resemble the girls in the red-light district?

His cell phone trilled and he checked the number. His superior, Lieutenant Phelps. He connected the call, his gaze catching sight of his partner combing the wooden dock.

"Lieutenant, what is it?" Jean-Paul asked.

"We just got a call I need you to check out."

"Do we have a lead already?"

"Maybe. You know that erotica magazine, *Naked Desires?*"

He grimaced. His sisters had mentioned it at one of their family gatherings. Apparently *they* thought some of the letters were titillating. "I don't exactly subscribe to it."

Phelps chuckled. "I wouldn't expect my pride-and-joy officer to."

Jean-Paul grimaced. He hated all the hype he'd received after the hurricane. Just because he'd stuck to his post, done his job and saved a few people, he'd received a damn commendation. Big deal. He'd lost his wife....

"So what is it?" he asked.

"Britta Berger, the editor of the Secret Confessions column called and said she had something we needed to see."

"Now?" Jean-Paul tapped his boot impatiently. "What is it, some letter that freaked her out?"

"Apparently it's a photograph, not a letter," Phelps said in a serious tone.

"But doesn't this case take priority?" Jean-Paul asked.

"It is about this case," Phelps said, deadpan. "According to her description, she received a photograph of a crime."

"What crime?"

"A murder," Phelps said. "One that sounds suspiciously like the one you're investigating."

HE STOOD OUTSIDE the door to Naked Desires, the urge to go in making him shake with need. The moment he'd seen her photograph in that magazine, he'd recognized her.

His Adrianna.

How ironic to finally have found her here in the city. So close to where he had first met her. So close to where everything had gone wrong.

What was she doing now? Studying the photograph he'd sent her? Staring in horror at the woman's vile, bloodless eyes? Wondering why he had sent her the message?

Adrenaline churned through his blood, heating his body.

He had to see her. Touch her. Watch the realization dawn in her eyes....

No. Not yet.

He'd waited years for this moment. Had searched in every face and town he'd visited. Had combed the edges of the bayou—hunting, hoping, yearning, praying she had survived.

So he could kill her.

Laughter bubbled in his chest. And now the moment was so near, his vengeance almost within reach. Yet he had to draw it out. Earn his redemption. Save the other sinners. Make them pay.

And make Adrianna watch them suffer.

With each one, she would feel him breathing down her neck. Coming closer. Know the pain of having death upon her conscience.

Just as he lived with his father's death upon his.

God made the world in seven days and nights. Seven days and nights *he* had been tortured after she took his father's life.

Seven more days until Mardi Gras.

Each day until then, a celebration.

Each day until then, a time to torture.

And on the seventh day, when Mardi Gras reached its grand finale, he would find salvation. He couldn't wait to see the shock in her eyes when she realized that she had never escaped at all. That she had to pay for her sins.

And that she had to die because he loved her.

CHAPTER TWO

THE DEAD WOMAN'S eyes haunted Britta.

She tried to tamp her nerves as the publisher of *Naked Desires*, R. J. Justice, paced his office. He'd been cursing ever since she'd shown him the photo. Of course her insides were knotted. The *last* thing she wanted to do was talk to the cops.

In fact, she had held on to the picture all day hoping to convince herself the note and picture had been a joke, but finally her conscience had worn her down. She hadn't been able to justify not showing R.J. the photograph.

Not even to save her own skin.

Hopefully, it wouldn't come down to that. This was an isolated incident. The police would investigate.

And she wouldn't have to be involved or divulge her secrets.

"I know you're shaken, Britta," R.J. muttered.

"I'll be fine. After all, this is probably a false alarm. We aren't positive the woman is really dead. The photographer could have staged the scene to look like a murder. For shock value."

"True. But he had to know we'd check it out before we printed it."

Britta shrugged and rubbed at her temple, appalled

that R.J. would consider showcasing such violence in their magazine. "Who knows what drives people. Maybe he's a photographer and wants to impress us so he can land a job here." Or maybe he meant for her to call the police because he wanted public recognition.

R.J. stopped pacing, his tall lanky frame silhouetted in the window, his laser eyes piercing her as if contemplating the possibility. Outside, gray clouds cast shadows across the office, making the room seem even smaller and more claustrophobic. Zydeco music pounded the air, the shouts of partiers from the street below echoed through the dirt-streaked window. Crowds of tourists still cheered and talked about the parade. Although it was early evening, tourists had already dipped into the happy-hour specials with tequila and pitchers of beer and were filing into the strip joints for their first peep show of the night.

"I have to meet with our legal team. Do you think you can handle the police?" R.J. asked.

Britta clenched her hands together. "Sure."

For a moment, R.J. reached for her. Twice when they'd discussed her column, debating over which submissions to print and which ones were too graphic, R.J. had hinted at wanting a personal relationship with her. Hinted that he'd like to share his secret sexual fantasies with her.

She backed toward the door. R.J. was barely thirty, only a few years older than her and was well-dressed in his Armani suits. Attractive. Single. Sexy. Mysterious.

But dangerous.

The collection of gargoyles on his bookshelf made her uneasy. And he had dozens of nude sketchings on his walls—all macabre with scenes of violence—along with an S and M calendar and bronze sculptures of mutant creatures—part human, part animal.

Some men had dark sides. R.J. was one of them. She'd witnessed his charm and ability to seduce a woman. Then his volatile temper.

His fantasies teetered on the narcissistic side.

And she didn't want to be any part of them.

THE HEAT FROM the New Orleans air simmered with sexuality and smelled of raw body sweat that only heightened R.J.'s lustful thoughts. The magic of Mardi Gras fed his addiction to the night life and celebration of man's greatest pleasure—the physical coupling of man and woman.

He wanted Britta. He had wanted her for a long damn time.

But she wasn't ready—yet.

In fact, if she knew the gritty cravings in his mind, she would run a million miles away.

She might even suspect that he'd sent that lurid photograph.

A soft laugh escaped him. But she couldn't run forever. One day she'd see that the two of them were meant to be together. That he had built this magazine with her in mind. That each day as he walked the streets of the French Quarter, he imagined seducing her in his office, ripping off her clothes and taking her on his desk. Each night he fell asleep with fantasies of her on top of him, her legs spread wide on his bed, taking his aching length into her warm body. With her tied to the post, the black leather squeaking as she shifted, the whip in his hand, passionate cries floating from her lips. And then vice versa.

His cock swelled, throbbing like hell. He intended

to unleash Britta's darkest desires. And she had desires…even though she refused to admit them.

Her terror over the photo might be his ticket to win her trust. She needed comfort. Protection.

And he'd open his arms and watch her fall right into them.

DESPERATE TO ESCAPE R.J., Britta raced away, but her breath caught at the sight of the hulking man in her office. Neon lights twirled and blinked intermittently, painting a kaleidoscope of colors across his angular face as he stared out the window overlooking Bourbon Street. A mixture of blues, jazz and gospel music engulfed her, its pounding mirroring her beating heart.

Who was he? The man who'd sent her the picture?

As if he sensed her presence without even facing her, he murmured her name. "Miss Berger?"

He knew she'd been watching him. "Yes?"

He slowly turned toward her, his intimidating stance personified by his huge masculine body. "Detective Jean-Paul Dubois."

She inhaled sharply as recognition dawned. His picture had been plastered all over the paper. That reporter Mazie Burgess had written a half-dozen hero-worshipping pieces on him. Apparently, Jean-Paul Dubois had risked his life to save hundreds after the latest hurricane disaster.

He was also a hard-ass when it came to the law.

Fear tightened her chest as she scrutinized him for signs that he wouldn't pry too deeply into her life. That he'd accept what she gave him and ask for nothing else.

But the steely expression in his eyes told her not to count on it. His masculine body screamed Cajun and his raw sexuality hit her in the pit of her stomach. He was rugged, much bigger than he'd looked in the newspaper, probably at least six-four. Tough. Not afraid to fight. His hands were broad, scarred, as if he'd wrestled alligators in the swamp and survived.

If he'd grown up in the bayou, then he probably had.

His razor-sharp eyes looked almost black in the dim light. A five o'clock shadow already grazed his angular jaw and his masculine scent triggered wicked fantasies of her own. Naked, he would look like an ancient Roman god.

"You phoned?" he asked in a deep baritone.

She nodded, searching for her voice and professional manner.

He glanced at the current magazine cover on her bulletin board, a half-nude couple donning elaborate Mardi Gras masks with black and red feather boas as their only clothing. She silently reminded herself she didn't have to be ashamed of her job or her affiliation with the magazine, either. Besides, it was a cover. "Yes, Detective. Please sit down."

His gaze slid over her, then lingered a moment too long on her breasts and a disapproving flicker followed. She cleared her throat, irritated at herself for letting it bother her. What did she care if the man found her sexually lacking? She'd never indulge her fantasies or pursue a relationship with a cop.

Recovering quickly, she claimed her office chair and waited until he settled into the wingback opposite her. "I don't know if this is important or not. It may be a prank, someone wanting to shock me. We…get some of those." God, she didn't want to do this. What if he asked too many questions?

Questions she didn't want to answer.

She'd lied all her life about who she was, what she was, where she'd come from. Sometimes she barely remembered the truth herself.

"I imagine you do." A suspicious smile tugged at the corner of his mouth. "You like reading people's secret fantasies?"

How could she answer that without sounding perverted herself? "There's nothing wrong with sexual fantasies, Detective Dubois."

"Ever include your own?"

Her chest tightened at the smoldering insinuation in his husky voice. The music outside intensified its beat, drawing her into its seductive lair. The odd love chant of New Orleans rippled through the paper-thin walls from the bar next door. "If ever I cease to love, may cows lay eggs and fish grow legs. If ever I cease to love…"

"No." She wouldn't openly reveal her private thoughts. Or her fears. And good heavens, she wished they'd stop that song. She didn't believe in love.

"This isn't about me," she said, struggling to redirect the conversation. "I phoned the police because I received something disturbing in the mail today."

His jaw tightened. "Yes, of course."

She handed him the envelope and their hands brushed, sending a shiver up her spine. She drew her hand back quickly. She couldn't allow this man to charm her. He was a pro.

He might extract information from her without her even realizing it.

Information she would take with her to her grave.

JEAN-PAUL DUBOIS SIGHED in disgust. What the hell was wrong with him? Granted he was a sucker for a woman in trouble but usually he handled his reaction better. But something about the challenge, the wariness, the spark of sexual attraction between him and Britta Berger had him on edge.

Not a good idea. He needed to get back to the crime scene. This visit was probably a waste of time.

Still she was intriguing. Her camisole top, coupled with that long whimsical skirt and sandals gave her a live-and-let-live look, yet he sensed she wore a disguise. She wasn't laissez-faire at all but as uptight as a wild animal in a cage.

And those dynamite full lips conjured up images of sultry kisses. Plus her fiery short, red hair triggered fantasies of wild, tawdry sex.

But her brown eyes skated over him as if he were the scum of the earth. He reminded himself he was here on business. He didn't care what she thought about him. A woman was dead, for God's sake, and he was the lead investigator.

"He left a note with the photo," she said in a strained voice. For a brief second, tension ruled her slender face, then she inhaled sharply, making her top stretch across her breasts and offering a glimpse of her tantalizing cleavage.

Shit.

He dropped his gaze to the desk while she slid a manila envelope toward him. "Who delivered it?"

"I have no idea. It was on my desk with the other mail when I arrived at work."

"You lock your door when you leave your office at night?"

"Yes."

"Who else has access to your office?"

"Just R.J., the head of the magazine." She ran a hand

through her hair. "And Ralphie, the young college kid we hired to sort mail."

"I'll need to talk to both of them."

Britta frowned. "Trust me, Detective, Ralphie had nothing to do with this. He's just a kid."

"He has male chromosomes, Miss Berger. Trust *me*, I know what young men are like."

Her face paled and he ground his teeth, hating to frighten her, but she shouldn't trust anyone. Especially with all the crazies in town. "How about your boss?"

A nervous look flickered in her eyes. "R.J. is hard-working, innovative and knows how to make money. We have a business relationship, that's all."

Jean-Paul arched an eyebrow, wondering why she'd offered that tidbit, then removed the contents from the envelope. Damn it to hell and back.

The picture was of his crime scene.

The auburn-haired woman was tied to the bed, her face contorted in agony, her chest pierced with the lancet. The torn red teddy, the mask of the part crocodile, part human head on the wall, the CD player, the obscene makeup—the details were identical to the murder scene he'd just processed.

Even more alarming, the victim faintly resembled Britta Berger. Not as good-looking or striking, but her hair color and complexion were similar.

"Did anyone touch the photo besides you?"

"Just my boss. I showed it to him to ask his advice."

"You weren't going to call the police?"

"I wasn't sure it was real, that...the woman was really dead."

He contemplated her answer, then nodded. "You have no idea who sent this?"

"No."

"Have you ever received anything like this before?"

"No. Most of the photographs are sent directly to our photography department. Our legal department handles any contacts with submissions."

He made a disgusted sound but she continued.

"Our magazine doesn't support murder or violence, Detective Dubois, just healthy sexual fantasies."

His gaze met hers, emotions flaring in her exotic brown eyes, but also defiance.

"Still, some of those fantasies border on the sadistic side," he argued. "They come from perverts, sickos, deranged individuals."

"Everyone has their own tastes," she admitted quietly.

And his lay toward sweet, simple, quiet, more domestic family-type women like Lucinda. Not with spooky redheads with fire in their eyes. Ones who looked as untamed as a hot July New Orleans night. This one, he imagined, had seen the seedy side of life and not cowered from it. A vixen in disguise.

One who had secrets.

"Did you know this woman?"

"No, I've never seen her before." She bit down on her lip. "Why, Detective? Is it real?"

He met her gaze head-on. "Yes. I just came from the crime scene. I'm afraid this woman was murdered."

A faint gasp escaped her. "Oh God, no." A heartbeat of silence stretched between them, taut, filled with unanswered questions. "Who was she?" she finally asked.

"We're still working on identifying her." He cleared his throat, lowering his voice. "I'd like for you to keep this confidential. No press. No publication of this picture. Don't tell anyone else that you received it. Understood?"

Britta nodded. "Of course. We'll help any way we can."

Her mouth twitched slightly as if she wanted to say more, but she clamped her teeth over her lower lip instead.

He shifted and tapped the envelope with one finger. "Has this man written you before?"

"You mean for the column?"

"Yes."

She massaged two fingers to her temple. "I...don't know. But I'll review our prior issues and see if I find anything that appears connected."

"I'd also like to take copies of the magazine with me. And don't forget the letters you didn't print."

Alarm shot through her eyes. "There must be hundreds."

"Bring them to the station. My partner and I will help sort through them."

Wariness pulled at her features but she agreed.

"You also mentioned a note?" He held out his hand. "Let me see it."

She handed him the sheet of charcoal-gray paper, and he read the message silently.

I know your secrets.
And you know mine.

His gaze rose again to meet hers. "What does he mean by that? He knows your secrets?"

She remained so still that he didn't think she was going to answer. But fear momentarily settled in her eyes. "I assume he's referring to the magazine," she said in a low voice. "My column is called Secret Confessions."

Liar. "It sounds more personal." He closed the distance between them. "I think you know more than you're telling. You may even know the killer. At least, *he* knows *you*."

She lifted her chin a notch. "A lot of people who write into the magazine think they know me."

"You're hiding something, Miss Berger." He leaned across the desk, so close his face was only a breath away. So close he inhaled the hypnotic scent of her perfume.

So close he felt the tension vibrate in her lean muscles.

"But secrets have a way of coming out. And before this investigation is over, I will find out exactly what you're keeping from me."

CHAPTER THREE

"I WILL FIND OUT exactly what you're keeping from me."

Detective Dubois's warning echoed in Britta's head as she searched her memory for any confession letters that might have hinted at violence or murder.

What if the killer had written to her in advance and she had ignored the warning or completely missed it? Maybe she could have saved this woman if she'd paid more attention....

Disturbed by the thought, she bagged the last two months' submissions to carry to the police station the next day. For now, she had to take a walk. Clear her head.

The stench of beer, alcohol, smoke, sweat, urine and garbage permeated Bourbon Street. The raucous laughter and horny, groping drunken strangers were a dreaded experience.

But living on the streets had taught her how to deal with them. The thought of holing up in her apartment above the office with back copies of the magazine—alone with her own demons—was something she couldn't face yet.

She'd walk to the Market, lose herself in the local musicians and artists, grab a bite of supper. Her stomach growled, reminding her she'd missed lunch. The possibility of a nice crisp crab salad or bowl of seafood gumbo made her mouth water.

She checked over her shoulder for the hundredth time to make certain no one was following her as she wound through the chaotic crowd. A man wearing a patch over his right eye whispered an invitation for her to join him in the pub next door, but she rushed past, aware the man tracked her as she disappeared into the throng. Next door, another club offered half-priced drinks along with pole-dancing, featuring the mammoth-breasted Moaning Mona. Two dregs wearing ratty T-shirts that read "I fuck like a Mack Truck," grunted an invitation for drinks and a threesome. And a group of bikers boasting tattoos of snakes and tribal symbols huddled around an outdoor table, guzzling beer and making catcalls to the girls flashing their boobs for free drinks and beads.

She plunged through the tawdry mob, south toward Jackson Square and the French Market where the less seedy side congregated in the outdoor cafés, finer restaurants, the open market and shops that comprised the *Vieux Carre*. Although street musicians and artisans normally flocked to the area, now an open-air festival had been set up with artisans showcasing their creations, demonstrating techniques, offering sketches for the tourists and squabbling over prices for their treasures.

A clown created balloon animals for the children in one corner, a mime entertained in another and a longhaired hippie rasped out music on a washboard for pocket change. Down the street, the famous jazz music of Louis Armstrong flowed from a restaurant while blues tunes paying homage to Fats Domino wailed into the steamy sultry air. Patio gardens and flowerboxes from the delicately carved balconies added color and a sweet fragrance. This was the N'Awlins she loved.

She seated herself at her favorite outdoor café, ordered a glass of pinot grigio and a crab salad, then studied the crowd as she sipped the wine.

But the hair on the back of her neck bristled. Someone was watching her.

She scanned the streets again. Oblivious to her unease, the air buzzed with activity and excitement, celebrating life and the renewal of the city. A mime plucked a coin from behind a little girl's ear, while puppeteers drew the small kids in droves. Families littered the streets, carrying tired children with painted faces, cotton candy and tacky souvenirs, tugging at heartstrings she tried to ignore.

She banished them quickly. She was not a family kind of girl.

Instead her past mocked her. And the whisper of danger echoed in her ear....

I know your secrets. And you know mine.

No. It was impossible. She'd never told anyone about her childhood. Especially about that night.

And her mother.... Surely she wouldn't have confessed to anyone. That is, if she'd survived herself.

Then again, her mother had done other unspeakable things.

The washboard player took a break and an earthy-looking saxophone player claimed his spot, adding his own jazz flavor to old favorites. She glanced behind him, toward the edge of the street, and noticed a tall, bald man holding a camera. Her fork clattered to the table. Was he photographing her?

She craned her neck to see more clearly and he lowered the camera. Shadows from the silvery Spanish moss shrouded his face as if he'd been cocooned in a giant spiderweb. Then he lifted his right hand and waved. Her breath caught in her chest.

A series of flashes flickered like fireflies against the growing darkness. Once. Twice. A dozen times. She blinked and threw her hand over her forehead, spots dancing before her eyes.

He *was* watching her. Taking pictures....

For what reason?

Panic and anger mushroomed inside her and she stepped forward to go confront him, but the waiter appeared with her check and blocked her path.

"*Chere?* You pay before you leave us? *Qui?*"

She sighed, removed her wallet and paid. But when she glanced across the street, the man had completely disappeared, lost in the darkness and the sins waging the city.

HOWARD KEITH STOOD nursing a Jax, a locally brewed beer, across the street, shielded by the exuberance of the Mardi Gras festivities. Britta Berger had actually noticed him.

Of course he was at a distance and she couldn't see his face.

Howard's right hand went to his prosthetic eyeball and he blinked, feeling it slip out of place. He popped it out, dusted it off, then slipped it back inside his eye pocket, blinking to create enough moisture to force the fake eye to settle.

Of course, he tried not to handle the ocular prosthetic in public, at least not in front of women. They tended to balk at the empty eye socket.

Although even with his eye in place, they were put off by his appearance. They never knew quite where to look, where to focus, so they averted their gazes and studied his feet, his stomach, his hands, anything but his face. And within seconds they rushed away, dismissing him as if he was a freak.

He would show them. Prove them wrong.

His fingers tightened on the camera. Even his interest in photography had garnered laughter and disbelief. How could he truly be an artist when he had no peripheral vision? No depth perception?

The camera compensated. Its powerful lens enabled him to capture the planes and angles, the light and shadows, the depth he wanted, and record it in vivid detail. And New Orleans certainly provided enough colorful characters, scenery and entertainment to feed his camera-frenzied mind.

Then he could do with it as he wished. Create masterpieces with his sketches, mold the faces into sculptures if he chose. Give the subjects life forever. Paint the eyes.

The eyes were the windows to the soul.

Did Britta Berger have any idea that he had seen into hers? That he had been watching her for months? That he knew her schedule. The food she chose for breakfast. The way she liked her coffee. The fact that she enjoyed a glass of wine on her patio at night before she retired. That she brushed her short red hair at least a hundred times before she crawled beneath the sheets.

That she slept without underwear.

That he'd seen her naked in the shower, her own hands stroking over sensitive private places that he ached to touch.

Yet, the seductress that he saw thrived on privacy. She was an enigma. He'd discovered that in his research. In her own way, she was hiding from life itself.

The vulnerability in her eyes had drawn him. She wanted someone to reach out and make the pain of her past dissipate. But she was afraid. After all, underneath her physical beauty lay lies, weaknesses, false promises. Evil.

Yes, a bad girl lurked inside Britta Berger and he would show the world her true self, just as he would with his other subjects. If it hurt them, then so be it.

His own pain had brought him to this point. He used it. Thrived upon it. It had inspired the theme for his work, which would hopefully gain him acclaim.

Then the beautifuls would be erased, their ugliness exposed forever.

IRRITATION KNOTTED Jean-Paul Dubois's shoulders as he drummed his knuckles on R.J. Justice's desk. Dammit. Time was critical. He had a murder to investigate and the magazine owner had kept him waiting for half an hour.

Long enough for him to decide he didn't like the man. That he was weird. His office collections indicated an interest in S and M, witchcraft, bestiality and photographs that bordered on porn.

Justice finally loped in, tugging at his tie. "Sorry about that. My meeting ran over."

Jean-Paul ignored the feigned apology and studied the man's features, sizing him up. The women might call him handsome but a cold hardness that Jean-Paul had detected in other suspects hinted that he was ruthless and calculating. He would do whatever he had to do to protect *Naked Desires*. And to get what he wanted in his personal life.

"You met with Britta already?" Justice asked as he settled into his desk chair.

Jean-Paul nodded. "She was very helpful." Britta had claimed she and Justice were simply business partners. Just how did Justice feel about her?

"She was upset," Justice said. "Were her fears justified?"

"I'm afraid so."

Justice ran a hand over his sleek desk. "Damn. So the crime scene was real?"

Jean-Paul nodded. "We found the woman in the photo murdered earlier." He leaned forward, his gaze penetrating. "You don't seem surprised."

Justice shrugged. "I realize our magazine caters to the...adventuresome side, so we get some odd mail. But we certainly don't condone murder."

Jean-Paul narrowed his eyes. "I asked Miss Berger to bring all the mail she's received in the past month to the station. It's possible this guy wrote in before."

Justice hesitated. "I suppose that sounds fair, although I would like to keep our magazine out of the investigation when you talk to the press."

"You don't want the publicity?"

Justice shrugged. "I can stand it, but I was thinking about Britta's safety."

"Of course." Jean-Paul cleared his throat, not certain he believed the man. What if Justice had killed the woman, then sent the photo to Britta anonymously to stir publicity?

"Do you keep a record of the submissions with the sender's name and address?"

"Yes. In a secure file."

"Who sent this photo?"

"I'm afraid I don't know," Justice said matter-of-factly. "I checked and the envelope wasn't logged in. Ralphie must have found it in the overnight-mail slot and put it on Britta's desk."

"Then I need to speak to him."

Justice punched a button on the intercom and ordered the boy to come to his office.

Jean-Paul stood. "Mr. Justice, can you tell me anything that might help us find the killer? Did you know the victim? Had you ever seen her before?"

Justice steepled his fingers as if in thought. "No. Should I know her?"

"Not necessarily, but I have to ask."

"What was her name?"

"We haven't identified her yet." Jean-Paul paused. "How about the cabin? Did you recognize it?"

Justice scoffed. "That shanty could be any one of a hundred tucked in the bayou."

Jean-Paul pushed on, "Have you received any calls or letters yourself that might be related?"

"I would have reported it if I had, Detective."

"Can you think of any reason the killer targeted Miss Berger with the photograph?"

Justice raised a brow. "She's a beautiful woman. Maybe the killer saw her photo in the magazine and wanted to get her attention."

"You're probably right," Jean-Paul admitted, although his gut instinct hinted there was more. And that Justice was holding back. Maybe *he* was the one fixated on her. Maybe he'd killed a replica of her to frighten her into his arms.

"How long have you known Miss Berger?" Jean-Paul asked.

Justice's hands tightened by his side. A telltale sign that the question stirred his anxiety. "A few months."

"And your relationship is…?"

"Strictly business," Justice said with a predatory gleam flashing in his eyes.

"Has she been involved with anyone recently? Someone who might want to hurt her?"

"Not that I know of," Justice said in a curt tone.

"You haven't noticed any strange men hanging around? Maybe outside?"

"No." Justice cleared his throat. "Well, except for that Reverend Cortain and his religious group. They're harassing us."

"By protesting the publication of *Naked Desires?*"

Justice heaved a sigh. "Yes. That idiot reverend is leading the madness. If you ask me, he's a psycho himself. Maybe you should check into him."

Jean-Paul made a note to do so. "Has he threatened you or Miss Berger?"

"He sent fliers to Britta about his protest rallies, touting some religious bunk about us leading others into sin," Justice admitted with a scowl. "And if this murder gets out, he'll probably accuse our magazine of triggering sexually related crimes."

"Where were you two nights ago, say around midnight?"

Justice snapped his head up, his eyes seething. "You can't possibly think that I had something to do with this. For God's sake, I encouraged Britta to report the incident. And like I just said, this crime will only be fodder for Cortain's nonsense."

"I have to ask so I can eliminate you as a suspect."

Justice shuffled his day planner. "I…was with a

woman. I can give you her name if you want. She'll vouch for me."

Jean-Paul indicated a pad on the desk. "I'd appreciate that."

Justice's lips thinned into a straight line, but he tore off the sheet of paper and shoved it toward Jean-Paul.

A knock rapped on the door and a skinny, blond kid appeared. "Mr. Justice? You wanted to see me?"

"Yes, Ralphie. Come in. Detective Dubois from the New Orleans Police Department needs to ask you a question."

Jean-Paul gave him a once-over. Young. Naive. Khakis and a designer shirt with Italian loafers. Green under the collar.

Not a murderer.

The boy paled. "Did I do something wrong?"

Jean-Paul explained about the photo and Ralphie collapsed into a chair. "I…I thought Miss Berger seemed upset when she asked me about the mail earlier, but she didn't tell me about the picture."

"What did she say?" Jean-Paul asked.

"She wanted to know if I'd seen the person who'd delivered the envelope."

"And did you?"

"No." He crossed his feet at his ankles, rocking sideways. "It was under the door this morning when I arrived."

Jean-Paul nodded. "So you put it on her desk? But you didn't open it first?"

"No. It was addressed to her." Embarrassment colored his face. "Miss Berger doesn't like me to read the mail. Says I'm too young."

"How did you get those scratches on your hand?"

"My dog." He stared at his knuckles. "I just got a boxer puppy. I'm trying to train him but, man, he chews on everything in sight."

Jean-Paul frowned. The kid obviously knew nothing. "Have you noticed anyone lurking around, maybe watching Miss Berger?"

"No one specifically. Although men always look at her."

Yes, they would. Although Britta could probably take care of herself, a sliver of worry tickled his spine, arousing protective instincts born of years on the job.

His reaction certainly couldn't be personal. Britta Berger was definitely not his type.

But the killer had chosen her for a reason.

Jean-Paul intended to find out exactly what it was.

And why his victim had resembled her, as well.

A GUST OF WIND from the impending storm rattled the trees and sent leaves swirling around Britta's feet as she rushed through the mob on Bourbon Street to her apartment. The storm clouds grew darker; the sounds of feet pounding the pavement became more ominous as the night swelled with the hordes of tourists. She glanced over her shoulder, repeatedly searching for the photographer, but a fog of drunken tourists obliterated any individual from standing out.

Still, someone was out there.

She sensed him watching her, felt his beady eyes on her skin. Studying her. Waiting.

Was it the photographer she'd spotted during dinner? The killer who'd sent her the photo?

Were they the same man?

She considered calling the cops but what could she tell

them? She had an odd feeling? They'd think she was crazy.

A beer can rolled across the pavement, clanging into a metal garbage can and she shrieked, pausing as a beefy hand reached down to grab it. "Sorry about that, ma'am."

She tensed at the lascivious look in his liquor-glazed eyes, and pushed past him, shouldering her way around more groping hands until she reached Naked Desires. Neon lights dotted the street with color, highlighting the painted print and logo on the door window. Several lurid males drooled, their faces pressed against the fog-coated glass as they tried to peek inside.

Ignoring their pleas for a sneak preview of the upcoming magazine and offers to share their fantasies with her, she maneuvered her way inside, slammed the door shut and locked it. But she froze at the sight of the darkened stairwell leading to the upstairs apartment. She tried the light, but it didn't work. Had someone messed with it or had the bulb simply burned out?

You're being paranoid. How many times last month had it done the same thing and she hadn't thought it suspicious?

Choking back fear, she clenched her keys, ready to use them as a weapon. Outside, the wind howled like an animal. She unlocked the door and hurried inside. With only three rooms to the tiny apartment, she raced through them all, finally muttering a silent thank-you to find them empty.

Still, she paused in her bedroom, the hairs on the nape of her neck prickling. The top bureau drawer which held her underwear was open slightly. Hadn't she shut it this morning when she'd left for work? Normally, she kept her garments neat, her bras on the left side, her favorite frilly underwear on the right. In the drawer below, she stored her teddies. Now, her underwear was jumbled as if someone had pawed through it. Frantic, she jerked the second drawer open and gasped. Her teddies had also been moved around as if someone had touched them.

Then she saw it—a red crotchless teddy lay in the center of her bed.

A low sob caught in her throat. It was just like the one the dead woman had worn in the photograph. She glanced up in horror and noticed the note stuck to the mirror.

"I always have one eye on you. You can't run forever."

Shaking with fear and disgust, she rushed to the bathroom and splashed water on her face to stem the nausea. What should she do? Could that photographer somehow have gotten into her place? Or the killer who'd sent her the photograph of the murdered woman?

Hands shaking, she reached for a towel, patted her face dry, then glanced in the mirror, expecting to see a madman staring at her. But only her terrified eyes were reflected back. That and images of a long-ago time she'd thought she'd forgotten. Of a terrified little girl and a man she refused to speak of....

She spun around, ran into the bedroom to grab her purse and retrieved Detective Dubois's card. She had to report the break-in. Show him the red teddy.

But if she did, he'd ask more questions. Want to know more about her and why this psycho had decided to stalk her.

She'd thought today's note had to do with the magazine. But what if it had something to do with her past?

D-day—the day she'd died and started a new life.

No, it was impossible.

Maybe she should just pick up and run again. She could start over. Find another job. A new name. A new city.

But the face of the young woman who'd died rose to haunt her. She was so young. Hadn't deserved to be left in the bayou for the mosquitoes, snakes and gators to feast upon.

Memories of the night she'd fled into the bayou rushed back. She'd been dirty, hungry, terrified and so thirsty she'd hallucinated. She'd seen the devil and other wild, mysterious creatures in the marshy swampland.

And now, thirteen years later, another one roamed the streets....

She couldn't run this time.

Not with the dead girl's face etched in her mind permanently. It would stay with her no matter where she went. And so would her guilt and the memory of her sins.

The only way to escape them was to pay her penance.

Maybe by helping to find this woman's killer, she could finally receive forgiveness.

LOUP GAROU—the swamp devil.

Jean-Paul grimaced. The local PD had already dubbed their newest killer with the name. The fabled creature lived on in the minds of the Cajuns as real as the day the legend started.

Only a devil could leave a woman the way this sicko had—helpless, dead, exposed in the heart of the untamed bayou.

Even though it was late evening, Jean-Paul met his captain and partner at the ME's office. When he showed the photograph to his partner, Carson, and his lieutenant, Phelps, cursed.

"I'm sending it to forensics, although I doubt we'll find prints," Jean-Paul said. "Maybe they can trace the photocopy paper."

Phelps frowned. "The son of a bitch is bragging about the murder."

"Did he really expect that magazine to print this?" Carson asked.

Jean-Paul shrugged. "I don't know. But for some reason, he wanted Britta Berger to see his handiwork."

"Because of her column?" Phelps asked.

"Maybe. Or maybe there's a personal connection." Jean-Paul recalled her reaction to the photo. She'd definitely been shaken. And he sensed she didn't like cops.

He'd run a background check on her to find out the reason.

"Maybe he knows her," Phelps suggested.

"Or wants to," Carson added.

Phelps nodded. "That's possible. If so, Britta Berger might be in danger."

A frisson of unease rippled through Dubois, heating his blood. He'd arrived at the same conclusion on the way back to the precinct. What if this psycho didn't stop at one victim? The symbols he'd left reeked of a ritualistic killing.

The ME, Dr. Charles, appeared in his office and waved them back to the crypt. "Have you identified our Jane Doe yet?"

Phelps snorted. "No, we're searching all the national databases but so far, no hits."

"We're checking the universities and clubs, too," Carson added.

Jean-Paul sighed, already tired and the investigation was only getting started. If the vic was an out-of-towner who'd come for Mardi Gras or to cash in on the heightened prostitute business during the festival, the identification process would be more difficult.

Phelps cut to the chase. "What did you find, Dr. Charles? Anything that might help us?"

"Nothing conclusive yet. Except that the girl didn't die from the chest wounds. I suspect she might have been poisoned."

"What kind of poison?" Jean-Paul asked.

"I don't know. I'm still running tests." Charles indicated one of the containers from his handiwork. "So far, her stomach contents don't reveal traces of a poison so she didn't ingest one. I didn't find any injection marks on her body, either."

"Keep looking," Phelps said.

"Any evidence of rape or a date rape drug?" Carson asked.

Charles shook his head. "Not so far."

"Which meant she agreed to have sex, then things got out of hand," Jean-Paul surmised. "Once we ID her, we'll start with her boyfriends, lovers. All her male acquaintances."

Jean-Paul's cell phone trilled and he unpocketed it and hit the connect button. "Detective Dubois."

"Detective...this is Britta Berger."

Alarm shot through him. Her voice sounded shaky, frightened. Had the killer contacted her again? "What is it, Miss Berger?"

"Someone broke into my place tonight," she blurted.

"I…think it might have been the man who killed that woman."

Jean-Paul's fingers tightened around the phone. "Keep the door locked and don't open it for anyone." His pulse kicked up a notch. "I'll be right there."

CHAPTER FOUR

BRITTA TWISTED HER fingers into the thin fabric of her skirt.

Stay calm, she reminded herself. *You don't have to tell him about the past. This killer has nothing to do with that. It's impossible.*

Still, she paced to the window and searched the busy street below. Was her intruder out there, watching?

Chilled by the thought, she wrapped a small throw around her shoulders. Then she poured herself a glass of wine and sipped it, trying to settle her nerves. But every whistle of the wind and every screech from the streets below alarmed her. Every man…posed a danger.

Dammit. She thought she'd left her fears behind. That she could finally look toward a future. But now this psycho wanted to take her peace of mind from her.

Why? What had she done to him?

She dragged in a breath and reminded herself she was being paranoid. She had her cell phone. And she knew how to fight.

Logic kicked in, along with the guts that had kept her alive. Even if this madman knew where she worked, he didn't necessarily know where she lived. She'd been meticulous about not listing her number or including her home address on any paperwork.

Anyone experienced with a computer could find her, though. And if he'd watched her office, he could have easily seen her climb the stairs to her apartment.

She could almost hear the killer taunting her in a sing-songy voice. See him sinking the spear into her heart. Feel the cold sharp blade puncture her insides. Then see the blood oozing out. Her nightmares rose again with icy fingers from the grave clawing at her. The years fell away as if it were yesterday. As if she was there again. Except this time she was even younger.

She was five years old. So small, so tiny that if she tried hard enough, she could make herself disappear. Then no one could find her.

And the monsters couldn't hurt her anymore.

Footsteps sounded outside. Loud voices. A man's dark booming laughter.

No!!!!!! Not again.

She crawled beneath the bed, closed her eyes and folded one bony arm beneath the other. Then she slid her hands into her armpits, hunched her knees up to her belly and curled into a ball.

Like a fleck of dust that no one could see, she'd stay there for hours. If she didn't make a sound, they'd think she'd gone. Then she'd be safe.

Free from the man. Free from the hideous monsters in the bayou.

The door screeched open. The scent of whiskey floated toward her. Thunder rumbled. She caught her breath. Tried to hold it.

Don't move. Don't make a sound. Be invisible and they'll go away. But the floor creaked. The wooden boards splintered. And she felt his hand on her arm.

He had her....

Britta heaved for air, sweating, disoriented. This memory was only one of many. The beginning. So many more afterward....

She had to banish them.

She stood, trembling, then moved to stare out the window into the starless night. It wasn't possible that this killer knew her. Or knew what had happened years ago. How she'd escaped. How she'd survived. How she'd lived on the streets like an animal.

No one knew but her.

More panic yanked at her and she rushed back to her bedroom and dug under the mattress for her journal. Inside it, she wrote all her private thoughts. Her own secret desires and confessions.

Her fingers finally connected with the thick velvet binding, and she tugged it out, flipping through the pages to make certain it was intact. She nearly collapsed on the bed when she realized nothing was missing. Her thoughts were still private.

A voice sounded through the intercom. "Britta? Are you in there?"

Jean-Paul Dubois. He was the last person she'd tell. He'd show her no mercy. He'd take her to jail, lock her up and throw away the key. No, he could never know her secret desires or get near her heart.

She'd die before she'd let that happen.

THERE HAD ALREADY been one woman's body found today. Jean-Paul held his breath as he waited on Britta to answer the intercom at her door. He hoped to hell there wasn't going to be another.

Dammit, why wasn't she answering? He'd raced over after her call. St. Charles Street had been unusu-

ally calm for Mardi Gras season. Various flags of kings
and queens of Carnival waved from the palatial
mansions, all symbols of the royalty: the professional
businessmen and politicians who resided in the city,
ones who funded the celebrations, rebuilt the city and
revitalized the traditions in the Big Easy after the last
hurricane. Although some businesses and people had
given up and moved on, others had rallied to resurrect
the historical district and the culture.

But here on Bourbon Street, the decorations boasted
of sex, voodoo, black magic and the live-and-let-live
attitude of the tourists seeking a good time, a stiff drink
and a good lay—anonymously of course. Which only
added to the crime.

Anger mounted inside him. *Bon Dieu.* Why the hell
had Britta Berger chosen to live on Bourbon Street?
Why not in one of the sleek condos on Decatur? Just
working at the raunchy magazine set her up for trouble.
But to live in the heart of it… She might as well hang
a damn sign on her body flagging her as an open target.

Did she enjoy living on the edge?

He didn't. He wanted the town back to normal, back
to the New Orleans he loved.

The image of her tied to a bed, naked, with a lancet
embedded in her heart, flashed in his head and he
grimaced as he punched the buzzer again.

"If you don't answer, Miss Berger, I'm going to
break down this damn door."

"I'm sorry," she finally said in a trembling voice.
"Come on up."

A click sounded and he opened the wrought-iron
gate in front of the door, then entered. Her office lay to
the right, a dark staircase ahead. He took the steps two

at a time. When he reached Britta's apartment door, he gave three quick raps. Seconds later, she opened the door, the chain still intact.

He arched a brow. "Are you all right?"

"Yes. I'm sorry, just shaken." She unlocked the door and stepped back, clutching a long robe to her throat.

"You said someone broke in?" He examined the door, but didn't notice any damage. "I don't see evidence of forced entry."

"He was here." She folded her arms across her waist, the movement making her look shaken and vulnerable. "In my bedroom."

He scanned the living room. Simple furnishings. Contemporary. A butter-yellow leather sofa accessorized by a few red and green throw pillows. A TV. Desk. Her laptop.

Perhaps the man climbed to her balcony and sneaked in through the patio window or the French doors. "Did he disturb anything?"

She inhaled, fiddling with her hands. "The bedroom. He went through my drawers. Then he left me something."

He followed her to her bedroom. Although the paint had faded in the hall, colorful artwork from the locals decorated the wall: scenes of a historic church, the bayou at sunset, the river. A collection of macabre Mardi Gras masks shaped like alligators and sea monsters occupied a decorative shelf, while gris-gris and beads she'd probably bought from the market dangled from hooks to create an eye-catching corner. Oddly, there were no personal photos in sight.

The bedroom appeared the same. A contemporary iron bed. A dark crimson comforter. A gray velvet lounging chair that looked decadent by the window. A few copies of *Naked Desires* were displayed on a bookshelf along with some self-help books. *Slaying Personal Demons. Overcoming Phobias and Fears. Black Magic. The Crocodile Myths.*

Another collection of Mardi Gras masks covered the walls. Some were beautiful, exotic, while others displayed the dark side of New Orleans—the voodoo priestess, the devil, a swamp creature.

It was almost as if everything in her apartment had been purchased in the city. As if she'd left any hint of a past behind. Or did the collection of masks symbolize her life? Was she a woman in disguise? Perhaps she had an assortment of wigs in her closet to change her appearance.

"He pawed through my lingerie," she said.

Jean-Paul spied the opened drawers, the sheer fabrics—all sexy, risqué. A pair of black and red thongs hung from one corner while a hot-pink camisole dangled from the edge of the dresser.

She walked over to the bed and leaned against the corner. "And he left me this."

A crimson red lace teddy lay in the center of her bed. His pulse clamored. It was almost identical to the one left at the murder scene that morning.

She recognized the similarity, too.

"This one didn't belong to you?" he asked.

She shook her head no.

Jesus. She had a right to be rattled. Leaving a note at work raised a red flag, but invading her home and leaving the same type of underwear he'd left with his victim was way more personal.

"He also left me this note." Her hand trembled as she lifted it toward him.

He read it in silence. *I always have one eye on you. You can't run forever.*

Instincts warned him Britta Berger was in danger. And that they might be dealing with a serial killer who was only getting started. "Did you notice anyone watching you today? A stranger who seemed suspicious?"

She hesitated, then cleared her throat. "While I was eating dinner at a café in the Market, I noticed a man with a camera taking pictures of me from the square."

His fingers tightened on the note. "Did you recognize him?"

"No, I've never seen him before."

"You're sure he was photographing you?"

"Yes. He paused when I caught him and waved to me. But his smile seemed sinister." She hesitated.

"Sinister?"

She glanced at the mask of the monster on her wall. "I suppose that sounds crazy, doesn't it?"

He shook his head. "You should trust your instincts. Especially after a day like today."

She nodded and he continued. "Can you describe the photographer?"

"He was tall." She swept her eyes over him, and their gazes locked. "But not as tall as you. Maybe five-ten. Thin, sort of wiry."

"Dark hair or light?"

"Bald. I got up to run after him," she added in a low voice. "But he disappeared in the crowd."

Christ. "Chasing a potential stalker is dangerous, Miss Berger. You should have called the police then."

"Are you serious?" Nerves made her voice high-pitched. "The cops would have thought I was being paranoid. Artists are always taking pictures, drawing sketches, painting the scenery and people in the streets."

True. But under the circumstances…

"I'll have forensics examine the note and lingerie. Maybe we can find out where he purchased the teddy." He cleared his throat. "And we should dust your place for prints."

She nodded, although turmoil filled her dark brown eyes. Eyes that bled with distrust. Eyes that were so hypnotic, the need to hold her tugged at his chest.

But he ignored the pressure. It was his nature, his job, to protect the innocent. And the only way he could protect her was to find the maniac threatening her.

To do that, he needed a clear head. Not one complicated by images of her wearing a teddy for him or whispering her secret confessions into his ear while he took her to bed.

Which only planted more doubts and questions in his mind. "Miss Berger, have you considered the fact that the killer might be someone you know?" She paled, but he forged ahead. "Maybe an old boyfriend? A lover?"

"No…that's not possible."

He ignored her protest. She was a heartbreaker if he'd ever seen one. "Are you sure? Do you have a current boyfriend? Or maybe someone you just broke up with?"

"No, Detective, I'm not dating anyone." Her voice dropped a decibel. "I haven't in a long time."

"How about an acquaintance? Maybe a man who asked you out? One you turned down?"

A faraway look settled in her eyes, but she shook her head. "No one that I can think of. Like everyone else after the hurricane, I've been trying to survive the past year and a half. There hasn't been time for personal relationships."

He nodded, unable to argue that point, yet something about her tone indicated that her lack of a social life was more of a preference, not a result of time restraints. And that she'd lied about no one asking.

"Not even since you started at *Naked Desires?*" he asked. "Your boss?"

"No." She shifted as if she'd lost her patience. "Now, I'm really tired, Detective. You can see your way out."

He was right—she was hiding something. But would she hide a killer?

"I'm not leaving now. Not until a crime-scene unit arrives to process your place. In fact, you shouldn't stay here tonight," he said. "Do you have a friend you can call? A family member?"

She shook her head. "No. No family."

"I hope you didn't lose them in the hurricane?"

She averted her gaze, picked at an invisible piece of dust on the end table. "No. It was a long time ago."

A note of sadness tinged her voice. "Where were you living before you came here?"

Panic slashed across her face. "In one of the small towns that got wiped out. I had nothing there and decided to move on."

"Have you always worked in journalism?"

Irritation flared on her face. "You certainly ask a lot of questions, Detective."

"I'm a cop. That's my job." He leaned forward again, this time so close he inhaled her citrusy scent. "What did you do before you came to work for *Naked Desires?*"

"Odd jobs," she said, meeting his gaze head-on.

"Now, I'm tired of this inquisition. You're supposed to be trying to find this madman, not dissecting my life."

He'd pushed enough for the night. She looked exhausted and had had a harrowing day. "Let me drive you to a hotel. We'll get your locks changed in the morning and add a deadbolt."

"With Mardi Gras in town, there won't be any empty hotel rooms," she said, pointing out the obvious. "And if this man wants to kill me, another lock won't keep him out."

"Maybe not, but we sure as hell aren't going to make it easy for him." He shoved his hands into his pockets. "If you're afraid to stay alone, I'll arrange for a guard tonight."

Wariness flashed in her expression, but she jutted up her chin. "No, I'm not afraid. New locks will do just fine."

Why did the mere thought of having the police around frighten her so? And why would having the police dust for prints bother her? Unless she didn't want them to pick up her own prints.... Which meant she might have a record.

Was she more afraid of the cops than a ruthless cold-blooded killer?

BRITTA STRUGGLED to maintain her composure while Detective Dubois conferred with the CSI team. He'd also called a friend who did locksmith work for the police department to change her locks and add a deadbolt.

"Come with me while they finish up," Detective Dubois suggested.

"I'm all right here."

"It'll do you good to get out for a while. Besides, I haven't had dinner and there's a quaint Cajun café near here. We can discuss the magazine."

"I've already told you everything I know," she said defiantly. "And I've eaten dinner."

Detective Dubois touched her arm gently. "Come on. They have great desserts at this restaurant. You can have coffee and tell me more about yourself."

Exactly what she didn't want to do.

"I don't need a babysitter, Detective. I'll be fine alone."

He angled his head toward her. "What's wrong? You aren't afraid of me, are you, Britta?"

She stiffened. "No, don't be ridiculous." Hadn't she learned long ago not to draw attention to herself?

His dark eyes pierced her, probing.

Unnerved, she nodded, knowing the only way to quiet his suspicions was to appease him. He couldn't seduce information out of her—not if she didn't let him. "All right. But I intended to search those letters tonight to see if this guy might have written to me before."

"You can review the letters tomorrow." His voice softened. "It's been a long day already."

He instructed the others that he would return within an hour and pressed a hand to her waist, guiding her outside. The gesture triggered another round of nerves. He was so strong that she felt safe by his side, yet not safe at all. She couldn't allow herself to depend on any man, much less Jean-Paul Dubois. He might stir desires and hungers that could never be sated. Might awaken a sexual beast within her....

Not something she could allow to happen with a cop.

The sultry evening air aroused another longing inside her, one that conjured images of a real date, of strolling hand in hand with a lover, listening to the sexy blues and jazz music wafting around them while the Mississippi lapped softly against the bank.

"We're here." He stopped at a small café that had cropped up after the hurricane and gestured for her to enter. *Dubois Diner.* Wonderful heady odors wafted toward them. Hot, spicy Cajun sausages and gumbo, jambalaya, shrimp po'boys....

"Do you own this?"

"No, my father does. It's a family business."

A tall, broad-shouldered, older man with wavy, gray hair and a slight limp met them at the door. One glance into his eyes and she recognized him as a Dubois.

He clapped Jean-Paul on the shoulders. "Ahh, Jean-Paul, so good to see you tonight, son. And here, you've brought a beautiful woman on your arm. Finally! Welcome, *chere*."

Britta froze, aware the detective shifted uncomfortably. "Papa, this is Miss Britta Berger. She's helping me with a *case*."

His father pinched his fingers together and slapped them to his forehead, then lapsed into a round of French Cajun dialogue. Detective Dubois's mouth tightened but he didn't argue.

Finally he angled his head her way. "My papa and *maman* think I work too much. But my job is my life."

"Those who do not take time to love will never find it," Mr. Dubois spouted. "Take heed of what the song of New Orleans says."

Britta smiled, remembering the strange verse. Then a pudgy woman with a bun swooped toward them.

"Maybe this was a bad idea. Maman is great, just very old-fashioned." Dubois shot her an apologetic look just before his mother pulled him into a bear hug.

A sharp pang slammed into Britta's gut as her own mother's face materialized in her mind. It had been so long since she'd seen her that her image was foggy. Her mother had never hugged her like that. She'd been too doped up. Her eyes hollow, not laughing. Her smile strained, her face gaunt.

And then Britta had lost her forever.

THE MOON BEAMED bright and full above the swampland as he made his way to his father's grave in Black Bayou. Only the land had shifted since the last big hurricane and the patch of dirt he recognized was no longer there. His father's remains had been swept into the tidal wave of the hurricane disaster, lost forever like so many others.

Just as his father had been lost to him the day Adrianna had destroyed him. Behind him, miles away, stood the city. New Orleans—the Big Easy. The town of sinners.

The city of the dead.

There the graves remained, at least the ones that stood above ground. An ominous reminder that the city could be lost again in a second.

No wonder Britta Berger had decided to hide in town. After all, technically, she was dead. Her new name stolen from one of those very graves just as he'd stolen a new name for himself.

Muttering a prayer to his father, he renewed his vow for vengeance as he made his way through the back-woods to the new meeting place of his people. As he approached the circle of light created by the bonfire, the dark memories dragged him back to his childhood and the reason he'd returned.

Yet, here he stood as an adult, trembling from fear, knowing he didn't belong—that he'd never earned his manhood in the clan's eyes. Hidden away among the backwater folks who worshipped Sobek, who feared the devil's wrath, who still believed in the ancient ways, they fought the battle between good and evil.

God would punish the sinners. But the devil was always working. Sometimes he walked among them, stealing souls and casting spells on innocents to convert them to do his service.

The clan had to pull together. Pray. Offer the gods a sacrifice so they could live among the bayou safe from the crocodiles and vermin the devil used as traps for the weaker.

The low hum of gospel singing echoed in the air, beginning the ceremony. The passage of boy to man, girl to woman.

One was always taken.

Adrianna's face remained etched in his mind as the young girls dressed in virginal white stepped before the altar. Their mothers shivered with fear, knowing that any one of their daughters might be the chosen one.

Only the girls knew nothing.

But Adrianna had known. The devil must have whispered in her ear. And she had chosen him.

Then the clan had cast *him* aside as if he was a leper.

He fisted his hands at his sides. He had to destroy all those wicked women who defied their religion. The cheap whores. Satan's messengers. Then the curse would be removed from him and he could once again walk among his people.

Fury twisted his insides as time spun backward.

He was back in Black Bayou on that fatal day.

Blood soaked his hands, his face, his clothing where he leaned over his daddy's body. Shouts and screams of terror and shock rocked through the clan. Suddenly someone yelled for them to hunt Adrianna.

Torches were lit, tempers fired and men dispersed. He had gone with them. Hours had dragged as they'd relentlessly fought through the bayou. Crocodiles had threatened. Attacked. Another brother had fallen prey to the swamp, his limbs ripped away one by one by a gator's sharp teeth.

Then one had shot out of the water toward him. His stomach rolled as he recalled the gator's teeth ruthlessly sinking into his arm, his torso, his ear. Fear had nearly crippled him.

But Satan had decided to let him live that night. Death would have been too easy.

Finally at daybreak they'd returned to the camp. Exhausted. He was half-dead.

They hadn't found Adrianna.

Then his next realm of punishments had begun. He'd bowed his head before the snake pit, the blinding pain swirling him into a vortex of eternal darkness. The clan chanted and prayed for the demons to be exorcised from his body. They'd thought him weak. A traitor. That he had warned Adrianna....

In their eyes, he was a failure. An outcast. He had not survived the trial by ordeal without looking guilty.

Then they had banned him from their presence forever.

Thunder clapped above, drawing him back to the present. He stood on the edge of another clan now, the work of the great Ezra Cortain in progress. The pounding drums echoed around him and the chants began, praising Sobek. Although forced to remain on the periphery, he clasped his hands and silently joined their prayer.

Adrianna might be able to run, but she couldn't hide.

And she had changed her name, but he knew it, as well as her real one. The Christian one her mother had given her.

The one he would call her when he finally offered her to the spirits.

CHAPTER FIVE

JEAN-PAUL SILENTLY CURSED his decision to bring Britta Berger to his family's restaurant. He should have called it a night. Left her at her apartment. Gone back to the precinct.

But once he'd ignored his family's welfare for his job and his wife had died. He'd never forgive himself. Lucinda's family hadn't forgiven him, either.

He had to warn his sisters and mother now that there was a killer preying on women.

A low jazz tune wailed in the background of the diner, wrapping tendrils of nostalgia around him—and a longing for what he'd lost. The comfort of a companion. The feel of a woman's touch.

Only Lucinda had never been a comfort about his job. She'd hated it and begged him to leave police work.

God, why was he thinking about her tonight?

Because another woman had died and you couldn't stop it.

"This is the rest of our family!" His *maman* gestured toward the wall of family photographs above the table, forcing Jean-Paul back to the present as she rattled on. "Jean-Paul is the oldest and of course, always the responsible one, taking care of everyone."

"Mother—" he growled.

"It's true." His mother batted her hand at him, then continued, oblivious to the fact that she was embarrassing him. "See all the pictures of him after the hurricane? He worked day and night, saved women and children. My boy is a local hero."

Jean-Paul gritted his teeth as she waved past the photo of him and Lucinda. Britta narrowed her eyes, obviously curious about the woman, but she didn't ask and he didn't offer the information.

How many times had he questioned his decision? Some men had lost their jobs because they'd left their posts to save their families. He'd saved strangers, kept his job, but lost his wife.

"And here's Damon, my next-to-the-oldest son," his mother continued. "Damon works for the FBI. Always the serious one, tough like Jean-Paul, but reserved, a methodical thinker." Her face beamed with pride. "And this is Antwaun, my youngest boy. He's hot-headed, temperamental like his papa, unpredictable." She pressed her hand to her heart. "He's too quick to jump into things sometimes, but ahh, a good boy at heart, he is."

"You have a beautiful family," Britta said quietly.

Her tone sounded so sad that Jean-Paul squeezed her hand beneath the table. A gesture of silent thanks for being so tolerant? The realization that he was sorry for whoever had hurt her?

"Now please, Britta, try some of my famous white-bread pudding." His mother pushed a dish toward Britta and she accepted it graciously.

"It's delicious." Britta sipped her latte. "In fact, everything looks wonderful. And the smells…I'm sure customers are drawn in from the streets because of the tantalizing aromas."

"Oh, thank you," his mother gushed. "You must come by for lunch. I work so hard to get the freshest ingredients and Catherine here, Jean-Paul's youngest sister, she helps me create the desserts."

"My daughter, Chrissy, likes to bake, too," Catherine said with a grin. "I think she might grow up to be a pastry chef herself."

"Yeah, but she usually wears more flour than goes into the dough." Jean-Paul ruffled his five-year-old niece's hair and smiled as she popped part of an éclair into her mouth and the cream oozed down her chin.

"So how long have you known my big brother?" Catherine asked.

Britta squirmed in her seat. "Actually we just met."

Stephanie, his dark-haired sister and the bookkeeper for the café, raised a brow. "Papa said you're helping Jean-Paul with a case?"

Britta nodded, but refrained from elaborating.

"What is it you do?" Catherine asked. "Are you a detective?"

"Or one of those psychic investigators?" Stephanie asked.

Jean-Paul rolled his eyes. "The festival has everyone's imagination running on overload, doesn't it?"

Stephanie shrugged. "I know you don't believe in anything supernatural, but that doesn't mean it doesn't exist."

Catherine cleared her throat. "That's right. Just like love. Just because it's not a tangible thing, doesn't mean it's not real."

Jean-Paul glared at them to stop the matchmaking. They both knew he'd vowed never to marry again, that he had no desire to get involved with another woman.

Britta cleared her throat. "Actually, I'm not gifted or a detective. I'm an editor for a magazine."

Stephanie's dark eyes lit up as recognition dawned. "Britta Berger. That's right. You edit that Secret Confessions column, don't you?" She stirred sweetener into her coffee. "I love that column. It's exciting to see the diversity of confessions. Do you have a difficult time choosing which ones to print?"

Britta shrugged. "Sometimes."

"I met the owner, R.J. Justice," Stephanie continued. "He's handsome. I bet he's interesting to work for."

Jean-Paul frowned at his sister as he finished his last bite of gumbo. He didn't want Stephanie anywhere near Justice, but if he told her so, she'd probably make it a point to see the man.

"The magazine, that's one reason we stopped by," Jean-Paul said. "We had a murder-rape case today, and the killer sent Britta a photograph of the crime."

"Oh my gosh, that's horrible," Catherine whispered.

"Why did he send it to you?" Stephanie asked.

"I think he wanted me to print it."

"But we're not playing his game," Jean-Paul declared.

His *maman* looked appalled. "Who did this awful thing?"

"We have no idea who the killer is yet. That means you all have to be careful." Jean-Paul fixed his sisters with a look that had intimidated cut-throat killers but didn't faze them. "Absolutely no going out alone at night. Hell, not even during the day."

"Have you talked to your brothers?" his mother asked.

"Not yet, but I will."

Catherine tapped her nails on her chin. "We can take care of ourselves, Jean-Paul."

Stephanie slicked her long dark hair behind one ear and angled her head toward Britta in a conspiratorial tone. "Honestly, our brothers can be so protective it's nauseating."

His *maman* waved a napkin, swatting at her daughters. "You girls listen to Jean-Paul. He knows the streets and works hard to keep us safe." She turned to Britta. "Your family would say the same thing to you, wouldn't they?"

Britta nearly choked on her coffee.

His mother patted her on the back. "Are you okay?"

"Yes. Fine, thank you." Her eyes caught Jean-Paul's for a moment, and he detected a wariness that made him more curious about her past and what she wasn't saying.

He lowered his voice, aware of the restaurant patrons. "Don't take this lightly, ladies. Trust me, this guy is one sicko. You don't want to wind up like the young woman we found." A shudder nearly tore through him at the very thought.

Catherine and Stephanie exchanged a silent sisterly look as if they were preparing to gang up on him. He didn't give a damn. Better they be mad at him and alive than the contrary. Tonight, he'd call Catherine's husband, explain the situation. Not that he'd have to force the man to protect her. In spite of Cat's protests, Shawn guarded her and their daughter like a watchdog. And he'd sic his other brothers on Miss Independent Stephanie. At least Steph carried a gun.

"Tell us more," Stephanie said over the rattle of silverware and dishes at the neighboring table. "The only thing the news reported was that a woman had been killed in the bayou."

"We haven't identified her yet or released any information, so I can't talk about it." Jean-Paul threw some money on the table, then did the usual dance with his mother about not paying.

"Maman, we've been over this before. I won't eat here free."

She huffed but kissed her pinched fingers, then placed her fingers on his cheek. "We will go to church Sunday and pray for the girl and her family, *oui?*"

"I'll try to make it, Maman."

"Bring Britta, too." She slanted Britta a sideways wink. "We always have room for one more at our table."

Britta shook her head. "Thank you so much, Mrs. Dubois, but I couldn't impose."

"Impose?" His *maman* waved the napkin again, this time at Jean-Paul. "You tell her she could never impose. We love company. Now, you bring her, Jean-Paul."

"We'll see," he said softly. He lay his hand over his *maman's* for a moment and squeezed, his gaze catching the odd look on Britta's face. Did she think it was strange that he and his family showed their affection in public? Or did the family scene make her uncomfortable?

Why did he care what she thought? When the hurricane had stolen his parents' home and business, they'd banded together to rebuild their lives.

The tragedies had taught him about what was most important. Material things could be replaced, but loved ones couldn't. But he didn't want his family getting the wrong idea about their relationship.

Besides, a madman might be after Britta. He'd

protect her with his life but he refused to lead the killer back to his own family's door.

His cell phone jangled and he pressed the phone to his ear to hear over the din of laughter and voices. "Detective Dubois."

"Dubois, it's Carson. Listen, there's a bartender down here at the House of Love who recognizes our victim."

A break they needed. "I'll be right there." He stood and gestured toward Britta. "We need to go."

"Always working," his mother hissed.

Stephanie punched his arm. "Stay safe, brother."

Catherine hugged him. "Yeah, watch your back. You're not invincible either, you know."

He nodded, then slid his hand to Britta's waist as they left the restaurant. It was out of the way to walk her home, but the House of Love was a divey bar with nasty floors, cheap strippers and raunchy patrons.

"What's wrong?" she asked as they stepped into the cloying humidity.

"My partner found someone who recognizes our victim. I'll take you home, then I'll go talk to him."

She lifted her hair off her neck to cool herself, drawing his gaze to a tiny scar beneath her right earlobe. "That's right around the corner."

"I know, but it's not the kind of place I usually take a woman."

Emotions flickered in her eyes...relief, surprise. Then she shrugged nonchalantly. "I've seen worse," she said. "Besides I'm not the sweet, domestic type like your little sisters. This is about the case. It's not personal."

He shook his head, but his body hardened at the way

her eyes darkened in the moonlight. "No, not personal at all."

And he would keep reminding himself of that, even if she decided to turn her seductive powers on him.

After all, she *wasn't* shy or the wholesome girl next door like his sisters. She didn't seem to like the family scene, either. And she had refused his mother's invitation to dinner as if a homey gathering would bore her.

Worse, she printed erotic confessions in a magazine. Watching a performer take money for stripping probably wouldn't even faze her.

THE NIGHT FELT as if it would never end.

Britta entered the wall-to-wall packed House of Love, fighting the memories that rose from the depths of the forgotten to haunt her. Thick smoke, sweat, beer and the stench of tawdry sex filled the air; the hint of drunken lust added a layer of tension over the sea of anonymous faces.

Nausea filled her. She'd grown up in places just like this. Had watched her mother entertain night after night. Then seen her duck into the curtained-off areas to perform private lap dances....

"It's not a bad way to make a living," her mother had told her one night when she'd caught Britta staring through the curtain. "It's just sex, nothing more."

No emotions. Just the simple exchange of bodily fluids and money.

Disgust gnawed at Britta's throat as she banished the images. She'd hated seeing her mother degrade herself. Hated even more the strange men's grunts and groans at night, watching her mother delve into booze and drugs, knowing filthy hands touched her....

"Come on," Jean-Paul mumbled, "I see the bartender over there."

The strobe light blinked to the beat of the contemporary rock music, the center stage occupied with two busty half-naked women gyrating and dancing around poles. A slender black girl tossed off her spangled top and double-Ds swayed as she rode the pole, tassels of silver and bright yellow twirling as she bounced her breasts. Beside her a brunette with three-inch red nails—and red stilettos to match—tossed her gold top into the groping milieu of men. Catcalls erupted as her pasties followed. Playing to the audience's excitement, she crawled across the stage on hands and knees, slithering her ass upward. The black girl shimmied, then began to slowly peel away her G-string, inch by inch, teasing the men thrusting dollar bills toward her.

Jean-Paul coaxed Britta through the crowd toward the opposite end of the bar, casting only a quick glance at the stage. "It's a damn shame girls turn to that kind of lifestyle. Didn't their mothers teach them any better?"

The censure in his voice raised her defenses. "Not every girl comes from a Cosby home like yours, Detective Dubois."

He slanted a frown over his shoulder. "Not everyone who has problems turns to drugs, alcohol or hooking, either."

The jab hit home and Britta clamped her mouth shut, humiliation heating her face. How could he possibly know what drove some people to make the choices they did? She'd never understood her mother, but she claimed she'd worked at the bars for Britta, so they could survive.

"You're a bad girl, Britta. Just like your mama."

The words echoed in her ear, reminding her of her roots and the vast difference between her and this cop. She wondered about his personal life, about the woman in the photo at his parents' restaurant. His girlfriend? Lover? Wife? Where was she now?

He wasn't wearing a ring. And his family would have mentioned if he was married. And the woman… she'd looked so sweet, delicate. Nothing like Britta.

Jean-Paul Dubois would not understand her childhood. Or what she had done later that had marked her for life.

He flicked his hand toward a man at the door. "That's my partner, Carson Graves."

She nodded, not bothering to try to speak above the noise. Jean-Paul shouldered his way through the mob, then up to the counter. A beefy man reached out and pinched her ass, and she flipped around and nearly swung at him. "Keep your hands off, buddy," Britta snapped.

Jean-Paul gave the man a lethal look, then slipped his arm around her waist, keeping her pressed close to him as they sidled up to the counter. Heat emanated from his hands and broad chest, and they were so close his breath brushed her neck. His protective gesture was subtle yet comforting, but after his comment Britta refused to allow herself to enjoy the feel of his hard chest against her back. She could stand on her own. She always had and always would.

He introduced her to his partner, who seemed to assess her the way the drunks in the room had when she'd entered. He was shorter than Jean-Paul, but still close to six feet, and handsome with short dark brown hair. When he shook her hand, she noticed an odd tattoo.

"A pleasure to meet you, Miss Berger. And that—" He indicated the three-ringed marking on his hand. "Was a gang tattoo," he explained without seeming offended. "I came up through the trenches but I finally got my head on straight."

She felt an immediate connection with him personally.

"Britta," she said automatically.

"I heard you've had a rough day, Britta," he said in a Southern drawl.

She shrugged. "Not as rough as the poor girl in that picture."

He conceded with a nod. Jean-Paul cleared his throat, his voice gruff when he spoke. "You have information on our victim?"

Carson pivoted toward Jean-Paul. "Yeah, this bartender says he's seen her. His name's Moe Leery."

Carson waved the thin, thirtysomething bartender over and Moe leaned across the bar and wiped the counter.

"What can you tell us about this woman?" Jean-Paul flashed the picture again.

The guy winced and pushed the photo away. "Her real name is Elvira Erickson. But she went by Pooky."

"She was a stripper?" Jean-Paul asked.

"Yeah, but she'd only been working here a couple of weeks. Told me she needed tuition money for school. Said she was planning to go to Tulane."

A muscle ticked in Jean-Paul's jaw and Britta saw the wheels turning in his mind. He was thinking about his sisters.

"Do you have an address?"

Moe scribbled on a napkin. "I think she lived in an apartment near the university."

"We'll check it out," Carson said. "Did she have a boyfriend?"

Moe smirked and grabbed two mugs to fill an order. "If she did, she sure as hell didn't bring him in here. Wouldn't be good for business or her tips."

Jean-Paul gave him a clipped nod. "Did you notice any guy hanging with her? Say two nights ago?"

Moe shook his head. "Naw, man. The girls come and go. I try to keep my head down. I don't want their pimps' wrath on me."

"How about any strange men who might have been watching her?" Jean-Paul asked. "A stalker maybe?"

Moe indicated the crowd. "Half the guys in here fit in that category."

Jean-Paul grimaced and Britta searched the mob of lust-starved, dollar-holding men, remembering similar scenes with her mother. More than once, a customer had jumped on stage and tried to drag her off with him.

Across the room, a man in a gray suit and wire-rims caught her attention. He seemed familiar, so she tilted her head to study him, then remembered that she'd seen him in the market. She'd thought he was watching her.

Always looking for ghosts from her past. In New Orleans, they were all around her....

He flashed some money at the black dancer, then spotted her and his eyes widened as if he was a deer trapped in a set of headlights.

Britta tapped Jean-Paul on the shoulder to get his attention, but by the time he turned around the man had disappeared back into the crowd again as if he'd never existed.

JEAN-PAUL INCHED CLOSER to her. "What's wrong?"

"I thought I recognized a man in the crowd," she said in a shaky voice.

Jean-Paul immediately scanned the smoky room. "Who? What does he look like?"

"He's gone now. But I saw him in the market earlier." A strand of her red hair fell across her cheek. "I guess it was nothing."

"Was it that photographer?"

"No, another man. It's probably my imagination."

"You're smart to stay alert," he said, itching to touch her hair and tuck it back into place. "We don't know that he wasn't the man who broke into your place. Or the killer."

"If he was after me, why not just approach me?"

Jean-Paul lifted an eyebrow. "In a crowded bar? No way." He stroked her arm gently, and a small tremor rippled through his body, stirring protective instincts. Dammit, the Dubois men were always suckers for a woman in trouble. "If he made me for a cop, he'd definitely run."

His logic made sense but only heightened her anxiety level.

"Come on," Jean-Paul said. "I'll take you home, then I need to see what information I can dig up on Elvira Erickson."

"You have to locate her family and tell them, don't you?" Britta asked.

Detective Dubois's jaw tightened. "Yeah, I might as well get it over with."

"I'll meet you at the station," his partner said. "Nice to meet you, Britta."

Jean-Paul glared at his partner. Carson was notorious for flirting and he seemed intrigued by Britta.

He shook off the disturbing thought as he took her home, instead concentrating on the call he needed to make to Elvira's parents. He hated like hell to tell them the details of her death, especially when he had no suspect or leads in the case to offer them.

His gaze shot to Britta. Was there a connection in her past that she hadn't told him about?

If there was and she'd been lying, he'd damn well make her confess her secrets.

A FEELING OF TREPIDATION overcame Britta as the detective walked her back to her apartment. The tension between them had been palpable since they'd left the bar.

He scowled at a wino lying near the garbage can next to her building, then at the poster of the magazine cover on the front window as she unlocked the door.

"You don't approve of the magazine I work for, do you?"

His dark eyes met hers as they entered the hallway, climbed the steps and stopped at her door. But he didn't reply until the locksmith left and they'd stepped inside.

"No." The short word was filled with disapproval. "You seem like a smart woman, but you live on Bourbon Street and you work with sickos. You put yourself in danger."

Her temper flared and she folded her arms across her chest. "I suppose you think that the way women dress invites rapists, so it's the victim's fault if she's attacked."

He leaned closer and braced his arm on the wall behind her. "That's not what I said."

"You didn't have to. It's obvious that you want your woman in an apron—tied to the kitchen, waiting with a martini in one hand and your slippers in the other when you arrive home."

His look darkened. "Tied to the kitchen?" A ghost of a smile played on his mouth. "Only if she's naked beneath the apron." His husky voice sent a tingle through her. "And I prefer a beer over a martini."

She lifted her brow at that remark. "One of *your* fantasies, Detective Dubois?"

"Jean-Paul."

His masculine odor made her dizzy. And that smile…his killer smile, mixed with that sexy rumbling voice was about to hack through her defenses. Dare she call him by his first name or was that too personal?

"Now tell me one of your fantasies, Britta?"

She wet her parched lips with her tongue. *For him to kiss her.*

"I… We weren't talking about me," she stammered, struggling for control. "We were talking about you not liking my job."

He lowered his hand, tucked a strand of hair behind her ear. "I'm simply pointing out the obvious about your safety. That's my job."

Yes, he thought she put herself in danger by way of her work and her apartment. What would he think if he saw her on the streets at night?

Emotions crowded her chest. "You can't always play it safe, Detective. And you can't protect everyone."

Pain flared in his eyes, then a shuttered look fell across his face. She instantly regretted her comment, but she couldn't discuss fantasies with this man and not want him to touch her.

And touching her would be too dangerous. She might lose control….

Then the demons that chased her would finally win.

"I can take care of myself, I always have." She ducked under his arm to escape his closeness and gestured toward the door. "You can go now."

He straightened, heat pouring off his body in waves. "You can't run forever, *chere.* Sooner or later, I will figure you out."

His words mimicked the killer's. A cocky smile tilted his mouth as he turned and walked away.

She closed the door, then faced her desk, trembling. A copy of the latest *Naked Desires* magazine lay open to the spread on her Secret Confessions column, mocking her. Other people might bare their souls for all to read, but her fantasies were private.

Yet the killer claimed to know them. And there might be another letter from him in the pile. She had to find it before Jean-Paul Dubois did, just in case the letter revealed too much.

She couldn't let him get near, close to her in any way. If he did and discovered the truth, he would destroy her.

DISGUISED BY HIS homeless man's attire, he hid amongst the shadows of the party-seekers and noise along Bourbon Street, so close to Britta Berger's apartment he could see the light as she switched it off.

It had taken him a long time to find his Adrianna. In fact, for a while he had given up. Had assumed she was dead. As dead as he had felt inside.

But he'd searched for her in every woman he'd met since that day. Hoping, yearning, dying to discover that she was still out there. That he could still have her.

And make her pay for the pain she had caused him.

Then one day he'd picked up a copy of *Naked Desires* and had seen the small photograph of her in the editorial section. She was so beautiful she looked like a hand-painted porcelain doll.

One look into those witchlike eyes, though, and he'd recognized her instantly. His Adrianna.

She had been so close all along. So near Black Bayou where they had met, where they had almost been joined together.

Running had only brought Adrianna back full circle. There was no escape for the sins that lived within her. But passing the trial by ordeal, the fact that she'd walked across the gator-infested waters and survived, did not mean she was innocent. Only that she had performed some black magic spell to keep the snapping gators at bay. That she was no *'tite ange*.

That she had been spawned by the devil.

The reason he had to destroy her. She was here now spreading her wickedness, enticing depraved men with her looks, casting a spell over the weak ones with her bewitching eyes—just as she had him, years ago. Through her column, she'd found the perfect venue to reach the masses.

He wanted to complete the ritual sacrifice. But he was a man and just as the crocodiles did during mating season, he had to mate with numerous partners.

Tonight he'd choose another.

He fell into the shadows and changed his clothing. Another disguise, this time one that would entice a woman. A white shirt and tie. A pair of dress slacks. An air of authority.

A wad of money.

And a mask over his face.

Another redhead, although her wavy hair was dyed an unnatural shade, tapped her foot at the corner of the House of Love, wearing a black micro-mini skirt, thigh-high boots and a flashy green top that looked like a bra. Her cleavage spilled over and through the mesh netting, her dark nipples stood turgid.

She twisted her head one way, then the other. Her nose jutted in the air as she took a drag from a menthol cigarette and flicked ashes on the grimy pavement. Finally aware he was watching her, she dropped the cigarette to the concrete, crushed it with her boot, then curled a finger toward him, beckoning him to join her. She looked impatient, primed, ready.

In need of some cash. Probably for drugs.

He had those in his pocket, as well. One that would give her the high of a lifetime.

He smiled, then smoothed his jet-black hair into place and strode toward her. Tonight, the whore would pleasure him. He might even draw out the fun a day or two if she was good, play with her, test her resistance.

Make her beg.

Then he'd force her to confess her sins before he killed her and added her to his kingdom.

CHAPTER SIX

Six days before Mardi Gras

RATTLED BY DETECTIVE DUBOIS and by the cozy family dinner they'd shared the night before, Britta settled in her bed the next evening with a cup of tea and more letters. The sooner she figured out who'd sent her the letter and photograph, the sooner the police could catch the murderer and put him behind bars.

Then she would have no need to see Jean-Paul Dubois again. Or be taunted by his sexuality.

And more importantly, she wouldn't have to worry about watching her back for fear he'd discover the truth about her past.

Determined to block out the sound of the partying below, she put in her favorite Harry Connick Jr. CD and allowed his seductive voice to soothe her as she read.

My secret confession:
I've fantasized about sex since I was a teenager and have just found the love of my life.

In my fantasy, we've just gotten married and my husband whisks me away to the honeymoon suite. Flowers fill the plush room, and a dozen candles shimmer with soft light across the heart-shaped bed. As he reaches for the champagne, a knock sounds at the door and his two groomsmen appear, still dressed in their black tuxes. My husband invites them in. At first, I'm confused, then one of them, a guy named Jim, smiles and says they are there to pleasure me.

A shiver goes up my spine as I realize he is talking about all three of them.

I've always dreamed of having multiple partners and the idea of the man I love and his two best friends all going down on me at the same time ignites a fire in my stomach.

"I don't know if I can take so much pleasure," I say.

My husband laughs, then presses a kiss to my hand. "It's your wedding night, love, I wanted it to be special."

He peels off my wedding dress, slowly unfastening each of the tiny pearl buttons down the back, drawing out the seduction with kisses and tongue licks along my spine, while Jim plucks the pins from my hair and runs his fingers through it. Chad, the other groomsman, kneels and removes my white satin shoes, while my husband plays his tongue along my lips. Soon, they lay me down, prop me up on pillows and caress my entire body. I tingle with need and hunger. Just as Chad tugs my nipple into his mouth, Jim slides his hand up my thigh and strokes my clit. Chad sucks my breasts then my husband enters me. Soon the three of us become a tangle of naked, throbbing bodies, frenzied, panting and sweating, rocking our bodies together until we finally climax all at once....

Heat rushed up Britta's neck, and she forced herself to skim the remainder of the letter for hints of violence, then placed it in the stack of possibilities for publication. Remembering her mission was to search for possible notes from the killer, she quickly skimmed the first paragraph of the next few letters, looking for details of S and M, violent tendencies or indications that the man hated women.

A blue envelope caught her eye and she opened it; the first line made her pause.

My secret confession:
I have an odd attraction to animals, especially golden retrievers. The guy next door is really hot—big with blond hair and gorgeous blue eyes. Every night when I see him walking his big dog, I start dreaming about what it would be like…

Britta slid the letter back into the envelope. Bestiality held no appeal to her, but it didn't mean the person was a killer. Besides, it was written by a woman.

The killer was male.

Using that logic, she sorted the letters by sex, so she could focus on male submissions.

In the next letter, the woman fantasized about bondage. Hmm. A perfect target for the killer.

A disturbing thought struck her. What if the killer chose his victims from her letters?

But how would the killer know who had submitted the letter or how to find the woman? He'd have to tap into their computer base….

Tomorrow, she'd verify that Elvira Erickson hadn't written to her. If she had, she'd alert R.J.

And Detective Jean-Paul Dubois.

The phone rang and Britta jumped, the last strains of Harry Connick's voice dying as the song ended. She stared at the caller ID, half expecting to see the detective's number, but the display read as an unknown listing. She must be crazy. Just because she'd thought of Jean-Paul Dubois, didn't mean he was telepathic. Or that he was thinking about her.

"Hello."

Heavy breathing rattled over the line. "Did you like the picture I sent you?"

Britta's breath caught in her throat. "Who is this?"

"The man who knows your secrets."

A bead of sweat rolled down Britta's neck. She started to slam down the phone, but hanging up on him would do nothing to help the woman he'd murdered. "Why don't you tell me your name?"

Laughter, low and sinister, rumbled from him. "One day I will. But I must build my kingdom first."

A frisson of alarm rang through her. His kingdom, meaning he was just getting started. Detective Dubois was right; her column had drawn sexual deviants like sweet molasses drew flies. "You're a coward," Britta whispered.

His voice held a threatening edge. "No, Britta, I'm the one in control now. You feel it, don't you?"

He'd never control her. No man would. "Then why hide behind the phone? Behind the notes?"

"Because my work has only begun." Another laugh, even more sinister, filled the silence.

"I must save those women, make them repent for their sins. Just as you must." Agitation made his voice raspy. "You run from town to town—changing your name, your hair—until you don't even know who you are anymore. You're as dead as the people whose names you steal. I can see it in your eyes." He lowered his voice. "Your fear controls you."

She twirled the phone cord around and around her fingers, winding it into a knot. He was right.

But how did he know so much about her? How long had he been following her?

"Please leave me alone. I don't want any part of your twisted games."

Again she started to hang up, but his next words stopped her cold.

"You don't want to know who I have now?"

Britta clenched her hands into fists. "Let her go," Britta whispered. "Please don't hurt anyone else."

"I can't, Britta. Not yet. Not until she learns her lesson and pays for her sins."

The phone clicked, then went dead in her hand.

A vision of the woman begging for her life taunted her. Then the crude mask of Sobek and an image of this man offering the woman as a sacrifice to the half crocodile, half man.

Time swirled backward. The smell of death, blood and the marsh assaulted her. Then the hiss and snapping of the gators as they churned the muddy water, anxious for their meal....

TWENTY-FOUR HOURS since they'd found Elvira Erickson. Jean-Paul Dubois sighed, loosening his collar in the smothering heat as he exited the precinct. Another long, frustrating day. And no headway on the case. He'd questioned the two mask-makers in town for the festival and neither of them made or sold one like they'd found at the scene. Both men had alibis, too.

The necklaces, however, were a dime a dozen.

Several reporters suddenly rushed him, jamming microphones in his face. A camera flash nearly blinded him and he threw up his hands to block another.

"Tell us about the woman murdered in Black Bayou!" a reporter shouted.

"Is it true she was stabbed with a lancet?"

"Did the gators get to her?"

"He raped her before he killed her or after?"

"Do we have a serial-killer case?"

Jean-Paul had to make some kind of statement. But what could he tell them? That so far they had no evidence, no name, no one to arrest? He spotted Mazie Burgess and headed toward her. She was a friend of sorts; had written stories on the hurricane and was fair. She'd also asked him out, but he hadn't been ready or interested in dating. She smiled and met him halfway and he took the mike.

"We did find a woman murdered yesterday," he said matter-of-factly. "At this time we have no suspects in custody, but the police are doing everything possible to find the woman's killer. Now, get out of the way so I can do my job."

Mazie thanked him. But instead of backing up, the mob moved in, surrounding him. He shouldered his way through, shrugging off a skinny guy who chased him to his car. "Come on, Detective, you have to give us more than that. Someone said that the killer contacted the editor of the *Naked Desires* magazine."

Bon Dieu! If they caught wind of the picture Britta Berger had seen, there would be widespread panic. "No comment," Jean-Paul barked. The last thing he wanted was the press hounding Britta. They might even scare off this guy from sending her information.

And he refused to give the swamp devil the pleasure of seeing a big write-up in the paper.

He tried to pry the man's fingers off his car door but the reporter resisted. "If you don't move out of the way, I'm going to arrest you for interfering with a police investigation and charge you with assault."

"I didn't assault you!" the man screeched, but he did back away. Jean-Paul hit the accelerator and bolted.

Next on his agenda—he had to check R.J. Justice's alibi. He drove to the pricey new lofts near the edge of town and met Carson. Debbie Waller, the woman with whom Justice claimed he'd spent the night, supposedly lived in one of the units. The inside of the building consisted of chrome and cement and showcased exposed beams and concrete walls. Apparently the artsy, rich twenties and thirties crowd had flocked to buy the units.

He knocked on the metal door, his shoulders tight. Loud rock music nearly drowned out the voice who yelled for him to hang on.

Carson shot him a wired look. "What do you want to bet that this chick has a sugar daddy?"

Jean-Paul chuckled. "Maybe Justice himself."

The door opened revealing a twentysomething platinum blond in three-inch metallic-black heeled boots, a leather skirt that…well, Jean-Paul wouldn't consider a skirt, because the front was split to her crotch and she wasn't wearing underwear. Damn.

Tattoos of scorpions danced along her arm as she gestured with her hands. "I didn't invite the cops."

"We invited ourselves," Carson said, inching one booted foot inside the door.

Jean-Paul quickly made note of the room. The place smelled of booze, weed and sex. Black netting formed a canopy on the wall like a spiderweb and draped a black-lacquer bed with rumpled sheets, sex toys and leather masks.

"Justice must have told you we'd drop by," Jean-Paul said.

She hitched out a hip. "Yeah, yeah, yeah. About that dead woman." A half-dozen earrings sparkled on one ear, while a network of tiny scars lined her neck. "Such a shame. But sometimes sex just goes too far."

"How far is too far?" Jean-Paul asked as he elbowed his way past her.

"Death," she said. "Otherwise, it's just a game."

"Murder is not a game," Jean-Paul muttered.

She gave him a pouty look. "I just meant that when two people want to do it their own way, they should be entitled to. Danger heightens the senses, makes sex more titillating."

"We're not arguing titillating," Carson said. "We're talking cold-blooded and vicious homicide."

"How did you get your scars?" Jean-Paul asked in spite of the fact that he was certain he already knew the answer. From his vantage point, he spotted a whip and mask on the bed, a vibrator with metal prongs and a wicked set of leather chaps. Blood stained the sheets of the unmade bed; leather wrist and foot bindings were attached to the four corners. The rope indicated the couple had delved into asphyxiation sex. Handcuffs and a silver-studded black-leather dog collar lay on the bedside table beside a ceramic hand-shape candy dish that would have held peppermints at his mother's house but contained an assortment of condoms.

Hmm. What would Britta's hold?

"I like it rough," she whispered, cozying up to Carson. "As long as I trust the person I'm with, anything goes."

Carson's eye twitched. "Just tell us about the night before last. Was R.J. Justice with you until morning?"

She nodded, then gestured toward a triangular table. "Yes."

"Are you sure?" Jean-Paul asked.

"Yes. He was my submissive. I turned him into my lamp."

Carson coughed and Jean-Paul gritted his teeth. He'd read about the latest tools the sex addicts were into—turning their partners into household objects to humiliate them.

She walked over to the table to demonstrate. "He was naughty, so I punished him. His head comes up through that round hole in the center of the table and serves as a fixture. I hung my panties over the shade and made him watch." She laughed at Carson's stunned eye-raise, then turned to Jean-Paul. "You know what I'm talking about, don't you, Detective?"

Yeah, pretty sick shit. But Jean-Paul refused to take the bait. He removed his business card and laid it on the table. Just imagining the man's kind of lovemaking sent a sour taste to his stomach. He sure as hell hoped Britta Berger stayed away from him.

How could she even work with a man like that?

Unless she wasn't aware of his sexual preferences. Maybe he should warn her....

No. Britta's sex life or romantic relationships were none of his damn business.

"Man, she's weird as shit," Carson said as they left the building.

"Yeah. And I have a bad feeling this case is going to get even more weird before we solve it."

His phone vibrated in his pocket and he connected the call. "Detective Dubois speaking."

"Detective, this is Britta."

Jean-Paul's internal alarm button sounded. "What's wrong?"

"He called my house," she said in a low voice. "And he has another woman."

ANOTHER VICTIM.

Jean-Paul's heart slammed into his ribs. Then they *were* dealing with a serial killer.

And to take the next victim so soon suggested something was pushing his buttons. Or *someone*. "What else did he say?" Jean-Paul asked.

"That she had to pay for her sins." Britta's voice cracked. "He talked about having control, about building his kingdom."

Dammit. A kingdom implied he'd only gotten started. "Stay put. I'll be right over."

"You don't have to come by," she said hurriedly. "I just wanted you to know about the woman, so you could look for her."

Carson narrowed his eyes and Jean-Paul mumbled an explanation, then gestured for him to drive toward Britta's apartment.

"Did he indicate where he might have taken her?" Jean-Paul asked.

"No."

"What about his number? Did it show up on caller ID?"

"No, it appeared as an unknown."

He grimaced and studied the busy street as they neared Britta's. It was midnight already, but party-goers still overflowed from the bars. Every man seemed to jump out at Jean-Paul as a possible suspect. Two guys wearing bandanas loitered outside Naked Desires, peering in the window, open beers in their beefy hands. Anger pounded through his blood as he glanced up and realized how easily they could gain access to Britta.

Carson parked and Jean-Paul jumped out, then ordered the bikers to move down the street. One of them cursed and staggered toward him, but Carson waved his badge. "Go on or we'll let you sleep it off in the tank."

The second man yanked his friend back. "Come on, man. Fuck the cops. They're not worth it."

Jean-Paul pressed the security buzzer, grateful when Britta responded immediately. He didn't know why his chest was so tight but a sharp pain had knifed through it. If the killer had called Britta at home, then he was growing bolder. He was showing off his crimes to her, touting his depravity to impress her.

And eventually he might target her as a victim.

GINGER HOLLIDAY'S DADDY would die if he saw her now. He'd always told her she was some no-account piece of shit, but she told him she was a victim of having stupid parents. Wrong answer. He'd beaten her sense-less and thrown her out on her ass.

At first, she'd wallowed in self pity, but finally she'd dusted off her butt and decided the best revenge was to prove the bastard wrong. She applied to a med-tech school. In two years, she'd have a decent job, one that helped other folks. Not some demeaning, boring-as-hell drone's job like threading fake alligator's teeth on chords to make those cheap necklaces they sold at the market or gutting fish all day like her sorry old man.

And not like the one she'd chosen last night. Why, he'd been quiet and intense. The artwork he collected was weird. Drawings and sculptures of crocodiles and black magic. And those eyes…man, they were some freaking shit. He'd even told her he wanted to paint hers.

But he had a Bible beside his bed so she figured he was safe.

Hell, so far she hadn't done anything to earn her money. Sure, he'd made her pose for him. And he'd tied her to the bed but then he hadn't touched her. He'd just drawn sketches of her while she lay there naked. He'd done a real nice job with her eyes, too.

Wondering what he had in mind tonight, she glanced toward him. He looked like he came from money—had nice threads and a sharp little Miata. Maybe he was a professor or something. Anyway, he wasn't half-bad.

For a man who bought sex on the streets.

Except his eyes were a little strange. One of them looked sort of blurred; or maybe it was his expression, as if he saw her through a fog. And his face felt funny, his skin sort of rubbery as if he was wearing makeup or a mask.

He shifted gears and glanced at her, the scar on his upper eyelid glimmering in the moonlight. He hadn't smiled since she'd gotten in the car; just told her he was taking her to a mansion where he promised to give her as much pleasure as she gave him.

Like that could ever happen. She never got involved with clients, never let herself feel. In fact, she barely remembered how she'd gotten into the business.

The moon slithered into the thick treetops in the bayou, the sounds of the backwoods echoing around her as they left the noisy town. Suddenly a frisson of unease skated up her spine. Maybe this wasn't such a good idea, going outside the city limits. What if this guy was some kind of pervert? Or what if he refused to bring her home? A cab would cost a fortune.

She automatically rubbed her hand over her purse where she kept her mace, then patted the edge of her thigh-high boots. She kept a knife inside, just in case.

"Where are we going?" she asked.

His breathing wheezed out but he didn't reply. She fidgeted and tried again. "You visiting New Orleans or you live here?"

Again he didn't answer. Only the whites of his eyes, big and unnerving, settled on her face, before he turned his attention back to the road.

The silence was near-deafening, which only accentuated the noises of the woods. He steered the car onto a long drive flanked by cypress and live oak trees that created a tunnel. A second later, she spotted a two-story antebellum home. He parked in the winding drive beside the garage, then gestured for her to get out.

"Are you restoring this place?"

He nodded. Then finally he spoke. "There are rumors that a mighty man of the cloth lived here, but one of his own clan murdered him and fed him to the gators." He slanted her an odd look, then cut his eyes toward the backyard. "Let me show you the river before we go up."

His story rattled her nerves. "As long as we don't get too close. I don't like the swamp."

The moonlight chased shadows across his face as he urged her forward onto a tiny bridge. Moss hung like clusters of spiderwebs from the trees, creating a trap for whatever stepped inside.

Water lapped and receded against the jagged rocks while frogs croaked and whined. The stench of swampland, decay and something else that smelled rancid floated from below. Several yellow-greenish eyes glowed in the dark on the water's surface—bodies submerged, only long snouts and scaly heads visible in the darkness. *The gators.* A pair of sharp teeth shimmered in the moonlight.

"Let's go back," she said in a shaky voice. "I don't like it out here."

He pushed her forward. "No. I have a surprise for you."

Fear ripped through her at his ominous tone. "Please, I don't like it here—"

"I bought you, Ginger," he said in a low voice. "You'll do whatever I want."

The legend about the house suddenly took on dire meaning. She reached inside her purse for her mace, but he twisted her arm and she cried out. Terrified, she kicked upward toward his knee, connecting with bone. He yelped and momentarily released her. She tried to run past him toward the car but he slammed her facedown onto the bridge. She tasted blood.

Dammit. She'd worked too hard to end up like this. She swung her loose arm toward his feet, but he stomped on her hand and she screamed in pain. Bones crunched and blinding pain shot through her. Dry brush, stones and bark clawed at her knees and face as he dragged her toward the shanty.

Suddenly a loud growling erupted, then another and another. Finally a hideous, terrifying cry. The gators' cry of warning before they charged.

Dear God, she'd thought he was safe. What a fool. This man was going to kill her.

Then he might feed her to the animals.

Or would he feed her to them alive?

CHAPTER SEVEN

BRITTA'S HANDS TREMBLED as she lifted the door latch and allowed Jean-Paul and his partner into her apartment. How much should she tell Jean-Paul about her conversation with the killer? If she confessed that the man had hinted that he'd known her in the past, she would open Pandora's box.

Yet, if *she* had drawn the madman to murder, if she had known him, not telling the police would only enable him to kill again.

"Are you all right?" Jean-Paul asked.

She nodded and gestured for them to sit, then offered coffee, which both men declined. Jean-Paul settled into the chair across from her, while Detective Graves claimed the loveseat.

"What time did he call?" Jean-Paul asked.

"Just before I talked to you."

"Tell us everything he said, word for word."

She knotted her fingers into the folds of her robe, wishing she'd changed into her clothes. "I'm not sure I can remember."

"Listen, Ms. Berger," Detective Graves cut in. "It's important that you try. At this point, everything we learn about our unknown subject, our UNSUB we call him, is a clue that might help us figure out his identity."

She chewed on her bottom lip, searching for the bravado that usually saved her. *Paste on a detached face. Chin up. Maintain eye contact. Don't let anyone know you're afraid.*

Up went her chin. She was in control now. These men had no idea who she was. She'd covered her tracks well. No paper trail. And there had never officially been any charges filed. Besides the only one she could think of who'd want to hurt her was the boy she'd run from. And he had died.

"Britta," Jean-Paul said. "Are you sure you're all right? Do you need something to drink?"

She shook her head. "No, I was just trying to sort through the conversation."

Sexual looks she was used to. But having a man worry about her launched her into uncharted territory.

"Britta?"

"I asked him who he was and he repeated what he'd written in the note."

"That he knew your secrets?" Jean-Paul asked.

She nodded, but her gaze latched on to his hands, which were folded in front of him. Dark hair was sprinkled over his large knuckles. His nails were blunt but neat, his fingers scarred. He had strong, capable hands. Could they also be tender?

"What else?" Jean-Paul prompted.

She jerked her attention back to his face. "He said one day he'd tell me his name, but he had to build his kingdom first."

"His kingdom?" Detective Graves made a note of it. "Maybe a religious reference. That could be important."

"It means he's going to kill again and again until we stop him," Jean-Paul said.

Britta's face paled. "I told him he was a coward for hiding behind the notes." She moved to the window, then closed the blinds so no one could look in. "He didn't like that. He said *he* was in control."

Jean-Paul gave her an odd look. "You intentionally angered him?"

"He called me to brag about hurting this woman and I refused to satisfy his twisted mind by acting afraid," Britta snapped. "I told him I wasn't playing his games."

"And how did he react?" Jean-Paul asked.

She raked her fingers through her hair. "He said he had another woman. I begged him to stop—not to hurt her—but he claimed she had to pay for her sins."

A muscle ticked in Jean-Paul's jaw, while his partner leaned forward in the chair with his hands on his knees.

"Did you hear anything in the background?" Jean-Paul asked. "A noise—maybe a boat, train, cars? A woman crying?"

Britta shook her head. "Just his grating, sinister voice." And the ticktock of the wall clock behind her.

She rubbed her arms.

How much time did this woman have left before she died?

JEAN-PAUL STOOD AND braced his hand on the back of the chair, his gaze fixed on the clock. Every second that passed lessened their chances of finding this woman alive. He could almost hear the woman's screams for help in his head.

Just as he'd imagined Lucinda had probably cried for him the night she'd died. Hoping he'd save her.

But he'd failed.

Would he fail this woman, as well?

"I'm calling in the feds," he finally said.

His partner snarled. "You don't think it's too soon?"

Jean-Paul shook his head. Pride be damned. The age-old territorial battle would no doubt ensue. Most of the cops didn't like working with the feds. But his brother could always be trusted. And what choice did they have? So far, they were chasing their tails.

They had to stop this psycho before he destroyed the town. The city had worked too hard in its recovery, had proven that the human spirit and heart of the Big Easy would survive no matter what. Just as his own family had.

Except there had been casualties.

Lucinda for one. And so many others….

The ceiling fan hummed, stirring the humidity, and he scrubbed a hand over his neck. The fact that their UNSUB had Britta's personal number worried him. "Do you want us to drive you someplace else tonight?"

"We've been over this before, Detective. I'm fine." Her voice broke off, emotions teetering on the surface.

Right. She had no family to call. She was virtually all alone. Jean-Paul itched to fold her in his arms and hold her.

But his job came first. He needed to act on this latest call. Except they had no idea where to look for this girl or any clue as to her identity. If the man had chosen to take her to the bayou, they could be anywhere in the miles and miles of endless marshy swampland. He had to organize some search teams.

"Carson, get a trace put on Miss Berger's phone."

Carson headed to the door to place the order.

Jean-Paul rubbed his hands up and down Britta's arms. "If he calls again, keep him talking. The longer he remains on the line, the better chance we have of pinpointing a location."

Her tired sigh mimicked his own weary soul. "I'll try."

He started to release her but the need to stay with her pulled at him, too. She appeared so strong on the outside, but beneath that tough facade, he sensed a lonely, troubled woman. One who didn't want anyone to see her fears.

One who knew she was in danger. But one who refused to whine or beg him to stay.

"You'll call me if he phones you again tonight?" he asked.

Tension sizzled between them as he waited for her response.

"He won't," she said matter-of-factly.

Their gazes locked and he wondered if she was thinking the same thing he was—that the psycho would be too busy murdering his second victim to phone. But neither spoke the words out loud. The silent look that passed between them was all the communication they needed.

He murmured good-night, then he and Carson left the building. Outside, he glanced up and down the street as they walked to Carson's car, searching for predators. The crowd had begun to thin, although music still wailed from several bars and the scent of stale booze and sweat permeated the air. He phoned the precinct, then reported the killer's call and alerted the night shift to be on the lookout for trouble. Two more units were dispatched to stroll Bourbon Street and keep order. Another four went out to drive along the country roads. And two more were ordered to check the location where the first woman's body had been discovered, just in case the psycho used the same shanty.

His stomach rolled. Even if they found the woman tonight, she might not be alive. And what about Britta? Would she be safe in her apartment alone?

There had to be a personal reason for the killer to phone her. Had he known her in the past or simply fixated on her now?

THAT SICKENING phone call echoed in Britta's mind, along with her conversation with Jean-Paul Dubois. The things she'd told him.

The things she hadn't.

That the killer had been looking for her for a while. Which meant he'd known her before....

Would another young girl die tonight because she refused to share her secrets?

Because she had to stand alone?

She opened the nightstand and removed the photo album, then flipped to the first page, to the one photo she had of her and her mother. The rest of the pages were empty. No family mementos. No Christmas-tree shots. No happy Easter Sundays. No hugs hello or tearful goodbyes. No promises of a future.

A dull ache settled in her chest—the longing for all that she'd missed. All that she'd never known. All that Jean-Paul Dubois had with his family.

She wiped at a tear, then removed the familiar white-satin box and gently lifted the lid. The simple white pearl combs winked back beneath the moonlight. They had been a special gift from her mother when she had turned thirteen.

Britta had been shocked. Normally, her mother had

preferred flashy, colorful costume jewelry. The cheap stuff that made her look even cheaper.

Her mother had saved for a long time to buy her the pearl combs. She wanted Britta to be beautiful. To be classy and sophisticated and to grow up with a nice life, not like hers.

But then her mother had betrayed her. She'd taken Britta to that cult and offered her up as if she was a piece of property.

What had caused her mother to change so radically? To give up her dreams and plans to escape? Drugs?

Britta's hands shook as the memories bombarded her. A lifetime ago.

The voice of Adrianna Small.

Crawling under the bed, folding her tiny body to make herself disappear. Hiding from the monsters.

Then years later…

The oils and ceremonies, the bathing rituals, the chants and prayers to ward off the devil. The young women sharing their beds with so many. The cries in the night from the ones who didn't want to be taken.

Then the sacrifices.

Shrill voices reverberated in the darkness. A girl screaming. Her own voice. Others.

Then the man's husky low voice in her ear. *You're a bad girl, Britta. You know where you belong. You must give your life to be saved from your sins.*

But she had refused to die.

So she'd run.

Found herself on the streets. The bayou. She was drawn to the evil and the darkness.

But on every corner, in every stripper or homeless face, she saw herself. And she continued to search for her mother. Sometimes Britta sensed she was dead. The uncertainty would nearly make her double over. Other times, she felt her mother was still out there. Maybe hurting. Maybe alone. Maybe needing her....

The familiar well of guilt weighed on her shoulders. She had to somehow make it all right, pay her own penance.

The need to be outside rippled through her veins. She had to smell the night air. The draw was strong.

It was also dangerous.

But she had lived too long on the edge to be frightened of those who wandered the town.

She slipped from her bed and dressed in a short skirt and flashy top—her other persona. Stiletto heels came next, then she dabbed mousse into her hair and fluffed the layers. A touch of blush and lipstick and she was ready. After all, she had to fit in. Mingle. Become one of them. In a place where she was comfortable. At home.

Not like the awkwardness of being with the Dubois family.

Shaking off any lingering thoughts of them, she grabbed her keys and headed downstairs into the sultry night. Booze and raunchy sex scented the air. Footsteps, laughter and the drums of the ancient witch doctors echoed around her. The stench of the marshy swampland teased her memory. The blood, the vermin, the swamp devil. The gators were the gods in the bayou. And all of Black Bayou should respect them.

Jean-Paul Dubois would never approve of her venturing into the night. He was so transparent. A cop all the way. Judgmental. He looked down at the lost ones on the streets, hovering around trash cans and alleys scrounging for food.

But what did she care about his opinion?

It was too late for her. She couldn't outrun the devil inside her or be a part of the all-American family.

And no one could change her.

NEARLY TWO in the morning. A woman lost. A life in jeopardy.

And Jean-Paul had no idea how to save her.

He and Carson had canvassed Bourbon Street asking questions, searching the bars, trying to get a jump on who might be missing.

So far, they'd had no luck.

His mind raced to Britta as they passed her apartment again. Why was she getting to him? Why did he want to go upstairs and hold her? Make sure she was safe? Comfort her?

Feel her beneath him?

Dammit. He had no right thinking anything sexual about her. Especially when she was involved in an investigation.

But logic had nothing to do with the insane desire that strummed through him when he was near her. Her eyes mesmerized him and made him senseless.

If it was any other time and he'd met her, he'd go ahead and let the heat between them sizzle. After all, he'd sworn off marriage, but he'd never promised to be celibate. And having sex with the woman would probably be explosive. He could do it without becoming involved.

Bright lights nearly blinded them from an oncoming car as they passed a graveyard, and Carson cursed. Shadows of the dead rose like mystic creatures in the murky night, bolted him back to reality. Elvira Erickson was among them, waiting for justice.

"Are you all right, Dubois?" Carson asked. "You seemed a little unglued around that Berger chick earlier."

Jean-Paul massaged his temple. "I'm fine. Just thinking about the case."

Carson dragged a Marlboro pack from his pocket, thumped a cigarette onto his thigh and lit it. "I thought for a minute you were digging her or something. She sure as hell looked as if she could eat you up."

Jean-Paul shot him a cold look. "She's part of the investigation," he snapped. "And I'm not interested in her or any woman."

"Hey man, I wasn't criticizing," Carson said with a wry smile. "It's been almost two years since your wife died. You probably need a good lay."

Was that all he wanted from Britta?

No, he wanted to know more about her, too. Dammit. "Drop it, Carson. The subject is closed."

Carson rolled down the window, the hot, thick air invading the car along with the heady smoke of the cigarette. "Hell. I'm just saying, the chick wants you. Use it to your advantage."

He gritted his teeth. Carson might be right. But he didn't make it a practice to seduce women for information.

And even if Britta was attracted to him, she wasn't jumping into his bed—she was running from something.

What was she so afraid of?

"Maybe we can pick up Swain tomorrow," Carson said. "Tonight, I'll check for any cases with similar MOs across the states."

Jean-Paul nodded. "I'll see what I can dig up on Britta's past."

Carson raised an eyebrow, but refrained from comment as he wheeled into the precinct. Jean-Paul jumped out, climbed in his SUV and drove toward his own house, scrubbing a hand over his bleary eyes. He probably wouldn't get a wink's sleep, but he didn't know what else to do right now. He felt so damn helpless.

The lieutenant had taken it upon himself to phone the Ericksons and they were flying in from Houston in the morning to identify their daughter's remains. He'd phoned Damon for a seven o'clock briefing to discuss the case. A task force was being put in place already. And later, Britta and he were supposed to review those confession letters.

The house he'd renovated—rather *was* renovating— stood like a monument to the old N'Awlins as he approached it. The basic structure had withstood the elements, but the paint had faded, shingles had been blown off and glass windows shattered during the hurricane. Over the past year, he'd restored it to at least livable conditions.

Hundred-year-old oaks with massive tree trunks dripped Spanish moss to the ground, while the wraparound porch with its porch swing and the intricate lattice work remained, reminding him of what life might have been like years ago.

Dry ground crunched beneath his boots as he strode up the clam-shell drive; the crushed shells resembled white powdery sugar spread across the parched grass. Lucinda had loved the veranda, had talked of redoing the garden with rosebushes and azaleas that would add color to the lush green landscape. But she'd never had the chance.

The shrill whistle of crickets and cicadas sang their nightly rituals. Mosquitoes buzzed and somewhere beyond, near the river, leaves were rustled from an unknown source. A snake perhaps, or maybe a gator who sought the shade of the night beneath the weeping willows and tupelos on his property.

He surveyed the land beyond, then turned back to study his porch. *Beau Monde,* his place was called, for the woman who supposedly worked to save her home while her lover went to war. She'd been raped and brutalized by foreign soldiers, yet she'd survived and had refused to leave her house for fear her beloved wouldn't know where to find her when he returned.

Lucinda had thought the legend so romantic. Yet she'd believed the man should have stayed home to protect his wife instead of leaving her to fend for herself.

Just as she'd wanted *him* to leave police work for her. She'd hated the violence, the fact that he might not come home at night. And she'd shudder if he mentioned what he'd seen, the cases....

But he'd been stubborn, just like the owner of *Beau Monde,* and insisted he was doing his duty, that he'd been called to save others.

How could a person outrun who they were inside? Who they were meant to be? He was a Cajun, born to serve the law, bred to fight the dregs of society. He could be nothing more just as Matthew Monde had been a hundred years ago.

But he'd failed Lucinda. When the hurricane had hit, he'd been spearheading rescue attempts while looters had killed his own wife.

Guilt nearly had him doubling over and sweat poured down his face. He deserved the guilt and more.

But the innocent woman struggling for her life tonight needed him to be strong and pull himself together.

Muscles tight, he straightened and went inside. He couldn't change the past, but he could find this maniac who was taking lives. Keep trying to save the innocents to make amends for the one he'd loved and lost. The one he should have protected and saved.

His head pounded as he entered through the mudroom, and he brewed a pot of coffee, knowing he couldn't sleep. Mug in hand, he booted up his laptop at the antique oak table, then began to search for information on Britta Berger. There was some reason the killer had phoned her specifically.

Maybe because she worked at the magazine.

But he claimed to know her secrets, which implied he'd known her in the past. A past she refused to share with him.

He opened the French doors, and sipped the hot coffee while he searched for information. Nothing appeared on any of the police databases, indicating that she didn't have a criminal record. In fact, a half hour later, he scrubbed his hand down his face, exhausted, confused and angry.

He stood, walked to the bar, poured himself a shot of bourbon and tossed it down, grateful for the slow burn rippling down his throat to his belly. The gnarled branches of the trees enveloped the bayou as if protecting its secrets.

Just as Britta's outward mask of control protected hers.

He had found absolutely zilch on her in the databases. Nothing except for the fact that she worked for

Naked Desires, and that she'd moved to New Orleans a year and a half ago.

Dammit, he'd been an absolute fool. She had sucked him in with those guileless bewitching eyes. But those pretty lips had told him nothing but lies.

Bon Dieu. Britta Berger wasn't even the woman's real name.

No, two years ago, Britta Berger had died. In fact, she was buried right here in one of the cemeteries in the Big Easy.

CHAPTER EIGHT

Five days before Mardi Gras

EIGHT HOURS SINCE THE killer's phone call and Jean-Paul still had no idea who the missing woman was or where the killer had taken her.

Or if she was still alive.

Elvira Erickson's parents wanted answers, too, and he had no idea what to tell them.

The muggy heat bore down on Jean-Paul as he stared at the grave. This one, the woman named Britta Berger. She was buried next to her folks, a man named Wally, a woman named Cassie. Apparently they had died in a car crash, all together. He'd looked them up last night and discovered they were a close-knit family.

So who was the woman at *Naked Desires* who called herself Britta Berger? Had she stolen the name from the obituary column? Had she known the real Britta Berger?

And why had he spent half the night thinking about her, searching for reasons to justify her actions?

He'd be better off if he'd never met her. Had never wondered what it would be like to kiss her. To touch her bare skin. To have her naked and writhing beneath him.

Damn. He shouldn't have read that magazine last

night, but he hadn't been able to sleep and had hoped he might find a clue to their killer between the pages. Instead, he'd found erotic pictures and a few letters that he begrudgingly admitted aroused him. He'd always thought men just got turned on by pictures but surprisingly, the written word had made him hard as hell.

Then he'd dreamed about Britta.

But when he'd awakened, he'd been haunted by the fact that she had lied to him. Then again, maybe she had a good reason for changing her name. She might have an abusive boyfriend after her....

If that was the case, why not tell him?

He'd witnessed the twinge of sadness in her eyes when she'd claimed she had no family, and that one real moment taunted him to want to trust her.

Or maybe she'd used that vulnerable, lost look to seduce him.

Whatever, he had to keep their relationship professional.

Yeah, like discussing sexual fantasies from her confession letters today wouldn't get personal.

A subject he and Lucinda had never broached. Lucinda had been old-fashioned, shy about her body, had insisted on lights off during sex. Simple white cotton gowns, not lacy lingerie as he imagined Britta choosing.

He damn sure bet she didn't have to undress in the dark. And he sure as hell wouldn't want her to.

No. He wasn't going there with Britta.

Hell, if she'd changed her name, she'd probably changed her appearance, as well. Maybe she *did* have a closet of wigs and disguises just like the masks on her wall.

Disgusted with himself, he shoved his hands into his

pockets, stalked back to his vehicle and rushed toward the precinct. Today he would get answers.

And hopefully he'd find this killer.

Just as he'd expected, more reporters stood on the front steps, pouncing on him as he neared. Damn leeches.

"Detective Dubois, any progress on that murder case?"

"You have to tell us something."

"Is it true the girl was a prostitute?"

"The cops don't care about the hookers, do they?"

Jean-Paul glared at the man, but refused to take the bait.

Mazie Burgess thrust a microphone in his face. "Come on, Detective Dubois, the public has a right to know if they're in danger."

She was right, but it was too early to talk. "I will make a statement when I have something to tell you. For now, go home and let me get on with the investigation."

Mazie stroked his hand. "Come on, Jean-Paul…"

He narrowed his eyes, warning her to back off. Unfortunately, they both knew he couldn't avoid the press forever.

Still, if word leaked about the second victim, hysteria would erupt. And if the public knew the killer was contacting Britta, her privacy would be shot and she might be in more danger. He rushed inside to the elevator. He had to find out why Britta had lied to him about her identity. And if she'd lied about one thing, she could have lied about others.

What if she knew the killer or had known him in the past? Her silence could cost more women their lives.

THE FACE OF THE DEAD woman rose like a ghost in Britta's dreams. Whispering to her for help. To find her killer.

She jerked awake, a myriad other faces swirling in front of her. Faces she had seen on the streets the night before. Innocent young girls turned to hooking. Girls who'd forgotten themselves and lost their souls to the debauchery of the city.

Predators waiting to pounce on every corner. Ones who might end up just like Elvira Erickson.

Yet she had still been called to the streets.

Jean-Paul Dubois would dub her an idiot. Tell her she was asking for trouble.

She massaged her shoulder where Shack's buddy had twisted her arm behind her back. But he had refused to let her see him. The bruise on her chin from his blow could be camouflaged by makeup.

Jean-Paul would say she deserved those, as well. But he didn't know the real Britta. After all, she was used to disguises.

And last night, she answered her calling.

Today she had to face reality. A killer was using her to alert the police about his murders.

Anxiety squeezed her already sore muscles, and she quickly showered and dressed in a black cotton skirt and crimson tank, donned her spangled bracelets and earrings, then fluffed the short racy ends of her hair. Her glasses came next, the perfect addition to her latest persona.

Then she grabbed her leather shoulder bag filled with the confession letters to take to Detective Dubois. Last night, after her return from the streets, she'd stayed up until four scouring the bundle for suspicious submissions. A handful stood out; she'd pass them to Jean-Paul Dubois.

She stopped in the office, but R.J. hadn't arrived so she decided to drop by the detective's office after she visited the café for her morning coffee and beignet. A noise outside startled her. Through the front window, she noticed a group in front of their building. A square-necked beefy man—a few years older than her, wearing a black suit and hat—lifted his hands to the gathering crowd. He shouted something she couldn't hear, then a chorus followed. Homemade picket signs sprang up as the protesters formed a circle on the street in front of the outer entrance to Naked Desires. "Get rid of the sinners! Cast them aside and build the kingdom of God in their place!"

Britta clenched her hands together as the jeers grew louder. A camera crew arrived and a reporter and cameraman jumped out to capture the scene.

Ever since the caravan of religious fanatics had rolled into town five days ago, R.J. had warned her that they might show up. They'd already staged protest marches in front of two strip joints, another bar and the voodoo shop on the corner.

Dreading the mob and worried about a photo of her on the front page of the paper, she ducked into the hallway to phone him. He answered on the fourth ring.

"R.J., it's Britta."

"Morning. Is everything all right?"

She'd forgotten that she hadn't told him about the phone call the night before and caught him up to date.

"God, Britta, maybe you should stay with me for a few days until this settles down."

"Thanks, R.J., but I'm okay. Except that Reverend Cortain and his mongers are protesting outside the office and a reporter just showed up."

"Shit. I'll be there as soon as possible."

"Wait. R.J., I promised Detective Dubois I'd drop by

and review these letters with him today. I'll see you when I get back. But I want you to do one thing."

"Anything for you, Britta."

Her shoulders tensed at his tone. "Do you think it's possible the killer chose his victims from one of the women who wrote into the magazine?"

"You mean he thought he was fulfilling their fantasy?"

"Maybe."

"That's a long shot," R.J. replied. "We have a secure database. Besides, it would be too much trouble. He can easily find a prostitute on Bourbon Street. And if he's into S and M, there are clubs that cater to that, too."

"Ones you frequent?" Britta instantly regretted her question. She'd tried not to show any personal interest in R.J.'s life.

"Ahh, Britta," he said in a low, husky voice. "All you have to do is trust me and I can show you how exciting sex can be."

She didn't trust any man. And she didn't need a bed of horrors. But neither could she be judgmental like Jean-Paul Dubois. "No thanks, R.J. I'd better go now. That detective is probably waiting."

A tense second passed between them. She could almost hear the disappointment in R.J.'s labored breathing. "What about the reverend and the reporters?"

"I'll dodge them."

"All right, but be careful. And if you do get cornered, don't comment."

"Don't worry. The last thing I want is to get caught up in the publicity."

She said goodbye, then raced upstairs to her apartment, grabbed a hat and sunglasses and hurried down toward the back entrance. As soon as she opened the

door, a camera flashed and a reporter jammed a microphone in her face.

"Aren't you Britta Berger, the Secret Confessions columnist?"

Britta gripped the door edge, ready to run back
inside, but a middle-aged woman clutched her arm.
"Please, Miss Berger, stop your porn column. We have
to save our children!"

"Shut down the magazine!" a man yelled.

"What do you know about the swamp-devil killings?"

They must have seen her with the detective. Britta
ducked her head and covered her face with her hands,
then shouldered her way through the crowd. The cameraman and reporter followed, along with others.
Someone tried to rip the bag of letters from her arm, but
she held on to it for dear life. Terrified of the escalat-
ing mood, she sprinted to the edge of the street corner
and merged into the crowd preparing to cross.

"Stop that heathen!" someone yelled.

"Shut down the slutty column!" another person
shouted.

Suddenly someone shoved her from behind. She
pitched forward and tried to grab something to steady
her, but her heel caught in a crack in the pavement and
she fell forward. She yelled and threw out her hands to
brace her fall, but her knees slammed into the concrete
and pain shot through her. Tires squealed and brakes
screeched around her.

She looked up in horror as a black sedan raced
toward her.

THE ELEVATOR DOOR opened and Jean-Paul headed to his
office.

Carson was waiting on him. "Hey, man, we've got
Randy Swain in custody. Ready to question him?"

Jean-Paul nodded. "I'll be right there." He threw down his briefcase and followed Carson to the interrogation room. "Has he said anything yet?"

"No. But he's pretty wired. I'm running his prints now."

"Good. Does he have an alibi?"

"Claims he was working on a new song the night the Erickson woman died. Guy's already got a big head. He's on his way to the top of the charts with that heartbreaker song."

"Heartache Blues." Jean-Paul chewed the title over in his head. Could the man have decided to murder to gain attention and spike ratings?

Seemed a little drastic, but desperation and ambition were powerful motivators. Plus Jean-Paul had discovered confession letters from women who'd fantasized about having sex with the singer. He'd also found a full page ad for Swain's CD in *Naked Desires*.

He stepped into the room, frowning. Swain looked skuzzy—as if he hadn't seen a shower or razor in a couple of days—and his eyes were bloodshot, probably from drugs or lack of sleep—or both. He was sprawled out in the seat, his arm draped over the chair back, as if he was pissed at being dragged away from his apartment.

If his fans could see him now, they might rethink their loverboy image.

"Mornin', Swain." A table sat in the center below a lamp hanging from the ceiling. Carson sat across from the man, while Jean-Paul situated himself at an angle, half sitting, half standing for intimidation purposes.

"What am I doing here?" Swain asked. "I haven't broken any laws."

Jean-Paul cleared his throat. "Your new hit 'Heart-ache Blues'?"

"Yeah, what about it?"

Carson leaned forward, eyes trained on Swain. "We found a copy of it at the scene of a murder."

The man's bushy brown eyebrows shot up. "So? There's been thousands of them sold in the last week."

"You don't know how it got there?" Jean-Paul asked.

Swain ran a hand over a hole in his jeans. "Listen, if you're talking about that girl they mentioned in the paper this morning, I don't know jack shit about her. Never even heard her name before I read it in the paper."

Jean-Paul zeroed in on the small scars on Swain's hand. They were burns. Some old, some new.

"How'd you get those?" he asked.

"I burn candles and incense at night. It helps me relax when I'm trying to write."

Jean-Paul frowned while Carson cut in. "Where were you last night, say around midnight?" Carson asked.

Swain tapped his temple as if trying to remember. Or formulate a lie.

"Working. I cut off from the band to write alone around eleven."

"So no one can account for your whereabouts then?"

Swain shrugged. "No one I want to tell you about."

"Being an ass won't help your case," Jean-Paul growled. "Did you make any phone calls?"

Swain worked his mouth side to side. "No."

Easy enough to check, but Jean-Paul had to push the guy harder. "And you don't have an alibi the night the Erickson woman was murdered?"

"If I knew I was going to need one, I would have made sure I had one," Swain shot back.

Jean-Paul slapped his palms on the table with a thud and glared into the young man's eyes. "You don't have an alibi, asshole, you're going to wind up in jail."

Swain shifted restlessly. "What the hell kind of motive would I have for murder? I don't know this chick that was killed."

"She was an exotic dancer," Jean-Paul said through gritted teeth. "You've been in the clubs while you were here?"

"So. Don't tell me you haven't?"

"This is not a game," Jean-Paul barked.

Swain's face paled. "Okay, so this girl that was killed, she was a hooker?"

Jean-Paul nodded. "Maybe you know her from the House of Love."

"Is that where you met her?" Carson cut in.

The corner of Swain's mouth lifted into a cocky grin. "I don't have to pay for sex. Since this record aired, women are throwing themselves at my feet."

"So much for their taste," Jean-Paul tossed back. "And that doesn't mean that you didn't hook up with a prostitute. Maybe she was a fan. It started out wild and a little kinky, but something she did pissed you off, reminded you of the woman you sing about in that song and you took out your anger on her."

Swain knotted his hands on the table. "That's crazy. I'm not violent, I write about love."

Carson cleared his throat. "Really? That's not the way the chorus to 'Heartache Blues' calls it:

"You broke my heart.
When you left my bed

Now I'm singing the blues
Because you're dead."

Jean-Paul folded his arms. "Sound like a threat to me."

"Even better, sweet revenge," Carson added. "She dumped you so you killed her and left your CD at the scene to hype your sales."

"That's ridiculous!"

Jean-Paul shoved a copy of *Naked Desires* toward Swain. "Really? Do you know anything about this magazine?"

Swain gulped. "It's an erotica publication."

"Yeah. And you placed a full page ad for your CD in the magazine," Jean-Paul said matter-of-factly.

"My publicist did that," Swain said in a panicked voice.

Jean-Paul rapped his knuckles on the table. "Do you know Britta Berger, the editor of the Secret Confessions column?"

He shifted, chewing on the side of his lip. "What's she got to do with all this?"

"You tell me," Jean-Paul said.

Swain leaned his head onto his hands. "I'm through talking to you guys. I want a lawyer."

THE SMELL OF BURNING rubber and exhaust assaulted Britta as she scrambled away from the car. The sedan swerved and barreled into a lamppost while she crawled to the sidewalk on hands and knees. Screams and shouts erupted around her. Someone's hands reached out to help her and a claustrophobic feeling engulfed her. Memories resurfaced…men clawing at her.

"Are you all right, miss?" a voice asked.

"Are you crazy! You jumped right in front of that car!"

The driver, a man in a black suit, jumped from the sedan and stalked toward her. "I tried to stop, lady. Why'd you dive in front of me like that?"

The cameraman pushed through the crowd. A camera light exploded in her face, nearly blinding her.

"I'm sorry," she whispered raggedly. "It was an accident."

"You got insurance, mister?" someone asked.

He mumbled "yes" and his eyes pierced Britta accusingly.

The menagerie of faces watching her jelled into a blur, like the mob from the clan. Memories bombarded her. She was running through the bayou trying to escape the men hunting her down like an animal. They swept the darkness with their crude lanterns and vile language. Bugs bit her legs and branches scraped her hands and face. Snakes hissed and alligators stalked her with hungry eyes. Eyes like the swamp devil's.

Panic rippled through her. She had to run. Save herself.

She turned and sprinted in the opposite direction. She had escaped that past once. She wouldn't let it catch up with her and destroy the life she was building now.

REVEREND EZRA CORTAIN SHOUTED a prayer at his followers as they chased Britta Berger. She'd either dove in front of that car out of guilt or—through God's hands—someone had pushed her. Either way, it was time for her to repent, or die and burn in hell for her contributions to the debauchery on Bourbon Street.

As he had done for his own sins so many times.

The past two years with the deadly hurricanes had

forced him to expand his mission attempts. He'd collected lost souls from Mississippi, the Louisiana border and all along the gulf coast. He went where he was needed. Was simply a vessel to carry out the word of God. But sin ran rampant here and the devil fought him every inch of the way.

Fingers of anxiety scraped his spine, though, as images of his past flickered back. Britta Berger—she had crossed his path before. Had been lost then.

Had been a temptress. Had Satan's eyes.

Memories plucked at the recesses of his brain, triggering fear and guilt. The bayou. A ceremony. Virginal girls in white.

His brother-in-law's blood.

Then the others.

Dead bodies everywhere. Mothers moaning. Babies crying.

The details materialized in vivid clarity, painful and debilitating. The shock. Grief. The lost, helpless feeling. The cries of emptiness. Their leader had been destroyed.

They needed another. Just as they'd needed to quench their thirst for revenge. But they had been denied.

Because they thought she'd died that night. That the crocodile gods had served their own brand of justice.

But today, when she'd exited that magazine office, he'd seen the evil lurking in her eyes. The blackness from the swamp creatures had overtaken her body, sent her to Sin City to gather her own followers.

And he had to stop her....

SOMEONE WAS STILL following her.

Britta ducked into a gift shop to lose whoever was

behind her, then into the restroom to clean her bloody knees and hands. Minutes later, she sneaked out the back door and headed toward Jackson Square, this time slowing her pace so as not to call attention to herself.

The stench of the night's celebrations flooded the streets, while heat sent a pool of sweat to her neck. She passed a few morning joggers and a man walking his dog. Two winos dug through the trash for breakfast and several shop owners were sweeping up the garbage from the night before, preparing for a new day.

Exhaustion weighed her muscles, but she turned the corner and collapsed into a chair at the café. A latte and beignet with strawberry jam helped to settle her nerves. Around her, tourists talked of the upcoming parade while she watched the local artisans set up their booths. An artist who painted abstracts hung a collection of colorful finished pieces, a voodoo and black magic display came next, then the dollmaker she'd seen for months settled into his usual spot. One by one he displayed his finely painted porcelain dolls, each one different and so beautiful they looked like real babies or children. In contrast, next to him a guy offered dark, ghoulish wooden carvings of demons and monsters along with Mardi Gras masks that portrayed the dark side of the city. She'd bought some of them when he'd first set up. The way he painted the monster's eyes was unnerving, but she'd been drawn to them anyway.

Jean-Paul Dubois's sister Catherine approached the dollmaker, her hand twined with her little girl's. Chrissy picked up a baby doll and hugged it. A baseball cap shaded the dollmaker's face and he kept his head bowed as if he felt uncomfortable discussing his art. But Chrissy oohed and aahed over the doll until Catherine purchased it. Britta's heart squeezed at the natural affection the woman and her little girl shared.

She'd long ago banished any hopes for a family of her own, but suddenly the longing swelled within her. The realization followed that she and Catherine would never be friends, that they didn't belong in the same circle. Catherine and her daughter would wear the pearl combs Britta kept hidden away.

Britta would look ridiculous in them.

Mother and daughter left, hand in hand, the little girl singing and smiling. Loneliness tugged at Britta's chest but she fought off the feeling.

Still, on a whim, she ventured over to the dollmaker's table. "You do nice work. The eyes, they look so real."

"Th...ank y...ou," he stuttered.

Sympathy for him warmed her smile. "You're welcome. You're very talented."

A sheepish grin crossed his face. "Th...anks."

She studied the different faces of the dolls, then purchased a miniature doll in a pink-and-white gingham dress and had him wrap it. She put it in her bag.

He mumbled his appreciation, then began to etch tiny lines into the eyeballs of another doll while other admirers crowded around. Feeling silly for buying the doll, she rushed toward the police precinct, determined to share the letters with Jean-Paul and escape from him as soon as possible.

Hopefully, he had a lead on the woman the killer had told her about the night before, and he wouldn't need her any longer.

A FROWN YANKED at Debra Schmale's face. She wanted Teddy for herself.

But she'd seen Teddy watch the woman stop by his table. Britta Berger—Debra recognized her from the magazine photo. Except she was even more beautiful in person than the picture.

The bitch.

She had been flirting with Teddy for weeks now and had barely gotten him to even glance her way. He sure as heck hadn't grinned at *her* like an idiot like he had that Berger babe. And she'd bought half a dozen of his miniature dolls.

Of course, she wasn't a looker like Britta Berger.

No, she had knobby knees, wore an A-cup and needed extra cover-up to mask the zits that plagued her when she got nervous.

What was she going to have to do to get Teddy's attention? Dance naked in the streets?

She licked her fingers and tried to comb down her mousy brown hair. The stupid stuff reacted to this god-awful heat by exploding into a frizzy mop. Finally she applied lip gloss that tasted like wild berries and yanked her jeans lower on her hips to showcase her flat belly and new bellybutton ring, a small blue and yellow butterfly.

All twisted inside from fear that Teddy would ignore her again almost made her nauseous. Even though she wasn't sophisticated or trendy like Britta Berger, she'd show Teddy she could be fun. She fingered the bright silver bracelets she'd bought, ones similar to Britta Berger's. She liked the way they clanged on her arm when she moved. Maybe she could even buy a push-up bra and jam her boobs up high so she'd have cleavage.

Heck, why was she worried about Britta Berger?

She was too old and sophisticated to go for a guy like Teddy anyway; she could have half the men in town.

But what if she decided to play with Teddy just because she enjoyed the attention? She might tease him. Lead him on. Keep him from falling for *her*.

Just like the sorority girls at school had when she'd wanted that boy Danny. Damn bimbettes.

Once she'd tried to be their friends. Tried to fit in and join them. But they'd laughed at her and blackballed her.

They didn't bother her anymore, though. Not since she'd pulled that switchblade and threatened to carve out their eyes.

No one was ever going to keep her from getting what she wanted again.

And if the Berger woman got in the way, she'd take care of her, too, just like she had the others.

CHAPTER NINE

ANOTHER HOUR TICKED by. Another hour the killer had to toy with his victim.

Another hour and no answers.

Frustration nagged at Jean-Paul. They still hadn't located or identified a second victim, and the police department had pooled as much manpower as they could spare to search the bayou. Carson was checking out Swain's alibi and his place.

The need to be out there looking himself made Jean-Paul antsy, but when he'd informed the lieutenant that Britta Berger was not who she claimed to be, Phelps had ordered him to stick with the woman. So far, she was their only connection to the swamp devil.

Banning her from his mind until he could confront her, he thumbed through the preliminary information they'd gathered so far on Elvira Erickson. According to the detectives who'd canvassed her apartment complex, victim one had been a loner. Had not had a steady boyfriend or brought anyone home. Her phone records indicated only a few local calls, one to a man named Shack, who he was almost certain was her pimp.

Jean-Paul had already talked to his brother Antwaun. He was beating the streets now in search of the guy.

A knock sounded at the door and he braced himself as Britta entered his office. She looked disheveled. Her glasses were slightly crooked, a sunhat dangled from one hand and a shoulder bag had been slung over her arm.

His temper teetered on the surface. It was time she talked.

But he zeroed in on her elbow and noted fresh scrapes and the fact that her right eye looked swollen. His question died on his lips.

"What happened to you?" Alarmed, he strode toward her, took the bag and sunhat and placed them on the desk, then gently took her arms and examined them. Her other elbow was bruised as well as her hands, and faint scratches marked her chin.

She shrugged. "I fell off the curb this morning."

He narrowed his eyes. "Try again."

"It's the truth."

"Really? Just like your real name is Britta Berger?"

Her face blanched. "What makes you think that it's not?"

"Because I visited the real woman's grave this morning."

She turned away but he caught her hand. "Tell me the truth, damnit."

"About my name or this morning?"

"Both."

She glanced down at where their hands were joined. "Ezra Cortain and his crew staged a protest at the magazine."

"Do they know about the killer's note to you?"

"No. And I certainly didn't share the information with them."

Jean-Paul's pulse hammered. "Then what happened?"

"They chased me. I tried to blend into the crowd but when I went to cross the street, someone pushed me."

"Did you see who it was?"

"No, I was too busy trying to scramble away from the car flying toward me."

"*Bon Dieu.* Do you need to see a doctor?"

Her chin quivered as she gazed into his eyes, emotions glittering before she drew a curtain down over them. "No, I'm fine now. But whoever pushed me, tried to grab my shoulder bag. I don't know if they wanted money or the letters."

Alarm bells clamored in Jean-Paul's head. "The letters from your column?"

She nodded. "Why would someone want them?"

"Because they might lead us to the killer."

BRITTA GLANCED AWAY from Jean-Paul's probing eyes and the questions.

Desperate, she focused on the map on his wall, then a smaller one which highlighted the bayou. Various pushpins protruded from different areas, which she assumed were ones where they had targeted search parties. Black Bayou was one of them.

Just the thought of the area made her shudder.

"You should have called me." He jerked up the phone. "Listen, send a team to check out the protest at Naked Desires. Miss Berger was accosted there this morning. Charge them with violating a peaceful protest if you have to but disband them."

Her gaze flew back to his. "That will probably cause even more trouble."

"Reverend Cortain *is* trouble. He gives religion a bad name." Jean-Paul rapped his knuckles on his desk and she noticed the open folders spread before him.

"Speaking of names," he said, his thick eyebrows pulling together in a frown. "Why don't you tell me your real one and why you faked your identity."

A surge of panic raced through her. "I can't believe you checked into me."

Temper flared in his brown eyes and Britta took a step backward. He looked mad as hell, as if he wanted to shake her.

"Come on, Britta, I'm a detective. You knew I was going to check you out. You're part of a homicide investigation."

Hurt swelled inside her, although she hated herself for the emotion. For hoping that there might be one decent man alive. One who'd take her at face value. Trust her. Not hurt her.

Not question her past. Not care that she'd been living a lie.

But it was obvious Jean-Paul Dubois was not that man. He'd do whatever it took to solve his case. Even expose her and put her in danger. Or jail....

"I thought the investigation was about finding this killer, not me. So why should it matter to you who I am?" Tears pricked at her eyelids, although she blinked them away. She would not cry in front of him. Not in front of any man, ever again.

"It is." He stalked toward her. "But if you lied to me about one thing, maybe you're lying about the note. Maybe you know this killer and you came here to play some lurid cat and mouse game to distract me."

Her heart pounded. "That's ridiculous. I called you

because I wanted to help that woman. Now I realize my mistake."

"If you really want to help, then be honest, Britta."

"I told you the truth about how I found that note and picture. I wish he hadn't sent it to me, but he did."

"If that's true, the killer is connecting with you, not me or anyone else. That means he knows you—or knew you from the past."

She closed her eyes, vying for composure. She couldn't look into his and see her lies reflected or the truth of his words. Doing so meant shedding the armor that protected her. Admitting that she'd never escaped at all.

That the people who'd chased her into the bayou had not given up their thirst for revenge. That she'd never be free of them.

And that she might be the reason this man was murdering innocent women.

That kind of guilt would be unbearable.

Her heart racing, she turned to run. By the time her hand closed around the doorknob, Jean-Paul was on her, his chest pressed against hers. His breath brushed her neck.

"You can't run forever, Britta." His voice reverberated in her ear. The killer's words. Jean-Paul's. "Now, tell me who you are."

His grip tightened on her arm and the world slipped into a black fog. Men chasing her. The swampland sucking at her feet. The alligators spitting and announcing their attack. The vile stench of a hand closing over her mouth….

A cold clamminess pervaded her and she began to shake with fear and anger. "Let me go."

"Talk to me," he growled.

"I was in foster care," she admitted raggedly. "My foster parents and sister died in an accident. I took their daughter's name because I liked it, because I missed them." Her voice broke. "Because I wanted to be part of their family."

His breath bathed her neck, hot and husky. "Then why run? Is someone after you now? An old boy-friend or lover?"

"No...I told you there's no one," she said in an anguished whisper.

She was running because she had to.

Time swept her back as if it was yesterday.

She had to escape, had to get out of the bayou. The snakes slithered toward her. The darkness engulfed her. The stench of blood and death. Of them closing in like hound dogs on a blood hunt.

Weeds and bugs clawed at her arms and legs. Vines trapped her, their tendrils wrapping around her legs like snakes. Darkness blinded her. She had to keep moving or she would die.

Panic gave her strength. She swung her elbow up as hard as she could and jammed it into the man's chest. A grunt followed and he released her, but his icy hands touched her and she tore herself from his clutches.

The room swirled around her. Lights suddenly flashed, shimmering through the leafy trees. No, they weren't trees. She was in a room. Brightly lit. The murky darkness lifted slightly, and strangers' faces broke through the fog. A tall man. Another in a cop's uniform.

They'd found her and were going to arrest her.

No! She had to keep running.

Her feet felt heavy, and the room spun. She needed water. A reprieve from the heat. She stumbled forward,

*clutching at the walls to guide her. A voice called out
her name, telling her to stop. But she couldn't. Finally,
a hall. She leaned against the wall, confused. Where
was she? Not in the bayou? A building somewhere.
Bright lights glared in her eyes like a white tunnel.*

*The man called her name again and she scrambled
away from the wall, feeling her way again until she fell
through an opening....*

Seconds later, reality slowly returned. She'd
stumbled into a bathroom. Heaving for air, she fumbled
for the sink and turned on the water. The cold spray felt
heavenly against her face. She cupped her hand, let the
water fill it, then sucked it down her parched throat.
Again and again, until the dizziness passed.

Her hands shook as she felt for a paper towel.
Suddenly one was thrust into her hand. She opened her
eyes and the room came into focus. Her reflection
taunted her from the mirror.

Her eyes looked puffy and red, one was swollen,
black and blue. Her hair was disheveled and a crazy
wildness lit her eyes.

She wasn't alone.

Behind her, standing with his arms folded, his expression stony and silent, stood Jean-Paul Dubois.

JEAN-PAUL'S PULSE raced.

Post-traumatic stress syndrome. Britta had been
traumatized and was terrified of something. He'd witnessed similar reactions—some from war veterans,
others after Katrina.

What exactly had happened to her?

Something to do with her past. His demands obviously triggered her reaction.

His physical touch made it worse.

The thought of a man violating her twisted his insides. How young had she been? Was that the reason she'd been in foster care? The reason she'd changed her name?

God, what a mess.

His brain continued to search for answers, for a way to understand. But he couldn't push her now. And if she'd changed her name to escape an abusive boyfriend, husband or stalker, she'd taken a chance on exposing her identity by calling him. In fact, she'd been courageous.

But if the killer was the man after her, then he'd found her anyway. So why wouldn't she confide in him? She couldn't possibly want to protect the son of a bitch.

Unless the man she was running from had been a cop.

The truth could be anywhere in between.

Tears stained her eyes and the black eye he'd thought he'd detected looked stark without her makeup in the bright fluorescent light. He inhaled sharply, struggling to control his emotions. He hated himself for pushing her into this.

And if his touch had done it…hell, he felt like a bastard.

He cleared his throat. "I'm sorry, Britta. Are you okay now?"

She swallowed, although her body betrayed her by trembling.

He jerked off his jacket and eased it around her shoulders, careful not to alarm her or crowd her space. Her head still bowed, she tugged it around her as if she wanted to crawl inside the garment and disappear forever.

"I'm sorry," she whispered in a ragged voice. "I don't know what came over me."

"You mean you're not going to tell me," he said, forcing himself to remain in place instead of reaching for her.

Her pain-filled eyes rose to meet his, a silent plea in the depths. "Please," she said softly. "It's not important. I…came to help you. I brought the letters. That's all I can give you."

The anguish in her voice nagged at him. He had to let the matter drop.

For now.

But he would find out what had happened to her. Why one minute she was strong and defiant, and the next—she looked as if she'd gone through hell and barely lived to tell about it.

He had to earn her trust. But doing so would be a monumental job, especially since she didn't trust anyone.

Maybe she never had.

Or maybe the ones she had trusted, the ones who should have taken care of her, had hurt her the most.

BRITTA FELT EXPOSED, vulnerable, raw. And she didn't like it.

Jean-Paul Dubois had seen too much already.

She had to get the situation back under control. "We should get to those letters."

"Are you sure you're up for it?" Jean-Paul's eyes probed hers. "I can get a team to sort through them."

"No, I…want to help." She fidgeted with her hair,

then slid her glasses back on. She needed them, used them to hide behind. "I need to know if I missed something so it doesn't happen again."

He nodded. "Take a few minutes. I'll be in my office."

She turned away from him and reached inside her bag for her compact. But he lingered for a moment, watching, studying her. Waiting to see if she'd explain herself.

But she couldn't.

Finally disappointment flared in his expression. He strode out the door. She leaned against the sink and closed her eyes, willing away the nausea that had gripped her earlier.

God knows what Jean-Paul Dubois thought of her now. She'd acted like a lunatic. Not that she cared about his opinion. He was just a man.

Another one she could live without.

Then why did she feel so bereft and alone? Why had she ached to let him hold her and make the pain go away?

Mortified at the thought, she stared at her reflection. The bruises, the dark circles, the tormented eyes. The disguise was gone and in its place the raw girl who lay beneath had been exposed. The little girl who'd tried to make herself disappear, to be invisible. The little girl without a home. A family. The woman so desperate she'd taken someone else's name.

Jean-Paul had seen her, as well.

Furious at her weakness, she washed her face, then carefully reapplied her makeup. Cover-up for the bruises. Powder for her pale cheeks. Although nothing could help the puffy eyes except rest. And she didn't foresee sleep in the near future.

Not until the swamp devil was caught.

She clutched her purse, contemplating what to do next. She should go back to her apartment and pack. She'd leave R.J. a note; tell him to hire someone else for her column. If the killer was after her, maybe he'd leave town, too. She could find a new place to hide. A new name.

Start over.

Suddenly loud shouts erupted outside the bathroom. Feet pounded in the hallway. She rushed to the door, opened it and stepped into the doorway. A middle-aged couple stood beside Jean-Paul outside his office, the man shouting questions. The woman buried her face into her hands, sobbing.

Jean-Paul called them by name—the Ericksons.

Britta's chest squeezed with compassion for the dead girl's parents. She couldn't run. She had to help them find their daughter's killer.

Even if it meant putting herself in danger.

Not wanting to intrude on their grief, she inched into the corner, giving Jean-Paul privacy to console the couple. But she watched through the glass window of his office, mesmerized by his gentle voice and the way he calmed them. Her feelings for Jean-Paul Dubois were growing. It was bad enough that she was attracted to the man, but now she actually admired him and *liked* him.

A loud voice bellowed behind her. An officer yanked a woman dressed in spiked heels, a flaming sequined skirt and enormous fake breasts toward a chair.

Jean-Paul's brother, Antwaun.

"I don't have to talk to you pigs," the woman snarled.

"Shut up and sit down, Candy. We just want to ask you some questions."

"I want a lawyer," Candy hissed.

"You don't need one, you're not under arrest. We just want to talk to you about Elvira Erickson."

Memories of seeing her own mother hauled in for prostitution resurfaced. The pity and disdain in the officers' faces. The same way Antwaun was looking at Candy.

The same way Jean-Paul would if he knew about her mother.

How could she even contemplate that he could accept her?

RANDY SWAIN cursed as he paced in the interrogation room. "Listen, Marty, things can't go wrong now. You have to get me out of this mess."

"Just stay calm, Randy," his manager said quietly. "The police have nothing on you."

Sweat soaked Randy's back. "They have the ad we ran in *Naked Desires*. And they have letters women have written to that broad fantasizing about me." Randy lowered his voice. "God knows what they'll find to incriminate me at my apartment."

Marty shot him a worried look. "All circumstantial."

Except for those pictures and the lingerie… Fuck, how could he have been so stupid?

"Just play nice," Marty advised him. "I've called Leonard Turner. He'll be here soon."

Randy was still sweating bullets. "If they look hard enough, they'll find out about my past."

"No one knows your real name or that you grew up in Black Bayou," Marty assured him. "We've covered our asses."

Randy cracked his knuckles. Maybe. Maybe not.

There were other bad things they could find, though. Things he hadn't even told Marty. Notes about old songs that could condemn him. Things about his mother.

That trouble in that small town in Mississippi. And the games he liked to play with women.

Then the truth about his identity.

Even worse, there was the fact that he had met Elvira Erickson. And that he and Marty *had* discussed using that magazine for publicity....

BRITTA BRACED HERSELF as Jean-Paul approached. She'd seen the Ericksons leave and prayed she could help him find their daughter's killer. At least then they could have some closure.

Something she had never had with her own mother.

"Come with me, Britta," Jean-Paul said. "We have that singer, Randy Swain, in custody. I want you to listen to his voice, see if you recognize him."

"Why do you think that he has something to do with the murder?"

Jean-Paul explained about the CD and Swain's ad in *Naked Desires*. "Did you meet Swain when he placed the ad?"

Britta chewed her lip. She'd forgotten about it. "Yes, but just briefly. The magazine was hungry for supporters."

"And he was hungry for publicity."

She nodded, his meaning dawning. "You think he might have killed Elvira and contacted me to boost his sales?"

"It's one possibility. Carson is searching his apartment now." He led her to an interrogation room. "Listen. Tell me if he sounds like the man who phoned you."

"But I've heard his song, Jean-Paul," Britta said. "I don't think it was him."

"You said the voice sounded muffled. He might have disguised his tone."

Britta nodded and sat down behind the two-way mirror. Jean-Paul left the room, then appeared in the window on the other side to question Swain.

"Listen, Swain," Jean-Paul said. "There're a couple of things I want you to say for me."

"What? That I killed that hooker?" He pulled at his chin. "I don't think so. I told you I want my lawyer."

"Your manager said he's on his way. But if you want to get yourself off the hook, this just might do it."

Swain's features tightened, but he conceded. "Bring it on then. I want to go home and get some shut-eye."

Jean-Paul shoved a pad in front of Swain. He squinted, then repeated, "I know your secrets and you know mine."

Britta flinched, trying to dissect his tone, enunciation pattern, anything concrete to identify him. *Could* he have been the man who called her?

She wanted to say yes, but she couldn't be sure. The voice from the phone…it had been gruffer. Maybe raspier, lower pitched.

Her head spun in confusion. She'd been terrified when he'd called and his words had resurrected bad memories.

But what if she said no, and Swain turned out to be the killer? If they let him go, he might kill again. Then it would be her fault.

JEAN-PAUL STALKED INTO the room, anxious for Britta's reaction. Her expression looked strained.

"I'm sorry, Jean-Paul, I can't be sure."

He nodded, but his cell phone rang, cutting into the tension. "Dubois."

"It's Dr. Charles. I'll be in your office in five minutes. We need to talk."

Jean-Paul agreed, then pivoted. "That was the ME. He wants to discuss his report. I'll fill you in later."

"Please let me stay," Britta pleaded. "Maybe I can help."

"Let me check with the lieutenant."

He left the room, then returned a few minutes later and guided her into a small room with a long table and several chairs situated around it. A chalkboard and a cork board with several notes thumbtacked onto it hung on one wall. The opposite wall held a huge eraser board. And a map with pushpins occupied the third.

She claimed a straight wooden chair in the corner. Seconds later, Detective Graves entered, along with a man Jean-Paul addressed as Lieutenant Phelps. Dr. Charles stalked in a minute later, tapping a file folder. Jean-Paul introduced Britta to each of them, and they shook hands.

"What's she doing here?" Dr. Charles asked.

"She's the only one who's made contact with this swamp devil," Jean-Paul explained. "I think she might be able to help."

"All right. Let's talk about the tox screen," Charles said as he spread the report on the table. "The woman did have evidence of alcohol and a mild sedative in her system."

"So he drugged her, then carried her out to the bayou?" Jean-Paul surmised.

Dr. Charles nodded. "Probably wanted her quiet in

the car so she wouldn't draw attention to them." He attached several X-rays to the marker board, then pointed out various bruises and injuries. Next came graphic photos of the stab wounds to her heart where the spear had torn into tissue and cartilage. Britta had to look away from the gruesome details.

"Did the stab wound kill her?" Detective Graves asked.

"No."

"Then what was the cause of death?" Lieutenant Phelps asked.

"Poison." The ME cleared his throat. "More specifically, he used arsenic poisoning."

Jean-Paul narrowed his eyes, trying to piece together the various elements of the perp's MO. "In the drugs?"

"No." Dr. Charles adjusted his wire rims on his blunt nose. "That's where it gets interesting. He sprinkled the poison on the outside of the condom and fucked the poor woman to death."

"Christ. It's a wonder he hasn't killed himself," Phelps muttered.

"He wanted the death to be painful," Jean-Paul said. "But it also had to result from the sexual experience. That's important to him for some reason."

Charles nodded. "Within a short time of taking a lethal dose, arsenic poisoning causes gastric distress. A burning esophageal pain. Sometimes vomiting and diarrhea with blood. Then convulsions and coma. The patient dies of circulatory failure."

"Damn bastard. He wants the victims to suffer." Jean-Paul paced the room. "But he's conflicted. He uses massage oil before he has sex with them—as if he wants to pleasure them first."

He turned to them all, continuing with the profile. "He also likes history, dabbles in religion, has twisted sexual fantasies," Jean-Paul said with a snap of his fingers. "He left the victim with a serpent necklace where the serpent is chasing his tail."

"He wants to turn them into what they should be," Britta mumbled.

The men turned to stare at her.

"I saw a display about the necklace at that history museum."

Jean-Paul nodded. "Right. And the lancet is a reproduction of one used in wars from medieval times, too. He tears out the women's hearts after he kills them because they broke his heart."

"I don't understand why he needs the poison if he's going to stab them," Lieutenant Phelps said.

"He's a sociopath. Maybe schizophrenic. Everything has symbolic meaning." Jean-Paul folded his hands and took the floor. "In the middle ages, there's a story about a Frenchman who loved all his beautiful rich wives, so he decided to pleasure them before killing them. He used a thin goatskin to protect his penis, but put a lethal dose of poison on the sheath. The poison seeped into the women's vaginas and killed them shortly thereafter."

Britta blanched. "So he loves these women, but he's conflicted by his own beliefs, therefore he kills them."

"He's saving them from themselves, making them repent for their sins," Jean-Paul said. "Isn't that what he told you, Britta?"

She nodded. "The mask above the woman's bed—the crocodile head with the human body—it represents Sobek, the crocodile god the Egyptians worshipped in medieval times. The people used to sacrifice women to appease the gods because they feared them."

The group turned to her, their mouths agape. Horror struck her. Had she given too much away?

"She's right," Jean-Paul said with a curious sideways look.

Images swirled in Britta's mind; another carving of Sobek haunted her—one she'd seen years ago. One that she was supposed to worship. The chants, the fire, the singing and praying. Then the man and his son….

This killer couldn't be the man she'd run from years ago, could he?

All the clues led back to that day. To the cult.

To the day she'd died.

The trial by ordeal. To test for evil, the medieval people forced the accused to cross a path or group of logs across the river. If the gators didn't get them, they passed the test.

As she thought she had—years ago.

But her escape had been temporary. Had she survived because evil blood ran through her veins? Because she had joined the devil's side when she'd become a killer?

Even as denial swept through her, she had to face the fact that the clan might have survived. That they were still believers. That they still sacrificed women as they had intended to do with her years ago. That this man might be their leader or any one of his followers.

That he had come back to punish her.

And that she deserved it.

CHAPTER TEN

R.J. CHOSE HIS CLOTHES carefully. A necessity for the perfect disguise.

The dark shirt with the button-up collar. The red tie. The black pants. All his favorite colors. Each garment tailored to hide the telltale marks on his body. And if that didn't suffice, he could always use a little of that pancake makeup he'd bought at the S and M shop.

He grinned at himself in the mirror, remembering the change in himself from the night before. The first time he'd delved into the dark side, he had felt intense physical pain, an agony that had forced him to question his destiny. But each time the pain had gotten easier to bear. Now he embraced it. Each lashing, each moment of torture—both mental and physical—excited him. Just the hint of animal pheromones, the bayou odors, the glimmering moonlight made him dizzy with desire. And launched him into new fantasies, secret ones he wanted to share with Britta.

But not everyone understood his dark fantasies or would welcome the black side of him. The reason for his disguise.

The time was right. Mardi Gras was all about disguises, the old culture, paying tribute to the legends that went before them.

Britta would never know what he did at night. Or that some of the confession letters had been penned by him.

Not unless she chose to join him.

He walked to his study, pressed the button that opened the door to his secret chamber and noted the mess. Blood sprinkled here and there. The smell of raw flesh. Man and beast.

He closed the door and settled the books back into place, then strode outside into the hot sultry air. Steam rose from the marshland beyond, the details of his foray the night before parading in front of his mind's eye.

His lover would be waiting when he returned tonight. After all, where else could she go? She was tied to the bayou now, deep in its depth, the shadows of the trees protecting her. The animals knew her well. They would surround her and hold her hostage until his return.

Sunlight bolted through the haze and he dragged on dark Ray Bans, battling the wave of discomfort the daylight brought. The headaches. The pounding in his temple.

He was meant for the night.

But Britta had already phoned, upset. And he had to deal with Ezra Cortain.

Blistering rage rippled through his blood as he drove to the magazine. Tourists and sightseers crowded the streets, the bars preparing for another influx while the massive horses who pulled the carriage tours panted in the heat. A panhandler thrust an old worn hat toward him; the sight of the man's gimp leg caused R.J. to dig in his pocket for loose change.

Ezra Cortain should be here helping the homeless, not pounding the pavement shouting about *Naked Desires*. The man was such a fraud he was surprised that

God didn't set him on fire so the world could witness his demise.

As R.J. rounded the corner, the protest march was in full swing. Signs waving, people shouting to shut down the sinful magazine, blaming *his* brainchild on the decadence in town. He chuckled at the irony.

Ezra Cortain had no idea the part he'd played in R.J.'s choices. But he would. Bloodlust filled R.J. with exhilaration at the thought of that day coming.

He pushed through the crowd until he stood face-to-face with Cortain. The asshole had plastered himself in front of the window as if he could hide the dirty secrets inside the office with his billowing robe.

But Cortain had his own dirty little secrets and R.J. knew all about them. He ripped off his sunglasses, glared at Cortain's cold gray eyes, reveling in the fact that his height allowed him to tower over the short, pudgy man.

"Go away, Cortain."

"We must build the kingdom of the Lord," Cortain shouted. "Destroy the sins and evil in the city that you entice with your depravity."

R.J. gripped the preacher's flabby arm. "If you don't leave my business alone, you'll be sorry."

Cortain's eyes bulged. "You're threatening me in front of God's children."

"You're not the saint you pretend to be," he muttered low enough so that only Cortain heard. "And soon everyone will know the truth. Then see if your God saves you."

Cortain clutched his Bible to his chest as if it was a suit of armor and could protect him.

R.J. laughed. The man had better gather his horde of

followers and leave town before his worshipers learned he was not sent from God, but from the devil.

R.J. would expose him now, but first he had to protect himself and win Britta's favor.

JEAN-PAUL CONTINUED TO assimilate the killer's MO in his mind. Knowing how the man ticked would help them catch him. But would they do so in time to save the missing woman?

The ME left, and Jean-Paul and Britta gathered around the conference table with coffee and po' boys he'd ordered from his parents' restaurant. They'd insisted he invite her to Sunday dinner the next day.

Hell, he didn't even know if he'd make it, not with this investigation still hot.

Britta glanced up from a stack of letters in her hand. "So, we're looking for any mention of a spear, a serpent necklace, Sobek or poisoned condoms?"

Her sarcasm wasn't lost on him. If the guy had submitted previous confession letters, he probably wouldn't have been so damn obvious. "You think this is a waste of time?"

She shrugged and absentmindedly massaged her neck, calling attention to her bruised skin. He'd kill to know who had hurt her.

R. J. Justice? Was she into the kinky S and M like her boss?

"No. We have to do something," she said wearily.

He felt her frustration. Hopefully, Carson would return with something from Swain's apartment to help them. And he was still waiting on Antwaun to find the pimp.

"Tell me about Justice," Jean-Paul said. "What do you know about his personal life?"

Britta fumbled through the stack, obviously sorting hers by male and female confessions. "Not much. He lives on the outskirts of town in a refurbished antebellum house. It's near the bayou."

"Have you ever been there?"

"No."

"Did you two date?"

"No. We've discussed this before, Jean-Paul." She glanced up at him. "Besides, you don't really think R.J. killed that woman?"

"I have to look at every angle." He used his fingers to mark off his points. "First, the guy owns a sexually explicit magazine. Like Swain, publicity could help Justice's sales."

"Not with Reverend Cortain's slanderous protests."

"Even negative publicity can hype business," he pointed out. "He had access to your office. What about your apartment?"

"I don't know," Britta said with a frown. "He may still have a key. He stayed there when he first came to town and was renovating the building for the magazine. When he hired me, he moved into his house and I took the apartment."

Jean-Paul clenched his jaw. "He has access, motive and he's into S and M. Definitely fits our UNSUB's profile."

"I thought R.J. had an alibi for the night Elvira Erickson was killed?"

Jean-Paul rocked back in his chair. "He does. But the woman could be lying. She's…strange herself."

"What do you mean?"

His chair hit the floor with a thud. "He's into some weird stuff sexually."

Britta nodded. "I gathered that from the items and artwork in his office. But being kinky isn't a crime."

Jean-Paul's blood ran cold. It certainly made him a more likely candidate. "If he keeps those things on display, think about what he might be hiding at home."

"Everybody has something to hide," Britta said softly.

He shook his head. "Not everyone, Britta. With me, what you see is what you get."

"Then why aren't you married with your own family?"

Pain knifed through him like a razor blade. She was right. He did have secrets. A part of his life he wouldn't discuss.

She leaned closer, her dark eyes probing his. "See what I mean? You want to tear apart my life and examine it, but you won't let me look into yours."

Her comment hit so close to home that emotions crowded his throat. "Just be careful around Justice," he ground out. "He could be dangerous, Britta."

"You really think he might hurt me?"

"I think he wants you," he said deadpan. Not that *he* didn't want her, too. But in another way. "And Justice strikes me as a man who gets what he wants no matter what he has to do to get it."

JEAN-PAUL'S COMMENT ABOUT R.J. disturbed Britta, but not as much as the pain she'd seen on his face when she'd asked why he didn't have a family of his own.

She should have kept her mouth shut. Shouldn't have tried to get personal. But the man was getting to her on more than one level. Sexually, she had to admit wanting him. Craving his touch. Even fantasizing about his hands on her body.

And God, he'd been so compassionate with the Ericksons. He was smart, too. And worried about R.J. hurting her.

He's simply doing his job. He doesn't care about you.

But what would it feel like if he did? She'd ruin it with the truth.

Reality intervened quickly and she forced herself back to the task.

My Secret Confession:

My sexual fantasy is to have a man love me in public. We've just shared a bottle of Chardonnay and fed each other strawberries dipped in chocolate.

He reaches beneath the table and slides his hand up my thigh, then strokes the inside of my leg, slowly, inch by inch until he reaches my heat. His look of surprise when he discovers I'm not wearing panties gets me more excited and I spread my legs wider under the table so he can feel my damp cunt. By this time, my breasts are heavy and aching and my breath erupts in small little spurts. He senses my excitement and slides one finger into my aching heat. I straighten in the seat, holding on to the edge of the chair with sweaty fingers as he moves deeper, deeper into me, then he slowly withdraws his fingers and licks them where my wet juices linger. My body cries out for more.

Realizing I'm on the brink of screaming his name, he crawls beneath the table to have his dessert. I lean back in the chair, sip my wine and pretend nonchalance as if he's searching for a missing cuff link, but the waiter pauses with a grin and begins to watch. Two other tables realize our game and wave. One of the men gets so turned on, he cups his wife's breasts while the woman at the adjacent table places her husband's hand on her crotch.

My own guy slides his tongue around and around my dripping mound, making me squirm. Then, finally, he dips his long, wet tongue inside me. I grip the table, shaking and heaving for air, as he delves deeper.

Spasms rock through my body, relentless and intense and all I can think about is having him make love to me. I can't wait, I'm already coming....

Britta licked her lips, her own body feeling hot and heavy, then glanced up to see Jean-Paul watching her. She had forgotten that she wasn't alone, had allowed the woman's fantasy to become her own. And Jean-Paul Dubois was on the floor in the restaurant giving her the orgasm of her life.

"Should I read that one?" Jean-Paul asked in a thick voice.

His dark gaze met hers, the telltale smile in his eyes indicating that he realized exactly what had happened. Humiliation flooded her cheeks and she shook her head.

"No. This one isn't violent."

His chuckle rumbled through the air, and she closed the letter, deciding to include that fantasy in her column. But it told her nothing about the killer, so she moved on to another submission, this time skimming for any mention of lancets, snakes, S and M, poisons or the swamp devil.

Just the image the killer's name produced destroyed any lingering sexual desires she might have had.

TWO HOURS LATER. All Jean-Paul had learned was how titillating the written word could be.

Each minute his awareness of Britta had grown stronger. He'd loosened his own tie and shirt, the air growing warmer and the room smaller with each letter. A few times he'd even forgotten his purpose because he'd become engrossed in the fantasy. And in each one, the woman he'd been making love with was Britta.

Not Lucinda.

This realization shook him to the core. His reaction had everything to do with proximity, he told himself, to the fact that Britta was a much more sexually oriented person than his wife had been. To the fact that he'd been celibate for two years.

And maybe to the fact that Lucinda wouldn't have been caught dead reading sexual fantasies. If he'd suggested they teeter on the wild side or branch out in new positions or…other things he'd dreamed about doing, she would have thought he was perverted.

He brushed sweat from his brow, silently cursing the infernal heat, and he began to read again, hoping this one might provide something more than arousal—like answers to the killer's identity.

My Secret Confession:

I am a sexually hungry man but not always able to get the girls I want. I have begun to fantasize about voyeurism. In my apartment I have a telescope that allows me to watch women in the apartments across from me.

Jean-Paul shifted in his seat. So far, suspicious, but not anything criminal.

At night I see the woman in 3B strip and walk around naked. She likes to touch herself. And the lesbians in 4F like do to it all over the place. Man, can they eat some pussy.

Sometimes I photograph them and have started a book of all the beautiful women in the city. Just walking in the Quarter, the Market or on Bourbon Street, I see dozens every day. Sometimes I try to talk to them but the pretty ones don't even look my way. So, I photograph them when they're not watching. Their beautiful eyes. Their perfect sexy bodies. Their made-up faces meant to hide their flaws.

Each time the camera captures their image and tells all. When I look at the pictures, I focus on their eyes. The windows to the soul.

Although some of their eyes hold emptiness. They are the lost souls. The tramps. The ones in disguise. I want to carve out their eyes, display them and show the truth behind the lies.

I have one eye on you, Britta, for I know the truth.

That you are one of them.

His suspicions raised, Jean-Paul searched for a signature, but found nothing. The envelope was postmarked from the post office in town but there was no return address, no post office box, nothing to indicate who had sent it.

He sighed, stood and handed it to Britta. "Read this. See if the guy sounds familiar."

Britta's face paled as she digested the letter. "It sounds like the photographer I saw watching me."

Jean-Paul nodded. He didn't like it one damn bit, either.

"I wonder if his work is on display at the art festival."

Jean-Paul stood. "Let's check and see."

"We still have a couple more hours' worth of letters to read."

"Let's divide them up and take them home for the night." Jean-Paul stretched his arms. "I'm getting antsy." If this guy had been watching Britta and was their killer, he wanted to find him now.

He didn't intend to take a chance on the sick bastard getting to her.

She nodded. "Let me call R.J. and tell him my plans." Jean-Paul frowned. He didn't want her anywhere near the man.

JEAN-PAUL WAS TENSE. Britta was tense. And the time was ticking by, counting off the seconds until another woman died.

Britta tried desperately to stifle the guilt that consumed her. At the same time, her emotions toward Jean-Paul ping-ponged back and forth. She wanted to be near him. She felt safe by his side.

And she wanted to trust him with the truth.

But not yet....

She couldn't bear to see the disappointment in his eyes.

Still, he kept her close to him as they toured the art

displays, his hand always guiding her along, his body always a buffer as if he had assigned himself her protector.

Booths lined the walkways and square, stretching on for miles. Artists' exhibits included ceramics, woodcarvings, wax sculptures, metal art, junk and auto-parts art, along with every type of painting imaginable—oils, charcoal, watercolors, textured art, sand paintings—and bubble art, homemade voodoo dolls, serpent necklaces, gris gris, woven clothing, baskets and Mardi Gras masks.

A fortune teller had set up camp, along with a psychic who claimed to talk to the dead. Lines for both of them snaked around the square. The dollmaker barely lifted his head to acknowledge Britta as she passed. The mask artist worked diligently, deeply intent on adding feathers to a morbid creation while admirers watched. Booths offering local foods ranging from beignets to gator on a stick, shrimp po'boys and gumbo scented the air.

An hour later, the sun disappeared behind dark storm clouds, causing a chill in the air. A life-size wooden carving of a crocodile from the Nile drew gatherers and a line formed for the wax museum's latest display.

Just as they neared the museum, they found what they were looking for. The artist had created a wall of photographs. Instead of faces, he had only showcased the eyes and mounted them in black. All female, although the pictures ranged with eye color, expression and depth. A very dark, imposing display.

"Some of them are the same subject," Jean-Paul said, "only in different situations. He wanted to capture their various moods."

He pointed to a series of blue eyes, the eyes wide with fear. "That could be Elvira's."

A chill slid down Britta's spine. He was right. And beside it rested a pair of brown eyes with amber flecks that could very well belong to her.

Her gaze flew to the sign advertising his work. A shot of one dark eyeball painted on a black background served as the logo.

Britta glanced up to see the bald man who'd been watching her stride toward her. "What do you think of my exhibit?"

"You're the artist?" Jean-Paul asked.

He nodded and extended his hand. "Howard Keith."

"You took pictures of me," Britta said.

He shrugged. "You're a beautiful woman. I take photographs of interesting subjects in the Quarter all the time."

"Why do you choose to only photograph the eyes?" Jean-Paul asked.

"The eyes are the windows to the soul. When you can look into a woman's eyes, you can see everything about her. What she feels. What she thinks. If she's hiding something."

Jean-Paul removed the letter from his pocket. "Mr. Keith, I'm Detective Dubois of the New Orleans Police Department. Did you mail this letter to Miss Berger?"

Keith stared at the piece of paper and shrugged. "It's not a crime to submit to the magazine, is it?"

"No," Jean-Paul said. "But stalking is a crime."

Keith drew back, his good eye raised. "Who said anything about stalking? It's a free country. I can take pictures of public property. I'm free to voice my opinion or fantasies if I like." He stared at Britta, his voice growing deeper. "Isn't that right, Miss Berger?"

Britta tensed. "Yes, but I don't want you to photograph me anymore. And I don't like being followed."

A small tattoo of a snake coiled on his neck made the hair on the back of her neck prickle. She'd seen one like it before, years ago. The men from the clan had worn it.

The clan that she had been running from ever since.

GINGER HOLLIDAY BLINKED through a drug-induced fog, the tiny room spinning in a pit of never-ending black. Darkness cloaked the room, the stench of sweat and mold nearly suffocating her. Her arms and feet were tied to the metal bedposts. She'd cried for hours. Dirt and blood from her brawl with her attacker had hardened on her face with her tears.

Night swept over the cabin and fear consumed her. When he'd left her this morning, he'd promised to return, each hour that passed drawing her closer to another insufferable attack.

At some point, she'd prayed he'd just go ahead and kill her, but then her resolve to live had returned.

Although hope faded quickly. This dilapidated shack was tucked so far into the backwoods that no one would look for her here.

On the heels of despair, thoughts of sweet revenge surfaced. If she could just free her hands and feet long enough to grab the knife, she'd cut off his damn balls, and he'd never again rape another woman. Then she'd tie him up and watch him bleed to death while *he* listened to the eerie sounds of the bayou. Let him envision the alligators nibbling at him while he lay dying alone in the bowels of hell where he belonged.

Footsteps sounded outside on the wooden planked

porch. He kicked the door and it swung open. Her blood ran cold. It was so black outside, the gnarled branches of the oaks looked like the hands of a sea creature reaching toward her.

A sliver of moonlight caught his shadow, then disappeared as if the bayou had snuffed it out. But in that brief fleeting second, she saw the mask. A dark, eerie one of a monster.

He slowly began to undress. The sound of buttons popping grated on her skin like fingernails scraping a chalkboard.

"Please let me get up and go to the bathroom."

He paused, a sudden stillness filling the room like the quiet before a storm. She expected him to deny her, but he slowly walked toward her, untied her and dragged her into the bathroom. She was so damn weak and disoriented from the drugs she could barely stand. But she used the dirty facility, then stood, ran cold water and splashed it on her face, trying to wash away the foul stench of his mouth on her skin. Her bloodshot swollen eyes pierced the darkness, shining with terror in the broken mirror. She jerked open the medicine cabinet, hoping to find a razor, can of hair spray, anything to use as a weapon, but a bug crawled across the rusted empty metal shelves and she slammed it shut.

"That's long enough." His fingers pinched her sore wrist as he dragged her toward the bed.

"Let me go," she whispered. "Please, I'll do whatever you want."

"You'll do that anyway," he growled.

This was her last chance. She spotted her boots on the floor and tried to reach them, but he slammed his hand into the side of her face. Pain exploded inside her temple and she blinked to clear her vision, but white lights swam in front of her eyes. Still, she kicked at him, but he flung her onto the bed. Another whack to her head and the room went black.

Sometime later, she finally regained consciousness. He had retied her to the bed, stripped his clothes and stood above her. He dribbled oil on her skin, then massaged it into her bare arms and neck. She tried to scream, but he'd gagged her so tightly, the fabric caught the sound. Another sliver of moonlight caught his silhouette, highlighting a crisscrossing of scars on his pale chest. Other red, fleshy, puckered scars that resembled burns dotted his arms, and bite marks that could have come from a gator attack marred his arms and torso. No wonder he wore the mask. He was hideous. A monster.

He removed a condom from the bedside table, then donned rubber gloves on his hands and sprinkled something on the outside of the rubber.

She watched in horror as he peeled it over his penis. Surely if he was using a condom, he didn't mean to kill her.

He bent over and whispered against her neck, "Say you love me."

She shook her head no, but he slapped her again and clenched her by the throat. "Say you love me. That you'll never leave me. Then I'll save you."

Desperation clawed at her as he loosened the gag. She gasped for air, coughing, choking.

"Say it now."

"No," she rasped. "Never."

He twisted her nipples, and his mouth bit down on her neck. She closed her eyes and blocked out the feel of him as he pushed inside her. Tears filled her eyes and dribbled down her cheeks, but she imagined that she was somewhere else. A beach. The mountains. Drinking in the fresh air. Looking at the heavens. The air was cool, crisp. She was all alone. She'd start over. Leave her past behind.

Start in a new place where no one knew that she'd spread her legs for strangers to pay her way through school.

"I said, 'say you love me,'" he groaned against her throat, "that you'll never leave me."

Exhausted, she choked out the words, sobbing as he bellowed his release.

Tears flowed down her cheeks and she silently begged him to leave her alone with her misery. Instead, a violent pain shot through her stomach. Bile rose to her throat and she sobbed as pain slithered through her limbs and splintered all the way to her head. Then her body began to jerk. What was happening to her?

He ran his hand over her quivering stomach and her past flashed like candid shots in her mind. Of her dressed in the pink-dotted Swiss Easter dress her mother had sewn for her when she was five. Then later, the dorky Christmas photo they'd taken every year. Her mother had insisted they all wear red and white. Then the fights with her parents when she was a teenager. Her mother's sad eyes. Her brother pleading with her not to leave. Her father... His shouts that if she left, she was not to come back.

God, she'd been such a brat. If she could take it all back. The pain and grief she'd caused them, the hateful words she'd said. Things she hadn't meant.

She'd get a real job, apologize, prove she wasn't trash.

Another horrific pain tightened her muscles and twisted her insides. She was being ripped apart. The condom…the stuff he'd sprinkled on it. What was it? Some kind of poison?

No…no! She didn't want to die. He'd promised if she said she loved him that he'd save her!

But her body spasmed again, her limbs useless and heavy. The world grew darker, as black as the bottom of the Mississippi. With one last gulp of air, she sank her nails into his arm, hoping to leave some DNA behind. Then maybe the police could make this man pay for what he'd done.

Finally death whispered her name. She closed her eyes and welcomed the unknown. Anything to be free of the agony. Still, she prayed again, this time that there would be a white light where she was going. That death would take her away from hell, not plunge her into its darkness.

And that someone would find her body before the gators destroyed anything that was left.

CHAPTER ELEVEN

TWENTY-FOUR HOURS since the second woman had gone missing.

Britta had to do something.

Maybe she could help figure out the woman's identity. If they knew her name, they could talk to her friends, search her apartment, maybe find a clue.

The night sounds of the city and bayou whispered to her, pleading and insistent. It was Saturday—the biggest night for partying. Drinking. Hooking up.

Jean-Paul Dubois had left her claiming he was going to join one of the teams and search for the second possible victim.

Now, it was midnight. Tendrils of fear slithered through Britta, reminding her of the dangers in Black Bayou. Had he found the girl yet? Was she still alive? Or had she already given into death and joined Elvira?

Dressing again to play the part, she dolled up her hair, donned a lacy bustier in bronze and a tight leather skirt with snakeskin knee-high boots. A little perfume behind her ears and between her breasts, then off with the wire-rim glasses and she'd cloaked herself with an aura of confidence. She'd done this before, she could do it again. And she would survive. She'd learned to fight. Of course, she always took a knife with her, as did all the street girls in case one of their customers got nasty.

Although she considered herself a good judge of character, men often masked their true identities just as the girls disguised themselves and offered phony names and telephone numbers.

She glanced at the miniature doll she'd bought, then down at her outfit and embarrassment flooded her cheeks. What in the world was she doing buying dolls? She'd never played with them when she was little and certainly didn't plan to marry or have a daughter to pass them on to.

Not like Jean-Paul's family. Not like Catherine and Chrissy.

Irritated with herself for forgetting her origins for even a moment, she opened the drawer of the corner desk and placed the doll inside. Other similar dolls— some baby dolls, some porcelain, some fairy-book story characters—lay side by side on a white blanket.

She shoved the drawer shut, putting the nonsense out of her mind as she closed the door to her apartment and hurried down the steps. Her heels clicked on the pavement as she wove her way down Bourbon Street, the raucous laughter, zydeco music and partying pounding in her ears. The pungent scent of cheap beer, urine and vomit permeated the dark alleys, and drunken patrons danced in the street, made out on benches and shouted obscenities. She parked herself on the corner, removed a cigarette and lit up. Cars honked their horns, while the people inside waved beads and Mardi Gras flags through their opened windows.

The sultry air hinted at impending rain, resurrecting memories of the floods that had destroyed so many homes and businesses after the hurricane. The stench of raw sewage, disease and vermin still haunted her. And then the looting.

Some of New Orleans' own had turned on their brothers and sisters in their bleakest hour. Yet heroes had also risen through the masses. Jean-Paul Dubois most certainly had been one of them.

Her gaze skimmed the crowd and streets, the skin at the base of her neck prickling. A dark sedan rolled to a stop in front of her and she braced herself for action.

"This corner is taken, baby. Don't you know that?"

She winked at the pony-tailed man with the spectrum of earrings running down his ear. "Ahh, surely there's room for one more, sugar."

His smile said he liked what he saw. "You have to talk to Shack. He owns the girls in this part of town."

Exactly. She batted her fake lashes and leaned forward, making sure he caught sight of her cleavage spilling out. "Then take me to him."

Britta's bracelets jangled, mimicking her rattled nerves, but she blew him a kiss anyway and climbed in the backseat. Her knees knocked together as he sped off, but she forced herself to remain calm.

Shack would be pissed as hell to see her. He hadn't liked what she'd done to him a few years ago. And he detested the fact that she'd been stealing his girls away from him. He knew she had her own agenda, and it conflicted completely with his.

Of course, he might rough her up a little before he finally listened. But a girl had to do what a girl had to do. And she couldn't change what she'd become.

No use trying, not for a man like Jean-Paul Dubois, a hero. A man who'd never understand.

She only hoped he found the missing woman tonight, before the swamp devil claimed another life.

TWO O'CLOCK. And they still hadn't found the woman.

She couldn't die tonight.

Jean-Paul would not allow it.

He and his team had been searching the bayou for hours, their legs and backs breaking, but he refused to quit. Bugs, weeds, swamp water clung to their clothes and skin as if they'd been bathed in the murk. Mosquitoes fed on their arms and faces, buzzing through the air ready to feed.

It was always like this in Black Bayou. More stories of ghosts and supernatural creatures originated from this stretch than any other part. Here, night never ended. The thick trees and silvery-gray moss created a cavern that reminded him of an ancient burial ground from medieval times. It was a dark, lost place where legends touted that any human who entered never emerged alive. A place where voodoo priestesses and witchdoctors had been born, where the lowest humans were condemned to lie with the night stalkers. A place where mutant creatures existed, living in the shadows, moving along the whispery darkness like ghosts banned from the other side.

Sweat streamed down the rescue workers' faces as they hacked their way through the weeds and brush choking the water.

"We might as well call it a night," his brother Antwaun said. "All the men are exhausted."

"But she's out here." Jean-Paul turned to survey the backwoods. "She needs us."

Antwaun frowned. "Listen, Jean-Paul, I know this is

getting to you. I understand why you're so driven. Lucinda should have stood by you—"

"I don't want to talk about her," Jean-Paul snapped. Or Britta, the woman he had been thinking about instead of his dead wife.

"Stop blaming yourself. You can't save them all—"

"I can't stop trying, either."

Antwaun's expression turned solemn.

"Just a little longer," Jean-Paul muttered. "We're close, I can feel it...."

Jean-Paul moved his flashlight along the weeds, aware of the gators floating like tree trunks in the water. Silent. Waiting. Ready to pounce any second.

He turned to their right, heading deeper into the shadows. Five minutes later, he spotted a rotting shanty practically floating in the mud and water. Jean-Paul eased onto the wooden slatted porch, then waved for the men to wait. His own need for vengeance surfaced.

This killer deserved to die.

He braced himself to fire. Antwaun moved up behind him, his own gun raised for back-up. Jean-Paul peeked through the dirt-fogged window. Although his eyes had adjusted to the darkness, the room was steeped in shadows. He couldn't make out anything except the outline of metal bedposts.

Slowly, he eased open the door to the cabin, pointed his gun, then swept the room with the flashlight.

The killer was gone.

But he'd left his handiwork behind.

The poor woman lay in a pool of blood and sweat in the middle of the rumpled bed, tied down as if she was an animal.

Rage pumped through Jean-Paul's stomach. She was

naked just like their first victim, bloodsoaked and wide-eyed with terror. The stench had drawn the flies and bugs, making her look even more helpless and degraded.

He rushed forward to check for a pulse, but visible signs indicated that she was dead. The heat had started rigor, but she wasn't completely stiff yet.

Antwaun radioed for a crime-scene unit and medical examiner, then searched the room. Within minutes, both teams rushed in to process the scene.

While they went to work, Antwaun and two other officers canvassed the parameter, but the Mississippi had already washed away any footprints. Inside the cabin, the killer had wiped everything down, everything but the blood and grime on his victim. Jean-Paul forced himself into the head of the killer. The swamp devil wanted them to see the woman naked and exposed for the dirty girl he deemed her to be.

The mask of Sobek had been hung from the ceiling, which meant the girl had been forced to look at it while she'd been raped and murdered. Had the killer prayed over her body, offered her as sacrifice to the gods as the medieval Egyptians had done?

And why? Where the hell had he adopted that sick practice?

Time of death: midnight. Dammit, just about the time he'd left Britta. Three hours earlier and they could have saved this woman.

But once again, he'd been too late. And she'd suffered....

What about Britta? Where was she now?

Was she safe or had the swamp devil contacted her again to brag about his latest victim?

A FRISSON OF ALARM rippled up Britta's spine as Shack's buddies surrounded her. Three giant men with tree-trunk bodies, scarred black faces and fists the size of grapefruits. They could kill her with one punch if they chose.

Shack puffed on a cigar, glaring down at her with his pithy eyes. His hair looked as black as soot, his skin so pale it resembled the white flaky skin of an albino croco-dile. Though they were rare, she'd seen one in the bayou the night she'd run away. The creature had actually pounced in front of another gator as if to save her.

Just as Shack had.

But he'd had another plan. Just as the albino gator probably had.

He'd intended to eat her himself.

"Why are you here, Britta? You know I'd like to strangle you."

"Let it go, Shack. I came to give you a warning."

Laughter boomed from his big body. "You're warning me? That's rich."

The silent implication of his words sent a shudder through her. Shack thought he owned his girls. Leaving wasn't an option. He'd told her that when she'd skipped. Every day she walked a tightrope knowing he might send someone back to force her to return to him, to the life. Why he hadn't done so yet, she didn't know.

She licked her parched lips, remembering her reason for braving this visit. "You need to watch out for your girls."

"What are you talking about, Britta?"

"Elvira Erickson, the girl who was murdered. Was she one of yours?"

He blew a ring of smoke into the air, and watched it curl upward. "I was recruiting her, yeah."

Britta crossed her leg, vying for calm. "The killer is targeting the street girls. *Your* girls."

Shack's eyelids turned to mere slits as he studied her. "So you want me to call my girls off the streets?" Sarcasm edged his voice. "I can't do that. I'd lose too much business."

Damn. She knew he'd say that. "Are any of your girls missing now?"

Shack sent one of the beefy men a questioning look but the man shrugged.

"Check and see," Britta said. "If you do, we can tell the police and maybe they can save her."

Shack drummed his diamond-clad fingers on his leg. "I'm not working with the cops, so don't even start with that shit."

"Then send word to me and I'll pass on a name. This guy's a real sicko, Shack. He ties up the girls, poisons them with a condom, then has sex with them. As if the pain from the poison isn't enough, he sinks a lancet into their hearts and leaves them as bait for the crocodiles."

"Jesus."

Britta forced herself to continue, "He leaves them in a ritualistic manner, as if he's sacrificing them to Sobek."

His features tightened, nostrils flaring. "That is some scary shit."

"He also leaves a mask of Sobek with the victim. Do you know any groups still honoring the medieval practices?"

The men behind Shack shifted uncomfortably. Shack leaned forward and lowered his voice, his diamonds sparkling against the dark. "There's a new clan sprung up—out in Black Bayou—might be doing some of that weird stuff you're talking about."

An icy cold numbness speared Britta. She'd thought the clans had disbanded. But at least one had resurfaced.

It was too much of a coincidence to ignore.

Shack stood, buttoned his gold double-breasted jacket and stared down at her, his eyes blazing. "Now, you listen to my warning. Interfere with my business again, mess with my girls and we're gonna have to talk. And trust me, Britta." He raked a nail across her cheek. "It won't be pretty."

"DAMON, IT'S JEAN-PAUL."

"What's up, brother?"

"We have a serial killer." Jean-Paul relayed the past few days' events, the MO of the murderer, Britta Berger's connection and their current location.

"I'll be there in twenty minutes," Damon said.

Jean-Paul thanked him, then stepped outside the shanty for fresh air and phoned Britta. He let it ring a half-dozen times, then checked his watch. Almost four o'clock. Hell, what was he thinking? She was probably tucked in bed, sound asleep.

Still, his nerves jangled with worry.

The CSU finished their tasks, the minutes crawling by. Another team had been dispatched to search the antebellum mansion near the shanty. One of the locals went into a tirade at Damon's arrival, but Jean-Paul cut him off. To hell with pride and jockeying over jurisdiction; they needed all the help they could get.

Damon took one look at the crime scene and muttered, "For the love of God."

"I know. Scary, isn't it?" Jean-Paul commented.

Damon nodded. "I want notes on every detail about the crime scene, the victims, any other evidence you've collected so far."

"You've got it."

"Do you have any suspects?" Damon asked.

Jean-Paul explained about the CD. "So far we've questioned Randy Swain, a local singer, R. J. Justice, the publisher of *Naked Desires*, and a photographer who sent Britta a personal message through her column. Justice's alibi for the night of the first murder checks out. Swain said he was alone working on a song. And the photographer claims he was in his darkroom."

"But you have nothing concrete on any of them."

Jean-Paul grunted. "Afraid not. My partner's supposed to get back to me on the search at Swain's place. Maybe you can run the handwriting sample through your guys. So far, we haven't matched it to any of our suspects."

"Sure. I also did some checking after you called," Damon said. "It turns out there have been a few cases with similar MOs over the past few years."

"Where?"

"Three murders in Savannah, Georgia, two years ago. They all occurred within a seven-day period, prior to the big St. Patrick's Day Parade." Damon removed a note pad and glanced at his notes. "Another similar group of murders occurred last year on the outskirts of Nashville the week leading up to Easter."

Jean-Paul rocked back on the balls of his feet. "Why didn't we hear about them?"

"Stories got buried and never made national news."

"Because the victims were prostitutes," Jean-Paul

said in disgust. "As if the girls didn't have families or deserve justice."

"You know how it works. Police are understaffed. They have priorities…" Damon rubbed at the back of his neck.

"We need to see if Swain or Justice was in either of those cities around that time."

"I'll get someone on it," Damon said. "You mentioned that the killer contacted the Berger woman?"

Jean-Paul nodded again. "He sent her a photo of the first murder, then called to tell her he had another woman."

Damon narrowed his eyes. "How much do you know about this woman?"

He knew she was beautiful. That she was a liar. That she was hiding from someone. That she had secrets. That she had him all twisted up inside.

That although she was nothing like Lucinda, he wanted her anyway.

"She's a loner. Has no family. Claims she has no former boyfriends or lovers that could be after her. Says she has no idea why this guy chose to contact her, except for her column."

"He wants the attention," Damon said.

"Yeah, but that's not all. His message was personal. He said he knows her secrets."

Damon raised a suspicious brow.

Jean-Paul leaned against the doorjamb. "Britta Berger isn't her real name," he admitted. In fact, he still hadn't figured that one out, although he'd searched. "She told me she lived with foster parents and assumed the name of the daughter after she and her parents died in a car accident."

Damon frowned. "Was there an investigation into the accident?"

Jean-Paul nodded. "No foul play."

"Do you think she's lying?"

Hell if *he* knew. "The Bergers were foster parents and took in a number of kids. I'm still looking into it. Why? Do *you* know something about her?"

Damon hesitated, his controlled expression not giving anything away. "Her name's come up before."

"What do you mean?" Jean-Paul asked.

"We have a special team investigating prostitution rings."

Jean-Paul sucked in a sharp breath. "How is Britta connected?"

"My guys have seen her on the streets. Word is that one of the pimps has it in for her because she tried to get out of the business."

His brother's words hit Jean-Paul in the gut like a fist. Britta had been a prostitute. If that was her secret, then she might have lied about knowing the victims.

He had to see her. He was sick of her lies and secrets. This time he'd damn well make her tell him the truth.

Even if he didn't want to hear it.

BRITTA WAS TREMBLING as she climbed from the taxi in front of her apartment. Things hadn't gone well after she'd left. She'd found another girl and had barely escaped with her.

She rubbed her arm and wished she'd brought her compact so she could hide the new bruise under her eye. But thankfully, no one would see her tonight. She would hide out in her apartment, then cover up the hazardous results of violence in the morning.

The Mardi Gras festivities continued around her as she reached for keys to open the door. A shadow caught her eye and dread suffused her. She turned and scanned the crowd, searching for the photographer, but instead, Jean-Paul Dubois stood in front of the entrance to her apartment.

Her breath caught at his tightly set mouth. Then the truth dawned. "You found the missing woman?"

He nodded, pain, then disapproval and anger darkening his eyes. "Let's go inside. We have to talk."

She grabbed his arms, desperate for answers, for the madness to end, but he coaxed her forward. "Inside," he barked.

She dropped her keys on the stoop and he yanked them up, opened the door, then half dragged her up the flight of steps.

She balked and tugged at his hands to release her. "What's wrong with you, Jean-Paul?"

"I spent half the night slugging my way through the swamps to try and save another victim. But I found her naked, brutalized, murdered and left for the gators. I'm exhausted, angry, frustrated—and sick to death of your lies."

He vaulted inside, leaving her to either join him or stay in the dark hallway. Remembering her attire and fresh bruises, she turned to leave. She'd go to R.J.'s, wait until Jean-Paul calmed down.

"Don't even think about running again," he snapped. "You say you want to help stop these murders, then get in here now."

She pressed her lips into a thin line and stepped into the foyer. He had no idea what she'd been through tonight. And yes, she wanted to help. *But—*

"My brother works for the FBI." He swung around and pierced her with laser eyes. "He claims to know a few things about you. Things you failed to mention."

Alarm strummed through her nerve endings. "What things?"

He towered over her, scowling, so angry she felt the tension vibrating from his big body. She fought the urge to back away. Then his gaze zeroed in on her face. To the bruise.

"Dammit, Britta." His voice thickened. "I didn't want to believe it, but it's true, isn't it?"

Her chest ached. She was tempted to beg him to help her, to trust her and not condemn her. But he'd already tried and convicted her.

"You tell me," she said, her breath whisking out with anger.

"It's obvious. Just look how you're dressed. I'm not an idiot." A muscle ticked in his jaw as he reached up and touched her cheek. It was throbbing so badly moisture burned her eyes. She needed ice and aspirin, not questions.

"You *would* think that," she said quietly.

He trailed his finger downward to pull at the lacy ties of her teddy and her body betrayed her by tingling in response.

"What else can I think?" He dropped his hand, then plastered it to his side. He looked so upset that she wanted to explain, to convince him to listen to her side.

But if she did, his image of her would be tainted forever. And then he'd walk away, maybe even decide that she deserved to face the wrath of the swamp devil.

"What does it matter?" she said. "When you catch this psycho, you'll go back to your life. And I won't be any part of it. "

Tension crackled through the air, hot and steamy as the mist from the bayou. Hurt tainted his expression. But desire flickered in his eyes, as well.

Desire that mirrored her own desperate need tonight. She wanted—needed—someone to banish the sordid images of the streets. The lost girls. The meanness and sick lust of the more depraved.

And so did Jean-Paul.

"Maybe I don't want you to wind up like the others," he said in a gruff voice.

"Or maybe you're just exhausted and frustrated and need some comfort," she said softly.

Unable to stop herself, she inched closer to him, so close her skin brushed his. His gaze flickered with heat. His eyes fell to the mound of cleavage her glittery top revealed. This time she didn't sense disapproval, only the heady ache of wanting his touch. Of him wanting hers in return. Her nipples hardened, straining against the flimsy fabric, begging for his mouth.

She licked her dry lips. "Jean-Paul—"

His mouth suddenly closed over hers, the raw need in his kiss so powerful his body shuddered as she raised her hands and shoved them into his hair. He threaded one hand behind her neck, the other around her waist, then plunged his tongue between her lips. White-hot fire speared her from head to toe as he deepened the kiss. As if he couldn't get close enough, he moved his hand to her breast and kneaded the mound before he dragged his mouth down to her neck, licked the sensitive skin of her earlobe, then trailed fiery kisses down her neck. She throbbed all over. Her legs buckled as he ripped open the ties holding the top together, then dipped his tongue to tease her nipples.

She moaned, low and throaty, and he drew her right nipple into his mouth and sucked it greedily while his hands played along her spine.

Outside, a shout rang out and something shattered against the window frame. He jerked back, shoved her down to her knees, then stared at her as if he was in a daze. They'd both lost control. "Cover up," he ordered.

With a muttered curse, he strode to the window.

Her heart pounded with unsated desire, regret, fear. She wanted him so badly her body trembled.

His breathing hissed in the silence and she followed him to the window and glanced outside. A group of staggering roughhousers had tossed beer bottles at the door.

"I'll get rid of them."

"No. They're just drunk," she said, her pulse racing. "They'll go away."

He waited a fraction of a second and the guys staggered down the street. But Jean-Paul didn't move to touch her again. She reached for him anyway, knowing he needed the release, that they both needed something physical tonight, that she wanted him more than she'd ever wanted a man. That she was finally ready to give herself to passion. "Please, Jean-Paul. I know you want me."

He pushed her away and shook his head, his expression tormented. "Sure. Part of me does, but the other part wants to know the real woman. Not the one you call by a dead woman's name. Not the one who hides under that makeup and hooker garb. Not the one who probably spent her night with another man." He swiped his hand across his mouth as if to wipe away her kiss. "Or *men.*"

Hurt and humiliation seeped through her. "You wouldn't like the real woman, either."

"Why don't you let me be the judge?" He rubbed a finger along her arm, stirring her arousal more. "Trust me, Britta."

"Don't you see? I don't want a judge and jury," she whispered.

"I can help you," he said in a gruff voice. "At least get you out. Save you from your pimp, from becoming like the others."

She lifted her chin, the heartache she'd lived with for years so intense that her courage waned. He thought she was a hooker. If he knew the truth, he would still walk away. And then she'd pay the price of being a fool for believing him. For trusting.

"It's too late for me," she whispered. "I can't be saved."

He shook his head in denial. "It's never too late."

"Go back to your perfect family," she said, certain now that she couldn't allow her heart to get involved. And with Jean-Paul it would be so easy for her to fall in love. "You know I would never fit in with the Dubois family."

The truth dawned on his face in the ensuing silence. He knew she was right. He couldn't even argue the point.

"My family has had our share of problems," he admitted quietly. "My brother Antwaun has been in trouble, our house was destroyed, so was the restaurant and Papa nearly lost his leg in the aftermath of the hurricane."

He didn't mention the woman in the picture on his parents' wall. But she stood between them as if she'd physically walked into the room.

"Your family pulled together because you love each other," Britta said.

He squeezed her arm, pleading. "That's what families are for."

"Not all families are like that, Jean-Paul."

"Britta, I'm sorry if you had a rough childhood." His voice was low, gruff, reverberating with emotions. "But I'm not sorry my family is close. I see the dark side— the underbelly of violence and crime—every day. My family grounds me and keeps me from crossing to the other side." He reached for her hand. "I know there's good in you."

Tears nearly choked her. "The bad stuff's easier to believe."

"Trust me," he said softly. "I can help you find it."

"No." He'd only end up hurting her. And she would hurt him. It was an impossible situation.

Britta pulled away, walked to the door and gestured for him to leave. He'd condemned her earlier. Thought the worst of her, and he didn't know half of her story.

She didn't want his pity. "The woman you claim you want to see is dead, Jean-Paul. She died a long time ago so I could be born. And no one can save her or bring her back."

CHAPTER TWELVE

Four days until Mardi Gras

SUNDAY MORNING DAWNED with thunderstorms mounting in the sky, the gloomy gray mirroring Britta's mood. Another woman had died last night.

Another one the killer had gotten away with.

Was Jean-Paul blaming himself? Beating his head against the wall wondering who might be next?

Hating her for letting him believe that she had been on the streets the night before?

She had almost picked up the phone a dozen times to call him and confess the truth. A longing to be part of a big happy family like Jean-Paul's had made her ache all night. Then another longing—one to comfort him.

But pride and fear had kept her home alone. Better not to open her heart and take the chance on him breaking it. Besides, it was best for him. How would it look for a hero cop to hook up with a girl who'd grown up on the streets?

Especially one who'd taken a man's life.

No, her only involvement with Jean-Paul pertained to the case.

But the feel of his touch, his lips, still lingered like a

phantom lover, and she feared it might already be too
late for her, that she was falling desperately in love with
him.

Regardless of her personal feelings or needs, she
had to help him stop this killer.

Had he sent her a picture this time? Or maybe a
clue?

Dread gnawed at her stomach. She had to know.

She quickly showered and pulled on a simple black
skirt and tank. Today she brewed her own coffee, poured
herself a mug, then hurried downstairs. The stairwell
seemed eerily dark this morning, Bourbon Street quiet
after the all-night party. In four days, the big Mardi
Gras finale would sweep the streets. The city would be
even crazier than ever.

She prayed Jean-Paul found the swamp devil before
then.

She let herself into the office, then glanced toward
the mail slot on the opposite wall. A brown manila
envelope lay on the floor. Perspiration beaded her neck
as she examined it. No return address, no postage
stamp, only her name written in bold black letters. Very
neat and straight print. She wondered if the writing
style had significance and tried to remember if the other
package had been addressed in the same handwriting,
but couldn't recall.

Jean-Paul Dubois would know.

Of course, this package might not be from the killer.
But she had a bad feeling in her stomach, and she
touched only one edge so as not to destroy fingerprints.
Her hand trembled as she opened the clasp and removed
the contents.

Another picture of a murder scene, this one just as

vivid and chilling. Tears burned her eyelids, but she blinked them back. The poor girl was so young....

Just like the ones on the streets. Was she one of Shack's girls? If so, did he know she'd been missing?

The urge to run assaulted her, but she stumbled to the desk instead and sat down. Hands shaking, she unfolded the note.

My Secret Confession:

The bayou beckons with its call of the crocodile. As its servant, and a servant to my own gods, I must obey. Sacrifices must be made.

At night, I dream of how you will taste. I see your porcelain face in my mind and know that it has always been you that I wanted. You that I need to be complete. You that will be my redemption.

Soon, very, very soon, I am coming for you.

Only after you repent, can you truly rest. Then our souls will be together forever.

Britta shuddered and collapsed deeper into the hard wooden chair. She had to call Jean-Paul and R.J. and tell them about the note.

The swamp devil might already be looking for his next victim.

And eventually he was coming for her.

THE KILLER WAS COMING for Britta.

Jean-Paul's anger mounted as he reread the note. His ironclad control snapped like twigs in the wake of a violent wind. He wanted to kill the man who'd sent it.

At the same time, he wanted to drag Britta into his arms and hold her. Keep her there and never let her go.

One look into her terrified face and he did just that.

She stiffened at first, seemingly shocked by his actions, but then she lowered her head and leaned into him. A shudder tore through her. He felt it in the trembling of her delicate body.

"He's not going to hurt you," he whispered. "You're safe."

"I...don't want to be afraid," she whispered. "I won't allow him to have that much control."

Her breath hitched and he rubbed slow circles on her back. "Don't worry. I'll find him and make him pay."

Questions assaulted him, though. How could he promise her that when two women had already died? When he'd let his own wife suffer? When he was no closer to finding the killer than he had been three days ago?

"I have to do something to stop this." She raised her head and he read fear in her expression, but also strength. Determination.

The realization startled him. She was more upset for the other women who'd died than afraid for herself.

Emotions welled in his chest. Unwanted, but they were there. Tenderness. Desire. A longing unlike anything he'd ever known.

"Maybe I should go public, make a plea." She clutched his arms, her voice growing more insistent. "Or I could offer to meet him somewhere. We could set him up."

"That's crazy," Jean-Paul growled. "Don't even think about it, Britta."

"But I can't let him kill anyone else." Her fingernails

dug into his arms. "And he will. You read that note. He'll kill again and again, then he'll still come after me."

"Listen to me." He cupped her face in his hands and traced one thumb down the side of her cheek. "This is not your fault, and you're not going to do anything crazy like try to trap him. You're going to let me handle it."

"But he won't stop," she whispered. "You heard him, he wants me. If I offer him that—"

"Shh." He tightened his hold on her, the thought of her putting herself in danger tearing him in two. "My brother, the FBI, we're all working the case now. Just give us time. We'll catch this psycho." She started to pull away, but he kissed her. He had to get through to her. He couldn't lose her now.

Her lips felt warm, sensual, pliant, giving. He felt her need in the soft whimper in her throat, in the way she held on to him, in the gasp she emitted when he pulled away.

"Damon discovered this guy may have killed before," he whispered. "In at least two other cities. Savannah, Georgia and Nashville, Tennessee. All his vics were prostitutes." He had to make her see his point. Didn't want her blaming herself. He'd done enough of that for both of them. "We'll request their evidence, compare notes. Damon's having his guys look at the handwriting samples now. I will catch him."

Her body tensed, but she finally relented and allowed him to pull her into his arms again. He cradled her against him and savored holding her. Last night he'd barely slept for thinking about Britta. For wondering about her past. Her secrets. The other men in her life.

Her lies.

Images of another man lying naked with her had driven him from bed, so he'd hiked to the edge of the bayou and listened to the animals in the swamp, hoping the noises would obliterate the sultry sound of her voice in his head. The softness of her skin. The touch of her lips on his. The heady feel of her body against his hardness.

The fact that he'd torn himself away earlier when he'd wanted nothing more than to drag her to bed and make her his.

The fact that she was alone, had been so starved for a family that she'd taken a dead woman's name, made his heart clench.

He'd failed with Lucinda even before she'd died. But Lucinda had nothing to do with today.

Or his feelings for Britta. The past was over. He couldn't change it or go back.

Britta was here now.

He'd always followed the letter of the law. Had lived by it all his life. Had even left his wife alone so he could stand up for what was right.

And they'd called him a hero.

Yet he hadn't been a hero in his wife's eyes. Because the law had been all that mattered.

What would he do if he had to choose this time— between what was right and Britta?

BRITTA'S FRIGHTENED VOICE echoed in R.J.'s head. She'd received another note, more photos and was terrified. She needed him. This was finally his chance.

He couldn't wait to get to her.

Traffic was nonexistent, allowing him to make it to the office within minutes of her call. He rushed inside, his pulse pounding. He could already feel her in his arms.

But Jean-Paul Dubois had beaten him at his own game. Son of a bitch.

He cleared his throat. Vowed to get rid of Dubois some way.

The two jerked apart. Dubois's eyes speared him. Britta's glittered with pain. R.J.'s blood heated with desire.

"I came as fast as I could."

She gave Dubois an odd, almost intimate look, then sank onto one of the chairs. "I…was rattled. The note…the killer hasn't finished yet."

Dubois folded his arms and glared at R.J., who knew what was coming. An inquisition.

"We found the woman's body last night," Dubois said in a gruff voice.

R.J.'s mind quickly sorted through his alibi for the previous evening. The woman tied to his bed. The blood on his hands. The sound of her cries.

Would she stand up for him if he needed it? Or would she let him fry?

BRITTA STUDIED R.J.'s reaction. He looked as if he hadn't slept the night before. Scratches marred his hands. She could see a fresh claw mark on his chest where his shirt lay open. And he smelled of sex and sweat.

She'd trusted R.J. Had worked for him for months. Could he possibly be a killer and she not realize it?

Her mind raced with possibilities. Had she known him from her past? If so, how? Where?

She glanced at Jean-Paul and tension thickened between them. His professional mask clicked back in place.

He had a job to do. And she was part of that case.

And so was R.J. He shot her a look of disdain as if by being in Jean-Paul's arms, she had cheated on him.

R.J. would accept her as she was; somehow she knew that.

So why did her body still yearn for the impossible— for Jean-Paul Dubois?

R.J. scribbled a woman's name on a note pad. "I was with Lena last night. We met at the Lover's Lair."

"The S and M club?" Jean-Paul asked.

R.J. nodded. "I'm sure she'll vouch for me."

Jean-Paul frowned, but accepted the information, then turned to Britta. "I'll run the killer's note and the photos by the precinct for trace. Maybe the handwriting or paper will tell us something."

She nodded.

"Stay here, Britta." His eyes implored her to obey. "You're not going out alone."

"Don't worry about me," Britta said. "He's not coming after me on Sunday afternoon, not in the broad daylight."

"You can't be certain of that. After all, we don't know exactly how long he kept the girls, when he abducted them." Jean-Paul's mouth tightened. "Although he most likely picks them up on the streets at night."

His silent warning echoed in her ears. She should stay home tonight.

"If you think of anything that might help, or if he phones you again, call me." Jean-Paul sent R.J. an intimidating look, then turned back to her. "Remember, keep him on the line so we can trace his location."

She nodded.

"After the task force meeting, I'll come back and you can stay with me the rest of the day."

Go to his family dinner? She didn't think so. "Jean-Paul, I can't—"

"I'll play bodyguard," R.J. said, angling a sideways grin her way. "In fact, we might take a trip over to that wax museum. There's an interesting display. That would make a good story for the magazine."

Jean-Paul moved forward as if hoping she'd disagree with her boss, but she'd already leaned on Jean-Paul too much today. And she had her own plans, ones that didn't involve either man. "Go on, Jean-Paul. Conduct your investigation. Visit your parents. I have plenty of work to do myself right here."

"I'll call you later." He hesitated as if he meant to say more, then glanced back at R.J. and his jaw went rigid. He turned and strode out the door.

She had the vaguest feeling she'd just made a mistake by declining Jean-Paul's request to dine with his family. But if they knew her identity, about her past, they wouldn't want her at their house.

Her heart swelled with desire for Jean-Paul anyway. She wanted to be with him. But pipe dreams didn't come true for girls like her. She'd visit her own family today just as she did every other Sunday.

Maybe somehow she'd figure out if this killer was a man from her past. If he was, she might be the only person who could stop him.

JEAN-PAUL CURSED HIMSELF for his actions with Britta. He'd let his feelings get too personal. Assumed that just because he wanted her, she wanted him in return.

But she was still holding back. Still not telling him everything.

He wheeled into the precinct and hurried inside. Even though it was Sunday, the task force gathered in the meeting room. His brother Damon, his lieutenant and his partner had arrived, along with a crime-scene guy and two locals. Antwaun hadn't made it yet. Maybe he was chasing a lead.

Jean-Paul began the meeting by reviewing the information they had so far. Then he turned to Carson.

"What did you find at Swain's?" Jean-Paul asked.

Carson removed his notes and skimmed them. "Nothing concrete. No murder weapon. His place is a mess, lots of takeout food, booze, cigarettes. I obtained samples of the paper he uses for his songs to compare to the paper our guy used for the notes, but I don't think they're the same. Oh, and I found some kinky photos of him and some chicks." Carson grinned. "Swain likes to dress up in women's clothing. Especially lingerie. But no masks of Sobek."

"Did the lingerie match the teddy at the crime scene?"

"Not the same brand color or style. Swain likes black. Wasn't from the same store, either."

Jean-Paul frowned. "How about his background? Any trips to Savannah or Nashville the past couple of years?"

"You have specific dates in mind?"

Damon recited the dates he'd uncovered regarding cases with similar MOs.

"I'll get right on it," Carson said. "In fact, I did some checking. Swain is not the guy's real name. He was born Jimmy Joe Letts. Father was a drunk, mother religious.

From the aunt's description, she was obsessive compulsive, forced Jimmy Joe to attend church night and day. She got so fanatical that in his teens, Jimmy Joe split, changed his name and started writing country-blues songs. She died a couple of years ago. Don't know what happened to the father yet."

"Swain or Jimmy Joe, have a record?" Jean-Paul asked.

"Some prior petty crimes. Drunk and disorderly. Two years ago, some chick accused him of roughing her up, but she dropped the charges."

"Talk to her," Jean-Paul said. "Find out what really happened. Maybe Swain's violent tendencies grew after his mother's death."

"How about the other suspects?" Damon asked.

"I just talked with Justice," Jean-Paul said. "Says he has an alibi for when the second victim died." Still, he didn't like or trust the man. "I'm putting a tail on him. And I want a search warrant for his apartment."

Phelps leaned back in his chair, sipping his coffee. "Do you have probable cause?"

Did he? "Just a gut feeling. He's into S and M, violent sex. He could be killing these women to spark sales for his magazine." And to make Britta run into his arms.

"We need more than that." Phelps frowned. "Have you found anything suspicious on him?"

"His alibi checked out. We ran a preliminary check on him but nothing turned up. I'm going to do a full background check on him now. I'll find something."

"Two of my men are investigating the cases in Savannah and Nashville," Damon said.

"Let's move, people," Jean-Paul said. "The clock is ticking."

The group dispersed. Jean-Paul rushed to his office, grabbed a cup of strong coffee at his desk and entered everything he knew so far about Justice into his computer. A few minutes later, information spilled across the screen. Justice was from the Black Bayou area. His parents were both deceased. He had two accounts at a local bank in New Orleans. A savings account that had over a hundred thousand dollars? Hmm—from Naked Desires? Or another investment?

Something illegal perhaps? He could be laundering money or any number of things. A few minutes later, he discovered another company that Justice owned. A filmmaking enterprise named Kinky Creations.

Did he feature some of his girlfriends in the movies? Was he trying to recruit Britta?

The mere idea sent bile to Jean-Paul's throat. Surely she wouldn't be swayed by his charm to play in one of those cheap flicks. Then again, she'd been dressed pretty racy the night before. He'd smelled the perfume, the cigar smoke, knew where she'd been.

So why did he still want her?

He knotted his hand into a fist, willing the sordid images to fade. Finally his vision cleared and he focused on Justice's personal data. A couple of arrests when he was a juvy—hmm, maybe the beginnings of his violent nature emerging. And another incident the year before; a woman had accused him of rape, but Justice had pleaded down to assault. Could be a pattern.

Had Justice been guilty? Or had his S and M habits landed him in trouble?

Curious about the man's family, he read further. Both parents had died when he was a teenager. The same date for both deaths. Not a car accident. Suicide.

Both of his parents? Suspicious.

Hmm. He sat up straighter and accessed an article about their deaths.

Mass Suicide Leaves Fifty People Dead in Black Bayou

All fifty victims fell prey to a religious cult practicing medieval customs including polygamy, snake handling, the worship of Sobek and animal and human sacrifices. Reverend Theodore Tatum and the remainder of his followers have disappeared and can't be located for comment.

The medical examiner has reported that the cause of death was arsenic poisoning.

Jean-Paul's instincts roared to life. Arsenic poisoning? Worshiping Sobek? Animal and human sacrifices? He scrolled the names of the victims and found a family by the last name of Cortain. But there was no mention of Ezra Cortain. He would have been much younger then, maybe early twenties.

Hmm, a coincidence? He didn't think so.

He rubbed the kinks from his neck. Dammit. Cortain might be related to the leader of that cult and Justice's parents had died there.

And he'd left Justice alone with Britta.

"REVEREND CORTAIN IS SPEAKING today. Are you ready for church, Debra?"

Debra Schmale paused at the kitchen door, batting at a fly. She'd hoped she could sneak out while her dumb-ass parents were getting ready for church, but her mama had ears as sharp as a dog's and at least ten eyes in the back of her head.

"What are you wearing, girl?"

She was busted. "A new skirt."

Sponge rollers in her hair, her mother grabbed her arm and jerked her around. "Good Lord, Debra, that's not a skirt, it's a Band-Aid. Your grandma would roll over in her grave if she saw you looking like some two-bit slut."

Debra yanked her arm free. "Mama, all the young women dress like this these days. Besides, I'm almost twenty now, all grown up. You can't tell me what to do anymore."

Her mother's nostrils flared. Debra backed away. Her mother always slapped hard and always got her right in the face. The hit resounded off the wood walls.

"Now, go change. You need Reverend Cortain's sermon today. He's gonna preach about the sins of the flesh."

"I don't want to hear him talk. He's archaic."

"You sound like that whore woman who works for that sex magazine."

Like Britta Berger? Debra knew her mama hated the woman and that magazine. She'd joined the protesters the other day and had gotten her picture in the damn paper. "That preacher is brainwashing you, Mama."

Her father walked in, all barrel-chested and pot bellied, trying to button the white shirt that was two sizes too small. "Get some clothes on for church, girl, before I tan your hide."

Debra shook her head. "I'm not going." She gripped the door knob and opened the door. Her legs were shaking, her stomach quivering.

"You leave looking like that," he snarled, "don't bother to come back."

Debra glared at them both, then ran outside. She didn't want to live with them anymore. She needed her own place so she could entertain whoever she wanted.

Maybe Teddy wouldn't mind some company today. After all, she'd read that magazine, knew the tricks men wanted. And she was tired of being a good girl.

She wanted a boyfriend.

And Teddy looked like a guy who needed some loving.

"WELCOME TO THE KINGDOM of the Lord." The sleeves of Reverend Cortain's robe swayed like the wings of an angel as he flapped his arms up and down. "We love all who enter. Members, visitors, deacons, sinners."

He silently scanned the crowd, searching for those who looked lost and vulnerable. They were the ones he needed to target his sermon to most. "Yes, sinners, I once walked amongst you. But now I offer you redemption."

The choir broke into an old-fashioned version of "Shall We Gather at the River," and the church members joined in on the chorus. Years of sin, acts of defiance and watching others suffer had brought him here. The river had always been regarded as the place to start over. As it had been with the clan in his youth, and then again when he'd grown into a lost teenager himself. He had to guide this new generation there today. They would be baptized in the Mississippi. Join their brothers and sisters to offer their sin-afflicted souls in exchange for salvation.

Sweat poured down his neck and back, his voice

rising toward the heavens as he blessed the congregation. A row of teenage girls dressed in paper-thin cotton dresses exchanged secret looks, deaf to his words, so he turned and spoke directly to them.

"Lest you not be lead astray, my children. The sins of the flesh are enticing. Temptation runs amok here in N'Awlins. The swamp devil spreads his will through the devil-besought whores. They have turned a blind eye to the sanctity of marriage and have given themselves so freely to men, spreading disease, tasting of flesh and seed that has already been shared with another. Guard your hearts, your souls. Save your bodies and worship them as a temple."

"Amen!" a man in the back row shouted.

A chorus of other comments followed, each one growing more intense and emotional. Yet the girls he'd targeted his lesson to giggled.

His temper flared. "The devil already lives within you." He strode forward, waved his hand above them, bowed his head. "Let us pray you see the light and find redemption."

The choir broke into a gospel tune born of the bayou and the crowd rose, chanting, clapping and singing as if their souls had been moved today. Two hymns later, people were crying in the aisle. Two women lurched forward, arms raised, begging to be saved. A man followed, then a family.

Yes. Soon he would have another following—enough to meet at the river for the baptismal. The parents would drag their young girls to the fire, screaming and kicking if they had to, anxious for him to save their wicked souls. They trusted him. They would let him lead the way. And he would offer the girls salvation.

As the mass left, some crying and hugging, others shaking his hand and welcoming him to town, he noticed R.J. Justice standing across from him.

And at the doorway, Detective Dubois, that hero cop working the swamp devil case, watched him intently.

Both men posed a problem and could cause trouble.

Justice stepped forward, his earlier warning reverberating in Ezra's head. Since that day, Ezra had done a little research. He knew the boy from his brother-in-law's clan. The sacrifices.

The pact.

A knot gathered in his dry throat. Had the boy been part of Theodore's congregation when he was younger? If so, and he came forward, he might destroy the reputation Ezra had been building.

He couldn't allow that to happen. He had worked too hard to redeem himself. He would do whatever he needed to protect his reputation and his followers.

HE WATCHED THE congregation disperse with mixed feelings. A sinner stood among them. A vixen disguised in her Sunday finest.

Each detail of her face, her narrowed eyes, her upturned nose, was perfectly outlined like an artist painting a canvas. Hide the flaws with her mask of makeup. Cover the shadows. Make it look beautiful.

Showcase the eyes.

Paint them with precision. Outline the lid. Shade the colors so they looked natural in the light. Hide the tiny veins and lines of the eyeball with long black lashes and vivid colors that matched the iris. Make the pupils perfect, dark and wide. Innocent.

But she was not innocent. Her surface beauty served

as a front for the ugliness that lay beneath. Her clothes—the long flowing skirt, the dark blue blouse buttoned to her neck, the plain flat pumps—created the disguise to convince the others that she belonged.

But like so many, every detail provided a cover for the real woman inside.

The one he'd seen the night before.

Last night, she'd prowled the streets, dressed not in low-heeled sensible pumps but in red stilettos. In lieu of the high-necked blouse, she donned the bewitching low-cut camisole, her skirt so tight she looked as if the leather had melded to her skin.

Yet today, she had come to pray for forgiveness that she had allowed herself to be swayed into joining the ladies of the night. But she couldn't fool him. His eye caught her naked desires. One Sunday's church couldn't atone for the sins she had sowed.

Seven days it took God to build the world. The seventh day was meant for rest.

But how could he rest when his work was never done?

He adjusted his tie and stepped from the edge of the magnolia tree as she sauntered toward her shiny silver Miata.

"Did you enjoy the sermon?"

She pivoted abruptly, then her gaze slid over him and a small smile creased her lips. "Yes, I was moved by the spirit."

Bon Dieu! She would be moved again tonight. Moved enough to ask for salvation.

And he would show her the way, just as he had the others.

CHAPTER THIRTEEN

ANXIETY PLUCKED AT JEAN-PAUL, and he stepped aside to phone Britta. She finally answered on the fourth ring.

"Jean-Paul?"

He exhaled in relief. "You're okay?"

"Yes, I'm fine. Why? Did something happen?"

"No, I just wanted to check. I made a connection between Reverend Cortain and Justice, and wanted to warn you about Justice."

"R.J. is not going to hurt me, Jean-Paul."

"He's not a nice guy, Britta. He's into all kinds of deviant behavior and he has an assault record. Let me come by and pick you up. We won't stay long at my family's house—"

"No." She cut him off so abruptly that he kicked the dirt with his toe in frustration. She didn't want anything to do with him personally or with his family. That was obvious. Even worse, she trusted Justice.

"I'll be fine, Jean-Paul. Enjoy your family. I'm going to work."

He couldn't force her. "All right, but call if you need me."

Silence stretched between them, then she whispered goodbye. Jean-Paul hung up, feeling oddly disturbed and knowing that she wouldn't call for help unless it was a dire emergency.

The reverend's words about building his kingdom replayed in Jean-Paul's head. Strange that the killer had used the same phrase.

Then again, maybe not.

Had Cortain immersed himself in religion to the point of believing himself God? Could he have made it his mission to clean up the streets by killing prostitutes?

Had he started a new cult that met at night in the bayou similar to the one his brother-in-law had built years ago?

He hadn't mentioned Sobek or human sacrifices. Nothing concrete that would justify a search warrant for the man's private home. In fact, Jean-Paul walked a fine line. If he harassed a minister, the press would eat him alive.

But he wasn't convinced that Cortain didn't possess an evil streak or that he hadn't appointed himself a savior and crossed the line to complete his goals.

His phone trilled. Carson's number appeared on the digital display. He connected the call. "Yeah, Dubois here."

"We identified the second victim. Her name was Ginger Holliday," Carson said. "Just applied to a med-tech program, but her prints were in the system from a past DUI. Apparently she was paying her way by selling her body."

Foolish, misled young girls. "What about her family?"

"Lieutenant Phelps notified them. They said she ran away two years ago. Hadn't heard from her since."

He couldn't imagine the hell they were going through. The need to see his sisters had Jean-Paul picking up his pace.

"Thanks, Carson. I just came from Cortain's sermon.

He's a real piece of work." He filled him in on Cortain's preachings. "Maybe Damon will have more on him."

"I'll hit the streets. See if I can find any of Ginger's friends. Maybe somebody saw her with our guy."

"Good idea. Keep me posted." He hung up, feeling anxious. He wanted to get into Cortain's house and take a look.

A quick stop at his parents', then he'd work on getting a warrant. A few minutes later, the family met him with hugs.

"Come on in, Jean-Paul," his mother coaxed. "The gumbo is hot and steamy. Just as you like it."

His stomach growled, reminding him he had skipped breakfast, and dinner the night before.

Damon took the chair opposite him, while Antwaun loped in wearing a pair of gritty jeans and button-down shirt, his beard scruffy. His mother gave him a disapproving look. But Antwaun was working undercover, trying to find out more about the street girls. He had to fit in.

Jean-Paul's sisters grinned as they joined them. "Antwaun, who's that girl I saw with you in the Quarter?" Catherine teased.

His mama's eyes brightened. "Yes, tell us, son. You have a girlfriend?"

Antwaun shot his sister a sideways glare. "No. Catherine's entertaining her overactive imagination."

His father brought a bowl of steaming crawfish to the table. "And where is this Britta woman of yours, Jean-Paul?"

He ignored the barb and his sisters' teasing smiles. "She had plans," Jean-Paul said curtly.

Catherine's husband, Shawn, and their daughter

Chrissy crowded around the table, thankfully ending the questions. His father offered a blessing, then the family dug into the Cajun meal with gusto.

"Any more information on the victims of that swamp devil?" Stephanie asked.

"We identified the second woman," Jean-Paul said. "But we haven't caught the guy yet."

"I saw an article on that reverend in the paper." Catherine sipped her tea. "His group was harassing Britta's magazine."

"It's not her magazine. She's just an editor there."

Damon and the rest of his family gave him a curious look and he realized he'd sounded defensive.

"I don't like Reverend Cortain's high-handedness," his mother said. "He's too judgmental. Always the hellfire and damnation speeches."

Stephanie and Catherine agreed. He cut his eyes toward Damon, who had been unusually quiet.

"We'll take coffee in the study," Damon said. "I need to talk to Jean-Paul."

"More about work." His mother tsked.

"Go ahead," his father said. "We'll clean up."

Antwaun raised a questioning brow and Jean-Paul nodded for him to join them. They returned to the study and closed the door.

"You missed the task force meeting," Jean-Paul said.

Antwaun shrugged. "Sorry, I got caught up with an informant."

"Anything you need to share?" Jean-Paul asked.

Antwaun shook his head. "Another case."

Jean-Paul filled them in on the second victim, her name and background, then explained his findings about Justice's background and Cortain.

"Do you think Cortain's trying to revive the old cult his brother-in-law started?" Antwaun asked.

"It's a possibility," Jean-Paul said.

"I did some checking," Damon stated. "Cortain has been traveling around a lot speaking in various cities. He was in Savannah and Nashville around the time of the other murders."

Jean-Paul's pulse pounded. "Then he might be our guy."

Damon shrugged. "We also traced the lancet from the first murder. It was bought off of eBay. There's a group of collectors, mostly men, who buy original and replica swords and weapons from the past."

"How about that specific one?" Jean-Paul asked. "Do you know who bought it?"

"No, not yet. But R. J. Justice's name appeared several times on the buyers' list. He must have an extensive collection."

Jean-Paul's blood ran cold. Justice had been a part of that clan years ago. He liked the dark side, was into S and M and perhaps bestiality. He worked with Britta and had access to her apartment and the office. And he collected medieval swords and weapons. He had also spotted him at Cortain's church.

And Britta trusted him.

"I have to go."

Damon nodded and Antwaun agreed to call him if they discovered any new information.

Jean-Paul said goodbye to his parents, then hurried out the door. On the way to Britta's, he called to push the search warrant for Justice's place and to request one for Cortain's. Getting them issued on Sunday would be hard, but Phelps promised to do his best.

Time was of the essence. The killer might already be seeking another victim.

And Britta was on his list.

BRITTA HAD ONE HAND on her apartment door, ready to leave, when the phone jangled. She froze. What if it was the swamp devil calling again? What if he'd taken another victim?

She didn't know if she could handle hearing his vile taunts. But she had to help.

Then again, the caller might be another reporter dogging her for information about the magazine or her relationship with Detective Dubois. Were the reporters looking into her past, as well?

Jean-Paul Dubois had uncovered that she had assumed the name of a dead woman. Had someone else?

Inhaling to steady her nerves, she released the doorknob and checked the caller ID. Mazie Burgess. The woman's interest in Jean-Paul was obvious from her previous articles and even more so in the segment where she'd interviewed him.

Trying not to let the woman's interest bother her, Britta walked out the door.

A man with a camera hoisted above his shoulder strode toward the magazine office as she exited the building. She cut down an alley to avoid him, rushing away. All she needed was to end up on the front page again. The picture of her sprawled in the middle of the road had already garnered attention.

Thunder clouds and the hint of winter dampened the air with the onset of a rainstorm. The Mardi Gras attendees wouldn't be happy about that. Neither would the parade founders with their decorative floats and costumes. But the weather would drive everyone inside, so the restaurants and bars would flourish.

She ducked into another alley, walking briskly and tugging the baseball cap lower on her head in hopes that no one recognized her. Footsteps sounded behind her. A pebble rolled across the pavement, the footsteps getting closer. She pivoted and checked over her shoulder through the fog. A dog barked, its blind owner stumbling over the oyster shells on the street.

Breathing a sigh of relief, she rushed on, weaving her way through the streets in case someone was following her, then dodging a few hungover drunks and crackheads as she drew closer to her destination. Finally, she ducked inside the warehouse and waved at the other helpers. A line was already forming outside.

"Another Sunday," Wynona, a heavyset black woman, muttered. "They'll be piling in for lunch in a few minutes."

"Your fried catfish and hushpuppies smell great," Britta said, surveying the huge cast-iron pans brimming with sizzling fish and the massive pots filled with creole.

Wynona patted her on the back. "You doing all right today, hon? Dat face of yores looks plumb wore out."

"Yeah, girl," a hunched-over man with gnarled fingers said. "We can handle it iffin' you sick or somethin'."

Britta almost laughed. Both Wynona and Eddie had at least twenty years on her. Wynona had arthritis and Eddie had nearly lost his leg the year before to gangrene.

"I'm fine. I'll dish up the creole and pour the sweet-tea."

Wynona nodded while two other volunteers rushed in to take their places as the doors of the shelter opened up and the homeless, sick, winos and addicts filed in. Britta's heart bled for them. Some were so thin their bones protruded. Their skin had turned sallow and they stumbled from weakness. Others looked high on crack or whatever substance fed their abuse, while a few young girls—new to the streets, probably runaways—timidly approached. Yet most were too proud to crawl back home.

But it wouldn't take them long to realize the petty jobs around town wouldn't pay them enough to survive. Then Shack or some other pimp would pretend to be their savior and rope them into prostitution before they even realized that was the predator's intent.

A vicious cycle that needed to be broken.

She jumped into the task wholeheartedly, forcing a smile on her face as she dished up the food. This shelter was where she belonged. With her family.

Not with Jean-Paul Dubois and his picture-perfect one.

In the back, someone stumbled. She glanced up and her heart sputtered. A tall man wearing a black cape and hat stared at her, but shadows blurred his face.

Then he raised his head and met her gaze and a shudder coursed through her. Was he the man who sold those Mardi Gras masks? She'd bought some from him but he was so intense. Odd.

No, it wasn't the same man. She'd never seen this man before. Or had she?

As if he sensed her unease, a sinister smile played on his lips, making her even more anxious. Then he disappeared into the shadows. She wiped her hands on a cloth in disgust. She was getting paranoid. Not only was she searching for her lost mother in every homeless woman she saw, now she was looking for the swamp devil in every person, as well.

A HUMBLE FEELING of surprise washed over Jean-Paul at the doorway to the homeless shelter. He'd followed Britta from her apartment, his pulse pounding as he'd watched her checking over her shoulder to see if anyone was following. Twice he'd had to duck into alleyways to remain hidden. He'd first thought she intended to meet a boyfriend or lover, then wondered if she had an appointment with a customer, but in her worn clothes and baseball hat, she looked about twelve years old, not like a woman on the prowl for a man or meeting a john.

It hadn't once occurred to him that she might be volunteering her Sunday afternoon to feed the needy.

All her false bravado, her acts of defiance, the magazine and her nights on the street—what did it mean? Today, she looked like a different person. Like a young innocent girl, all scrubbed clean, void of makeup and show, free of the disguise. Or was this persona the disguise and the dolled-up version the real one?

Determined to make her come clean, he strode forward. The chatter in the room abruptly came to a stop. A few men and two young girls hid their faces. A hushed whisper of fear reverberated through the sudden silence. He realized his badge was showing.

The people in the line turned around and he froze as Britta's gaze landed on him. Her brown eyes pierced him with anger. Then she raised her hand to the crowded room and spoke calmly, "Relax, he's not here to harm you or arrest anyone."

A second later, she handed over her task to another volunteer and rushed toward him. He wanted to grab her, but she jerked him outside beneath an awning. The mist in the air added a chill that matched the cold look on her face.

"Are you following me, Jean-Paul?"

Guilt flared, along with his own anger. "Hell, yes. I followed you. But I wouldn't have to if you weren't so secretive."

"You had no right to invade my privacy." She released his arm and paced in front of him. "I thought you were eating with your family."

"I did, but I was worried so I left to check on you."

"You mean to check *up* on me?"

Their gazes locked, tension rippling between them. A thunder cloud rumbled above, the gray sky painting shadowy streaks along the grimy, graffiti-covered walls. The vile scent was barely tolerable, yet Britta didn't seem to notice.

"When I left you, you were with Justice," he barked. "I found out some things about him that aroused my suspicions."

"And when you called, I told you I was fine."

"You also said you were going to stay home and work."

She sighed. "So you showed up here and scared the bejesus out of these homeless people. All they want is a hot meal, not to be harassed by the cops or treated like criminals."

He hadn't considered their reaction. "I didn't come here to hurt anyone, Britta."

"They don't know that." Her voice rose with such passion that he nearly smiled. "Half of them are junkies or winos, all of them are homeless and a few probably have records or minor offenses that put them where they are now."

"So you come here to help them?" he asked in a low voice.

"I come here because they're my family." Britta pressed a fist to her heart. "This is where I belong, Jean-Paul. Now, go back to your family and leave us alone."

WITHOUT ANOTHER WORD, Britta stormed into the center. How dare Jean-Paul Dubois check up on her? Didn't he realize she could take care of herself? That she didn't need him around?

Good grief. What did she care what he thought? She wasn't trying to fit in with the Duboises.

And he's not here because of anything personal. He's just doing his job.

She'd overreacted. Heck, she should have told him about the man with the cape. But she scanned the crowded room again and didn't see him. He was long gone by now.

Besides, he hadn't approached her. He was probably just a tourist or another wino and she was panicking.

Suddenly, Jean-Paul stepped back inside, removed his jacket and tie and tossed them on a side table. He seemed oblivious to the fact that several men eyed them with envy. The clothing probably wouldn't be there when he returned to retrieve them.

The next two hours, he worked alongside her, pitching in to clean and bus tables, empty the garbage and wash dishes. She tried to ignore him, but watched out of the corner of her eye and noticed a few of the women tidying their appearance as he approached them. Then he paused to assist a physically handicapped war veteran to a table and her heart squeezed.

By the time they finished and the last person left fed and happy, she was not only physically exhausted but mentally drained. Her feet and body ached from tension and lack of sleep.

As always, she'd searched each face for her mother but hadn't found her. Someday, maybe she would accept the fact that she'd lost her forever.

Jean-Paul spoke to each of the volunteers, then leaned close to Wynona and murmured a Cajun expression that made the heavyset woman giggle.

Britta rolled her eyes. Even Wynona had fallen prey to Jean-Paul's charm. And he'd made friends with the others as if he'd always been a part of their team. She had no idea why she resented it, but she did.

If he didn't go away, she was going to fall for him.

"Come on," he said as he dried and stacked the massive pots. "I'll walk you back to your apartment, Britta."

"I can find my own way, Jean-Paul."

His smile faded and he fixed her with an intense stare. "We have to talk. You're not running from me again."

She ran a hand through her hair, knowing it was sweaty and that she smelled like creole and soapy dishwater. And he was standing so close, smelling the same way, yet still so sexy and brooding that she had the strongest urge to kiss him.

His dark eyes skated over her, a sultry smile curving his mouth as he reached up and plucked a bread crumb from her hair. "What do I have to do to earn your trust, *chere?*"

Her throat closed, emotions warring inside her. Trusting a man was impossible.

But it didn't stop her from wanting him or aching to have his arms around her.

"I WANT YOU, Sissy. Say you want me, too."

Sissy Lecher struggled against the bindings, a tear dribbling down her face. "Why are you doing this?"

He tightened his fingers around her throat. Felt her muscles contract. The breath whoosh out. Her eyes flared with panic and fear. God, she had beautiful eyes. "Say it. Say you love me."

She shook her head, but he jerked her neck, shoving her into the pillow. "Say it."

"I...love you," she whispered, choking on the words.

Heat fired his blood. The more resistance she offered, the more excited he became. The more she strained against the bindings, the harder he got.

He stroked his cock, then shoved his full length toward her mouth. He'd make her eat out of the palm of his hand.

Laughter escaped him at the double entendre. But he'd better not indulge. He might leave evidence. And he had to be careful. Couldn't get caught.

The muscles in his thighs tensed and she tried to press her legs together. But he pried them apart, rolled on the condom and straddled her. Her bare nipples stood erect, begging for his mouth but he twisted them with his fingers instead. Dressed in the crotchless red teddy, her pale skin looked like an angel's yet her eyes held a devil's desires.

He'd finish with her now.

Then he'd take another. One that nobody would guess. A stray from his pattern that would have the cops jumping up and down with shock.

Two more days until Mardi Gras.

Two more days until he had Britta.

But Dubois was in the way.

His plan took shape in his mind. He knew the perfect way to get back at Dubois for interfering. A way to assure himself that Britta would come to him.

A way to hurt them both.

And show them that he would win.

Sissy began to convulse around him, and he emptied himself inside the poisoned condom, then watched as she clawed the sheets from the pain.

Seconds later, it was over. She screeched a ragged breath. Gasped and choked on the bile. Then her chest ceased to move up and down.

He climbed off and studied her in disgust as he raised the lancet toward her heart. The blade pierced her skin, then ripped through cartilage and muscle. Bones snapped and cracked. Her organs appeared, exposed and raw. She looked so ugly. Her eyes aghast.

He'd had to do it.

Satisfied she had been punished, he snapped a photograph to send to Britta.

"WE MUST WIN THE WAR OVER sin!" Reverend Cortain shouted.

Hilda Holliday bowed to him in front of the fire, desperate for answers and relief. Ever since she'd heard her baby girl Ginger had been killed by the swamp devil, she'd been sick.

She'd cried till her tear ducts had dried up, had yelled and screamed at her husband and blamed him. If he hadn't been such a tough son of a bitch, her little princess never would have run away. And Lord Almighty, to have turned to selling herself on the streets— No, no, no, it just wasn't possible.

"Thank you for having this special prayer service, Reverend," Hilda whispered raggedly. "I'm just so hollow with grief."

He pressed his hands gently over hers. "To lose a loved one, even though we know they've gone to a better place, is hard for the mortal soul."

"The police, they don't know who did it yet. But I want justice." Her hand shook violently as she removed an old worn photo of her daughter at age three and laid it on the altar. "I know she strayed, but she didn't deserve this. The Lord forgives all, don't he, Reverend?"

Reverend Cortain shifted, tugging at the white-collared shirt. "Yes, sister, he heard your daughter's whispered plea to be saved before she met her master."

Sweat created dark pools on his shirt below his armpits as he raised them to spread his fingers across her head. "The Lord told me himself."

She nodded, grateful to hear his words of comfort. She'd waited for answers to her prayers when Ginger had first left home, but she'd never made a connection like some of the sainted chosen people claimed. But then again, she'd been lost herself when she was young. Her pappy had told her she weren't worth nothin' and then she'd married Jim Bob and proved his point.

Only good thing she'd ever done was birth Ginger.

"Reverend, someone has to pay the price for killin' innocent children, for leading them astray."

You're right," Cortain said. "The ones who entice our children into temptation should suffer."

"You mean my husband and me?"

"I mean the other street girls. The pimps. All those who run the strip clubs and bars. Feeding alcohol and drugs to ravage the young people's minds." His voice rose with conviction, "Just look at that magazine *Naked Desires*. They're positively shameless the way they print pornography. They emphasize the rewards of sinning and entice girls to cross over into the dark side. Britta Berger, the confessions columnist, encourages sex with strangers. The hussy must be stopped."

Hilda nodded, finding a new focus for her anger. She could crusade against the bars and strip clubs. And she could help destroy that magazine. Especially that Berger woman. Women ought to be helping one another, not glorifying sin.

She spotted Elvira Erickson's mama and headed toward her. Debra Schmale's mother claimed that her daughter had run out that day looking like a whore. Together they could band together to try to save the children.

Maybe they could even run that Berger woman out of town.

"WHY WOULD YOU keep it a secret that you help the homeless people, Britta?" Jean-Paul rushed to keep up with her as she practically sprinted through the streets.

She swung around as if desperate to escape him. "I'm not looking for rewards or attention," she said. "Like I told you, they're family to me just like yours are to you."

Silence lapsed, taut and thick, charged with tension.

They passed a walking ghost tour, a cool mist falling, making the air gray with fog. Up ahead, the daily parade had started with dozens of floats, motorcycles, dancers, horse-drawn carriages filled with sponsors, a train of voodoo princesses and other cultural displays. Britta wove through the side streets, avoiding the crowd.

"You don't have to follow me home," she said.

"Dammit, Britta, I'm trying to keep you safe."

"I can take care of myself. Why don't you go work on the investigation?"

Her jab hit home and he sighed in frustration. "That's just it. We're checking leads, but so far nothing. Well, except for Justice."

She paused, planted her hands on her hips and fumed at him. A smudge of creole sauce had splattered and dried to her cheek, her hair was flat and sweaty, her clothes damp with perspiration and food. She'd never looked more beautiful.

"What about him?"

"Justice has a collection of medieval weapons. I'm talking swords, lancets and spears. I've requested a search warrant now for his house. If we find out he bought the ones used in the murders, we can nail him."

"You're determined to pin this on R.J., aren't you?"

"And you're determined to defend him." He arched a brow. "What kind of hold does he have on you, Britta?"

"He doesn't have a hold on me," Britta snapped. "No man does."

Or ever would. He heard the underlying message and wanted to know more. Like why she wouldn't let him get close. "Justice also knows Reverend Cortain."

"Everyone knows the reverend, Jean-Paul. He's been all over the place—in the papers, on TV."

"No, I meant he knew him before. From his past."

Britta's wary gaze swung back to him. "How?"

"Apparently Justice lost his parents in a suicide pact. The pact was made by a religious cult near Black Bayou about thirteen years ago."

Britta cast her eyes toward the ground. She looked nervous. Shaken. Bothered.

His comments about the pact had obviously struck a nerve. "You know something about the suicide pact, don't you?"

Britta shook her head. "I…maybe I heard about it somewhere. You know how the worst stories are passed around in New Orleans."

"Stop lying to me, Britta. I need to know the truth."

BRITTA TRIED TO temper her reaction. But she had no idea that R.J. had been involved in a cult. Had it been similar to the one she'd escaped? Or could it have been the same one?

She searched her memory bank for details. After she'd escaped, she'd lived on the streets. Occasionally, she'd seen a newspaper. Had read something about all those people killing themselves. And she had scanned the names to see if her mother had been listed among them, but she hadn't.

"I did read about the mass suicide in the paper," Britta finally admitted. "I was only thirteen at the time."

"Cortain's brother-in-law, Brother Theodore Tatum, apparently led the cult," Jean-Paul offered.

Britta shuddered at the sound of the man's name. And if Jean-Paul was right, then Reverend Cortain was related to Tatum, the man she'd shot.

Britta began walking again, heading toward her

apartment. She hated being out in the open now, exposed. Raw. If Jean-Paul had figured out Justice's past, he would figure out hers, as well.

But Jean-Paul didn't back down. He moved up beside her, keeping pace with her as they threaded their way through the streets. Silent. Waiting for her to open up and offer information.

"Even if Justice's parents did commit suicide because of Cortain," she finally said, "what would that have to do with these murders?"

Jean-Paul tugged her to the left to avoid a guy on rollerblades. "I don't know yet. Probably the suicide traumatized Justice. Maybe he's killing these women and spinning a religious angle on to it, so he can frame Cortain."

In a bizarre way, his theory made sense. But why frame Cortain? Because his father convinced R.J.'s parents to kill themselves. Then again, if Jean-Paul spoke the truth, R.J. should hate her, want to punish her, because the people killed themselves out of grief for their leader. The man Britta killed.

"I saw Justice at Cortain's sermon," Jean-Paul said.

Panic slammed into her. "I didn't think he went to church," she admitted.

"Like I said, there's a history with Cortain." He placed his hand at the small of her back as they crossed the intersection. "Has he ever mentioned his background to you?"

She shook her head. "No, we've never talked about it."

The storm clouds above suddenly darkened. Grew more ominous. A gust of wind shook the trees, the Spanish moss wavering like a ghost had shifted through the branches.

Maybe it had.

If Justice or Cortain had been involved in the original cult, they might know her real identity.

And that she had killed Reverend Tatum. And if Cortain was, he might want to see her dead out of revenge.

CHAPTER FOURTEEN

MARDI GRAS WAS ALMOST upon them. His favorite time of year.

R.J. could feel the excitement mounting. The partiers growing anxious. The costumes and masks becoming more prevalent. The celebration of the New Orleans customs heightening the anticipation in the air.

The city of the dead was truly alive.

Dusk settled across his bedroom, cloaking the corner in shadows of day and night. The woman below him moaned and R.J. settled himself between her legs, trying to find fulfillment when his urges cried out for another woman.

Not the one who lay beneath him. She was a temporary fix.

Soon he would be with Britta. Just to touch her skin, finally show her some of his coveted collections, to have her in his bed…he could hardly stand the wait.

The woman below him wrenched at the bindings around her arms and wrists, the agony of her imprisonment only heightening his sexual drive. She was the second woman he'd taken like this today.

He plucked a feather from his nightstand and traced it over her bare breasts. She whimpered, fighting the pleasure, waiting to see what he did next. He lowered his head and bit her nipple, tasting the sweet droplet of blood that flowed into his mouth. He glanced at the clock, gauging his time. Another hour and he'd be done with her.

Another hour to kill.

He lowered his head and took another bite.

"STAY AWAY FROM JUSTICE," Jean-Paul declared as he and Britta entered her apartment.

Britta shivered at his ominous tone. "That's impossible. He's my boss." She dropped her keys on the black lacquered end table. "Besides, I told him I'd meet him at the square this evening. We're going to look at that new exhibit in the wax museum."

Jean-Paul bit back a nasty reply. "It's not safe, Britta. Cancel the meeting."

"If he *is* your killer, he's not going to do anything to me in public, Jean-Paul." She fidgeted with the tail end of her stained T-shirt. "And I can take care of myself."

"I'm sure the other hookers thought the same thing."

He realized his gaffe a second later when fury flattened her lips into a thin line. "I'm going to take a shower. When I get out, I want you gone."

"Britta—"

She held up her hand in warning. "Don't apologize, Jean-Paul. You said what you meant."

"But—"

She cut him off by storming into the bedroom and slamming the door. The lock clicked a second later.

He cursed himself for fouling up with her again. They'd been going rounds ever since they'd met. He'd never win her trust with insults. But dammit he didn't understand her. And she had his emotions in a knot.

The shower water clicked on, unnerving him more as images of Britta assaulted him. Britta naked, her flesh coated in bubbles, warm water running a path over her face, her breasts, her abdomen, then down to her heat. Unable to leave her alone and desperate to understand her, he searched her den. Maybe he'd find some clue as to who she really was. He checked the tiny desk in the corner. More confession letters and notes she'd made about upcoming magazine pieces.

He looked in the end tables, then the drawers on the entertainment unit. A white blanket held several miniature porcelain dolls. He'd seen similar ones at Cathy's; his niece collected them from a local street artist.

Odd. He wouldn't have pegged Britta for a doll collector. Then again, she was the most complex woman he'd ever met. They especially seemed out of place next to the macabre masks and bayou creatures on her walls. Why had she hidden them?

In the next drawer, he discovered a photo album. Britta had claimed she had no family, so he opened it and looked inside. A lone photo of a small child with dark red hair and big eyes stared back. It was Britta. She looked so small and alone that his heart clenched. And with her was a woman, probably in her late twenties, although the misery in her eyes aged her considerably.

Britta's real mother? What had happened to her? Had she died? Or had she abandoned Britta for some reason?

And why did Britta have only one photo? His mother had dozens of albums filled with pictures, along with numerous videos of him and his siblings.

Curious, he checked the next drawer but found it empty. Frustrated, he sat down in her armchair to wait and confront her. But he felt something hard beneath the cushion. He dug underneath and found a velvet-covered book wedged between the cushions. Curious, he examined the outside.

Secret Confessions.

Guilt nagged at him and he started to put it down. But dammit, he had to know more about Britta. Women's lives were at stake.

The first entry described her move to her current apartment. Her excitement over the job. Another described her job interview with R.J. She thought the man was attractive. Enigmatic. Frightening. And the job posed an opportunity that would pay well.

It was also a perfect cover.

He frowned. A cover for what?

Could she possibly be in cahoots with Justice?

Hmm, she didn't go into the details. He skipped a few pages and found an entry about him.

Jean-Paul is the sexiest man I've ever met. Sometimes I fantasize about him at night. I close my eyes and pretend that he is touching me, holding me, making love to me.

But he's a cop. I can't get too close to him or he might discover the truth. The darkness that I am.

When I think about my past, I see the bayou and I fall into the endless abyss of tangled vines and trees. The monsters live with me. They follow me everywhere I go.

Even in my sleep.

But sometimes in the early morning, I dream that I have escaped. I see light, the colors of the rainbow. I have a clean slate and I paint over the black and gray until I see vibrant colors of red and gold, blue and orange.

But when morning comes, the big dark hole is back. It's a black so dark that no light or color exists, only the tentacles of evil that lie below, feeding on my fears and the bad things I did in the past. Then it swallows me, and I know I can never climb out or escape.

Disturbed by the entry, he skipped over and read another one, this one much different.

Secret confessions:
I want to make love to Jean-Paul Dubois. I imagine his arms around me and close my eyes, wanting, craving his touch. I can hear him whisper how much he wants me, that nothing can keep us apart.

Then I know that I'm not like my mother. That the past doesn't matter and that I'm not alone.

That I never will be again because someone loves me.

"WHAT ARE YOU doing?"

Jean-Paul jerked his head up just as Britta snatched the journal from his hand. "How dare you read my private thoughts."

The look of utter anger and hurt that lined her face made his chest ache. Dressed in that terry-cloth robe with her hair damp from the shower, she looked young and vulnerable. Then he saw the moisture in her eyes.

"Get out, Detective Dubois. And this time don't come back."

He started to apologize again, but she rushed to the door, opened it, then tapped her foot, waiting.

He thought about the killer after her. About her initial reaction to the threats. And to *him*. To the fierceness with which she was determined to keep her secrets. To the way she responded to his family and the fact that he'd seen her feeding the homeless. To those tiny little dolls.

To the journal entry where she'd admitted she wanted him.

He could fulfill her sexual fantasy.

And God help him, he wanted to.

But afterwards, he'd have to walk away and that would hurt her.

"I'll leave for now." He paused and brushed a tendril of wet hair from her cheek. "But I will be back, Britta." He cupped her face in his hand and forced her chin up, but she tried to turn away. Instead of allowing her that reprieve, he lowered his head and pressed his lips to her mouth. He kissed her so gently his body throbbed for more, but the fact that she didn't reciprocate warned him to stop.

He'd break down that wall with Britta. If anyone knew about darkness, he did. He lived it every day with his job. No grays, just black and white. Right or wrong.

But sometimes there *were* grays…and he was slipping into the murkiness now. Crossing the line with Britta. Wanting her even though he knew she harbored secrets from him. Secrets that might be relevant to the case. That she might have done bad things in the past. That she might be a street girl.

But she wasn't all bad.

He would prove to her that every man wasn't a bastard. That she could trust him with her secrets. That he wouldn't let this crazy man hurt her.

That he'd protect her with his life if he had to.

BRITTA CLOSED THE door behind Jean-Paul, her insides quivering. How much of her journal had Jean-Paul read? Had he seen the notations about her secret fantasy of making love with him? And not just making love, but making a family. And those silly dolls…

But other entries were more damning.

The ones where she'd described D-day—the day she'd died and been reborn?

Outside, the storm clouds moved in front of the window, obliterating the sunlight. Winter screamed its arrival. The dark black sky looked like the empty canvas she'd written about. One void of colors and hope where silence echoed around her.

The phone rang, startling her, and she rushed toward it, half-hoping Jean-Paul was calling, that he'd insist he'd take care of her. But leaning on him would be too easy….

The caller ID read out-of-area. She frowned and almost turned away, but remembered that the killer's number hadn't shown up before. No reason for it to now.

Bracing herself, she answered. "Hello."

"I have made another offering."

Britta tightened the robe around her waist. "Who are you? Why don't you just tell me your name?"

"You know me. You just don't want to admit it."

She glanced out the window to see if someone was outside, watching her, but no one seemed visible from the street in front of Naked Desires.

"Where are you now?"

"I'm close by." The voice was whispered. Muffled. "Watching you. Waiting."

She scanned the building across from her and detected movement in an apartment on the corner. The curtain shifted and she thought she saw a shadow move. Then it disappeared and there was nothing.

"Are you across the street?" she asked.

His breathing wheezed out. "Only four more days until Mardi Gras, Adrianna. Until the final sacrifice."

She shivered and sank onto the sofa. Adrianna? He knew who she was. Had known her in her former life.

Someone from the clan. Maybe the boy she had run away from…. But he was dead, wasn't he? His name had been listed in the paper among the suicide victims.

She opened her mouth to call him by name, but the phone clicked into silence. Barely a minute had passed. Probably not long enough to trace, although it had felt like forever. And she'd learned nothing helpful to tell Jean-Paul—nothing except that another woman was dead.

Shaking with helpless fury, she punched in his number. "Jean-Paul?"

"Britta?"

"He just called again. He's killed another woman."

His heavy sigh reverberated with frustration. "I'll see if we got a trace. Did he give any indication where she is?"

"No."

"I'll be right there."

"There's no need. I'm all right." Britta dropped her head into her hands. "Just find the girl, Jean-Paul."

Silence stretched for a painful heartbeat. "All right.

But I'll send a uniform by. Stay put and keep your doors locked."

Britta hung up, then once again walked to the window and stared out. Stay put?

No, she couldn't do that. She had to help him find this murderer. He knew her real name. Knew her past. Knew that she was a killer herself.

That was the reason he'd called her. He thought she'd understand.

Tears burned her eyes, but she blinked them away. He was wrong. She had shot Reverend Tatum out of fear. Self-preservation. And not a day had passed by that she hadn't felt the weight of guilt upon her.

But this man…he had no conscience. He killed innocent women for the game. In the name of sacrifice. And he wouldn't stop until they caught him.

Jean-Paul thought R.J. might be involved. If he had lost parents to the clan, if he was taunting her now, she'd find out that, too.

Jean-Paul would say it was too dangerous. But maybe she could assuage the guilt of the other girls' murder if she could prevent another.

Three days until Mardi Gras

THE LAST TWENTY-FOUR hours had been maddening.

More search parties were dispersed. The woman's body was found. Her name was Sissy Lecher. And Britta had received another photo.

Thankfully, the ME had found trace evidence beneath Ginger Holliday's fingernails, but it would take time to test it. Other than that, clues were nonexistent.

Jean-Paul's anger rocked back and forth between

fury at the killer, his own ineptness and being angry at Britta for not confiding in him. But he didn't have time for emotions.

Carson was following Howard Keith, the photographer. Antwaun was assigned Randy Swain. Jean-Paul was going to talk to Reverend Cortain. And he'd hunted for more info on Britta. But the social worker who'd handled the Bergers' foster care had died and her records had been sketchy, so he hadn't learned Britta's real name.

A chill dampened the air as he drove to the reverend's house at the edge of Black Bayou. The weather seemed more ominous, the evening sky turned darker by the minute. The silvery Spanish moss seemed weighted with gray, the tendrils of the weeping willows waved like an old woman battling to stand up against the force of the impending storm.

The cacophony of night sounds echoed around him as he walked up the cobblestone steps toward Cortain's house, a wood-frame structure with peeling paint and faded curtains. He knocked, then identified himself. Several minutes later, the stubby man appeared in baggy black pants, his tie loosened, an open Bible in his hands.

"What can I do for you, Detective?"

Jean-Paul narrowed his eyes and removed photos of each of the victims. "Did you know any of these girls?"

Cortain adjusted his wire-rim glasses and studied the photos. "No, I've never seen any of them before. The paper said they were prostitutes?"

Jean-Paul nodded curtly. "They might have attended one of your sermons," Jean-Paul said. "Or maybe you met them *elsewhere?*"

Cortain's eyes bulged with anger. "I'm a man of the

cloth, Detective. If I visited the red-light district at any time, it would be to try to save the lost souls."

"So you've never tried to *save* these three women?" Jean-Paul asked, not bothering to hide his sarcasm. He didn't believe for a minute that Cortain was all that holy.

"I've already answered that question. Now, is there anything else? Perhaps you have something on your mind—a confession of your own? Perhaps you need repentance?"

He sure as hell did, but he wouldn't ask Cortain for it. "Tell me about the clan your brother-in-law led. The one where fifty people committed suicide."

Cortain's fingers flitted nervously over the Bible pages. "I was only a young man myself back then."

Jean-Paul produced a newspaper clipping. "Then let me refresh your memory. Your brother-in-law used medieval practices. He worshipped Sobek and offered sacrifices to the gods."

Cortain arched a brow. "That was a long time ago."

"Not so long that you've forgotten?"

Sweat rolled down Cortain's ruddy cheek. "Like I said, I was only a kid myself. It was a confusing time. We all loved my brother-in-law. We were devastated when we lost his leadership." He choked up. "And then the deaths—my sister was among them."

"The man we're calling the swamp devil is practicing those same medieval practices. He might have belonged to that original clan. You probably knew him."

Cortain reached up as if to shut the door. "I don't know anyone left from the group."

Jean-Paul caught the door edge with his hand. "Then you won't mind if I take a look inside your house, will you?"

Cortain's face blanched, but he stepped aside and allowed Jean-Paul to enter. "Go ahead, Detective. Search away. I am a messenger from the heavens. I have nothing to hide."

R.J. WAS HIDING something.

The nerves at the back of Britta's neck tingled. He had made an excuse the day before, begging off from visiting the wax museum with her.

Then today he'd called and insisted they go together.

Frank DeCamp, the creator of the masterpieces in wax and director of the wax museum, was now showing her a mask collection made by an artist who used the initials SW. The series of masks on display intrigued her. They were detailed—dark, each one depicting an evil force of black magic.

DeCamp indicated a second wall behind him. "These masks represent some of the famous ghosts who haunt the city."

She studied DeCamp's features as he described a few of the local ghost legends. She had seen him before, but couldn't place him. Probably in the market. Or at one of the restaurants.

Or perhaps from her past. From the bayou?

She searched her memory, but still couldn't place his face. His eyes, though, seemed odd. Intense. Sinister. They were different colors. One brown, one hazel. Glassy-looking.

A scar crisscrossed his hand, another carved a red path up his arm and a third skated up from his shirt to his neck. They resembled bite marks from an animal. Or maybe someone had used his sculpting knives on him?

"We have a special historical display of religious memorabilia portraying customs through the ages," he said as he led them to the next exhibit.

DeCamp showed them into a dark room filled with plastic shrubbery, trees and displays of crocodiles from different regions, then past the biggest bust of Sobek she'd ever seen.

Several low-lit cordoned-off areas showcased replicas of medieval gods and the history of religion from Judaism to Protestant origins. Opposite those, she noticed a sacrificial scene of natives dancing around an open fire while snakes hissed in a nearby pit. Lambs, calves and wildlife lay slaughtered and bloody on stones and grassy mounds—their predators down on bent knees offering their sacrifices. On a cloth of velvet lay a young girl dressed in virginal white. Four natives held the poles of her bed as if they'd carried her to the cross that they lit in honor of the ultimate sacrifice.

"Is it not totally captivating?" DeCamp asked in a low voice. "The loved ones were so unselfish."

Britta glanced up at DeCamp's unwavering, intense eyes. Then to R.J. whose face held a smile as he studied the exhibit.

"What do you think, Britta?" R.J. asked.

That it resurrected memories from her own near-death experience. "The customs were barbaric."

DeCamp laughed. "Some historical practices were indeed so." He guided them to another room. "Now, you must see the heads. My personal contribution to the museum."

The sight of the intricate, lifelike wax figurines stirred Britta's unease. The busts looked as if they were real heads that had been removed from humans.

"These are the queens of Mardi Gras," DeCamp pointed out. "And here are the famous voodoo priest-esses that came before us."

R.J. brushed his hand along her waist, then tugged her closer to him. "The details are magnificent, are they not, Miss Berger?"

The man's choice in mediums disturbed her. It was almost as if he had known each of the women he'd sculpted. As if he'd sculpted them from memory.

"They look real," she said in a low voice, "as if the women have been beheaded."

DeCamp's smile sent a chill down her spine. And R.J.'s reaction—the more she learned about him, the more he frightened her.

And the more she suspected he might be the killer.

DEBRA WANTED TO SEE Teddy's secret room. All his artwork. Even the pieces he'd never shown another living soul.

But Teddy could not allow it. His fantasies were private.

She batted her long brown eyelashes at him. She had worn more makeup today and looked like one of the pretty girls on the street. The ones who usually didn't give him the time of day.

But Debra claimed she *loved* him.

Maybe she could make him forget the other girls. The ones who'd turned him down. The ones who'd laughed when he'd approached them. Maybe this thing with Debra *was* the real thing and he could finally love a woman.

Debra's eyes floated over him as if she might lap him up like an ice-cream cone on a hot day. He wanted to want her.

But when she ran her fingers along the inside of his thigh, his body refused to respond.

Fuck. It was happening again. Just like the other times.

He had to focus. He couldn't fail her and have her laugh at him. Then she'd run away.

Frustrated, he rolled her over and pinned her to the bed. Her eyes flared with desire. "That's it, baby," she whispered. "Make love to me, Teddy."

For the next twenty minutes, she tried her damnedest to turn him on. Teddy tried his damnedest to let her. He wanted real love but it escaped him.

And nothing she did with her fingers or mouth was working.

The *Naked Desires* magazine, the pictures of the girls…the Secret Confessions. They always aroused him.

And so did the picture of Britta Berger.

Frustrated, he left the bed and went into the other room. Debra called his name, but he shut the door and stared at the dolls. So pretty. So perfect. So beautiful.

The jars of eyes stared back at him. They did look real. He brought them to life.

He opened the curtain the rest of the way and studied the pictures of the naked girls. At the one of Britta he'd bought from that photographer.

A smile creased his lips. And his cock finally hardened. He slid his hand down, ready to satisfy himself, but the door opened and Debra stood watching him. Her gaze fell to his hand then to the photograph of Britta.

Anger reddened her cheeks and she slammed the door in his face.

He cursed himself then ran after her.

BRITTA KNOTTED HER hands together as R.J. parked in the drive to his house. She had to get him alone. Get inside his house. Get him to open up.

And find out if he was the killer.

His house, a gray Victorian with white lattice work, dormer windows and an attic window, was cloaked in darkness. The five-acre piece of property hugged the swampland, shrouded in trees. It looked…haunted.

He rushed around to open her door and she hesitated as she noticed a crocodile resting lazily in the pool of water below the tupelo tree. Years ago, some rich family probably entertained on the wraparound porch. The ladies wearing sun dresses and bonnets while they sipped mint tea and nibbled on tiny wafer cookies.

Now the ghosts of the dead whispered of danger.

R.J. took her arm and guided her inside, helping her dodge the uneven ground and sticks the wind had tossed around. A light sprinkling of rain fell on her face, adding to the chill.

"Why did you choose this place?" Britta asked as they entered the dark foyer. "It's so deserted out here."

"I prefer the quiet," he replied in a thick voice. "And I like my privacy."

Tension clawed at her muscles. All the swamp devil's victims were found in the bayou in run-down shanties. All in desolate areas just like R.J.'s place.

He smiled, then walked to the minibar in the corner of the living room while she studied the dark veneered wood paneling. A library of books held works of science fiction and fantasy creatures, while an array of others included titles of erotica, bestiality, S and M and half-human creatures.

The temptation to run snaked through her. But then

she'd never learn the truth. And she was tired of running.

"Quite an accumulation," Britta commented.

"If you think that's impressive, come and look at my collection of swords."

Anxiety tingled inside Britta at his tone, but she followed him to a connecting room. Ancient swords and knives filled the walls. She surveyed the room, noting the sizes, shapes, golds, bronzes and wooden handles. Each weapon had a carved gold plate below specifying its origin, history and former owner.

"You must have been acquiring these for years." A gold-plated lancet that resembled the one the killer had left inside the dead women's hearts caught her eye.

He smiled. "Yes, that one resembles the one the swamp devil uses, but his are replicas," he explained. "Cheap imitations."

He handed her a crystal wine glass filled with a bloodred merlot. "I'm glad you finally came to my house, Britta."

He moved so close she inhaled the scent of his heavy cologne. So close she fought a shiver. "Jean-Paul Dubois mentioned that you grew up in Black Bayou."

His eyes turned a smoky hue. "Yes."

She sipped her wine, gauging his reaction. "He said you lost your parents to a cult thirteen years ago?"

The coarse bristles of his five o'clock shadow made a scraping sound as he ran his hand over it. "Yes, that's true. But then again, you know all about the cult, don't you, Britta?"

A cold knot of fear clenched her stomach. "Why would you say that?"

"Because we were both there." His low voice

rumbled with insinuations. "Don't you remember, Adrianna?"

Denial stabbed at her. Thirteen years had passed. The day she'd run, she swore she'd never look back. But she'd also thought she'd never forget the boy's face.... Had he survived?

Had he taken on a new identity as she had?

She searched R.J.'s features. His seething brown eyes. His muscular frame. There was no way R.J. could be the young boy who had tried to make her his wife. Could he?

"Why didn't you say something sooner?"

He traced a finger along her arm, then up her shoulder to her cheek. "I didn't want to scare you away. I had to get to know you. Earn your trust."

But she didn't trust him. She didn't trust any man.

Except maybe Jean-Paul....

"I know what happened to you that day," he murmured. "I saw you run into the bayou."

Her breath caught. He knew her secrets. Her shame. Everything about her. "Then you blame me for your parents' deaths?"

"No." His lips thinned into a straight line. "I blame Cortain."

She backed away, ready to flee in case Jean-Paul was right, but R.J. caught her around the waist and dragged her to him.

"Don't you see? We were meant to be together, Britta. Once the bayou gets in your soul, it won't let go."

Britta shook her head, unable to accept his words as true. She had escaped. This couldn't be happening.... "What happened to my mother after I left? Did they hurt her?"

"I don't know. I never saw her. But I heard rumors

that they killed her, then other rumors that she ran off, too."

He paused, his expression pained. "A few weeks later, Cortain suggested everyone make a suicide pact. He was convinced that if the authorities found out about the cult, that they'd disband the cult and arrest us all." He hesitated, his voice lower, more ominous when he continued, "He convinced the others he was right. But Cortain chickened out at the last minute."

She shivered, realizing the trauma he'd suffered. "I'm sorry about your parents, R.J. I didn't know."

"Shh, it's over." He gripped the elaborately carved handle of the scepter and raised it to her neck. "The past, the secrets, the darkness, they bind us together— forever."

She felt the first prickle of pain as the sharp blade grazed her skin. Felt a drop of blood slide down her neck. He caught it in his finger, lifted it to his lips and sucked it away.

Fear caught in Britta's throat. He was crazy. A killer.

But why would he murder innocent women? To get back at Cortain, maybe frame him? Or to get back at her? Became he blamed her for his parents' deaths? He claimed he didn't but the predatory gleam in his eyes indicated otherwise.

What was he going to do to her now? Torture her like he had the other women, then leave her for dead in the bayou?

CHAPTER FIFTEEN

THREE VICTIMS SO FAR. The killer was probably searching for another one already. In fact, a woman named Winifred Schmale had reported her twenty-year-old daughter Debra missing.

Another day had passed. Night had fallen. And Jean-Paul was desperate for answers.

He drove up and down the edge of the Mississippi, checking isolated areas in search of a gathering place for a new cult. Finally, in the heart of Black Bayou, he found an abandoned campsight that looked suspicious. Animal feathers and blood were splattered on a pile of rocks. A decapitated chicken lay in the center. Other signs of mojos were evident.

Voodoo. Black magic. Whoever had been here was a believer.

He stooped by another mound of rocks and noted freshly turned dirt. A thorough dig revealed several pouches of black magic potions. Various roots and herbs, probably frogs legs or other animal parts were inside and urine soaked the outside. Had someone cast a spell to ward off evil or to conjure the Devil?

The scent of opium lingered in the air as he stirred the embers of the fire. A black piece of cord like the string of the serpent necklace found with each victim lay half-charred in the dirt. He bagged it for evidence.

Hoping he might be on to something, he searched the campsight one more time, then ducked into the thicket of trees to hunt for a shanty or clearing where the group had banded or a cabin where a killer might take a victim.

The picture of Debra that Mrs. Schmale had shown him replayed in his head, and he grunted in frustration. Debra was so young. Not a prostitute or stripper. But if she wound up on the streets for long, she might end up turning tricks to survive.

He had officers checking with her friends, questioning neighbors. They were running her picture in the paper and on the news. Maybe someone had seen her or would spot her.

Twigs snapped and leaves rustled beneath his boots. Lightning streaked through the thick vines and leaves; the wind whistled like an animal's screech before it attacked.

Yellow-greenish eyes peered at him in the darkness—waiting, watching. Suddenly his cell phone vibrated. He jerked it up, surprised he had service. The signal was weak, but one of their beat cops, Henderson, came through.

"Dubois, listen, you asked me to tail Justice."

"Yeah, what's he up to?" Jesus, he hoped this was the break they needed.

"That Berger woman is with him at his house."

Jean-Paul's blood ran cold.

Justice's house was only a mile away.

"I'll be right there." Jean-Paul hung up, then rushed back toward the car. As soon as he climbed inside, he punched Phelps's number. "I'm on my way to Justice's house now. You got that search warrant?"

"In my hands as we speak."

"I'll stop by and get it. I'm going to search his house tonight."

And he'd find out what Britta was doing there, then get her out before Justice hurt her.

"R.J., STOP IT," Britta whispered. "This game has gone far enough."

His low chuckle echoed in her ear. "Isn't your adrenaline pumping?" he asked softly. "Can't you feel the excitement between us? The connection on the most intimate level?"

"Is fear the most intimate level for you?" she whispered.

He slid the knife lower on her neck, scraping bare skin. "That edge only heightens the pleasure, darlin'."

"Is that what you told the other women?"

He hesitated, his breathing erratic. "I don't deny I've had other lovers."

"I'm not talking about your lovers, R.J." Britta sucked in a sharp breath. She had to confront him. Seduce him into talking. Make him stop. "I mean the swamp devil's victims."

"You think I killed those women?" His voice reverberated with barely controlled anger.

"You hate Cortain. You blame me for your parents' deaths."

He released his grip, but swung the knife down by his side, then handed her the glass of wine and led her to his bedroom. "I'm not a killer, Britta. I want to be your lover."

Dark red velvet curtains hid the outdoors while a matching coverlet draped the antique four-poster bed. Sheers hung from the wooden posts and thick gold ropes encircled them—to hold back the sheers or to imprison whoever lay inside?

He gestured toward a massive bar in the corner complete with crystal flutes and champagne chilling on ice, then opened a small wardrobe. Dozens of red and black lace teddies, nightgowns, camisoles, stiletto heels and mesh stockings occupied the cherry cabinet along with an assortment of gothic masks.

"See? I mean to seduce you, Britta. Not hurt you."

The sword glinted in the soft glow of the candlelight as he laid it beside the bed. Instincts told her to run.

Would he let her escape?

He picked up a black scarf from the end table and approached her. Britta's pulse pounded. He slid the scarf around her wrists. She stiffened, but he jerked her to him and pressed his lips to hers. Britta suddenly shoved against him.

"No. R.J., I can't do this."

"Britta, relax—"

"No!" Memories flooded her. One man handing her over to his son. Planning to take what she didn't want to give.

Panicked, she turned and darted from the room. R.J.'s footsteps clicked behind her. He called her name, but she raced toward the door and grabbed the knob, anxious for air. He caught her and manacled her wrists with his hands. "Stop running, Britta. We were meant to take down Cortain together. To be lovers forever."

The doorbell rang and someone pounded on the door. "Open up, Justice. It's Detective Dubois."

A muscle ticked in R.J.'s jaw. Then he pressed a kiss to the back of Britta's neck. "It's not over between us,

Adrianna. You will be mine one day, and you'll come willingly."

JEAN-PAUL'S HEART RACED with worry. What if he was too late? What if Justice had hurt Britta? He couldn't bear the thought.

He pounded on the door again.

"Detectives Dubois and Graves," Jean-Paul shouted. "If you don't let us in now I'm going to break down the damn door."

The door finally swung open. A growl erupted from the gargoyle knocker and Jean-Paul grimaced. Justice stood in the foyer, his tie askew, his shirt unbuttoned, his cheeks flushed as if he'd been exerting himself.

Behind him, Jean-Paul spotted Britta and fury slammed into his chest. Her hair was mussed, her cheeks pale and her clothes rumpled. What in the hell had they been doing?

Jean-Paul held up the warrant. "We have a search warrant for the premises, inside and out."

Justice lifted one brow. "What do you expect to uncover?"

He hoped to hell something to put the man behind bars. "We'll let you know when we find it." He slanted Britta a worried look. "Are you all right?"

She nodded, although she avoided his gaze. He could tell she was shaken. He had the insane urge to touch her, to make sure she was really okay, but he refrained. She sat down on the sofa and folded her hands together in her lap while Justice poured himself a Scotch and settled in his recliner.

Jean-Paul and Carson wasted no time searching. They examined the sword collection first, taking photos before they checked for prints.

Next came Justice's bedroom. Several paintings of nudes in various sexual positions graced the walls and a wooden carved crocodile decorated the chrome-and-glass bar. An assortment of lotions and body oils were situated on a glass tray. The decadent bed, bar and piped-in music verified Justice was a seductor. So where did he keep his whip and chains? Velvet ropes hinted at romance, but not necessarily S and M.

Then Jean-Paul found a wardrobe full of lingerie. Red teddies similar to the ones the victims had worn. He studied the brand label. Not the same. But that didn't mean Justice hadn't purchased others. And then there were masks. S and M ones made of leather, gothic renditions that were morbid.

A more thorough search turned up several porn tapes. All recorded by Justice's film company. What if he'd taped his victims' deaths? Jean-Paul dug around inside the cabinet, but couldn't find any personal tapes. Dammit.

He spent the next hour searching the remainder of the house. The closets, additional bedrooms, then the basement, looking for a darkroom or even the camera used to take the photographs of the vics.

They found nothing.

Carson checked out Justice's computer and they confiscated his files to search for evidence. As he entered the den again, Britta was perched on the sofa's edge with her hands entwined, as if she might run any second. Justice had moved over to sit beside her. Anger tightened Jean-Paul's throat—he didn't like seeing them together.

"You have another room somewhere," Jean-Paul said. "One where you entertain."

Justice's black eyes scoured over him. "You mean a secret room?"

"Yes, one that's reserved for special guests."

Justice smiled, the whites of his teeth so bright they appeared eerie in the dim interior. "And if I do?"

"Show it to us," Jean-Paul snapped.

Seemingly relaxed, Justice stood and crossed the room, then pushed a button inside one of the built-in bookcases that flanked the fireplace. The bookcases swiveled, revealing a hidden door. He gestured with his hand. "It is my private lair. But it is to protect my guests' privacy as much as my own."

Jean-Paul stepped into the small room, half-expecting to find a naked woman tied and tortured inside. But it was empty.

A bed dominated one corner, while various S and M paraphernalia was stored on black metal shelves. Cameras hung from the ceiling, candles and oils sat on a low table and a tripod occupied the corner. Ropes made of silk, velvet and thick cord lay near the bed.

Jean-Paul narrowed his eyes at the space above the bed. "Those spatters on the wall look like blood."

Carson nodded, and reached for his phone. "I'll get a forensics team here ASAP."

Carson stepped outside to make the call while Jean-Paul opened doors to the entertainment unit. At least two-dozen homemade videos filled the shelves, each one dated and titled.

Jean-Paul would view each and every one of them. Maybe he'd get lucky.

Maybe Justice had videotaped his murders.

THE WAITING WAS driving Britta crazy. Curiosity made her want to see what R.J. had inside that secret room, while another part of her didn't want to face it.

If R.J. was the killer, would he reveal *her* secrets if he was arrested?

She needed to tell Jean-Paul herself before that happened....

Jean-Paul strode back to where she and R.J. sat, a tape in his hand. "I'm going through each and every one of these," he said. "If you've filmed the victims' murders, we'll find it."

Justice glared at Jean-Paul. "Knock yourself out, Detective. But you won't find anything incriminating because I'm not a killer."

"Come on, Justice. There're too many connections here," Jean-Paul reasoned. "Either you're the swamp devil or you know who is. Maybe Cortain? What I don't understand is why you'd protect him."

"I wouldn't," Justice barked. "Cortain was the reason my parents died. He started that suicide pact. He was the damn leader. Then he chickened out at the last minute." Justice ran a hand over his forehead, wiping off the perspiration. "He just stood by and watched idly while my folks and the others killed themselves."

A real holy man, Jean-Paul thought. "Then maybe you're murdering these women so you can frame him."

Justice gave a nasty laugh. "If I was going to do that, I'd have pointed the finger at him from the beginning."

"Maybe you plan to kill him, then."

Justice tossed back his Scotch, fury radiating from him. "He deserves to die for what he did."

That was the one and only thing he and Justice agreed upon.

"I think you'd better come down to the station."

"You can't arrest me," Justice protested. "You don't have enough evidence—"

Jean-Paul pushed the man forward. "I can hold you overnight for questioning."

"I want a lawyer," Justice demanded.

"You can call one when we get to the station." Jean-Paul pushed Justice outside, questions drumming in his head. Was Justice their killer or was he just another deranged psycho on the streets of New Orleans?

RANDY SWAIN COULD NOT let anyone discover his true identity or his pastime.

Then his career would be over. He'd be back to begging for girls. Back to being alone.

Back to being a nobody.

He sipped his beer, smiling from the barstool as country music blared from the speakers. His song, "Heartache Blues," wafted through the smoky haze. He grinned at the females who crooned the words along with his recording.

Thank God the police hadn't found anything on him earlier. Lucky for him. Just as he'd get lucky tonight. He could have his pick of women. Take one or all of them to bed if he wanted.

Damn if his dick wasn't hard as a rock just thinking about it.

He'd screw them, then send them on their way without having to make a commitment. So different from before when he'd been nothing but a poor old country boy with nerdy glasses.

He was no longer that nerdy country boy.

In fact, no one he'd known before would even recognize him. He'd squashed that loser identity and taken on a new persona.

"I could never be with a guy like you," one girl had told him.

He'd been so mad he'd wanted to strangle the life from her.

Anger tore through him, vile and hot, and he found himself squeezing the neck of the beer so hard his fingers ached.

What would that girl say if she saw him now, surrounded by young and beautiful women always touching him, wanting him?

"Come on, Randy," a brunette pleaded in his ear. "Dance with me tonight."

A blonde wearing red stilettos and a top opened down to her navel brushed her tits over his chest. "No, take me, Randy. You know you want me."

He grinned and wrapped his arms around her shoulders, then pulled the brunette onto his lap.

"What if I want you both?" he growled.

They giggled together as if a threesome was right up their alley. He planted a kiss on the blonde's mouth, then slid his hand down the brunette's thigh. He'd pleasure them both tonight if they wanted. He already had his condoms.

Then he'd add their names to his list of conquests. The shrine to Randy Swain he called it.

The face of the girl who'd denied him long ago flashed in his mind and adrenaline pumped through his system. One day he'd let her know he was here in New Orleans.

And she'd be sorry she'd turned him down when he was done with her.

ON THE OUTSKIRTS of town where the fresh scents of the bayou heated the chilly wintry air, Hilda Holliday listened to Reverend Cortain's sermon with an open heart. She missed her girl Ginger like the dickens and wished she could bring her back. But Cortain was right. Ginger had moved on to another place. Was resting now with the angels. Had the purity back in her soul.

A stiff wind bit at her neck and face, the shrill whistle of the gators echoed through the spiny trees and limbs protecting the secrets of the backwater folks. The bonfire popped and crackled, lighting up the black sky with flickers of orange and yellow that danced in symphony with the words their leader belted out to the heavens.

Hilda latched hands with Elvira Erickson's mother. She'd come to another special prayer service that the good preacher had organized. This one for the latest victim, some girl named Sissy Lecher.

Winifred Schmale clung to her other hand. She had poured out her heart, crying that her daughter had run away. They had all prayed that the girl was safe. That she wouldn't fall prey to the demons roaming the streets.

Reverend Cortain strolled by, arms raised, his black robe waving in the wind like a bat's wings as he pressed his hands above their heads and stopped to murmur kind words.

The women knelt at his feet, grateful that someone so connected to their savior understood their pain.

They had to rid the town of the sinners who were taking over. He would show them the way. Tell them how to extinguish the evil that was pervading the town.

And they would do whatever he said.

BRITTA HUDDLED IN the comfort of Jean-Paul's car, but the silence on the ride to her apartment was strained.

She had to make Jean-Paul talk instead of just staring at her so intently. "Do you think a night in jail will make R.J. confess?" And would he reveal her sins, as well?

"Who knows? I'll look at those tapes tonight. Maybe they'll prove something."

Britta frowned, doubts still plaguing her. But the memory of the knife blade pressed to her throat returned, vivid and haunting. "I just want this to be over."

Jean-Paul muttered agreement, his shoulders stiffening with tension. She itched to comfort him. But she had no right.

Still, she'd never felt such an emotional connection with anyone. Never wanted to risk giving part of herself away.

Or confiding the truth about her past.

Would it make a difference in the case? He already had uncovered the connection to the cult. They were investigating Reverend Cortain. And they knew that R.J.'s parents had died in that suicide pact.

Jean-Paul parked in front of her building. "I'll walk you up, then I'm going to check out those tapes."

Britta pressed a hand to his cheek. "I'm okay alone, Jean-Paul."

He cut off the engine and turned to her. An odd look settled in his eyes. Concern? Hunger? "Tell me the truth, Britta."

Her hand stilled. The truth about her name? Her past?

"What would you have done if I hadn't shown up at Justice's?"

She licked her dry lips. "What do you mean?"

"Would you have slept with him?"

The air collected in her lungs, but she had to be honest. "No. How could I when there's another man in my head now?" She took a deep breath, her chest aching. "When it's you I want touching me?"

His breath whooshed out. "Britta…"

"You don't have to say it back, Jean-Paul. I…didn't mean to push you."

"It's the case…there's too much at stake." Jean-Paul rubbed his hands over his face but he didn't touch her. Disappointment filled Britta but she quickly squashed it.

What had she expected?

JEAN-PAUL FISTED HIS HANDS beside him so he wouldn't take Britta into his arms. The silence between them yawned long and tense. His blood heated at the simmering way her eyes rested upon his face. He saw the hunger. And her admission… God, it fueled his desire.

She was so tempting.

He had nearly come unglued when he'd seen her with Justice. The man was a predator and had his fangs bared for Britta. She thought she could take care of herself, but the other swamp devil's victims had probably felt the same way.

He had to go to the station and interrogate Justice, push him for that confession.

He wanted to follow Britta upstairs and make love to her instead. Make them both forget the horrors of the investigation that had brought them together.

Still, she was in danger and another woman might already have fallen into the hands of the killer.

Outside, the street hummed with activity. He scanned

the area to verify that no one was waiting for Britta. A group of religious protesters marched in front of a pub, two hookers sashayed by in shocking red outfits and a group of bikers chugged beer. A young teenage girl in jeans and a pink T-shirt sporting the word *Princess*, stared silently from a table—by herself, looking helpless and scared. A runaway?

Maybe. But it wasn't Debra, the girl he was looking for.

He climbed out and walked Britta inside her building. That damn light was out again, so they fumbled up the steps in the dark.

Britta unlocked the door to her apartment, then flipped on a small lamp. A warm glow permeated the drafty room.

"Thanks for bringing me home, Jean-Paul."

His gaze fell to her face. She looked worried, vulnerable, frightened. And she'd admitted she wanted him.

Unable to stop himself, he tilted her chin toward him, and lowered his head. "You have no idea what it did to me when I saw Justice touching you. And then when I saw that sword…"

His breath hissed out, then he closed his lips over hers and kissed her. Need rose like a demon inside him, hungry, raw, desperate. She tasted like sin and sweetness all rolled together, like the finest pinot noir, one that had suffered, yet blossomed and aged to be a blend of sensual, erotic taste.

She kissed him back, plunging her tongue into his mouth, and his blood heated. He shoved his hands into her hair, then dragged her up against him. Her lush breasts brushed his chest. Even through the flimsy fabric of her blouse, he felt her nipples stiffen. Desire surged through him, battling with reality.

But hunger won.

He traced his tongue down her neck, suckling and biting her gently while she tunneled one hand into his hair. A hungry whimper erupted from her, fueling him even more. He cupped her breasts into his hands, his cock throbbing. She leaned her neck back and flicked open the buttons to her blouse, offering her tantalizing cleavage. He felt like a starving man as he nipped at the black lacy bra, then miraculously realized the garment had a front clasp. He popped it open, awed as her breasts spilled into his hands.

"God, you're beautiful," he growled.

She ran her hands over his back, her chest heaving as he licked one nipple, then drew it into his mouth. He suckled her until she writhed against him. He traced kisses to the other nipple, running his tongue in circles around her aureole.

"Jean-Paul, that feels wonderful." She shoved at his jacket until he tossed it off, then quickly unbuttoned his shirt. They were like two wild animals—lust stricken, hungry, possessed.

It had never been like this with Lucinda.

The thought of her name drove a nail of guilt through his conscience and he slowed his movements.

"Please don't stop, Jean-Paul." Passion laced her whispered voice. "Please, I need you."

And he needed her, too, like he'd never wanted or needed another woman. But he still didn't know the truth about her past.

Did it matter?

He knew he wanted her. That she was in danger. That he didn't intend to let anyone hurt her.

She trailed kisses down his neck, teasing him with

her tongue. Down his torso. Lower. She reached for his zipper and he moaned. His cock was so hard that he thought he might explode.

"Let me taste you," she whispered as she rubbed her hand over his shaft.

He groaned again, then shook his head and backed her against the wall, tugging at her skirt until he had it up around her waist. He kissed her again—hard, long, desperate—then slid his fingers inside her panties.

"Jean-Paul..."

He caught her cry of pleasure with his kiss as he moved his fingers inside her. She bucked upward, a tremor rippling through her. He flipped them around, so his back was against the wall and he could see her in the wall-length mirror in the foyer. His own wild-eyed expression shocked him. Blood pumped through him as he imagined tearing off her panties and her legs wrapping around him while he pounded himself inside her.

The realization that he hadn't even shut the door behind them shocked him into reality.

What the hell was he doing? Attacking her as if he was some street thug who couldn't even take her to bed?

He had a damn suspect waiting for him and a girl was missing.

Slowly, he removed his fingers from her folds, then lowered her skirt and grabbed her hands. "Britta, stop."

Her breath rasped against his cheek. "Please, Jean-Paul, I want you."

He leaned his forehead against her, struggling for control. "*Bon Dieu, chere,* I want you, too."

Still he set her away from him, refused to look at her.

"I have go, though... Question Justice...." He grabbed his jacket, rammed his hand through his hair and rushed to the door.

"Jean-Paul?" Her voice sounded small. Uncertain. Still quivering with passion.

"I'm sorry, Britta." His head spun with confusion as he stepped through the door. He paused, tormented by leaving her. But he couldn't stay, so he closed the door behind him.

The image of him taking Britta against the wall dogged him as he drove back to the station. Dammit, he'd never treated his wife that way. But Britta was different. She aroused more than just the need to have sex. She stirred his animal instincts. And deeper, more primal emotions.

Emotions he wasn't ready to deal with now.

They had no future.

He couldn't trust her. Hell, he'd seen her wearing street garb like a hooker. He had to end the craziness before he allowed her to totally seduce him.

His stomach knotted. Maybe they could just have sex.

If it was just sex, then they would both be free to move on when the case ended. There would be no commitment.

Acid burned his throat at the thought. No, he couldn't do it.

If he made love to Britta, she couldn't go from his bed to another's.

HE WATCHED THROUGH the window, his blood hot, spiked with fever. Britta Berger—no, his Adrianna—had almost made love to that fuckhead detective. Anger

churned through him. She'd let the man maul her like
a common tramp. Hadn't even bothered to close the
door. As if she wanted the whole world to see her half-
naked, writhing and begging to be fucked.

Now she leaned against the door, her face flushed,
her breasts still exposed, the dark brown tips wet from
Dubois's mouth.

A bellow of rage swelled within him. Once she'd
acted like such an innocent, had pretended to be a good
girl. Had had such innocent eyes. And she'd run from
him like he was a monster.

She had to be punished.

And so did Dubois.

She folded her arms in front of her chest as if
suddenly realizing her shame, then rushed to the
bedroom and stripped her clothes off. He watched,
horny. Angry. His body steeped in rage.

She would go out now.

He knew her routine. She hadn't been satisfied. The
streets beckoned her each night, begging her to return
to the den of inequity that had been her home for years.

Britta—*no*, Adrianna—belonged with the creatures
of the night. The vixen.

Her prim persona was only a disguise.

Tonight, she would head toward the red-light district.
She had desires that hadn't been sated.

He rubbed his hand down his cock, feeling the life
pulse between his fingers. His fury fed his erection.

Soon he would find her and satisfy her dark side.

He could almost hear her soft whimpers. See her
lying tied to his bed. Exhausted but hanging on to hope
that she'd escape.

But he'd never release her.

He imagined shaping her face in his mind. Molding the mask to her features. Painting her eyes. Mixing just the perfect shades of white and pink, of brown and gold for her irises. And black, lots of black for when her pupils dilated as fear bled into her.

He thought of the other faces he'd created and his pulse clamored. Once he shaped the features, painted on the details, the mask would set. Harden. Grow cold.

Just as their bodies did in death.

Yes, soon Adrianna would pay. He could see her eyes—wide open in death.

He could feel her sweet, hot blood dripping between his fingers.

CHAPTER SIXTEEN

BRITTA'S HEART SWELLED with emotion as she lathered and washed away Jean-Paul's scent. What exactly had happened between them? One minute they'd been talking about R.J., the next, passion had exploded between them.

She had wanted Jean-Paul so much she'd begged him to love her.

But he had stopped. He was sorry. Why? Because he knew she wasn't worthy of him.

You're just like your mother.

No, she wasn't. She didn't take money for sex. She tried to help others....

Yet hadn't she acted like a street girl tonight? She'd shamed herself by asking for Jean-Paul's body. And she'd blown her chance to confess to him before he talked to Justice. Would he have understood if she'd told him the truth?

No. No one could understand.

The last remnants of hope faded as she stepped from the hot water into the chilled bathroom. Wind whipped against the window panes, making them rattle. She toweled off, grabbed a robe and curled into it.

Downstairs, a loud sound split the night. She hurried to the window in her den and studied the scene below.

The religious protesters still rallied strong. Two women looked violent. Another wild group of partiers danced through the street. A brawl broke out and shouts erupted. The crowd grew thicker, merging to watch the fight. Protesters yelled and moved closer to her building. Then someone threw a beer bottle and hit the street light, pitching the area in darkness.

Chaos erupted. Suddenly glass shattered. She opened the door to the hallway and glanced down the dark stairwell. A shadow moved. Was it inside?

Then bright orange flames flickered in the opening.

A fire? Had someone thrown an explosive through the window? She turned to grab her cell phone to call for help, but another noise chilled her to the bone.

A voice. Calling her name.

No. He whispered the name Adrianna.

Certain she'd imagined the sound, she inhaled to calm herself, then ran for the stairs. She could escape out the back or through R.J.'s office. But just as her foot hit the stairs, someone's hands closed around her neck. She struggled and lashed out, but she lost her footing and she and her attacker careened down the stairs.

"I DID NOT KILL those women," R.J. said calmly.

Jean-Paul braced his hands on his knees. How could Justice act so damn serene when he was a murder suspect? Was he a sociopath? A man without a conscience? Pure evil inside?

"If you cooperate, we can cut you a deal."

R.J. leaned forward on the table; tiny scars along his arm were visible beneath his shirt-sleeve cuffs. "You're wasting your time, Detective. Both with me and in pursuing Britta."

"This has nothing to do with Britta," Jean-Paul snapped. "It has to do with the fact that you're a serial killer."

R.J. chuckled. "That's where you're wrong. I haven't killed anyone." He paused, confident. "But I understand his obsession with Britta. He wants her the same way you and I both do."

"No, he wants to hurt her. I want to protect her." Jean-Paul stared him in the eyes. "And you want to own her, then punish her."

R.J. rapped his knuckles on the table. "You know I have an alibi for each murder. And you found nothing at my apartment to indicate I killed anyone. No evidence. No woman hidden away in my bed or tied in my secret chamber. That's because I'm innocent."

Jean-Paul fisted his hands, itching to punch Justice. "Did Elvira want it rough? And Ginger...did she beg to be tied up and screwed to death?"

R.J. merely stared at him. "You're chasing your tail because you don't have a clue as to how to stop this guy."

Jean-Paul stood and flexed his hands. Justice was right. Jean-Paul didn't have anything concrete on him. Just the gut feeling that he didn't like the man and that he was violent.

Could he be wrong about him as the killer?

The door squeaked open behind him and his partner cleared his throat. "Dubois, I need to see you for a minute."

Jean-Paul glared at Justice, then stalked through the door. "Dammit, he's not talking."

"Listen, Jean-Paul," Carson said. "A call just came in. There's a fire at that magazine office."

Jean-Paul's heart stopped. "God. Britta?"

"The firemen are on their way. But the building is in flames."

Jean-Paul raced for the exit. "Her apartment is above the office." He jogged toward the stairs. He had to get to Britta. He'd already lost one woman he loved. He couldn't let Britta die.

He had to save her.

A SCREAMING SOUND tore through the night. A siren? Her own cry of terror?

Britta stirred from unconsciousness, and tried to focus but the dark emptiness swirled around her. Her head throbbed. Heat scalded her face and neck.

She coughed and rolled sideways but smoke clogged her vision. Suddenly bright orange dots flickered into the darkness. Dear heavens, the building was on fire. She had to get out.

She tried to crawl toward the door, but pain stabbed her temple and she collapsed, coughing.

A siren wailed outside. Flames rippled toward her. Glass shattered and exploded and men's voices rose through the blaze. They were trying to get in but fire consumed the entrance.

Forcing herself into motion, she dragged herself toward the back door, but wood split and cracked, crumbling into a fiery blaze ahead of her. Tears filled her eyes. Both exits were blocked. There was no escape.

She closed her eyes, fighting panic. Seconds later, self-preservation kicked in. She had escaped the bayou monsters. She'd save herself now, too.

Smoke was rising; the flames crawled toward the steps. She covered her mouth with one hand and belly-crawled forward. One step. Two. Another. And another. She batted a patch of flames with her foot, then managed to make it up one step. One more. Then another.

Wood cracked and splintered behind her, trapping her. Panic welled in her chest. The acrid scent of burning wood and metal scorched the air and singed her skin. Another step. Another. A few more and she'd make it.

Then what? Her head felt fuzzy. Not a smart move to go up, but there was nowhere else to go. Make it to the window and crawl out the fire escape. Or jump if she had to. She would not die in this inferno.

Two more steps. Her head spun. Her arms and legs were so heavy she could barely move.

She collapsed on the landing. Wondered if R.J. had confessed. If Jean-Paul had found that missing girl, Debra.

She should have been honest with Jean-Paul. Trusted him for a moment. Despair nearly choked her. She wished she'd spent at least one night in his bed. But death was coming for her.

And she was running out of time before it claimed her.

HE WATCHED THE FLAMES in horror.

No! It wasn't time for Britta to die. Not like this. Not without his hands upon her. Not until she looked into his face and realized who he was. And why he'd come for her.

Not until he received the glory.

He started to run in to save her, but the fire truck raced up and police arrived. Too risky for him. They would rescue her.

A shadow moved in the distance. The alley. A man or a woman? The person who'd set the fire? Jesus. It was a woman. And she was running away, slinking into the darkness, leaving the havoc and the pain she'd caused behind her.

Rage splintered through his blood! He'd waited too long for his revenge for this girl to kill her. She had to pay for trying to ruin his plan.

Mindless with anger, he tore off after her.

As he ran through the alley, the night he'd chased Adrianna into the bayou bled through his fury. It was as if that night was happening all over again.

He was back in Black Bayou. Chasing the woman who'd hurt him. The backwoods screamed with the sound of the gators chomping. Bones crunching. Drums pounded out the ancient chants, the voodoo priestess hummed her spell and the witches made black magic.

He had tried so hard to be good. The perfect son. To please his father.

But the goddamn girls had taunted him just as the whores did today. Dancing naked. Skimming their hands over a man's body. Showing off flesh and skin that made a man's mouth water. Looking at him with lust in their eyes.

He had to destroy them.

The girl paused and leaned over to catch her breath in the corner alley. He grinned.

He had her.

Another one he'd add to his kingdom. At Mardi Gras, he would offer the ultimate sacrifice. The one who had started it all. The one who would redeem him from hell and allow him to enter the pearly gates of heaven.

A COLD KNOT OF FEAR cramped Jean-Paul's stomach as he ran toward the burning Naked Desires building. The entire downstairs was in flames, smoke swirling through the sky and street. Bystanders gawked as the firemen attached hoses and began to douse the flames. Two rescue men darted toward the back entrance and Jean-Paul followed.

"Britta Berger lives upstairs!" Jean-Paul yelled. "We have to rescue her." He lunged forward but the first guy grabbed him.

"Stand back and move out of the way, sir."

"Detective Dubois." Jean-Paul flashed his badge. "I know the woman. She might be trapped inside."

"We'll get her," the fireman shouted. "Wait here!"

The bigger man attacked the door with an ax while Jean-Paul ran to the side of the building where the fire escape snaked upward. He didn't see flames in the upstairs window yet. Maybe she was safe.

But why hadn't she climbed down the fire escape?

Sweat poured down his face from the heat, but he grabbed a metal trash can, scooted it over, then climbed on top of it so he could reach the fire escape. He caught the wrought-iron and swung himself upward. Once he latched on to the rail, he took the stairs two at a time. Smoke curled from the top of the building. Inside, wood shattered and boards splintered. Where the hell was Britta?

A crowd gathered around the side, gawking and watching. Someone shouted at him to stop but he forged on. Seconds later, Jean-Paul kicked the window and sent glass raining to the inside.

"Britta! Where are you?"

He covered his mouth with a handkerchief, then

climbed through the window and rushed through the apartment. She wasn't inside.

His heart raced as he hurried to the front door and checked the stairwell. Darkness cloaked the stairs while orange flames flickered and crawled toward his feet. The building was so old it would go up in minutes.

"Britta!"

Flames hissed and a board crashed to the floor in the hallway. He heard a low moan and spotted Britta lying on the landing. Heat scalded his face as he ran and checked her over.

Blood dotted her head and she moaned. "I've got you, baby." He hauled her up into his arms, turned and ran up the steps to her apartment. Fire nipped at his heels, eating the wood behind him.

A fireman met him at the top of the steps. "I'll take her."

"No, I've got her!" Jean-Paul pushed past him and carried her to the window. He climbed through the opening and started down the fire escape. She whimpered and he clutched her closer, his heart beating wildly.

"Jean-Paul…"

"Hang on. We'll be down in a second."

She snuggled into him, and faded back into unconsciousness. Jean-Paul's lungs tightened as the smoke choked him. A few minutes later and Britta could have died.

He climbed down the last two steps, then over onto the fireman's ladder and hurried to the ground, then ran around the building toward the ambulance. The paramedic jumped into action: helped him settle Britta onto a stretcher, placed an oxygen mask over her face, then checked her vitals.

Through the pandemonium, his partner headed toward him.

"Is she all right?" Carson asked.

Jean-Paul gripped his hands into fists. "I think so. But it was close."

"What happened?"

"I don't know. Get a couple of locals and canvass the crowd. See if anyone noticed anything."

"You think the fire was intentional?"

Jean-Paul shrugged. "My gut says this wasn't an accident. Either someone was attacking the magazine or trying to kill Britta. Or both."

BRITTA'S HEAD POUNDED. She struggled to open her eyes, but a haze of smoke and chaos clouded her vision. What had happened?

The last hour was a blur but she remembered seeing the fire. Jean-Paul...where was he? She was in an ambulance on the street. She whispered Jean-Paul's name, searching for his face. Then suddenly he was beside her.

"Shh," Jean-Paul murmured next to her ear. "You're safe now, Britta. I'm here."

She clutched his hand. She'd almost died tonight. She never wanted to let him go.

"Can you tell me what happened?" he asked.

She fought with the oxygen mask and nodded. "I heard the window crash. Then saw the fire."

He narrowed his eyes. "Someone started it?"

She nodded. "I think so. There was a noise outside. A fight. Protesters. Then a crash. And flames..." Her words faded into a cough, so Jean-Paul shoved the mask back over her mouth. She inhaled, felt the air soothing her throat, then lifted it again. "Jean-Paul, I tried to get down the steps. But someone attacked me."

"Did you see his face? Did he say anything?"

She shook her head; the world was spinning again. She felt light-headed, dizzy, as if she couldn't keep her eyes open. "No, it was too dark. And he came at me from behind."

She struggled to remain conscious. She owed Jean-Paul the truth about everything. But did she have the courage to tell him?

FOUR HOURS LATER. Midnight.

Jean-Paul had been called away from the hospital and had left Britta resting. Then he'd driven like demons were on his tail until he'd gotten here. The ME, Damon, locals and crime-scene techs swarmed the place. The location—only five miles from where they'd found the last victim.

He stared at the young girl's body, seething. Debra Schmale. A local hermit had found her and called it in when he'd happened onto the shanty after getting lost in the bayou. The poor guy had thrown up all over the rotting porch.

Jean-Paul sympathized. He'd seen the first three victims and it had looked ugly. But this time seemed more vile. More violent. Her eyes were painted grotesquely with black lines feathering all around her lids.

And blood was everywhere. It was almost as if this crime was more personal. Either that or the killer's blood-lust had grown stronger. He was more emotional. More enraged with hatred and anger. Not as methodical.

Which made him wonder if they were dealing with the same killer. Or if something had set the guy off.

Maybe he'd made a mistake, gotten sloppy, left some evidence.

The wind whistled through the dilapidated eaves of the shanty. Gators hissed in the background while the Mississippi churned through the labyrinth of waterways in the swamp.

Damon muttered a curse, and conferred with the ME.

In her desperation to escape, the poor girl had twisted her arms and wrists, causing layers of raw skin to peel away, exposing bone. Blood soaked her chest and had splattered the white sheets and walls. The mask of Sobek hung above her head by a rope attached to the ceiling.

Frustrated mumbles rumbled around him, everyone asking the same thing. Why hadn't they found this killer? Would they ever?

Damon's eyes shot to Jean-Paul and a moment of silent horror passed between them. Thankfully the parents weren't here to see their daughter in this condition.

"You have Justice in custody?" Damon asked.

Jean-Paul nodded. "What's the estimated time of death?"

"She's been dead a couple of hours."

"Then Justice couldn't have done it." Jean-Paul clenched his jaw.

"How about your other suspects?"

"Let's pick them up for questioning." Jean-Paul explained about the fire.

"Is the Berger woman going to make it?"

Jean-Paul nodded. "A few minutes later and she wouldn't have."

"Fire…" Damon arched a brow. "That doesn't fit our killer's MO."

"Neither does the level of violence here." Jean-Paul's phone jangled and he answered it. Antwaun. "Yeah?"

"Listen, Jean-Paul, the fire was definitely not accidental. Someone threw a torch inside. And trace discovered a female's acrylic nail on the landing where you found Britta."

"It's not Britta's," Jean-Paul said.

"I didn't think so."

"I'm with the fourth victim now." Jean-Paul scrubbed a hand over the back of his neck. "Our killer is male, he couldn't have been inside Britta's apartment attacking her."

So what the hell was going on? Were they dealing with two different killers? Or maybe two perps working together?

REVEREND CORTAIN WATCHED the frenzy on the streets, his blood sizzling. Firemen and rescue workers were still trying to save the building. Why in the world didn't they just let the place burn down to the ground?

Mazie Burgess, one of the popular local reporters, continued to talk into her microphone. The camera focused on her, but occasionally panned the crowd.

"Sources tell us that R.J. Justice, owner and publisher of *Naked Desires,* the building that caught fire tonight, is being held by the NOPD for questioning in the swamp-devil murders. No formal charges have been filed, but we'll keep you posted.

"Apparently, the editor of the popular Secret Confessions column, Britta Berger, who lives in an apartment above the magazine's office, was trapped in the fire. She has been hospitalized for smoke inhalation and has a slight concussion. No more details have been released at this time."

A man in a dark coat rushed over to speak to her, then she turned back to the crowd. "It appears that Britta Berger, the woman hurt in the fire earlier, has been receiving photos of the swamp devil's victims. Police have not divulged her part in the crimes, but an inside source claims that Miss Berger may be connected to the murders. We'll bring you more on this turn of events as it becomes available."

Cortain removed a cigar from his pocket, rolled the slender length between his fingers then removed the wrapper and sniffed the rich aroma. His gaze shot around the crowd and he noticed several followers at the scene. His sermon painting Britta as a guilty accessory to the debauchery on the streets had obviously fired up the mothers of the victims.

His plan was working perfectly.

The cold air chilled him and he hunched his shoulders, then slipped into the bar across the street. Decadent partiers were in full swing. But his gaze was riveted to the TV on the wall. Several patrons had gathered to watch the news coverage. He stepped into the thick group, wanting to remain anonymous.

Mazie cleared her throat. "More news, ladies and gentlemen. We've just received word that another woman has been found dead tonight at the hands of the swamp devil."

The cameras panned to Black Bayou, then zoomed in on a shanty in the midst of the bayou. Cops milled around the outside searching for clues. Anticipation boiled in Cortain's veins. He wished they'd show the inside of the shanty, let the world see the vile place where the woman had been left, how ugly she looked in death. How her flesh had already begun to rot. Her bones would soon be turning to dust. To know that the evil had been flushed from her body, her spirit now freed to return to good.

But the police forced the reporters behind the crime-scene tape as if to protect the world from the tawdry reality of death and her sins.

"So far, police have not revealed the woman's name or any details," Mazie continued, "but Detective Jean-Paul Dubois is collaborating with the FBI on the case. Unfortunately, there's no indication that the police are anywhere close to finding this serial killer and stopping his heinous murdering spree."

Cortain laughed at the foolish cops. Chasing their tails. They didn't have a clue as to how to catch this guy. Oh, well. The man was cleaning up their city for them, one whore at a time.

He was a hero.

The public should be cheering him on, not hunting him down like an animal.

CHAPTER SEVENTEEN

THREE O'CLOCK in the morning.

Dark shadows bathed the hospital room, sending chills cascading up and down Britta's arms. Thunder clouds rumbled outside, hinting at a storm. Where was Jean-Paul? With a fourth victim? Out searching for the killer?

Had he found him by now?

Britta's head throbbed and her throat was raw. Irrational desires made her wish that Jean-Paul would come to her during the night. But she had no right to wish for the impossible.

The familiar guilt stabbed her chest. Disturbing images of her past haunted her like choppy clips from an old horror film. The night she'd died in the bayou. Sometimes the gators gnawed at her flesh. Other times the monsters were men, the maniacs from the cult. Then she'd plunged from the dangers of the backwoods to streets where dark sinister beings stalked. Homeless, drug addicts, predators combing the alleys and bars for innocents.

And then there was Shack. The offers of prostitution. The thrill of some pretty clothes. The promise of independence.

"Stay with me, sugar," he'd whispered. "A girl like you will get rich in no time."

"It's simple," one of Shack's recruits had said. "One john. Another. Soon you get regulars. Beats Dumpster diving for food."

But Britta had fought the obvious. Then one day she'd finally understood. She had no choice. Desperation had driven her to Shack. After all, she'd been starving and had run out of fight.

Until the first man had touched her.

Then something had risen within her, a kind of angry self-preservation that she hadn't known she possessed. Or maybe she had—the reason she'd shot Reverend Tatum.

That fight had saved her from the cult and the bayou. It made her strike back again. The man had never known what had hit him. Then she'd run like hell.

Shack had beat her senseless.

But she'd sworn she'd never give in to him. And she'd found a way out. Ms. Lottie, a middle-aged woman who'd seen her own side of hell and back, had found Britta crying in a corner. She'd given her a room and helped her regain her self-respect. Since that day, Britta had sworn to do the same for others.

She wouldn't stop now. But all the good she'd done didn't change the fact that these women's deaths lay at her feet.

And that the killer remained at large.

Jean-Paul had been convinced of R.J.'s guilt. But R.J. was in jail. If he wasn't the killer, then who could it be?

The photographer who liked to capture women's eyes? Cortain or one of his followers? Maybe the boy who had chosen her as his bride—to be sacrificed, had survived. Maybe he was here in disguise, hoping to make her pay for killing his father.

Restless, she rolled into a ball. When she was little, she'd fold her body so small that it almost disappeared. Then she'd become invisible, like a fleck of dust on the wall.

But the monsters always found her, as if they had eyes in the back of their head. Not this time, she thought groggily. Jean-Paul would find the swamp devil and destroy him.

For just a moment, she allowed herself to dream that the monsters were gone. That the world was full of beautiful colors. That she was lying in bed with Jean-Paul.

That nothing could tear them apart.

But she was lying to herself and she knew it.

JEAN-PAUL DROVE LIKE a maniac to the precinct, his system wired. The press had launched an attack on him as if *he* was the swamp devil. Only Mazie had defended him.

Dammit, he'd never deserved the hero status they'd given him. And he didn't want it now. All he wanted was to do his job.

He heard Debra Schmale's mother's sobs as he entered the station. Saw his lieutenant tackling the impossible. Promising her parents that everything would be all right when they all knew it wouldn't. Uncomfortable with emotional outbursts, Carson gave him a helpless look as if he needed saving. Jean-Paul sucked in a sharp breath, joined them and offered his condolences.

Mrs. Schmale dabbed a tissue under her red-rimmed swollen eyes. "My Debra was a good girl. She wasn't like those hookers that got killed."

"She barely even dated," the father said. "I don't understand how this could happen."

"Why would he kill her?" Mrs. Schmale cried. "Why? She didn't dance at those strip bars like those other girls."

"And she didn't have sex with strangers," Mr. Schmale argued. "There's some kind of horrible mistake."

"Had your daughter been acting odd lately?" Jean-Paul asked. "Maybe hanging out with some new friends?"

Mrs. Schmale frowned. "She refused to go with us to church on Sunday. Came out dressed in a short skirt. Said she was twenty and would do what she wanted."

The girl's father bowed his head into his hands. "I was mad. I told her not to come back." He choked on the words. "But I didn't mean it…."

Jean-Paul chewed the inside of his cheek. Poor guy. He understood the guilt. "She didn't mention a name?"

They both shook their heads, looking bewildered.

Carson cleared his throat. "I'll take a look at the house. Maybe there's something in her room that might tell us more."

"Does your daughter have a computer?" Jean-Paul asked.

Mr. Schmale nodded.

"We'd like to look at that, too," Carson said. "Maybe her e-mail will tell us who she's been seeing."

The couple agreed, still protesting that they wouldn't find anything incriminating against their daughter in the files. But often enough parents didn't know what there kids were into. Then again, what if they were right? What if the killer's MO had changed?

It happened. A slight variation just to up the game. A different kind of victim—not just hookers now, but any girl who dressed a certain way. Something to throw off the cops.

Sweat beaded on his lip. Any MO change would make it harder for them to catch this guy. And if word spread that the swamp devil was targeting all young girls, not just prostitutes, panic on the streets would rise.

Phelps headed to the coffee machine, while Jean-Paul and Carson ducked into a side office. "Did you find out anything about the fire?" Jean-Paul asked.

Carson shrugged, noncommittal. "A bystander saw two women hanging around who looked suspicious. One of them sounds like Ginger Holliday's mother."

Jean-Paul arched a brow. "But why attack the magazine?"

"Maybe they saw the story on Miss Berger and the fact that the killer contacted her."

Jean-Paul gritted his teeth. "And Cortain's rantings against the magazine haven't helped. He's encouraging violence by stirring up emotions."

Carson made a clicking sound with his teeth. "Probably. His sermons tend to create a rise in people instead of calming them down."

Exactly what Cortain wanted. More publicity for himself. And he was practically glorifying the swamp devil. And Britta was caught in the middle.

"Did our UNSUB send the Berger woman a photo of Debra Schmale?" Carson asked.

Jean-Paul shook his head. "Not so far. If he heard about the fire, he might not. But I'm going to take one by and show her. See if she recognizes the girl."

"I'll check out the house," Carson said. "And the computer."

"Let's put a team on the street, too," Jean-Paul said. "If Debra wasn't a hooker or dancer, maybe someone in the Quarter saw her."

SHADOWS DARKENED the corners of the bayou where monsters lay in waiting. Britta's nightmares launched her back in time.

She struggled to make herself small as she scooted deeper into the corner of the tiny cabin. After running miles through the brush and mud, terrified of the gators and snakes, she'd stumbled upon the shanty in the dark and had crawled inside, hoping to seek shelter until morning. Once dawn broke and sunlight shone through the massive trees, she would find her way out. From there, she didn't know where she'd go.

But she would not go back to the cult.

Fresh tears rolled down her cheeks. She brushed them away, battling back the sobs that wracked her. She was all alone now. She had no one to help her. No one to protect her.

Her mother's face flashed into her mind. What was she doing? Were the cult members blaming her for Britta's escape? Would they hurt her?

She should go back but terror seized her.

No, her mother had to be all right. She had done what they'd said. It was Britta who'd defied them. In fact, her mother was probably drugged again. Furious with Britta for running away.

And for killing their leader.

If they found her, what would they do? Lynch her from a tree? Send her to prison?

The hiss of a snake broke the silence, its warning stirring other night sounds outside. The gators. The birds. Maybe bats that survived in the woodlands.

The whisper of someone's breath floated over her. Footsteps sounded. Then a man's hand clamped down over her mouth. She bit into flesh. Tasted sweat and dirt. Nausea clawed at her stomach.

She kicked and screamed but he shoved something over her face. He was going to smother her.

She shoved her feet at him and tried to buck upward, but he was too heavy.

She couldn't breathe…she was choking.

Outside, another sound rose above the forest. Not an animal. Voices.

Human voices. The rattle of machinery.

She jerked her eyes open, but darkness filled the room. The stench was acidic. The pressure on her throat so strong and forceful that she couldn't breathe.

The nightmare was real. Except she wasn't in the bayou but in a hospital bed. And someone was trying to gag her. One of the doctors. He was dressed in surgical scrubs and mask.

She tried to pry the pair of steel hands from her mouth, but his grip tightened and he raised a hypodermic.

Desperate and weak, she kicked at him and reached out for something to protect herself, something to use as a weapon. The sheets, bedding…the metal tray…. She fumbled but grabbed the edge and slammed it into his side. He loosened his grip for a fraction of a second and dropped the needle.

She rolled off the bed. "Help!" Her voice was so hoarse from the smoke inhalation, the sound died in the air.

He lurched toward her and she fumbled again and knocked the chair. It skidded into the wall and slammed against the night table. A metal pan rattled.

Outside, footsteps sounded.

The shadow hesitated, then must have realized

someone was coming because he growled, grabbed the hypodermic from the floor, and ran through the door.

She crawled sideways, gasping for air, her head spinning.

JEAN-PAUL'S CELL PHONE rang. This time, the hospital. His heart thumped wildly. "Detective Dubois."

"Detective, this is Dr. Samson at New Orleans General. I'm calling about the woman you brought in last night—"

"What's wrong? Is she all right?"

"Yes, but we had an incident a few minutes ago."

His jaw tightened. "What kind of an incident?"

"Miss Berger claims that someone attacked her."

Jean-Paul cursed, then rushed toward the door. Dammit, he'd thought she was safe there.

He never should have left her alone.

Vowing not to do so again, he jumped in his car. Time passed in slow motion, but when Jean-Paul looked at the clock as he entered the hospital, he saw that it had only taken him ten minutes to reach Britta. His pulse raced as he rushed into her room.

She looked pale and shaken and so damn beautiful his heart clenched. She'd almost died twice tonight. It was all he could do not to take her in his arms.

"Jean-Paul?"

"What happened?"

The doctor glanced up over bifocals. "She's going to be all right."

"Someone tried to gag me," Britta said.

Jean-Paul barely smothered an obscenity. "I want to look at your security cameras."

The doctor nodded. Jean-Paul ordered a local who'd

responded to the call from the security office to stand by Britta's door. Seconds later, he viewed the tapes. Nothing too suspicious at first. Then a person in a green surgical suit had quietly slipped off the elevator onto the third floor. He kept his head down, avoiding the camera and a cap and surgical mask hid his face.

Jean-Paul continued to search through the tapes, watching as the figure ran from the room a few minutes later. Again, he maintained a low profile, kept his head low, avoided the cameras. He'd merged into the elevator with a group of doctors as if he belonged. When the doors opened on the main floor, the man slid out unnoticed, still wearing the surgical garb.

Damn. He hoped he'd discarded it in the hospital so they could find it and look for forensics. No such luck.

He took a copy of the tapes so Damon could have the FBI's forensics team analyze it. Maybe if they enlarged the photo and zoomed in on the face, they'd find something.

He'd get his team on it. *He* had to get back to Britta.

She was in danger and he didn't trust anyone else to protect her but himself.

BRITTA WANTED TO GO home. But where was home?

Her apartment was in shambles. Her belongings probably had smoke damage. And there was really nothing personal there to save.

Except for the photo of her mother. Even if the rest of the album was empty, that one picture was the only connection she had. Was it safe and intact?

Jean-Paul strode in, looking haggard. She saw the guilt, the self-recriminations on his face. He didn't deserve to blame himself for what happened to her.

"We reviewed the tapes," he said quietly. "There was a man in surgical scrubs. I saw him come in, then leave your room. But we couldn't get a look at his face. I'm sending the tapes to the feds for them to review."

Britta nodded. "It happened so fast. I wish I could identify him."

Jean-Paul clenched his jaw, then closed the distance between them. "The girl we found earlier, Debra Schmale." He removed a picture from his jacket and thrust it toward her. "Do you recognize her?"

Britta's fingers trembled as she studied the picture. "Oh my God, Jean-Paul. She's just a kid."

"Twenty," Jean-Paul said. "Her mother swears she wasn't a hooker. She just ran away on Sunday."

Britta narrowed her eyes at him. "So she's not the swamp devil's usual target?"

"No."

She studied the picture again. "You know, I think I saw this girl. In the market, just the other day."

"What was she doing?"

Britta tried to sort through the haze of scattered memories. "Looking at the art. At the dolls one of the street guys sells."

"Voodoo dolls?"

"No, porcelain ones." Britta thought back. "A guy named Teddy sells them."

"Like the ones in that drawer you have?"

Britta twisted her fingers together. "Yes."

"My niece has some like that."

"I know, I saw Catherine and Chrissy buy one the other day."

Jean-Paul sucked in a sharp breath. "I have to talk to this guy."

A cold chill engulfed Britta. "You think Teddy might be the swamp devil?"

"You don't?"

"He seems really harmless," Britta said. "He's shy. And he stutters. He certainly doesn't talk to women or seem violent."

"Appearances can be deceiving. Do you know his last name?"

"No. He doesn't have a business card or a Web site, either."

Odd. Jean-Paul knotted his hands in frustration. "Then I'll have to wait until morning to find him."

"I'll go with you and show you where he sets up his stand."

"No, you have to rest. I'm standing a guard outside your door. And I'll pick you up when the doctor releases you."

Britta fidgeted with the sheets. "You try to protect everyone, Jean-Paul."

He ran a hand down his neck, his voice gruff when he spoke. "I've already failed miserably. He almost got you." His voice cracked. "Twice."

"I'm still alive," she said softly. "I told you I could take care of myself."

He shifted awkwardly, started to reach for her hand, then seemed to withdraw and backed away. "I'll be back later."

She nodded and he left, leaving her alone. He'd said he'd pick her up when the doctor released her, but where would he take her? She wanted to go home with him.

But what would Jean-Paul want?

One day before Mardi Gras

JEAN-PAUL HIT THE STREETS at daybreak. The newspapers and TV had splattered news of the fourth victim all over the place. His name was virtually mud along with the killer's.

He staked out the street, waiting on Teddy to set up his booth. Time crawled by. Hours passed but the guy didn't show. Meanwhile, Jean-Paul questioned dozens of artists and locals. They remembered the dolls, although no one knew Teddy's name, where he lived or anything else about him. He was quiet. Shy. Nondescript. He wouldn't hurt a fly.

Not exactly the profile of a serial killer.

Then again, in other ways, he fit the profile exactly. He was a white male, early twenties. Stuttering was a sign of inferiority. Although Britta hadn't mentioned him stuttering on the phone, perhaps the anonymity eased his nervousness, made him feel more in control. The fact that he was withdrawn, didn't call attention to himself, that he lacked self-confidence and was a loner were indicators.

He blended into the crowd perfectly.

And any woman he approached would probably trust him because of his demeanor and the nature of his craft.

If only he had a last name. But Britta had been right. He hadn't passed out business cards as most of the artists did. And Jean-Paul found no evidence of a Web site or that his work had been displayed in any of the local shops or museums. It was almost as if he existed only on the streets.

An ideal cover for a serial killer. He'd left no paper trail. No way to trace him.

Once again, the police were stalled for leads.

By late afternoon, Jean-Paul wanted to hit something. He'd had a police artist visit Britta and they were now passing around a sketch of this guy Teddy. He'd even called Mazie Burgess and asked her to run it. And he'd spent the rest of the day trying to track down all their suspects and account for them.

Adding more fuel to the flame of questions tormenting him, Antwaun phoned to say that the fingernail they'd found in Britta's stairwell had belonged to their fourth victim, Debra Schmale. He hadn't quite put the pieces of the puzzle together. Were Debra and this guy Teddy involved? Had she known about the murders and helped him or hidden his identity? But why would she attack Britta?

His gut still told him Cortain was involved somehow, maybe even Justice. But how?

Reverend Cortain had a horde of worshipers who would vouch for his whereabouts the night before. Randy Swain had been seen at a local bar, then he'd had his own private party with two fans he'd met over drinks. Justice had still been in jail, but they'd had to release him midmorning. Jean-Paul had stopped by the booth where Howard Keith's "eyes" display had been, but Keith claimed to have an alibi, too. Jean-Paul had called in for a search warrant to the man's place, although Keith had insisted that he had been painting the night before. He even had a live subject. One of his customers from the street had commissioned him to do a portrait of her eyes.

Sounded like the two of them belonged together.

Before heading to the hospital, he stopped by Britta's apartment to pick up some clothes for her, but the entire contents of the place smelled like smoke. He didn't have a clue as to what size she wore or how to buy her clothes, so he stopped at his parents' restaurant and explained the situation. Stephanie and Catherine jumped into motion, running to shop for Britta.

His mother forced him to sit down and eat some gumbo. "You look exhausted, son. You need to rest."

"I'll rest when this guy is locked up, Maman."

She patted his back as if he was a child. "You aren't the world's keeper, son. You do your best—that's all anyone can do."

"I let Lucinda down," he said in a low voice.

Unshed tears glittered in his mother's eyes. "She let you down, too, son. She admitted to me that she begged you to quit the force. I told her she was wrong to ask such a thing. You love a man for who he is. You do not try to change him."

Jean-Paul sipped his tea with a frown. He had no idea his parents were aware of the problems in his marriage. "Maybe she was right. If I had quit, she'd still be alive."

"You are a man of honor." She shook her head. "And we are proud of you, Jean-Paul. Lucinda's death was unfortunate, but you saved countless others. And you've punished yourself enough." She refilled his tea. "Now, don't let guilt keep you from finding happiness with another."

His gaze swung to hers. *"Maman—"*

"Shh. Don't argue with your mother. Eat up and remember what I said."

His sisters rushed inside in a flurry of chatter.

"We put together an overnight bag with some clothes," Stephanie said. "Britta's about my size so I hope things fit."

"We also stopped at the drug store and bought some toiletries," Catherine said.

Jean-Paul hugged his sisters. "I'm sure she'll appreciate it."

"Let us know if you need anything else, Jean-Paul," Stephanie told him.

Catherine gave him a peck on the cheek. "For what it's worth, I agree with Britta. I can't imagine that dollmaker as the swamp devil. He's too nice, too...nerdy."

"Just stay off the streets until this guy is caught," he warned them. "Most serial killers look sane and blend in with the rest of us. And some of them were nerds, targets for bullies as kids."

The Lundi Gras celebration by the river was in full swing as he left. He ducked through the alley to avoid the congestion, then climbed into his car and headed toward the hospital.

It was crazy to take Britta to his place. She was a potential witness in a crime. A possible victim.

And he was not supposed to be involved with her.

But he refused to let her return to that smoky apartment alone. If he had to play bodyguard to keep her safe, then he'd damn well do it.

BRITTA PACED THE hospital room, her nerves on edge. The sky was dark, daylight disappearing once again, and the swamp devil was still roaming the streets.

She had watched the news. Seen the paper. Knew the press was crucifying Jean-Paul. And that he must be going crazy.

She had to see him. Get out of this room. She felt like a virtual prisoner.

The guard outside had not left his post, but stationing him by her side had invaded her privacy. When she'd tried to walk down the hall to the nurses' station to beg them to dismiss her, he'd refused to let her leave the room. Then she'd summoned the doctor to check herself out, but he'd insisted she stay a few more hours until all her tests came back clear.

This was what it would be like if she told Jean-Paul the truth about her past, that she had taken a man's life. She'd go to prison. Only jail would be worse because she'd be locked up with other dangerous criminals.

Did she deserve to be punished?

Jean-Paul Dubois, local hero, would say yes. He was the letter of the law. Even now, he was tracking down the swamp devil.

The door screeched open and she spun around. Jean-Paul stood in the door with a small overnight bag. He looked haggard. He needed a shave and dark circles rimmed his eyes.

Their gazes locked and she wanted to launch herself into his arms. But would he want her?

"My sisters gathered some things for you. I hope it'll do."

Emotions surged through her. She'd never had sisters, never had anyone do something so thoughtful. "Thank you."

He set them on the bed. "If you want to get dressed, the doctor's preparing your papers to release you."

Thank God. But the memory of her burning building rose, gray and depressing. "Did the firemen save my apartment?"

"The structure's intact," he said. "But there's smoke and water damage inside. It'll take time to repair."

She hugged her arms around her waist, feeling lost.

"I stopped by and got this. I thought you might want it."

She narrowed her eyes as he reached inside his pocket. Then he handed her the photograph of her and her mother, and tears filled her eyes. "Jean-Paul..." She hugged it to her chest, overcome. "Thank you."

He gave a clipped nod and she wanted to hug him but forced herself to remain still. Her lies still stood between them.

"You're going home with me," he said in a quiet voice.

Britta stared into his eyes, searching for any hint that his intention was personal. But the steadfast hero cop was looking back at her. God help her, she wanted him so badly she hurt. But he deserved so much better.

He stepped into the hallway and she opened the overnight bag and dug inside, anxious to leave. Jeans and a soft cotton shirt; both fit her although the shirt was a little tight. She blushed, wondering what his sisters had thought when they'd chosen the sexy undergarments for her. Did they have any idea how much she wanted to sleep with their brother?

Jean-Paul knocked on the door, then pushed it open slightly. "Are you ready?"

She nodded. "Yes, let's get out of here."

During the ride to his house, she tried to remind herself that she didn't belong to Jean-Paul or his world. Getting involved with her might jeopardize his career, especially if the public found out about her past. She was selfish to want him. To even contemplate being with him. But she couldn't stop herself. She'd never known what it was like to crave another human being so much that you physically ached.

And she'd never wanted to please a man the way she wanted to please him.

For the first time in her life, she wished she could change the past. She'd still have run on D-day, but she wouldn't have picked up that gun. Then the preacher wouldn't have died and that suicide pact would never have been made.

Her heart clenched. She had all those deaths on her conscience, too. Just as she did the swamp devil's victims.

JEAN-PAUL COULDN'T SHAKE the feeling that Britta was on the killer's list. That she would be next. And that the killer's pattern had changed to throw them off.

"Did you find Teddy?" Britta asked.

"No. He's disappeared. And none of the other street artists seemed to know him very well, either." Which made him look even guiltier. "I sent the sketches around. Hopefully we'll get a lead and find him."

The gray sky mimicked his dismal mood as he pulled into the long oak-lined drive leading to his house. He felt so damn helpless. But the FBI and police were working round the clock. Antwaun was watching the House of Love for anyone suspicious and he'd taken Teddy's picture to see if the bartender or dancers recognized him from the club. Carson checked Debra Schmale's computer but that was another dead end. No secret love affairs on the Internet, notes to strangers or dating services.

"I wish he'd contact me again," Britta said in a low voice. "Maybe I should go back to my apartment for that reason."

"I've already arranged to have your phone calls routed to my house," Jean-Paul said. "That way if he calls, we can talk to him."

"But if he's watching my place and I don't return, he'll know I'm not home so he won't call."

Jean-Paul gave her a sharp look and cut the engine. He knew what she was thinking and it scared the crap out of him. "You're not going to go back and set a trap, so don't even suggest it."

"But, Jean-Paul—"

He pressed a finger to her lips to cut her off. "Shh. Trust me, Britta. I don't want you hurt."

The look of guilt that crossed her face mirrored his own emotions. "Stop blaming yourself, Britta."

"But he's killing these women to taunt me."

Her voice broke and his heart clenched. "He's killing these women because he's a sociopath. You didn't make him that way." He squeezed her hand. "Now, let's go inside. It's starting to rain."

She grew quiet as they entered his house. The familiar scent of wood and fresh paint usually soothed him, but his body was wound too tight tonight for his home to offer comfort.

Britta seemed to survey the remodeling, her gaze landing on the photos on the sofa table. His family, sisters, brothers, Chrissy. Lucinda.

He had an entire shelf of pictures while she had one lone photo of her mother.

Britta gestured toward the picture of his wife. "Who was she?"

Jean-Paul cleared his throat. He didn't want to talk about her tonight.

"Jean-Paul?"

The way she said his name tore him in knots. "My wife."

Britta's gaze met his. "She's beautiful. Where is she now?"

Jean-Paul closed his eyes and spun around. He couldn't bare to admit the truth and watch the disappointment in her eyes. "She was killed after the hurricane."

Her soft gasp filled the silence. "I'm so sorry, Jean-Paul. You must have loved her very much."

He had, once, when he was just a kid. "It's my fault she died."

There, he'd said it. The truth was out.

Now Britta knew he wasn't a hero.

He was a man who'd failed his family.

BRITTA'S HEART SWELLED with grief. "Jean-Paul, outside you told me not to blame myself for the swamp devil's victims. You can't blame yourself, either—"

"But it *was* my fault." His voice sounded gritty, rough with pain. "She was working in a small store when the hurricane hit. She begged me to come and pick her up, for us to evacuate, but I refused to leave. I told her to go on without me."

"You had to work," Britta argued. "You were doing your job."

"My job was to protect the town, to protect my own damn wife." He scrubbed his hand over his face. "But I failed that, too. Looters went in, things went crazy. She tried to call me, but some guy panicked and shot her. She died before I got there."

"You didn't pull the trigger, Jean-Paul," Britta said. "It was a horrible time. Everyone was crazy, panicked, scared. All those prisoners were released."

"Excuses. Don't you understand, Britta?" His voice

was harsh. "She died while I was out playing hero to someone else."

"She died because she was in the wrong place at the wrong time," Britta said earnestly. "And she should have listened to you and left earlier."

He looked so tortured that she closed her hand over his. "It's all right, Jean-Paul. Let it go." She traced a finger along his cheek, then pressed a kiss to his jaw. He was the most honorable man she'd ever known and she wanted to erase his pain.

He didn't deserve to carry the weight of the world on his shoulders.

Jean-Paul gripped her arms, his dark eyes piercing. "Britta…"

"I know I'm not Lucinda, I could never be like her," she whispered. "But I'm here, Jean-Paul, here with you tonight." She pressed another kiss to his lips, this one soft and inviting, filled with the whisper of desire. She needed him. Wanted him. He had to know that.

Silence stretched between them for an excruciating second, emotions warring in his eyes. But finally, he lowered his mouth to her ear and groaned. "I don't want her," he said in a gruff voice. "I want you, Britta. I have ever since I met you."

Then he cupped her face in his hands, lowered his head and kissed her.

CHAPTER EIGHTEEN

JEAN-PAUL TOLD HIMSELF to stop.

But his brain refused to listen.

He had wanted Britta for so long now, and she was in his arms, alive and wanting him in return. Hunger burned his veins as she threaded her fingers into his hair, and he forgot about Lucinda and conversation as he deepened the kiss.

Britta was everything he'd ever wanted in a woman. Strong. Brave. A fighter.

Yet a tenderness lay beneath her toughness. He tore his mouth away and looked into her eyes, unsure he should continue. "Are you certain you want this?"

"I've never wanted anything more," she whispered raggedly.

Her eyes looked stormy, her breath was erratic and her fingers sank deeper into his hair. She teased his lips apart with her tongue and he dragged her closer, so close he felt her breasts press against his chest. She moaned and darted her tongue along his lips and then down his neck, until he groaned her name.

The one thing he'd learned from his wife's death was that life could be taken in a nanosecond.

He had to live for the present.

And tonight, for just a little while, he wanted to

forget that a killer was out there. That he had failed to stop him from murdering more than once.

That he wanted Britta.

Because as long as she was in his arms, the man couldn't touch her. No other man could.

One second, logic and reason warned him to go slow. The next, she rubbed her hand down to his crotch and resistance fled. He grabbed her hand and held it to his chest, unable to stand the torture. He wanted to touch her, to taste every inch. And she was driving him wild. Whispering his name. Teasing him with those luscious touches. Pleading with him to take her with fiery eyes.

His body caught on fire with sensation as he walked her backward to the sofa, then he unfastened the top button of her shirt. She kissed his neck while he trailed his tongue down her ear and to the soft swell of her breasts. She yanked at his shirt, practically ripping the buttons free and he pushed it off his shoulders and tossed it to the floor. A sliver of moonlight painted her body in a golden glow. He savored the moment, memorizing the sight of her bare skin as he stripped off her bra and held her breasts in his hands. His mouth came next, hungry and hot, licking and lapping her up, suckling her until she cried out his name. Shivers of anticipation rode through her and she clung to his arms but he didn't stop. Hunger consumed him, drove him faster and he tore at her jeans, stripping them off as he eased her onto the couch. Her hair was mussed, wild around her face, while her big eyes danced with desire.

He licked his lips at the sight of her bare legs. They went on for miles. Then the lacy panties, black, see-through, they covered nothing. Yet they were still too much.

He peeled them off, licking and teasing her

stomach, then down to the insides of her thighs. She quivered and reached for his hands, but he pushed her back on the sofa, spread her legs and buried his head between them. He hadn't tasted a woman in two years, had never had the desire to eat her inside out, but he did with Britta. She clawed at his arms, then moaned and whispered his name. He drove his tongue inside her, his body hardening as her sweet juices filled his mouth.

She tasted like sweetness and spice. Innocence and sin.

He relished the moment, delving deeper and holding her tighter as her body spasmed its release.

"Jean-Paul…"

He finished licking her moist center, then rose above her, a satisfied man. But only for a moment. His cock twitched, begging for fulfillment, to be inside her hot center.

He kicked off his jeans, threw them across the floor, then crawled on top of her and braced his hands on the couch beside her face. A sultry look darkened her eyes, and she cupped her hands on his butt, then raked her nails downward, pulling him to her. His cock rubbed her belly, twitched again with arousal and thickened more. The waiting was almost painful, the most seductive torture he'd ever endured.

Then she wrapped her bare legs around his waist and kissed his lips. He lowered his hips enough to stroke her folds with his length, then saw her face flame with passion. She wanted more.

His heart pounded as he pushed himself inside her. She was so tight. He hesitated, giving her body time to adjust, then thrust deeper, deeper, all the way inside her wet heat. But she cried out and he stilled.

His gaze swung to hers. Shock hit him in the gut. She felt so tight, as if she'd never been with a man. Impossible. He'd seen her on the street, his brother had said…

"Britta?"

She bit down on her lip and pulled at his hips, embedding him deeper inside her. "Please don't stop, Jean-Paul. I want you so much."

He searched her face. Saw a small flicker of pain in her eyes, yet he also read desire mingled there. The questions he wanted to ask had to wait. They were both hurting, yearning, on fire.

If this was her first, dammit he should have taken it slow. Not mauled her on the sofa like a sex-starved teenager. Recriminations raced through his head. What kind of man was he?

Certainly not a hero in her eyes….

He pulled away slightly. Stood. But she grabbed his hand. Her fingers suddenly found his cock. Stroked him. His cock pulsed harder, throbbing for release. Tension built inside him, all the way to his soul.

More than anything, he wanted this woman, wanted to be closer, deeper, wanted her harder and faster.

"Please, Jean-Paul. We need each other tonight."

Her soft plea echoed in his head. Drove him crazy because she was right.

She dropped to her knees on the floor and flicked her tongue across the tip of his penis. A sharp bolt of excitement shot through him. Naked, on her hands and knees, she looked like a vixen.

He wanted to be inside her, coming completely.

He grabbed his pants, removed a condom and rolled

it on, his hands shaking. She smiled, sultry and catlike, then pulled him to the rug. He cupped her face in his hands and kissed her and traced her fingers over his length, urging his cock to stroke her. He growled and rubbed his length over her belly. Her hiss coaxed him on, making him even more engorged and greedy.

Then he thrust inside her, sucking in a sharp breath as she spread her legs wider to take him in. His pulse raced with desire and he pounded her harder, sliding his hands beneath her hips to angle her so he could grind deeper. Hungrily, he kissed her neck, then lower, teasing her nipples with his tongue, biting and sucking until she cried out, mindless with pleasure. He moved faster, stroking and building the rhythm, faster and harder, deeper, then more. Over and over until they were one, dancing together, making love. Over and over, until his body stiffened and shook with tremors.

She whispered his name. He moaned hers in return.

Together they climaxed, their bodies jerking and quivering out of control. He was lost in the intensity of the moment. Lost to stop his emotions from rocketing through him.

Lost as to how he'd ever tell her goodbye.

But he would when the case ended. He'd go back to his job. She'd go back to her life. He'd never marry again. Never fall in love.

And he knew Britta wouldn't cling to him. Wouldn't ask him to change or give up his job.

She'd accept that it was over.

But tonight…he pressed a kiss to her neck and rolled them to his side where he could take his weight off her. Where he could hold her all night. They lay there, panting and stroking, murmuring words of lust, whispering their pleasure. Finally, the air grew cool and he stood and carried her to bed, then wrapped them in the covers.

He fully intended to show her a romantic night. Prove to her that a man could make slow love to her. That he didn't have to be an animal and take her on the floor.

The gift she'd given him was as pure and unselfish as any a woman could give a man. He didn't deserve it.

But she'd given it to him anyway.

He would find the man who was after her and take him apart limb by limb. To hell with his job.

If the man hurt one hair on Britta's beautiful head, he'd kill him with his bare hands. He'd even give up his badge to protect her.

BRITTA'S BODY TINGLED with the aftermath of their love-making. She'd never thought she'd be able to share her body with a man as she had with Jean-Paul. They had made love three times now and it was only midnight. She wanted him again.

But guilt splintered the euphoria that had spread through her limbs. Jean-Paul had needed her tonight and she needed him on the most elemental level. But she also needed him on another level.

One that she had no right to ask.

She had to confess the truth.

But would she lose what little respect she'd gained from him?

Still, Jean-Paul didn't deserve for the town to look down upon him. And she couldn't continue lying to him and keeping secrets.

He nuzzled her neck, then propped two pillows

against the headboard for them and looked down at her. His eyes searched her face, his expression probing.

"Why did you let me believe you were experienced?"

His gruff voice skated over her nerve endings, arousing, but his question cut straight to the issues at hand.

She finger-combed her hair and tugged the sheet up to cover her bare breasts. Renewed tension filled the air, this time threatening her newfound closeness with the man beside her.

"I…don't know," she said. "Maybe it was easier than trying to explain."

He angled himself sideways, tucked a strand of hair behind her ear. The gesture was so intimate she wanted to cry.

Damn, she never cried. Not over a man.

"Britta?"

She twisted the sheet in her fingers, her heart thumping. God, she didn't want to ruin this moment. She wanted it to last forever.

He covered her hands with his, pried them loose from the sheets, then kissed her fingers. "Trust me. Tell me the truth."

She blinked back emotions. Took one look into his eyes and her heart swelled in her chest. She was in love with Jean-Paul Dubois. She had no idea when or how it had happened. She had known better than to let her heart get involved.

But she had lost herself to him anyway. Maybe the first time she'd seen him.

Still, the guilt…the other girls' lives rested on her head. All because she'd selfishly protected herself.

So she had to tell him the truth. But she couldn't look

into his eyes. Instead, she lowered their hands, stared at their entwined fingers and prayed that he could forgive her.

"When I was a little girl," she began, "my mother… she worked as a dancer at one of the clubs in town." She heard his breathing, but refused to look at him or she'd lose her courage. "I saw her turn tricks, give herself to earn money. I…hated it, but I loved her. She was doing what she had to do, she said, to take care of me."

He didn't comment, but she remembered his reaction to their conversation at the House of Love. Still she had to finish.

"When I was twelve, my mother joined a religious cult."

His fingers tightened on hers. "The one that Justice's family belonged to?"

She nodded. "Maybe. I swear, Jean-Paul, I didn't remember him. I didn't know him at all."

"But he remembers you."

Because of what she'd done. "My mother and I weren't there long." She paused, recalling her mother's excitement over joining the group. "My mother thought the group would be our salvation. She would become one of the reverend's wives and it would get her off the streets."

"One of his wives?" Jean-Paul asked.

"Yes." Britta shivered, remembering the disgust she'd felt when she'd realized the truth. "The cult had a lot of odd practices." She expounded on some of the rituals. "Polygamy for one. They were afraid of the gators, so they offered sacrifices to them just as the people did in medieval times. The women were submissive, taught to share their husbands. And the young girls and boys went through a rite of passage as they aged. At sixteen, a boy chose a girl to become his first wife."

"At sixteen?"

She nodded, lost in the past. "Any girl thirteen and older was up to be offered. They built a big bonfire, dressed the girls in virginal outfits and presented them to the boys. The girls were also bathed earlier, anointed with body oils, made to smell sensual to entice the boys to choose them."

Jean-Paul cleared his throat. "You were one of them?"

She heard the censure in his voice. Glanced up and saw his eyes darken to a stormy hue. "Some of the people came from witches' covens. They chanted and concocted spells to ward off evil."

Jean-Paul's jaw tightened and he released her hand. She stared into the darkness as he rose and went to the window and stared out. If she finished her story, he would look at her differently.

He already was. She sensed him pulling away from her. Felt the anger radiating from him. The condemnation. Knew that he'd never want her again.

She drew her legs up beneath the covers. Wrapped her arms around her knees and curled into a knot. She had once been so small she could roll herself into a ball. Make herself disappear. Become invisible. She wanted to do that again.

Run. Hide. Make herself like a little piece of dust in the sand. But she had to finish now. Had to finally own up to what she'd done, to the bad girl inside.

Because her confession might help him find the killer.

JEAN-PAUL'S JAW ACHED from gritting his teeth. He'd wondered about Britta's past. Had guessed that she'd grown up on the streets, that her mother might have even been a hooker.

But he'd never suspected that she'd traded her daughter for a safer existence, a way to get off her back. And she'd agreed to a polygamist relationship?

Why? Had she thought one night a week with a man more appealing than a night with twenty johns? He supposed the deal seemed sweet. But at the expense of marrying her daughter at thirteen? Forcing her into sex?

No wonder Britta didn't trust any man. God…

But she gave herself to you.

What had he done to deserve such an honor?

"Jean-Paul?"

Uncertainty laced her voice. He had to hear the rest. But it pained him to know how she'd been treated, that no one had loved her or taken care of her.

"Go on. Please."

He tried to bottle his reaction, but anger coiled inside him. She'd tucked her legs up and leaned her head on her knees. She looked impossibly small, as if she might disappear under the covers any second, never to come out again. He couldn't imagine her childhood and hated the people who'd hurt her. Her mother included.

"A few weeks after we went there, they had one of the ceremonies. One of the boys, Porter Tatum, the reverend's son, he chose me."

"What happened then?"

Britta rocked herself back and forth, her features strained. "When his father took my hand to make me go to him, I told him no. And then I ran."

She hesitated and he started to go to her, but his cell phone rang. He glanced at it as if it was a rattlesnake, then back at Britta. She looked so pale and sweet, had trusted him with the truth. He could see the anguish on her face.

"Do you know what happened to this guy Porter?"

"I thought he died in that suicide pact."

Jean-Paul silently cursed. He'd search for the son's name.

The phone trilled again. He had to answer it. He connected the call, wishing he wasn't a cop. He wanted to go to Britta and hold her. Love her again. Tell her he'd never leave her.

Instead, he answered the phone. "Dubois."

"Jean-Paul, it's Damon. Listen, we have a warrant for that photographer's place. Apparently, two women filed stalking charges against him in Savannah last year. He was showing his artwork there around the same time as the murders in the city."

Adrenaline surged through him. If Teddy wasn't the swamp devil, maybe it was Howard Keith. And tonight, they might find the evidence to put him away.

ONE SECOND BRITTA and Jean-Paul had been making love.

Then she'd told him about her past and seen the disgust on his face.

The phone call had been his excuse to leave her. But he would have done so anyway. His perception of her had changed. Was tainted. And he still didn't know that she was a murderer. She had to accept that. His leaving was inevitable.

It had only been a matter of time.

She tugged the robe around her, feeling cold and alone. Maybe Howard Keith was the swamp devil and they could end the madness.

Then she and Jean-Paul could go their separate ways.

Pain knifed through her, yet she forced herself to stand tall. A heartbeat later, the landline phone jangled. Britta frowned and checked the caller ID. Unknown.

She paced to the window and stared out into the dark night. Three o'clock. No one knew where she was. Jean-Paul was on his way to Keith's house. And she sensed that the killer was getting ready to strike again.

The phone trilled again. Five more times. A solicitor wouldn't be calling in the middle of the night. Jean-Paul had said he had her calls routed to his house. The cops would be tracing it.

Her fingers trembled as she reached for the handset. "Hello."

"I have another girl, Adrianna."

She closed her eyes, biting down on her lip. Not another one.

"If you want to save her, then meet me."

"Where?"

"I'll let you know."

The phone clicked before she could reply.

Rage and fear rode through her in waves and Britta screamed at the walls.

She had to help Jean-Paul stop this guy. If only she knew who the girl was.

She had to call Jean-Paul.

And tell him what? That the guy had someone else? She had no information to give him. He'd spend the rest of the night going nuts, searching the bayou. And blaming himself.

She had to do something. This was all her fault.

Shack. Maybe one of his girls was missing. It was

the only lead she had. She grabbed the clothes Jean-Paul's sisters had given her and dressed in the jeans and shirt. But what about a car?

Desperate, she called a cab. Ten minutes later, she was heading into town. She'd make Shack call all his girls. Show the sketch of Teddy and Howard Keith around.

And when she saw Jean-Paul again she had to finish her story. He had to know about the man she'd killed.

Maybe Cortain would know where Reverend Tatum's son was. If he had survived.

A cold dread washed over her. She'd suggest a trade. It was a dangerous move, but another woman's life was at stake.

And Britta had to save her.

JEAN-PAUL HATED TO LEAVE Britta alone but they might have a lead. The photos the killer had sent Britta were taken from a camera just like Howard Keith's. So far, they hadn't pinpointed that it was the same camera but the information would earn a search warrant.

Damon met him at the man's home, a small apartment off the corner of Bourbon Street.

"He's inside," Damon said. "I don't think he knows we're coming."

"Good, we can use the element of surprise to our advantage."

Damon rang the doorbell and Jean-Paul prayed that Britta would be okay alone. No one knew she was at his place. He'd told her to stay put. But he couldn't wait to get back to her.

The door swung open and Keith stared at them with his one good eye. "Detective Dubois?"

"Yes. And this is Special Agent Dubois from the FBI."

"A relative no doubt," Keith said with a wry grin.

Jean-Paul nodded. "We have a search warrant for your premises."

The man's thin face turned sullen, but he stepped aside. Jean-Paul and Damon strode in, anxious to begin the search. Keith's apartment was in a warehouse that also housed his photography studio. They were connected by double doors.

A thorough search of his bedroom and den turned up little. No swords or scepters. No red lace teddies. No religious paraphernalia. No masks of Sobek.

Frustration gnawed at Jean-Paul, but he refused to give up. If something was there, they'd find it.

He moved on to the studio. Studied Keith's art. Photos of women hung on the wall. Dozens of Britta on the street. Some in her office. Some in her home. All candid shots. Some of her in her bedroom in her nightgown. One of her climbing from the shower, wrapped in a bath towel.

Ones that exposed the vulnerability on her face.

Keith was definitely talented. He could look at subjects and capture the secrets in their eyes.

But did that make him a killer?

He dug through the files of photographs. Found dozens of other women Keith had watched. Probably stalked. Some clothed. Some nude. But no photos of the victims or murders were among them. Did he have another hiding place?

"Search his computer," Jean-Paul told Damon.

"I'm on it. What about trophies?" Damon asked. "Find anything?"

Jean-Paul frowned. So far, they hadn't noticed anything missing from any of the girls. Unusual.

An hour later, and they'd gotten nowhere. Except Keith had a negative attitude pertaining to beautiful women. He hated them. Wanted to show the ugliness that lay below the beauty.

Because so many women had rejected him.

His admission substantiated Jean-Paul's belief that Keith fit the killer's profile, but he needed evidence. So far, he could hold him for twenty-four hours, but unless someone came forth and filed stalking charges, he'd have to let him go.

"We're confiscating your photos and computer files," Damon told Keith. "And you need to come with us for questioning."

"Do I need a lawyer?" Keith asked.

"Did you kill those women?" Jean-Paul asked.

Keith shook his head. "No. I only take photographs, Detective. If I want to expose a woman's ugly side, all I have to do is catch her at the right moment when her guard is down."

"You mean when she thinks she's alone in her apartment or bedroom," Jean-Paul snapped. "When you're invading her privacy." The realization that the man had watched Britta in her private quarters, had photographed her nude in her bathroom stepping from the shower, at night in her bed, turned his stomach. "You're nothing more than a peeping Tom, you bastard."

Keith smiled, revealing crooked teeth. "I am an artist."

"How did you get those shots?" Jean-Paul asked. "You have a telephoto lens or did you break into her apartment and watch her?"

Keith's good eye fluttered. "I want a lawyer."

"Let's go." Damon jerked the man's arm. "Maybe you'll feel more like talking once you sit in jail for a while."

Jean-Paul ground his teeth as they left the man's apartment. They needed more evidence and Keith knew it. Their only chance of making a murder charge stick was if Keith confessed to the crimes. But Keith was too cool a number to do that.

Which left them back at square one—with absolutely nothing.

Britta's story about the cult ran through his head. The connection to Cortain. The boy she'd said had chosen her.

He and Damon would review all the articles about the cult and that suicide pact. He'd check on Porter Tatum. Maybe they'd find a picture of the boy. Damon's people could run it through a program to age the boy and they might get an idea of what he looked like now.

It was a long shot, but they had to pursue every angle.

"WHAT IN THE HELL ARE you doing here, Britta?"

Britta stood tall, refusing to let Shack intimidate her. "There's another woman missing. I wanted you to check your girls, see if it might be one of them."

Shack gestured toward his cohort, a shorter black man with fists the size of melons. The man nodded and left the room, hopefully to do as she'd requested.

"Look at the sketch of these men. Pass it around, see if any of your people recognize the man. Maybe he's a client."

Shack's diamonds glittered beneath the dim lighting as he accepted the flier. He glanced down at the drawing of

Teddy and narrowed his eyes, then cracked his knuckles. "I don't recognize him, but I'll check with my girls. You think this man might be the one killing the girls?"

"I'm not sure. But the police want to question him." She explained about the porcelain dolls and the girl Debra. "The other man is a photographer. He has an odd display where he features women's eyes. Calls it, 'The Windows of the Soul.'"

"Sounds like an interesting character."

Britta shivered, but the sound of a girl crying reverberated from a back room and she stiffened.

Shack rapped his knuckles on the table. "Time for you to leave now, Britta."

"Not yet." She gestured toward the door. "I want to see her."

"Stay out of my business, Britta."

"I can't do that, Shack. Not when a girl is in trouble."

"I'll take care of her." He stood, towering over her. "Now leave or one of my guys will show you out."

Britta shook her head. "How old is she?"

"I don't answer to you. And you know it."

"A teenager? Thirteen, fourteen maybe?"

"Old enough to know she didn't want to live at home with mommy and daddy."

"Not old enough to make those decisions wisely," Britta said. Remembering her own brush with Shack and his enticing invitations to join his business years before, Britta pushed past him and headed to the door leading to the back.

One of Shack's men grabbed her arm and twisted it behind her.

She glared at him, knowing he could kill her if he wanted.

But the crying girl needed her and she would find a way to help her. If she didn't, this girl might end up as another casualty on the street. Another victim of the swamp devil or a psycho just like him.

JEAN-PAUL FELT LIKE pounding the wall in frustration. Instead he paced his office.

Howard Keith refused to cooperate and had called a lawyer. Jean-Paul and Damon had reviewed the articles about the cult, the suicide pact and Cortain. According to all their information, the reverend's son was thought to have died in the suicide pact but there was no conclusive evidence.

His phone jangled and he checked the digital display. Antwaun. He clicked to answer, "Jean-Paul here. What's up, little brother?"

"I located that pimp you wanted to talk to. Shack."

"Yeah?"

"You won't believe this, Jean-Paul, but guess who just went in to see him?"

"I'm not in the mood for games, Antwaun. If you have something, tell me."

"The Berger woman."

Jean-Paul's throat closed. Britta? God, what was she doing there?

He'd left her in bed, naked and sated. Scared, too, although she wouldn't admit it. And he'd told her to stay put.

"Jean-Paul, are you there, man?"

His brother's voice hurled him back to reality. "Yeah. Where are you?"

Antwaun recited an address in the low-rent district and Jean-Paul headed to his car. He had to get to Britta.

Find out why she'd do something so foolish. She was in danger, for God's sake. And the killer picked his girls off the streets.

Did she have a death wish or what?

Anger spurned him forward and sent him racing toward the pimp's place. He took the corner on two wheels, his heart pounding as he steered into a side alley and parked. The warehouse building had been divided into apartment units. The street was dark, the smell rancid.

Antwaun met him outside at the corner. "She's been in there about half an hour."

"I don't understand what she's doing," Jean-Paul said.

Voices echoed from the steps. Jean-Paul stepped into the shadows and waited. A big burly black man stepped outside, his hand folded around Britta's arm.

"Get lost," the man bellowed. "And if you mess with Shack's girls again, you'll be sorry."

Britta raised her chin, angry. "I'm not leaving without the girl."

Jean-Paul and Antwaun exchanged curious looks, then Jean-Paul stepped forward. "What's going on?"

The burly man cut his gaze down to Britta, then his right hand inched toward his back pocket.

"Police. I wouldn't do that if I were you," Jean-Paul warned.

Antwaun circled the man and patted him down. A smile flickered on his mouth when he held up a .45. "You have a license for this?"

The guy glared at Antwaun but released Britta and stepped away. "Look, man, I don't want any trouble."

"Then don't threaten Miss Berger again."

"No problem." The man sent him a sour look but backed away.

Jean-Paul turned to Britta. "What in the hell are you doing here? I told you to stay at my house."

"The killer called after you left. He has another girl."

Jean-Paul knotted his fists. "Why didn't you phone me?"

"I thought I'd see if one of Shack's girls was missing. If we had a name, it would be easier to find her."

Antwaun glanced at Jean-Paul, but he ignored his brother's curious look.

"Was he any help?" Antwaun asked.

Britta shrugged. "He's checking with them. I also showed him the sketch of Teddy. He's going to pass it to the girls. Maybe they've seen something that will help us."

Jean-Paul moved closer to her, then reached for her arm. "Dammit, Britta, I told you to let me handle things."

"I was trying to help."

"How?" Anger hardened his tone. "By getting yourself killed?"

She licked her dry lips; a soft rain was beginning to fall. "Shack wouldn't hurt me."

Jean-Paul indicated the gun Antwaun had confiscated and the guy who'd been manhandling her.

Britta winced. "I'm all right."

Jean-Paul tugged at her hand. "Let's go."

Britta dug in her heels. "Not yet. I'm not leaving without the girl inside."

"What girl?"

"She's a runaway," Britta said. "I have to help her."

Jean-Paul's gaze locked with hers, then shot to Antwaun's. His little brother was studying him intently, but he ignored the questions in his eyes. He finally understood Britta. She had been lost herself, had almost ended up on the streets. Now she hid behind a bad-girl disguise while she helped others.

His throat swelled with emotion. He started to speak, then had to clear his throat to get rid of the knot. "Show me where she is and we'll take care of her together."

Britta gripped his arm, her voice soft and pleading. "Jean-Paul, please, if she sees the cops, she'll run. Let me do this my way."

"She doesn't have to know who I am."

Britta hesitated. "Then just stand back and let me do the talking. If she agrees, you can drive us to Miss Lottie's."

Miss Lottie?

"Yes. She helped me. She'll give her a place to stay. Help her get on her feet. Maybe convince her to call her parents."

The same Miss Lottie who'd taken Britta in years ago. She must have been her salvation. He wanted to thank her personally. If she hadn't helped, what would have happened to Britta?

The reality of their situation sobered him. What would happen to her if he failed her as he had his wife and the other swamp devil victims?

BRITTA APPROACHED the girl with caution. She looked hungry, dirty and terrified.

Shack had protested, but when Jean-Paul intervened and pulled his badge, he had become resigned.

"I can't go back home," the girl whispered. "My parents...I can't face them."

"What's your name?" Britta asked.

The teenager's green eyes appeared huge in her slender face. "Please…"

"I won't call your folks right now," Britta promised. "But please, just tell me your first name. I want to help you."

The girl's chin quivered. "It's…Carol."

Britta smoothed a strand of blond hair behind the girl's ear. She had a half-dozen earrings crawling up and down her lobe, a hickey on her neck and bruises along her jaw. No telling what atrocities she had suffered so far.

"Okay, Carol, that's a start." She smiled and took the girl's tiny hand in her own. "My friend, Jean-Paul, and I, are going to drive you to another friend of mine's. Her name is Miss Lottie. She's someone really special."

"She takes in girls who work on the streets?"

Britta barely suppressed a shudder. "Yes and no, sweetheart. She's not a madam. She gives you a place to stay. Some meals. A clean start." Along with counseling and advice. If Carol's parents were worth calling, Miss Lottie would figure that out. Britta had no desire to put her back in an abusive home or throw her to the wolves of foster care.

Carol pulled her ratty sweat jacket around her trembling frame. "But she'll think I'm awful. I'm not cleaned up."

Britta put her arm around Carol's shoulders and helped her to stand. "Honey, Miss Lottie has seen everything. She can't be shocked."

"How do you know?"

Britta's chest squeezed. Jean-Paul was watching. She hated to reveal any more of herself. Because Miss Lottie had not had a prim existence herself. Another reminder that she and Jean-Paul were worlds apart.

But Carol needed the truth. The very reason Britta had put herself out here now. The very reason she would continue to do so when Jean-Paul Dubois went back to his perfect family and hero status in the town.

"Because Miss Lottie took me in a long time ago, honey." Britta hugged Carol. "She was the best friend I've ever had."

Jean-Paul was polite but quiet and he allowed Britta to coax the girl into the car. She tried to read his thoughts, but he'd slammed that ironclad mask of control over his face.

A deep-seated anger darkened his eyes when he saw Miss Lottie's shack. Britta should have warned him that the housing wouldn't be fancy or up to the Dubois standards. But it had sufficed for her and it would for Carol for the night.

Miss Lottie had connections to folks who helped young girls like Carol. Some were social workers who abided by the law. Others worked underground to help women and girls start over if they needed a new life or identity. The arrangements were made in private. Britta never asked. She just delivered the girls to Miss Lottie and trusted her to do the rest.

JEAN-PAUL DIDN'T ASK questions as Britta escorted the young girl to her friend's house. But his cop instincts urged him to find out the girl's last name. Who her parents were. And how to contact them.

They must be worried sick.

He drummed his fingers on the dash, his hands beating a staccato rhythm like the rain pounding the sidewalk. It was almost dawn and another girl was missing.

He had no idea who.

And Britta and he were at odds again. Two people who'd slept together who didn't know how to scale the walls that stood between them. He wanted to tear them down but anger and bitterness toward the people who'd hurt her kept him tied in a knot.

Britta hugged the elderly woman at the door, then rushed through the rain to his car. He gritted his teeth, aching to take her in his arms.

"Thank you," she said softly as she shut the door.

"We should call her parents," he said gruffly. "They're probably out of their minds with concern."

Britta ran a hand through her damp hair. She looked exhausted and worried. And so damn beautiful he wanted to hold her. But he had to convince her that she couldn't go running off in the night, confronting pimps and their bodyguards, putting herself in danger, forgetting that a killer was out there. Targeting her—maybe next.

"Jean-Paul, trust me this time. If Miss Lottie decides that Carol's parents are worth calling, she'll do everything within her power to reunite them."

"Everything except call the damn police." Frustration sharpened his voice. "For God's sake, Britta, hundreds of girls go missing every year. The system is clogged with them. If she'd cooperate with us, it would make our jobs a hell of a lot easier."

Britta's eyes shimmered with rage. "Yeah, but the cops would send them back. Some of their homes are horrible, Jean-Paul. The parents, they're the reason the girls run away. They don't deserve to have them back."

"But the others—"

She cut him off. "I told you to trust me this once. Miss Lottie will get to the truth. She'll do what's right."

He wanted to trust her. And he did trust that she wanted to help this girl.

Dammit. He had pegged Britta wrong from the beginning....

His phone buzzed, and he read Damon's number, then connected the call.

"Jean-Paul, listen, I may have found something. Meet me at Reverend Cortain's house."

Jean-Paul pressed the gas pedal. "I'm on my way."

THE EARLY MORNING FOG rose through the bayou like misty rain above a grave. The bayou stretched beyond, the backwoods filled with the mysteries of the night. Rain drizzled onto the ground, making the Spanish moss droop with its weight. Britta's shoulders sagged with despair. She had to confess the truth.

But she couldn't find her voice for the deluge of dread that filled her.

"Damon's meeting us at Cortain's to question the reverend. If the killer is from the cult where the suicide pacts took place, then Cortain may know who he is. Or he may be Cortain himself." Jean-Paul pulled up to Cortain's house, then cut the engine. "He already has a God complex. And his background and history fit the profile. The suicides could have sent him over the edge."

She touched his hand wanting to explain, but his brother pulled up in a dark sedan. Damon's look turned to ice when he saw her with Jean-Paul.

Jean-Paul climbed out, then started around to her side but she climbed out herself, her stomach knotting as the three of them rushed through the rain up the porch steps.

"What did you find out?" Jean-Paul asked.

Damon shot Britta an odd look but the door opened, cutting off his reply. She felt as if she'd just walked to her own trial and had already been judged and declared guilty.

Reverend Cortain stood in the doorway, a black and gold cape billowing around him. Images of Brother Tatum flashed before Britta's eyes. His haunting voice had chilled her to the bone. And when she'd realized that he intended to sacrifice her in a medieval ritual, she'd been terrified.

Cortain greeted them with a smirk on his face. "What can I do for you?"

Jean-Paul introduced his brother and Damon spoke up. "We need to talk to you about your brother-in-law's death."

"Really?" Reverend Cortain's gaze pierced Britta. "So you're finally going to confess and ask forgiveness for your sins?"

Britta bit her lip, but Jean-Paul grabbed the reverend's arm. "Cut the bull, Cortain. You feel guilty for those suicides? Did you push your brother-in-law to kill himself first, or did you kill him so you could take over his clan and gain his power?"

Reverend Cortain's gray eyebrows furrowed. "Me?" A nasty chuckle reverberated through the air. "You've got your facts wrong, Detective."

Britta's heart clenched as Cortain leered down at her.

"Your girlfriend here, she was the who murdered my brother-in-law. If you don't believe me, ask her yourself."

HE SMILED AS HE STUDIED the woman.

She was terrified. Trembling. All tied up and waiting for him to begin. Mardi Gras had finally come.

But this woman was not his type.

No, it was time to take Britta.

And he had the perfect plan. The way to hurt Dubois for interfering. For turning his Adrianna into the whore she should have been for him.

Laughter bubbled in his chest. All these years and Britta had remained uninvolved. Had kept her identity a secret. The truth about who she was a lie.

But hell was about to break loose for her. And they would meet again.

He unpocketed his phone and clicked the detective's number. Wished he could be a fly on the wall to see the man's face when Dubois learned who he had kidnapped.

But at least he'd get to hear the pain in Dubois's voice when the detective learned that his sister's life lay in his hands.

And that if he wanted her back, he had to sacrifice Britta.

CHAPTER NINETEEN

CORTAIN'S ADMISSION HAD thrust Britta back in time.

It was D-Day—the day Adrianna Small had died.

The day the thirteen-year-old had killed a man so Britta could survive.

Britta had relived that day so many times, but hearing Reverend Cortain accuse her in such a cold way resurrected her guilt full force. She could see the blood spurting from the man's chest....

You're a bad girl, Britta.

Yes, she was. She was a murderer.

She'd never be able to escape that truth, no matter how far she'd run. No matter how many other girls she saved.

"Britta?"

Jean-Paul's gruff voice made her head jerk up. She heard the shock in his steely tone and knew that she had waited too long to confide in him.

"Tell him," Reverend Cortain bellowed. "It's about time you owned up to what you did, young lady."

The rain intensified, pounding the wooden porch rails. Droplets stung her cheeks as she angled her face toward Jean-Paul.

"What is he talking about?" Jean-Paul asked.

"I told you I found something," Damon said.

"You killed Reverend Tatum, didn't you, Miss Berger?"

Jean-Paul's eyes flashed with pain. Britta started to reach for his arm to steady her shaking legs, but he stiffened. "Britta?"

"It's true," she admitted in a low voice. "Reverend Tatum wanted me to marry his son." Her voice grew stronger. "He also intended to sacrifice me that day. I heard the other women in the cult whispering about the rituals. The fire. The chants. *The covens.* They were alive in the group and believed in black magic. And they were terrified of the gators."

"So they sacrificed young girls to them?" Jean-Paul asked in an incredulous voice.

"It was the ancient beliefs," Reverend Cortain interjected. "My brother-in-law was old-school. He thought that getting rid of sin today required taking religion— values—back to the basic beliefs of our forefathers."

Jean-Paul's eyes looked stormy in the predawn light. Damon's condemning look twisted her insides. Behind them, the wind whistled through the tupelos and a gator hissed its attack call. Britta remembered Jean-Paul's face filled with passion for her, then watched his feelings die as he saw her in a new light.

Just as the photographer had said, she had darkness, evil beneath the beauty. Ugliness in her soul. And now it was exposed.

"I tried to pull away from Reverend Tatum," Britta admitted. "But he grabbed me and was going to force me to go through with the rituals. So I panicked. I…" She hesitated, mentally replaying the scene. "I grabbed the shotgun and aimed it at him. I was shaking so hard. And he lunged at me and the gun went off. I…shot him." Her voice broke. "Blood was everywhere. People were screaming. I…threw the gun toward the fire and then ran."

Jean-Paul's gaze remained steadfast on her face, his body stiff and rigid, his jaw a tight mask, his eyes glittering with rage.

"We searched the bayou all night for you," Reverend Cortain said. "We decided that the gators ate you and we were glad."

Jean-Paul jerked his head toward Cortain. "So you've hated her all these years. Now you're punishing her by killing innocent women, by continuing the sacrificial practices of your brother-in-law?"

"No." Cortain leaned against the doorjamb. He looked old and tired. "I'm trying to atone for my own sins. After my brother-in-law died, the cult fell apart. People were lost without their leader. There was dissension. Some of the women spoke out about the marriages, protested men having more than one wife."

"And you suggested the suicide pact?" Damon asked.

Cortain nodded. "I was a young man, an idealist myself."

"But when it came time to take the poison, you were afraid to die," Damon added.

"So you watched the others?" Disgust laced Jean-Paul's voice.

Cortain nodded, and stared at his feet. For the first time since she'd met the reverend, real pain and grief twisted his face.

"I still hear the women and children's cries at night. The ghosts of the dead haunt me. The men who gave up their lives… I had to do something to make amends."

"So you became a preacher?" Britta asked.

He nodded and swiped at his tears with a handkerchief. "I swore I'd do everything I could to spread the word and fight evil."

"So you tried to stop us from publishing *Naked Desires?*" Britta asked.

"Yes." Cortain sighed. "But I'm not a serial killer."

"Did you set fire to the building that housed the magazine?" Jean-Paul asked.

He shook his head. "No. But there are some in the congregation who blame Miss Berger and the magazine for corrupting the town."

Jean-Paul grabbed Cortain's collar. "Because you planted the idea in their heads. I want names."

Cortain nodded, his look haggard. "You know them, Detective, but you can't really blame them. They're the mothers of the swamp devil's victims."

JEAN-PAUL WAS CONFUSED. He'd thought Debra Schmale had attacked Britta and set the fire. But what if the mothers had started the fire?

Damon was scrutinizing him, too. His brother had known about Britta. And he had looked like a fool in front of Damon.

God, how had he let himself lose perspective? He'd slept with her. Had listened to her explanation with compassion.

Yet she still hadn't trusted him with the entire truth.

No, his brother and a murder suspect had delivered that blow. They should take his badge for this.

Still…her horror story turned him inside out. As much as he'd seen on the streets, the idea of a cult actually sacrificing a young girl to save themselves, in the name of religion, was even more vile than he'd imagined.

And how had Britta survived after she'd run away? Where had her mother been when the group was about to murder her daughter?

And now…geesh. He had to bring the mothers of the victims in for questioning. They'd already been through hell.

But if they'd set that fire, no matter their justifications, they had almost killed Britta.

She wasn't the bad guy here—she had been a victim.

"Jean-Paul?"

"I'm going to have the Erickson woman and Ginger Holliday's mother picked up for questioning."

"I can't believe this is happening," Britta murmured.

Jean-Paul's phone rang, slicing into the tension. Cortain's head was bowed. He didn't look godly now, only worn and demented.

Jean-Paul checked the number. His sister Stephanie. His pulse hammered in his throat as he connected the call.

"Jean-Paul…"

"What's wrong?"

"It's Catherine," she said in a ragged whisper. "She never made it home last night. Shawn and Chrissy are here and they're both frantic."

Sweat exploded on Jean-Paul's forehead. *God no,* his sister had to be okay. Yet on the heels of his denial, reality whispered.

Another woman had been taken….

Pure panic ballooned in his chest, robbing his air. He leaned against the porch rail for a moment, his head spinning. No…not Catherine. Not his baby sister.

The swamp devil couldn't have kidnapped her.

"Jean-Paul, what's wrong?" Damon asked.

His brother's voice dragged him from his shock. Stephanie was calling his name on the other end of the line.

"Where are you?" he asked.

"At Mom and Dad's." Her voice broke, laden with tears. "I've had a bad feeling for days, Jean-Paul. A premonition that something would happen to tear apart our family. But this…God, not this."

Stephanie and her *feelings*. He wanted to pretend they didn't mean anything but she'd been right before.

"Damon's with me," Jean-Paul choked out. "I'll call Antwaun and we'll meet you at home."

He disconnected the call and turned to his brother. "Catherine's missing. We have to go."

Damon blanched white and cursed. Britta reached for his arm to soothe him, but he stiffened and refused her touch.

Jean-Paul glared at Cortain. As much as he wanted to vent his frustration on the man, he didn't think Cortain was the killer.

"Where is your nephew, Reverend Tatum's son?" Jean-Paul asked.

Cortain's eyebrows furrowed. "I don't know."

Jean-Paul gripped the man by the collar. He'd choke the answer out of him if he had to. "Tell me the truth, Cortain. If he hurts my sister, I'll hold you personally responsible."

Cortain's eyes bulged. "I…really don't know," he rasped. "I haven't seen the boy in years. Not since a few days after my brother-in-law died."

"What happened to him?" Jean-Paul asked.

Cortain sucked in a sharp breath. "He was punished

by the clan. Some of them...they thought he had warned the girl about the sacrificial ceremony, so they forced him to take the trial by ordeal."

"What the hell is that?" Damon barked.

"It's another ancient custom. They sent him into the bayou, he was forced to cross the river. The gators attacked him, meaning he didn't pass. But he didn't die, so they banned him from the clan."

And turned him into a killer, Jean-Paul thought. And he'd come back to exact revenge on Britta.

And now him—through Catherine, his baby sister.

Lucinda's accusations echoed from the grave. *Your work puts us all in danger.*

And so had his personal involvement with Britta.

His mind swirled for answers. Who was the swamp devil? If not Justice or Cortain, then who? Keith was still in custody. Randy Swain maybe? Perhaps that guy Teddy. Debra Schmale had met with him right before she'd turned up dead.

Britta had seen him almost daily. Catherine and Chrissy had bought dolls from him, as well. He could easily have approached her without her suspecting a thing.

Bile rose in his throat. The images of the other dead women floated before him in a foggy haze of horror. No, he couldn't let the man do that to Catherine.

THE DAY DRAGGED BY, the waiting excruciating. Britta moved through each painful hour on autopilot.

Jean-Paul's sister was missing. Police were combing the bayou. The dollmaker Teddy hadn't been found. And Catherine might be hurting or worse.

It was all Britta's fault.

Damon's accusing eyes sought hers in the dawning

light. She wanted to plead with him for understanding, assure him and Jean-Paul that she hadn't meant to hurt them. But the apologies lay lodged in her throat, along with the tears she refused to cry. Terror for Catherine had completely immobilized her.

On the other hand, Jean-Paul and Damon had both taken charge. They rushed into their parents' with Antwaun on their heels. Stephanie was calming their mother. Jean-Paul's father paced the den, looking shaken and in shock. Shawn had put their daughter to bed and promised to wake her when her mother arrived home. He hadn't revealed how worried they all were, but his face was ashen and he obviously hadn't slept all night.

Jean-Paul phoned the precinct, filed a missing persons report on Catherine and had an APB issued for Teddy. He and Damon had also consulted with forensics and the police in Savannah and Nashville and he'd called Mazie Burgess.

Ironic. They'd avoided the press for the past few days. Now they were begging for their help. Within minutes, the camera crew arrived.

Mazie stroked Jean-Paul's arm, leaning toward him in an intimate gesture that made Britta's stomach clench. Mazie was attractive, businesslike, Jean-Paul's equal. They would make a good match. She would fit into his family.

A place where it was more obvious by the minute that she didn't belong.

"Tell me everything, Jean-Paul," Mazie said. "I understand that the killer has been contacting Miss Berger?"

Jean-Paul's dark tormented eyes found hers. "Yes. Apparently they met when she was a child. But she hasn't seen him in years and doesn't know what he looks like now." He showed her the sketch of Teddy to run on the air, then explained about the cult, Reverend Cortain and the suicide pact.

"We think his nephew, the son of the preacher back then, may be the killer. It's possible he's this guy Teddy, but we can't be sure. I spoke with forensics again. They found traces of acrylic paint and pancake makeup at the second crime scene, underneath Ginger Holliday's fingernails, and at the scenes in Savannah."

"So he might be a makeup artist by day?" Mazie asked.

"That or he's into another art form. At best, he's using the makeup to disguise himself." The acrylic— hell, with all the artists in town, they had to narrow down where it was bought, the exact type and its use... Damon had guys working that angle now.

Britta twined her fingers together, feeling helpless. Today was Mardi Gras. A day when half the town would be in disguise, wearing masks. How would they ever find him?

"He wants me," Britta said. "Let me go on the air."

The commotion in the room came to an abrupt halt. Jean-Paul's mother looked up at her with tear-stained eyes. His sister Stephanie bit down on her lip but refrained from a reply. Shawn gave her an accusatory look that matched Damon's and Antwaun's.

"We can arrange a meeting," she said into the silence.

Tension whistled through the room as if a ghost had walked by. Jean-Paul shook his head, but Damon caught his arm. "Jean-Paul, think about it."

Antwaun cleared his throat. "It's worth a shot. This is our sister we're talking about."

A muscle ticked in Jean-Paul's jaw. Jean-Paul knew they were right.

But Britta knew he wouldn't ask her to take a chance. He was after all, a hero at heart.

He couldn't save everyone, though. And Catherine, who had a daughter, was an innocent in all this. She didn't deserve to die.

"Let's get a trace in place," Jean-Paul commanded. "We'll make a plea, offer a ransom and give out phone numbers for the killer to call or for leads."

He was calm, poised. Seething below the surface. Britta could read him so well.

God, how she loved the man.

And his family…they huddled together as if they were one. Painted a heartrending picture as the camera zoomed in to capture their terrorized faces.

"Please," Shawn said. "My daughter needs her mother. Send Catherine back to us alive."

Mazie took the mike next. "Please help this family and N'Awlins stop this reign of terror by the swamp devil. If you have any information regarding the recent murders, about a suspect. If you've seen this woman, Catherine Dubois—" the TV station flashed a photo of her, then Teddy on the screen "—or this man, please call." She repeated the phone number, then they displayed it on the screen again.

Chrissy, Catherine's little girl, suddenly appeared at the bottom of the steps in tears. "Daddy, where's Mommy?" Her big eyes stared at the reporter in horror. She'd heard the news report. Knew her mother was missing.

Shawn rushed to her and tried to comfort her. And the family encircled her.

"Please, Uncle Jean-Paul," Chrissy cried. "Get my mommy back."

Antwaun gestured toward Britta. "Come on, Jean-

Paul, give Britta a shot. It might be the only chance we have."

Jean-Paul jerked his finger toward the kitchen. "In there, now. We have to talk."

The family moved together into the kitchen, leaving her behind. Mazie Burgess raised her brows in a confused frown.

Britta had started this mess thirteen years ago when she'd killed a man and run into the bayou. She had to make things right.

As soon as the Duboises were out of earshot, she turned to the reporter, then took the mike.

JEAN-PAUL TRIED DESPERATELY to soothe Chrissy's cries. Finally his mother took her in her arms and she seemed to calm. But the little girl's red-rimmed eyes held expectations, and Jean-Paul wanted to erase her fear.

"Why are you protecting that Berger woman when your own sister's life is at stake?" Anger deepened Antwaun's voice.

"You don't understand," Jean-Paul argued.

"I understand that Catherine is in trouble," Shawn snapped, "and that we're standing here arguing over whether this stranger should help us."

Jean-Paul's mother leaned into his father. He patted his wife's back. "We have to stick together," his father said. "Stay strong. Trust our boys to find her."

"Britta is more than a stranger. Isn't she, Jean-Paul?" Stephanie asked.

Jean-Paul frowned, wincing internally. How could he possibly make them understand his relationship to Britta when he didn't understand it himself? She was so complicated, so lost.

So brave.

How could he trade one life for another?

"She's a victim here," he said in a gruff voice. He filled them in on what had happened to Britta as a child, not surprised when horror struck their faces.

"We can't ask her to face that man," his mother said softly.

"Mom, it may be our only chance to save Catherine," Antwaun argued.

"It's going to be night soon," Damon interjected. "We need to move."

"Let her make a plea," Antwaun suggested. "Agree to meet him somewhere. We'll wire her, follow her and let her lead us to him."

Jean-Paul wavered slightly. Every hour that passed lessened the chances they had of finding his sister alive. No telling what kind of pain the man was inflicting upon her….

But bartering an exchange for Britta, sacrificing her? He'd be no better than her mother…. It was too risky. "Even if we set up Britta, if the guy sees us tailing her, he might kill Catherine anyway."

Tension vibrated between his family as they exchanged frantic looks. The air was charged with the question nobody wanted to ask. What if Catherine was already dead?

Mardi Gras day

THE PARTIES WERE IN FULL swing. Children raced to catch candy as the parade leaders tossed to the street. Beer and liquor flowed freely. A maze of drunken partiers wearing Mardi Gras masks and costumes overflowed the bars.

But the Dubois family and Britta Berger were not in the Quarter. Not celebrating. No, they were huddled together discussing *him*. Wondering who he was. Where he was. What he had done with their beloved sister.

Laughter bubbled in his throat.

After running from the press for days now, Jean-Paul Dubois had finally gone public. To save his sister.

Would he trade Adrianna to have Catherine back?

He fingered the mask he'd designed for Britta. He'd most enjoyed painting the wide, stricken eyes.

Why hadn't *she* appeared on the news? Didn't she know that it was her he wanted? That today, Mardi Gras, the day of celebration, was the day he had to make his sacrifice?

He peeled back the mask he'd donned when he'd captured Catherine and breathed out deeply as he stared at his scarred face in the mirror. The dead, mangled skin, the reddened patches, his disfigurement—it had all been Adrianna's fault. Her fault that he'd never been normal, that the women hadn't wanted him, that they'd turned away in horror.

That he'd been forced to hide in disguise.

Catherine moaned in the background and he glanced over his shoulder. He should show her his hideous face, watch the terror streak her eyes.

But the news reporter's voice broke into the quiet. "Folks, Britta Berger is with us now. She has been in contact with the killer and wants to make a statement."

His pulse clamored as he turned toward the rickety set in the corner. Bloodlust thickened in his veins as Britta appeared on screen.

She was finally going to talk to him. When she

finished, he'd give her a call. Tell her that if she wanted to save Catherine, she had to meet him in the bayou.

Back to the place where it had all begun.

The bayou killed. It took lives. And gave them, as well.

It was his home.

And the place where Adrianna would die.

CHAPTER TWENTY

"MY NAME IS BRITTA BERGER. I want to address the man who has Catherine Dubois-Cramer," Britta said into the microphone. "You knew me as Adrianna Small. We belonged to the same cult a long time ago. And the night your father was killed, the night I shot him, I ran away." The reporter's eyebrows lifted and shock settled on her face. But Britta ignored her reaction and forged on.

If she went to jail after this, so be it. She could live with whatever happened, as long as her plan worked and they saved Catherine.

"It's me you want," she said calmly. "Not Catherine. She is innocent in all this. She has a daughter herself. You remember what it's like to lose a parent and you don't want to do that to this sweet little girl." She prayed he still had some conscience left. "Call me on the cell phone listed and let's talk. I'll meet you anywhere you want." She lowered her voice. "Please just don't hurt Catherine. Let me take her place."

Mazie was frowning. The cameraman gaped as if she'd lost her mind. But Britta had hidden long enough.

And Jean-Paul...he still blamed himself for his wife's death. She wouldn't let him lose his sister, especially because of her.

The reporter repeated the number again, and Britta

startled as her cell phone rang. She grabbed it quickly and pressed it to her ear. "Hello."

"I saw you on television, Adrianna."

She angled herself away from the reporter's watchful eyes. "Is Catherine all right?"

A long pause. "For now."

"Let me talk to her."

"No." His quick, low reply sent a shudder through her. "You want her released?"

"Yes."

"You'll meet me?"

"Yes. Wherever you say."

"You have to come alone. " His voice was harsh, muffled. "If you bring Dubois or anyone else—police, the feds, even that reporter—Catherine will die."

Britta closed her eyes, willing herself to be strong. "I'll come alone. I promise."

Heavy breathing rattled over the line. "Then I'll see you where we first met."

"Black Bayou?"

"Yes. At Devil's Corner," he specified. "You do remember it, don't you, Adrianna?"

"Yes." The whisper was ripped from her as an image of the area resurfaced. How could she forget the place where she'd nearly lost her life as a child—and lost her soul?

He ended the call with a click and she glanced up to see Mazie approaching her. "What did he say?"

"I have to meet him," Britta said.

"I'll get Jean-Paul."

"No." Britta grabbed the woman's arm, pleading, in-sistent. "This man will kill Catherine if I don't come alone. I can't take that chance."

"You can't face him alone," Mazie argued. "Jean-Paul—"

"Shouldn't have to watch his family suffer," Britta finished. "Or choose to trade someone to get Catherine back."

Emotions flickered in Mazie's eyes. Compassion. Worry for Jean-Paul. Maybe even for her.

"Please," Britta whispered. "Let me go now. I started this years ago. I have to finish it now."

Their gazes locked, their admiration for Jean-Paul binding them together.

"All right," Mazie agreed, resigned. "But you can't go unprotected."

Footsteps clattered on the wooden floor, Jean-Paul's voice growing closer. The family would be back in the room in seconds.

Mazie gestured toward the drawer where Jean-Paul's mother had made the boys store their weapons when they'd arrived. "Take a gun with you."

Britta found the key, unlocked the drawer, then removed Jean-Paul's gun.

"Do you know how to use it?" the woman asked.

Britta nodded, tucked the weapon inside her jacket, then grabbed the keys to Jean-Paul's car and rushed out the door. She prayed she'd survive this meeting. If not, hopefully she'd at least send Catherine back alive.

JEAN-PAUL HAD MADE A decision during the hurricane and lost his wife, and had to live with the consequences. No matter what he did now, someone he cared about might die. But he couldn't sacrifice Britta….

Antwaun poured himself a cup of coffee. "I'd never let a woman come between me and the family."

"Boys, please don't argue," his mother pleaded. "We have to stick together."

Stephanie worried her lip with her teeth. Jean-Paul didn't want to ask if she'd had a premonition. Damon gave him a silent questioning look. Shawn and Chrissy's expression was pleading, tormented.

Jean-Paul's chest clenched. If he agreed, he'd be throwing Britta to the wolves just as her mother had done. She'd never had a family to take care of her.

And dammit, he wanted to do so now.

"I've negotiated hostage exchanges before, Jean-Paul," Damon said. "Trust me. We won't let the killer get Britta. We'll protect her."

Damon's phone jangled, cutting him off. The air was so tense that his niece's breathing sliced into the silence. Damon connected the call and listened.

"All right. We'll be right there." Damon disconnected his phone. "One of my agents found your guy Teddy at a service station near Black Bayou and is bringing him in. I told the agent we'd meet him at the precinct."

Jean-Paul nodded. "Let me tell Britta."

Damon and Antwaun followed him into the den. Jean-Paul's gaze scanned the room. Mazie was tucking her notes in her briefcase while the cameraman headed outside with his equipment to load it into their news van.

"Where's Britta?"

Mazie bit down on her lip. "She's gone, Jean-Paul."

"What?" He grabbed her arm and made her look at him. "Gone where?"

She cast her eyes toward the door and his heart stopped.

"She went on air while you were in the other room. She asked the swamp devil to meet her."

A bead of perspiration trickled down Jean-Paul's back. "And you let her leave! Why didn't you call me?"

"She wanted to do this, Jean-Paul." Mazie squeezed his arm. "For you. For your sister."

Her gaze met his and Jean-Paul's throat closed with emotions.

Damon moved near him and Antwaun shuffled up beside him. They had obviously overheard. "We can try to track her," Damon said.

"Then let's go." Jean-Paul turned to the desk to retrieve his gun and saw the opened drawer.

Damon and Antwaun noticed at the same time and retrieved their weapons.

"She took yours for protection," Mazie said.

Jean-Paul gritted his teeth. He'd be in deep shit at the precinct. But he didn't care about the law this time. Not one iota.

"I hope to hell she knows how to use it," he muttered. In fact, he hoped she killed the bastard just like she had that Reverend Tatum.

BRITTA PRESSED THE GAS peddle, accelerating as she veered onto the highway leading out of town. The lights and party sounds of Mardi Gras echoed in the background, mocking her with their frivolity. The afternoon rain had stopped long enough for the parade, but now it splattered the windshield. Storm clouds thundered ominously, the occasional streak of lightning that flashed off the cemeteries making the gravestones look as if they were about to come alive. She imagined ghosts walking the land and wondered if Brother Tatum was among them. Had he been trapped in the city of the dead all these years, waiting on her to re-surface so he could watch her pay the price for killing him?

Would he be satisfied when she was arrested and finally move on? Or did he want to see her in the grave beside him?

Fatigue pulled at her muscles, reminding her she hadn't slept in over twenty-four hours. She sighed and turned up the defroster, glad the truth was out in the open. It was a relief not to carry the burden of her secret.

Her only regret was that she'd hurt Jean-Paul and en-dangered his family.

Wind made the branches on the trees sway and dip, its shrill whistle chilling her as she approached Devil's Corner. Some claimed they'd actually spotted the swamp devil at the corner of the two dirt roads that intersected the swampland. Some left offerings— voodoo mojos and gris gris—for protection.

The cult had met there years before to fight the evil. Only they had lost.

Because she had destroyed their leader?

Or because they were trapped by superstition and the barbaric practices of the past?

The last bad hurricane had altered the property slightly, so she had to drive a couple of miles to the west. But she recognized the gigantic rock shaped like a devil's horn and parked beside it. The rain softened to a drizzle, the fog barring her vision as she searched the darkness.

If the swamp devil had Catherine, then he must have found a shanty nearby to hold her prisoner. Britta killed the engine, then took a deep breath and checked her coat pocket for Jean-Paul's gun.

The eerie sounds of the bayou echoed around her as she waited....

R.J. RACED TOWARD THE police station, his heart pounding. He couldn't believe Britta had gone on air and offered to meet the killer.

What in the hell was she thinking?

He slammed on the brakes, tires squealing as he turned into the parking lot, then cut the engine. He'd been so furious when he'd been released from jail that he'd gone to see one of his girlfriends. He'd needed release and she'd given it to him.

Then he'd heard about the fire at the office and gone into shock. His building, his magazine, all in shambles. And all because of that damned Cortain and this fucking serial killer.

And now Britta, the one woman he actually had feelings for, was in even more danger. She'd put her life on the line for that cop Dubois, he was sure of it.

That and the guilt over Reverend Tatum's death. She didn't deserve that guilt.

She didn't deserve death, either.

He had to talk to Dubois. If the killer called her, R.J. had a hunch where he'd want to meet her. And Britta would be walking into a trap....

HOWARD KEITH HAD BEEN wrong about Britta Berger.

She had substance to her. An unselfishness below the surface that she had hidden from the world. Even he, the master of capturing the windows to the soul, had not seen it.

So maybe he was flawed. Had been wrong. In spite of her physical beauty, she was brave. Go figure.

He and the camera had both been incorrect in their perception of her. He wanted the whole story now. After all, the police were trying to pin the crime on him and he was innocent.

Why had Britta Berger chosen to face a killer and put her life on the line rather than run again?

Howard had understood her hiding out. He'd been running most of his life. Hiding his face because of his imperfection.

In that way, he could relate to the killer. Howard shot beautiful women's faces and revealed their ugly sides. The killer exposed the pretty girls with dirty souls.

Just like his friend...Sedrick offered masks to hide behind, although some of his masks were grotesque themselves.

He knocked on his friend's apartment door, then tapped his foot, impatient. Sedrick had first pointed Britta out to him. Maybe he knew more about her. He'd claimed Britta had snubbed her nose at him because of his looks. And lately, Sedrick had behaved oddly. Even made comments that had made Howard wonder how long he'd known Britta. And Sedrick's face...his scars.

How had he gotten them?

Sedrick was so secretive. Mysterious. Intense. Remote. He never discussed his past. And he was methodical. A perfectionist. Detail oriented. Which served him well in his profession.

Howard knocked again, but his friend didn't answer. Maybe he was working on a new art project.

Another mask. Or more eyes.

The guy was a wizard with design. He'd started his masks as a hobby, but today many of the more intricate Mardi Gras masks sold in town could be attributed to his talent. He even designed masks for the S and M shop and had a display in the wax museum. Of course, Howard understood his obsession with the art form.

His friend had his own flaws, imperfections.

In fact, the two of them had bonded at first sight because of them.

When Howard had lost his eye and decided to get a prosthetic one, he'd met with the ocularist. Sedrick suggested a custom prosthesis instead of the stock variety because it fit better and looked more natural.

But plastic surgery, his new fake eye, nothing had been able to compensate for Howard's flaw. He was scarred. Disfigured. Just like Sedrick. Except Sedrick's scars were physical, so deep he was forced to either wear a custom mask or heavy makeup.

Deciding Sedrick wasn't home, Howard removed the key from his pocket and inserted it into the lock. A sudden cold feeling split down his spine, as if fingers of ice had touched his skin. Bits and pieces of conversation with Sedrick rattled back in his mind.

Sedrick had grown up in Black Bayou. He hated women. He created masks of Sobek. Sedrick thought the swamp devil's victims deserved their fate. That Britta Berger was being contacted because of her magazine.

Suspicions skated through his head. Twice, on nights when women had died, he'd dropped by and his friend hadn't been home.

His pulse clamored as he let himself inside the apartment. He made a quick walk through but Sedrick wasn't home.

Nerves on edge, he hurried to the studio. Two new masks lay half-completed on the work table. Both dark, sinister—like some kind of mystic gothic creature.

His gaze shot to the locked door, Sedrick's private

room. Sedrick had gotten upset when Howard had tried to open it.

His heart hammering, he hurried to the work table and found a small knife. He had to see what was behind the locked door. And why Sedrick kept it a secret.

JEAN-PAUL WAS GOING out of his mind.

They had lost Britta. And they hadn't been able to trace the call to her cell phone.

"Dammit, Damon, we have to find her."

"Hang in there, Jean-Paul." Damon drove along Bourbon Street, his methodical mind checking streets, while Antwaun had driven to the station to question Teddy. Jean-Paul had hoped Britta would return to her place. Maybe meet the guy there or at the office.

But so far nothing.

The windshield wipers scraped the glass, rain pinging off in a steady drizzle. The timing of the killer's call to Britta didn't feel right. If Teddy was in custody, he wasn't meeting Britta. So who had Catherine? "What if the killer has Britta and Catherine now?"

Damon cut his eyes toward Jean-Paul. "This woman has really snuck under your skin, hasn't she?"

His brother didn't know the half of it. He couldn't deny it. "She has me in knots, Damon. She's this lost kind of woman, afraid and secretive. And she kept the truth from me about killing Reverend Tatum, but she had her reasons."

"Yeah, she was afraid you'd arrest her."

He ran his hand over his stubble, barely cognizant of the fact that he hadn't showered or shaved or slept in almost two days. "You heard what she said, that Tatum was going to sacrifice her. She was thirteen, Damon, just a kid."

Damon's jaw tightened. "I know, that's pretty horrible."

"If she hadn't escaped the cult, she'd be dead. She's a gutsy lady. She killed that guy in self-defense." His breathing wheezed out, choppy. "Just look at her now. She's putting herself in danger to save our sister." Because of guilt. Because she felt all alone. Because she thought no one loved her.

Because she wanted to spare Catherine and his family pain.

At any cost to herself.

"You're sure it was self defense? She wasn't a street girl—"

"Hell, no. She let me believe the worst, but she's been out there helping girls, Damon. Getting them off the street. She even spends Sundays feeding the homeless." And probably searching for the mother who'd abandoned her.

"If it had been Steph or Cat or, for God's sake," he continued, "Chrissy in her shoes, wouldn't you have wanted Britta to fight back?"

Damon gave him a long concerned look, then nodded. At least he and his brother saw eye to eye. Convincing Antwaun to accept his view would be a different story, but he'd worry about that later.

Right now all he could think about was finding Britta and Catherine. Where was Britta? Was she all right?

And what about his sister? Was she still alive?

DÉJÀ VU STRUCK Britta. The bayou looked different tonight. Felt different. The winds had changed. Some of the topography.

But the sounds were the same. The incessant trolling of the gators. The Mississippi churning against the bank. And the smell of blood and danger permeated the air.

She climbed from the car, searching the dense trees, knowing the swamp devil was out there somewhere. Waiting. Watching. Hungry for the kill.

Her breath felt painful in her chest as she checked the inside of her jacket for the gun. A twig snapped somewhere in the distance. Rain sluiced around her feet. The mud pulled at her shoes like quicksand trying to drag her into the bowels of the ground. She refused to give in.

Then she saw his eyes. Glowing dark embers of fire bursting through the night. They almost didn't look real.

An animal howled, low and throaty.

Then he whispered her name.

She wanted to curl into that teeny little ball of a girl she'd been once. Disappear. Become invisible.

But she couldn't abandon Catherine.

"I'm here." Her voice carried into the wind like a ghost's cry. The rustle of leaves reverberated behind her. Then to the right. Evil filled the air, and she sensed the swamp devil watching, ready to pounce.

She stood her ground, waiting on him to show his face. Then she'd follow him wherever he wanted to take her.

Suddenly a memory broke through the fog of her brain. The shanty she'd discovered when she'd been running from the clan. Deep in the heart of the backwoods, surrounded by water and weeds. It was close by.

That's where he'd taken Catherine.

Her heart pounding, she stepped into a knot of trees,

letting them swallow her shadow as she blended into the world that she'd once tried to escape. A second later, she felt his cold hands.

"I knew you'd come, Adrianna. We were meant to be together."

Thirteen years ago, she'd spit in his face and run.

She was tempted to shoot him now, then search for Catherine. But what if she was wrong? What if the shanty was somewhere else or what if it had been demolished in the hurricane?

She couldn't take the chance. She had to let him take her to Catherine first.

CHAPTER TWENTY-ONE

"I DIDN'T KILL Debra."

Jean-Paul studied Teddy and wondered if Britta had been right—on the surface, Teddy didn't appear capable of sadistic murder. But what if he had a hidden personality?

"Then why were you leaving town?"

Teddy's pale face turned ruddy. "Be…cause I saw the news. I knew p…olice would think I killed D…ebra."

Jean-Paul slapped the table. "She was last seen with you."

Teddy sniffled. "I know. We…she came home with me, but she was alive when she left."

"What happened between you?"

Teddy ducked his head. "We had…started to have sex…she said she loved me. But…she got mad when she saw me l…ooking at that magazine and ran out."

"Her fingernail ended up in Britta Berger's apartment after that fire. We think she attacked Miss Berger."

Teddy's eyes widened in shock. "I…don't know."

Jean-Paul hit the table with his fist again. "Where's my sister?"

"I told you, I don't know your sister."

Antwaun shoved a photo of Catherine and her daughter in front of his face. "Try again."

Teddy rubbed a hand over his runny nose, his body shaking. "I...wait a minute. I've seen them in the market. They bought some of my dolls."

"That's right." Jean-Paul gripped the man's arm with steely fingers. "Now, tell me what you did with Catherine. Her little girl wants her back."

Teddy's Adam's apple bulged. "I didn't do anything with them. W...w...why would I?"

"Because you wanted to hurt Britta Berger and me," Jean-Paul snapped.

Teddy shook his head violently. "I...I'd n...ever hurt Miss B...erger. I...l...ike her." He hugged the edge of the chair. "And I'm not the only w...w...one your s...sister bought from. She bought a m...m...ask from the guy next to me."

Jean-Paul had questioned the guy one time on the street after the first murder, but he'd had an alibi. And the masks he made were different from the one they'd found at the scene. But maybe he'd missed something.

"What's this guy's name?" Jean-Paul asked.

"Sed...rick..." Teddy whined. "Whitehead. He... also paints eyes."

"What do you mean he paints eyes?"

"He's an oc...ularist. Said he started p...ainting dolls' eyes like me, then got asked to apprentice with an ocularist."

"Prosthetic eyes are made from acrylic now," Damon said. "I'll check him out." Damon's heels clicked as he left the room, and Jean-Paul paced across the floor. He hoped to hell they weren't wasting time.

Britta had been gone for over an hour. No phone calls. No citings by the cops. No confession from Teddy.

In fact, the poor guy seemed genuinely upset that Britta was missing.

He felt like he was coming apart, that he might blow if something didn't break soon.

He stepped into the hallway and dialed Stephanie. Maybe she'd heard something.

"She hasn't called," Stephanie said. "Do you have any leads, Jean-Paul?"

Jean-Paul sighed, his nerves strung tight. "We're working on it. We've received a few calls about the other victims. I have uniforms checking out the leads. And we're interrogating a suspect now." And weeding out the crank calls. He'd expected some after they'd aired on the news, but the craziness of Mardi Gras had accentuated the problem.

"We're also looking for an ocularist now. Apparently, he also makes masks and sells them on the street."

"I've seen his work. He has a display in the wax museum," Stephanie said. "There's something eerie about that place. About his work."

Lieutenant Phelps strode toward him, then gestured for Jean-Paul to meet him in the hallway, so he promised to keep Stephanie posted, then hung up. Phelps was already pissed at Jean-Paul for losing his gun to a civilian. Now his job was on the line.

But he didn't give a damn. He'd do whatever necessary to save Catherine and Britta.

"Did you learn anything from Swain?"

Phelps shrugged. "He admitted that he's not who he says he is. Apparently he stole that song, 'Heartache Blues,' from a chick who dumped him in Nashville." Phelps popped an antacid. "He's a liar, a cheat and a crossdresser, but he's not our killer."

Now they knew the reason the guy had acted guilty.

Phelps put his hand on Jean-Paul's shoulder. "Look, Dubois, this one is too personal. I'm taking you off the case. Let the other boys handle it."

"You can't do that, Lieutenant."

"I can and I will. You've already lost your gun. And I watched you with that guy Teddy. You're losing it, Dubois. Sit this one out."

Jean-Paul removed his badge and shoved it into his lieutenant's hands. "Take it. I don't care about the job. I'm not stopping until I catch this maniac." And he fully intended to kill him.

He didn't wait for a reply. He'd chosen his job over his first wife. He'd be damned if he'd choose it over his sister or Britta.

His cell phone rang, and Jean-Paul answered it. "Dubois."

"Detective, this is Howard Keith. There's something you should see," Keith said, sounding out of breath. "I think I know who your killer is."

"Don't play games with me, Keith. My sister and Britta Berger are missing. If you have them—"

"I don't," he said sharply. "But I may know who does. A...friend of mine, another artist. His name is Sedrick Whitehead. He's the reason I started photographing Britta Berger in the first place."

"What do you mean?"

"He paints eyeballs, prostheses. That's how we met. But he also paints and makes Mardi Gras masks on the side. It's a hobby."

The ocularist, the mask maker, the same one Teddy mentioned. "Why do you think he's the swamp devil?"

"He has scars on his face, and wears a mask to

disguise it. I think his scars have something to do with a woman. Maybe Britta." Keith's breath was erratic. "Come to his apartment and you'll see what I mean." He rattled off an address.

Jean-Paul memorized it, then told him he'd be right there.

He rushed to inform Damon about the possible lead. They agreed to go together and leave Antwaun to keep pushing Teddy.

Ten minutes later, he and Damon met Keith at Sedrick's apartment complex. Jean-Paul was shocked as the photographer showed them inside the studio.

"I...never would have noticed Miss Berger if Sedrick hadn't pointed her out."

So this guy could have stalked Britta. He would have seen Catherine and Chrissy at Teddy's doll stand, too. And he could have seen Debra Schmale with Teddy.

Jean-Paul sucked in a sharp breath at the disturbing contents as he entered Sedrick's locked studio. The walls were filled with Mardi Gras masks in every conceivable form and shape. Leather ones that resembled the S and M ones he'd seen at Justice's apartment and at that costume shop, handpainted ones with beads and feathers and ribbons. Sinister ones that resembled fantastical mythical horror creatures. Feathers, sculpting wax, plaster, leather, paints, beads and assorted items to finish the masks occupied more shelves. Masks of Sobek filled one complete wall.

And another shelf held eyeballs that he'd painted for the masks. They were lifelike, so real. An ocularist would fit the profile. The man was detailed, meticulous, methodical. The art form had originated in ancient times. And the eyes were made of acrylics.

Jean-Paul dragged his gaze from the array of disturbing eyeballs to the opposite side of the room and his stomach clenched. Masks made for each of the victims of the swamp devil were displayed on the wall. Whitehead had labeled each one with the girl's name. And he was midway through making one for Britta—it was on his work table.

"He didn't take trophies," Damon said.

But there wasn't one for Catherine. Maybe he planned to spare her.

"Because these were his trophies," Jean-Paul added.

Panic stabbed at his chest as Damon opened a cabinet and found jars and tubes of makeup. A trunk also revealed a half-dozen lancets. Another one held red lace teddies and the serpent necklaces.

Damon cursed. "Where the hell is Whitehead now?"

Jean-Paul tried to get into the man's head. "He intends to end this with Britta. He'll want her back at the place where it all began. To the place where he was going to sacrifice her years ago."

Damon nodded. "That makes sense."

Jean-Paul had a general idea of where the first cult had formed, but Justice would know the place. "Let's pick up Justice. The hurricane changed the land slightly. Maybe he can show us the exact location."

Damon phoned for a CSI team to confiscate the evidence.

"I didn't know he was the killer," Keith said weakly.

Jean-Paul glared at him. "We want you at the station for questioning." He phoned Antwaun to fill him in and learned Justice was at the station waiting to talk to him. Then he and Damon raced back to the station with Keith.

Damon gave him a worried look as Antwaun took charge of Keith. "Your lieutenant told me you gave him your badge."

"He wanted to pull me off the case," Jean-Paul snapped. "I'm not sitting around with my thumb up my ass while my sister and Britta are missing."

Justice looked haggard when Jean-Paul walked in. "I saw the news report. Where's Britta?"

"I don't know," Jean-Paul said. "Apparently she received a call from the killer and left to meet him."

Justice launched forward and grabbed Jean-Paul by the neck. "You let her go to meet this guy by herself? What kind of cop are you?"

A piss-poor one, Jean-Paul thought. He pried Justice's hands off his neck and shoved the man backward. "I didn't let her leave. She ducked out without telling me, dammit. We think we know who the killer is."

"There's an old cabin near the place where the cult met years ago," Justice said. "He may have her there. I think I can find it."

The three men hurried to the car. Jean-Paul turned on his siren, and sped toward Black Bayou. If Sedrick had taken Britta and Catherine to Devil's Corner, they needed to hurry.

He just hoped when they found them, they would still be alive.

THE HIDEOUS MASK hid the killer's face.

His voice was low, grating, a whisper of evil. His hands—hard, rough, calloused—felt like ice as he pushed her along the swampland. Rain drenched Britta's hair and clothes, the winter wind sending a deep chill through her that cut all the way to her bones.

She nearly stumbled over a broken tree branch, but he caught her and yanked her along. Gators lay low in the water, watching, waiting, their bodies submerged but their eyes piercing the darkness.

He didn't act afraid of them. Instead he seemed to have a silent connection with the creatures as if he had bonded with them through his ugliness.

Through the fog and underbrush, she spotted a shanty in the distance. A tremor ran through her. Was Catherine inside? Was she alive?

The urge to run shot through her, but she stifled it. She wouldn't run until she got closer.

A few more steps, and he dragged her through a thicket of fallen trees that were rotting and mangled from a previous storm. Vines tangled and clawed at her legs and a snake hissed from its perch on a low tree branch above her.

He pushed her forward, across a small dilapidated wooden bridge over the river, and she looked down to see the sharp teeth of a gator glowing in the dim moonlight. It snapped at her feet, barely missing as he jerked her to the landing.

She was only a few feet from the cabin now. "All right. You have me. Now let her go."

He folded his arms and laughed. "You don't tell me what to do, Adrianna."

"I did what you asked. Now show me you'll honor your word."

"As you did with my father?"

"I never agreed to marry you. That choice was made without me, Porter."

"My name is Sedrick now. I'm growing quite famous with my masks. And even more famous as the swamp devil." He gripped her arm, squeezing her so hard her legs buckled. "You killed my father and you have to pay."

"He deserved it," Britta said. "But those women didn't. Especially that girl Debra."

He bared his teeth. "That girl Debra tried to kill you. She hooked up with your friend Teddy, but she was jealous of you, so she set your apartment on fire and attacked you."

Britta fought back a sob. "Still, Catherine's done nothing. Let her go and I'll do whatever you say."

He leaned closer to her face, the corners of the hideous mask scraping her jaw. "Say you want me, Adrianna."

"Take off the mask so I can see your face first."

He shook his head and released her, a growl erupting from him, then he stroked a finger over her shoulder. Britta reached inside her jacket for the gun, but he lunged toward her. The gun flew from her hand and fell to the ground. Desperate, she tried to retrieve it, but it was too dark to see. He grabbed her and she clawed at his mask and tried to pull it off but he slapped her so hard her ears rang and she collapsed on the soggy ground. Then he dove on top of her. She struggled and hit at him, clawing for a tree branch or stick, anything to use as a weapon. Finally, she latched on to a thick branch and slammed it against his head.

He bellowed in pain and rolled sideways. She jumped up and ran for the cabin. It took her a second to adjust to the darkness, then she spotted Catherine, gagged and tied to a rickety iron bed. She raced forward and began to untie the ropes.

"We have to get out of here," she whispered.

Catherine nodded, wide-eyed and panicked looking.

But at least she was alive. Finally she got the bindings undone and Catherine yanked out the gag.

Britta helped her to stand. "Come on, he'll be here any minute!"

Catherine staggered, weak and disoriented, then leaned against Britta, and they made it down the steps outside. But Sedrick swaggered toward them with a growl. Britta spotted Jean-Paul's gun in the weeds and shoved Catherine into a thicket of trees. "Run! I'm right behind you."

Catherine stumbled forward and Britta reached for the gun. He saw it at the same time and dove for it. They fought for the weapon and it went off. He knocked the gun from her hand and they both fell into the muddy swampland. Brambles and vines tugged at her ankles as she kicked at him. He slapped her again and again until her head spun. Somewhere in the distance a gator screamed. She prayed he didn't get Catherine.

Then Sedrick hit her one more time and she sank into the darkness.

JEAN-PAUL HAD JUST CLIMBED from the car when he heard a gunshot. God, he hoped Britta had killed the son of a bitch who'd kidnapped Catherine.

Justice jerked his thumb to the left. "The shot came from that direction. That's where the cabin is."

Jean-Paul pulled the weapon that Damon had loaned him and they ran into the woods. Rain beat at his face, the downpour creating a smoky mist inside the forest. Panic gripped him as Justice led the way. The thick foliage slowed their trek and Jean-Paul hacked his way through with his knife. Tangled vines and Spanish moss created a maze, making the night even grayer.

Justice stumbled, then cursed and crawled over a

fallen tree. Jean-Paul jumped it, then paused. Damon scanned the darkness.

A noise reverberated in the silence. Feet pounding. The swish of branches and leaves. Breathing. Someone running.

He angled his head to listen again, then motioned for Justice to wait. The sound grew closer. Footsteps slogging through the marsh. Suddenly Catherine broke through the clearing.

He grabbed her and she screamed. He shook her gently. "Cat, it's me, Jean-Paul. I've got you now."

Her legs wobbled and she clung to his arms to remain standing. "Britta...I thought she was right behind me."

His blood turned to ice. If she'd killed the man, she would have been.

He must have caught her.

"Jean-Paul..." Catherine cried. "She saved me. You have to find her."

Damon slid an arm around Catherine. "Are you okay, sis? What did he do to you?"

"I'm fine, really," she rasped. "Jean-Paul, please save Britta."

"I'll take Cat to the car and call for an EMT," Damon said.

Jean-Paul frowned. He might need back-up. But did he trust Justice with his sister?

"We need to hurry," Justice said.

"Go with Catherine," Jean-Paul told Justice.

"I'll call for back-up and an ambulance," Damon said.

Justice curved an arm around Catherine to help her through the woods.

Jean-Paul didn't wait. He darted toward the direction

of the cabin. Britta had to be all right. She was a fighter. The strongest woman he'd ever known.

She had saved Catherine.

Now he had to save her.

BRITTA'S HEAD ACHED. She wanted to curl into a ball. Be so tiny no one saw her. Become invisible like a fleck of dust on the wall.

No.

She had to fight back.

She struggled to open her eyes. Sedrick was hauling her across the marsh by one arm and had twisted it so hard she thought it would wrench from the socket. Rain pummeled them and she made herself into a dead weight, dragging her heels into the muck. Maybe Catherine would escape and get help.

But she couldn't count on that. She was all alone. She had to save herself—just as she'd always done.

Her body bounced over the rough tree branches, then he yanked her up the steps to the shanty. The wooden steps bit into her back and pain knifed through her. Where was the gun?

Oh God, she'd lost it. She had to find something else to fight with. Another weapon.

The door screeched open and he tossed her inside like a sack of garbage. Her head slammed against the wall and stars sparkled. Mud and rain soaked her clothing and hair. She tried to push herself up, but he dug his knee into her chest, pinning her down, and tore at her clothes. She screamed and shoved at his hands, then yanked at his mask again, determined to see his face. Finally she stripped it off and hurled it across the floor.

His eyes blazed with rage and one hand automatically flew up to hide his disfigurement. "See what you did to me! See how ugly I am now."

"Your scars aren't what make you ugly," Britta whispered raggedly. "Your soul does that."

"No! You did it." He grabbed her throat and shook her. "I've had to wear a disguise in public because I tried to save you when you ran into the bayou." His hot breath seared her neck. "You owe me."

"I don't owe you anything, you monster."

He hit her again, and pain split her temple. Then he growled against her throat, "Say it, Adrianna. Say you want me."

"No."

"Yes." His fingers dug into her neck tighter. "Yes, God dammit! Say you want me. That you love me."

"Never," Britta whispered.

He jerked her up like a rag doll, twisting his fingers into her throat, cutting off her vocal chords. "I've waited thirteen years for you to tell me. And you're going to say it before I kill you."

Britta remembered her last words to him the night she'd killed his father and ran. She repeated them. "I could never love you."

Rain pounded above like nails driving into the tin roof. Thunder grumbled. In the back of Britta's mind, she heard the ancient chants and drums of their medieval ancestors.

Sedrick's angry roar resounded off the walls as he hauled her across the room and threw her on the bed. She saw the red teddy. The oils. A condom. The virginal white gown.

And the mask of Sobek and the serpent necklace.

She lashed out. He grabbed the scepter and pointed the tip of the blade at her chest and she froze.

A sinister smile curved his scarred mouth as he flicked the blade under the edge of her blouse, then ripped the fabric. She sucked in a breath, trying not to move. Then he jabbed the blade at her chest and pierced her skin, bringing blood to the surface.

A sob escaped her as he pressed the sharp blade to her throat and tore her blouse the rest of the way off. She had to fight back but if she moved, the blade might slip and he'd behead her. Still, dying was better than being raped. And he was going to kill her anyway.

Using every ounce of energy she possessed, she shoved at his hands. The scepter clanged to the floor, then he bellowed his rage and his hands slid around her wrists. He slammed his fist into her jaw, then crawled on her and reached for the ropes.

Suddenly a gust of wind blew into the cabin. Cold air and rain pelted her legs. The bayou sounds filled the darkness.

Britta gasped for air. She was going to die here tonight. All alone in the bayou.

Sedrick suddenly threw his head back and bellowed again, but this time his body jerked backward. Pain and shock flared in his eyes and he convulsed, then collapsed forward on top of her.

She cried out and saw blood spurting from his back.

Her chest heaved and she tried to push him off her. Then she saw Jean-Paul.

He was standing over them, the scepter in his hands. He had stabbed the swamp devil with his own weapon.

Over Sedrick's body, Jean-Paul's dark eyes sought hers. He was angry, breathing hard. He looked like a wild animal. He must hate her.

She opened her mouth to say she was sorry, but a sob

escaped instead. Jean-Paul dragged Sedrick off her, then knelt and scooped her into his arms.

"God, Britta, you had me scared out of my mind." He rocked her back and forth, stroking her hair, her face, brushing her tears away as he kissed her.

Britta clung to him. It was finally over. Catherine was safe. The swamp devil was dead.

And for the moment she was in Jean-Paul's arms.

CHAPTER TWENTY-TWO

JEAN-PAUL WAS STILL RAGING with fury when the paramedics, his lieutenant and Antwaun arrived. The sight of that psycho tearing at Britta's clothes, trying to kill her, had unleashed something inside him that he couldn't calm. His body was literally shaking and wouldn't stop.

He watched the paramedics help her onto a stretcher and felt helpless. Britta should have never set out on her own to catch the killer.

Yet she had done so to save Catherine.

Damon assigned two agents to wait at the shanty for the CSI team and medical examiner to remove Sedrick's body.

Phelps pulled him aside before he climbed into the car and shoved his badge into his hand. "We need you. You're too good a cop to leave us."

Jean-Paul accepted the badge, a silent understanding passing between them. If he had to do it again, he wouldn't do things any differently.

Catherine and Britta swore they were okay, but Jean-Paul insisted they be taken to the hospital. He felt humbled and confused as he and his brothers followed the ambulance.

Antwaun phoned Stephanie and fifteen minutes later

his family met them at the hospital emergency room. As soon as Catherine saw Shawn and Chrissy, she held out her arms and they went into them. A tearful family reunion ensued, with everyone hugging and crying.

His mother finally calmed enough to wipe her eyes. "Damon told us what happened with your Britta. Is she all right?"

His Britta? He didn't bother to correct his mother or hide his feelings. "I think so. I'm waiting to go in now."

"She's a very brave, special girl."

"Yes, she is."

His father pounded him on the back. "I knew you boys would bring Catherine home safe and sound."

"Thank Britta, Dad," Jean-Paul said in a gruff voice.

"We intend to." His father put an arm around his mother's shoulders and Stephanie slid up to his other side and squeezed his arm.

"We want to see Britta."

He hugged Stephanie. Britta thought that she wouldn't fit in, that his family might judge her, but she was wrong. They would welcome her if she let them.

"Let me check on her first." He walked over to the nurses' station. "Detective Dubois. I'm here with Miss Berger. Can I see her now?"

"Why don't you take a seat—"

"I don't want her to be alone," he said. For some reason that was important to him. She'd saved his family and they were together, but she was by herself as she'd always been.

He wanted to change that forever.

The nurse must have realized that he was about to come unglued, because she showed him to the room where they were examining Britta.

They had cleaned some of the mud and dirt from her body, but the bright fluorescent lights of the hospital made her bruises more pronounced. He winced, emotions pummeling him as he entered. Rage, anger, sorrow…love.

"Britta?"

She jerked her head around and pulled the sheet up but not before he saw dark bruises on her neck and chest. Fury surged through him again, resurrecting the animalistic rage he'd felt when he'd killed Sedrick.

"Jean-Paul, how's Catherine?"

She was so unselfish; his heart swelled. Even now, when she'd been battered, she was worried about his sister, not herself. Just as she was with the girls on the street.

"She's going to be fine." He smiled, glad his sister was spunky. "Shawn and Chrissy and the rest of the family are with her now."

"Thank God. I…I'm glad he didn't hurt her."

Silence stretched between them, an awkward moment where he wanted to go to her but wasn't sure what she wanted. After all, he'd almost been too late to save her.

"Thank you for coming to my rescue," Britta said softly. "But what happens next? Are you going to arrest me?"

He frowned. "Arrest you? Why would I do that?"

"I killed a man, Jean-Paul. I know the statue of limitations on murder doesn't run out."

Jean-Paul stared down at her, willing his voice to work. "You defended yourself, Britta. There's no court in this land that would say any different."

"I wonder sometimes…" She hesitated and he lifted her chin with his thumb so she had to look at him.

"Wonder what, Britta?"

"What would have happened if I hadn't shot him—"

She might not be alive. Then he would never have known her.

He traced a finger over her cheek. "You did what you had to do, and I'm proud of you for it. If one of my sisters or Chrissy had been in your place, I'd want her to be a fighter like you." His voice choked. "I don't know how to repay you for saving Catherine."

"I don't want you to repay me," Britta said tightly.

An image of her being mauled by that maniac came to him again. She shouldn't have tackled him alone. She should have trusted him and waited.

Anger hardened his voice, "And I don't want you to ever do anything so foolish as to put yourself in danger again."

She blinked, moisture in her eyes. "I did what I had to do, Jean-Paul. Now go back to your family where you belong."

For a moment, he felt as if she'd hit him. He was about to admit he loved her, but she'd just been attacked and nearly killed by a madman. She didn't need him unloading his feelings. Pressuring her.

He turned to leave, knowing he had to give her time. Maybe romance her. Show her that he didn't have to live for his job.

That he'd give it up for her, anything to keep her with him.

EMOTIONS WELLED IN Britta's chest. She didn't understand Jean-Paul's reaction. One minute he was tender, the next angry. He was obviously touched that she'd saved his sister, but the last thing she wanted was for him to feel indebted toward her.

But she loved him so much her heart was breaking. Why couldn't he love her back? She knew the answer but couldn't seem to accept it....

He suddenly turned back to face her. A charged electricity filled the air, vibrating between them. "I'm not leaving. I belong here with you, Britta."

A tear slid down her cheek. "What?"

He strode back to her, then lowered his head and kissed her. "I love you," he said in a gruff voice. "I think I have for a long time. And I...never want to be without you."

"Oh, Jean-Paul." Her voice choked on her. She'd never cried for a man. He'd said he loved her.

"What is it, sweetheart?"

She memorized his face. He was what she'd always wanted. "You...me...it would never work."

He stiffened, his expression hardening. "Why not?"

"Your family must hate me for putting Catherine and you in danger. And you're a hero. How would it look for you to be with a woman who was a murderer?"

"You are the hero here, honey." His voice sounded husky. "And when I get through talking to the press, they'll know it."

"But your family..."

"My family thinks you're wonderful." He leaned over and brushed a strand of hair from her eyes. "And even if they didn't, they'd have to accept you because I love you."

"Jean-Paul—" Her voice broke again. "I love you, too."

His eyes flickered with a smile, then hunger, and she slid her arms around him and kissed him. Jean-Paul would make all her fantasies and dreams come true. She knew it in her heart. Because her heart belonged to him.

And she would spend the rest of her life making his fantasies come true, as well.

A second later, the door opened and Jean-Paul's family rushed in and surrounded her. Britta smiled through her tears as they welcomed her into their family.

* * * * *

*Don't miss Rita Herron's contribution
to the Harlequin Intrigue continuity* LIGHTS OUT.
*Look for ANYTHING FOR HIS SON,
on sale August 2007!*

Reader's Group Guidelines

1. Have you ever visited New Orleans? What significant elements about the town, culture, people and customs do you like? What do you think makes the city so special? What about your own hometown— what makes it unique? What would you miss most if the place was destroyed?

2. The natural disasters that affected New Orleans affected us all in varying degrees. We heard stories of tragedies and uplifting, touching moments of bravery and heroism, as well. Share some of the stories you heard.

3. What kinds of problems/tragedies have caused havoc in your life? What makes some people able to overcome adversity and pain and rebuild their lives, while others fold beneath the weight?

4. The story incorporates folklore and a legendary swamp devil. What kinds of folklore have evolved around your own hometown or the area you live now? Do you believe in superstition, and if so, what superstitions?

5. Britta Berger is a complicated character with a dark past that has traumatized her. Are there events in your own life that have affected you either negatively or positively? Elaborate. If they were negative, how did you overcome them? Do you believe that finding love can help overcome adversity?

6. Although they have encountered problems, the Dubois family is close. What holds them together? What about your own family? Do you handle problems together and offer support? How can you bring your own family close together, and what family values do you hope to teach them?

7. Do you see any underlying themes in the book? If so, what are they? Discuss.

8. Although the author incorporates in the book a religious cult that proves dangerous to the heroine, what positive influences do you think religion plays in our lives? In your own? Your family's?

9. The Mardi Gras masks are inherent in the story, and are used both literally and figuratively. They represent the faces the characters show to the world, which may differ from the ones beneath the surface. What kinds of masks do you hide behind? What about others you know? Do they wear disguises, and why?

10. What kept Britta and Jean-Paul apart when they first met? What ultimately do you believe brought the couple together? Do you believe that love can conquer all?

*Now turn the page for a sneak preview of award-winning author Rita Herron's next book for HQN,
DON'T SAY A WORD, featuring Damon Dubois.
On sale September 2007....*

Prologue

May, New Orleans

THE WOMAN HAD NO NAME. No voice. No face.

Dr. Reginald Pace studied her near-lifeless form as she lay on the shiny surgical table. The harsh fluorescent lights glowed off of her charred skin and raw flesh, painting a sinister picture.

Her silent, pain-filled, vacant eyes begged for mercy. For death.

But the voice inside his head whispered that he could not fulfill her wish. That her body craved the transformation that only his gifted hands could offer.

As a plastic surgeon, he had seen the ruins of people's faces and bodies on a daily basis. But never had he beheld a sight like the one before him. She looked almost inhuman.

Mangled, charred skin had peeled away from the severed tendons and crushed bone. Lips that might have once held a feminine smile now gaped with blisters and raw flesh. Eyes blinded by pain had flickered with a plea for death to end the agony before he had swept her under the bliss of drugs.

His healing hands would piece her back together.

His healing hands and time....

Layer by layer he would rebuild her. Repair severed nerve endings, damaged cartilage. Replace tissue. Mold the monster into a beauty.

Without a face, a name, a picture, he could shape her into whatever he chose.

The woman of his dreams, God willing.

He gently brushed the remnants of her singed hair from her hairline. She would be in agony for a while, but he would be there with her every step of the way to offer her comfort.

And she would recover; he wouldn't rest until she did.

A smile curled his mouth as he picked up the scalpel to get started. Yes, she would thank him in the end.

And then, she would be his creation.

His to keep forever....

REQUEST YOUR FREE BOOKS!

2 FREE NOVELS
FROM THE ROMANCE/SUSPENSE
COLLECTION PLUS 2 FREE GIFTS!

YES! Please send me 2 FREE novels from the Romance/Suspense Collection and my 2 FREE gifts. After receiving them, if I don't wish to receive any more books, I can return the shipping statement marked "cancel." If I don't cancel, I will receive 4 brand-new novels every month and be billed just $5.49 per book in the U.S., or $5.99 per book in Canada, plus 25¢ shipping and handling per book plus applicable taxes, if any*. That's a savings of at least 20% off the cover price! I understand that accepting the 2 free books and gifts places me under no obligation to buy anything. I can always return a shipment and cancel at any time. Even if I never buy another book from the Reader Service, the two free books and gifts are mine to keep forever.

185 MDN EF5Y   385 MDN EF6C

Name	(PLEASE PRINT)	
Address		Apt. #
City	State/Prov.	Zip/Postal Code

Signature (if under 18, a parent or guardian must sign)

Mail to **The Reader Service:**
IN U.S.A.: P.O. Box 1867, Buffalo, NY 14240-1867
IN CANADA: P.O. Box 609, Fort Erie, Ontario L2A 5X3

Not valid to current subscribers to the Romance Collection,
the Suspense Collection or the Romance/Suspense Collection.

Want to try two free books from another line?
Call 1-800-873-8635 or visit www.morefreebooks.com.

* Terms and prices subject to change without notice. NY residents add applicable sales tax. Canadian residents will be charged applicable provincial taxes and GST. This offer is limited to one order per household. All orders subject to approval. Credit or debit balances in a customer's account(s) may be offset by any other outstanding balance owed by or to the customer. Please allow 4 to 6 weeks for delivery.

Your Privacy: Harlequin is committed to protecting your privacy. Our Privacy Policy is available online at www.eHarlequin.com or upon request from the Reader Service. From time to time we make our lists of customers available to reputable firms who may have a product or service of interest to you. If you would prefer we not share your name and address, please check here. ☐

BOB07

RITA
HERRON

77105	IN A HEARTBEAT	___ $5.99 U.S.	___	$6.99 CAN.
77102	LAST KISS GOODBYE	___ $5.99 U.S.	___	$6.99 CAN.
77030	A BREATH AWAY	___ $5.99 U.S.	___	$6.99 CAN.

(limited quantities available)

TOTAL AMOUNT	$ _____
POSTAGE & HANDLING	$ _____
($1.00 FOR 1 BOOK, 50¢ for each additional)	
APPLICABLE TAXES*	$ _____
TOTAL PAYABLE	$ _____

(check or money order—please do not send cash)

To order, complete this form and send it, along with a check or money order for the total above, payable to HQN Books, to: **In the U.S.:** 3010 Walden Avenue, P.O. Box 9077, Buffalo, NY 14269-9077; **In Canada:** P.O. Box 636, Fort Erie, Ontario, L2A 5X3.

Name: _____
Address: _____ City: _____
State/Prov.: _____ Zip/Postal Code: _____
Account Number (if applicable): _____

075 CSAS

*New York residents remit applicable sales taxes.
*Canadian residents remit applicable GST and provincial taxes.

HQN™
We *are* romance™

www.HQNBooks.com